DOUGLAS WOOLF

HYPOCRITIC DAYS & OTHER TALES

Edited By
SANDRA BRAMAN

Preface By
EDWARD DORN

Black Sparrow Press Santa Rosa 1993

ACKNOWLEDGMENTS

Many of these stories originally appeared in the magazines *Big Table, The Black Mountain Review, Bombay Gin, The California Quarterly, Evergreen Review, Granta, Interim, Island, Kulchur, New Mexico Quarterly, Outburst, Perspective, Prairie Schooner, The Second Coming, Sir!, Southwest Review, Story, Western Review,* and *Wild Dog,* and in the collections *Signs of a Migrant Worrier* (Coyote's Journal) and *Future Preconditional* (Coach House Press). The Divers Press (Robert Creeley) originally published *Hypocritic Days,* Jargon Society (Jonathan Williams) originally published *Spring of the Lamb*; Wolf Run Books originally published *HAD*; and Tombouctou (Michael Wolfe) originally published *The Timing Chain.* Thanks to you all.

Black Sparrow Press books are printed on acid-free paper.

LIBRARY OF CONGRESS CATALOGING-IN-PUBLICATION DATA

Woolf, Douglas, 1922–1992
Hypocritic days & other tales / Douglas Woolf ; edited by Sandra Braman ; preface by Edward Dorn.
p. cm.
ISBN 0-87685-912-0 (cloth) : $$25.00. — ISBN 0-87685-913-9 (deluxe) : $30.00. — ISBN 0-87685-911-2 (paper) : $15.00
I. Braman, Sandra. II. Title. III. Title: Hypocritic days and other tales.
PS3573.0646H97 1993
813'.54—dc20 93-29924
CIP

Table of Contents

Preface

"... where the wolves are killed off, the foxes increase"
HERMAN MELVILLE, *The Confidence Man*

DOUGLAS WOOLF was strangely in advance of documentary fiction in one way or another his whole career. Through his incessant wandering he had an empirical grounding in the tradition of Herodotus, while at the same time, because of his intellectual instincts, he developed the compactness of style and accuracy and the critical savvy coming down from the school of Thucydides.

Your glance catches something out the window. A bright summer evening. Mythopoeic sky peopled by stars. The virtual library of the bygone and the doggone. You see the woolf—he's got his cap on backwards, way before anybody else. He's come down from Kellogg or Wallace—Idaho camptowns, feathery silver markets on the far tip of the right wing. He's got a couple of quarts of blackberries in his arms, picked with the morning dew, five hundred miles away. It's the professional way to treat western space—speed overcomes space until it just turns into it. The only difference between the new west and the old west is speed—the space is the same space. Some glaciers travel a foot a day. Given the mass, that's invisible.

This is an energy flow over which post-modern critical theory can have no destructive control—any attempt to replicate this system results in immediate prophylaxis of the syntax. Woolf's most radical and projective stylistic device was to embody "what is not there" and to echo "what is not said"—the reading mind is arced across the gaps in the mental terrain—the spiritual imago of abandonment, the late-modern holocaustic onslaught on humanity and its animal relatives. For the race of live readers, these linguistic chasms switch on the enterokinase and the whole tryptic cognizance between the text and the story. It's the record.

This kind of traditional sensory trap is not supposed to exist in the late half-millennium. The cold matter-of-fact wretchedness which has become the proud *modus operandi* of current *america,* was considerably more overt in the days when "Bank Day" was written. Sanguinity was still a rush, not a smart bombing run. It was blood, and if it came down to it, you could sell it. But you weren't supposed to know that down the road they'd give it back to you totally deconstructed by virus—the ultimate weight-watcher's short-term solution. And the upper-class plague of moral corruption. But Woolf revealed the psycho-social precursor of said very retro agent.

The citizens and aliens who gave blood with Douglas Woolf didn't need to notice that. They were all skinny and hungry just like their witness. You had to look twice at Douglas Woolf—he had a very fleeting presence, something like a thirties' photograph: monogram buckle, baggy work pants, baseball cap, or a laborer's fedora—at a distance he could have been a gas station attendant, the lowest official in the uniform hierarchy. Unfortunately, now officially one-stop-shop clerk.

It is an interesting fact that Oregon, a state Woolf knew well, sees no reason to trust the gasoline customer enough to let it pump its own gas. His documentation of the incompetent and driven state of the public is equal to Mayhew, with a lot less evidence to work with. Less evidence in documentation means you have to fill the holes. That procedure seems very presumptuous to the unobservant and the faint of heart. But—it's what Everybody does about Everything. And Woolf was among them, impartial as an ethnologist among savages.

How many cops can we afford? As many as the traffic will bear, plus a few more. Douglas Woolf's micro-study of the Highway Patrolman leaning over the engine block, wiping the road grease off the number, is a deep study of the business-end of the State—one twitch and possibly that's it. It isn't so much like where the rubber meets the road as where the whole tire meets the toad.

Woolf's oecological perceptions were extra pertinent and again prophetic—his rag-tag transculturalists patrolled the litter prone highroads of Chihuahua poking kleenex and wall to wall carpet into long, plantation class cotton-pickin' bags. They live in Rug Towns, they are serious, conscientious and altruistic—they are the paleo-NAFTA retro-trash pickers, Woolf's metaphorical model of the eternally self-cancelling efforts to simultaneously use it and save it.

It should be said, that in its significant social projections, his greatest public canvas was *Fade Out*—the mischievous 1956 picture of two old guys—a clerk and an ex-boxer (not senior citizens) who are wily and canny and rebellious enough to escape the clutches of their respective cigar-store indian daughters and take a bus trip from New Jersey through Dixieland to Arizona. It's a trip through the south where the pecker-wood's peckers are still made out of wood. They meet the pied piper of Tucson and are taken to a mountain with a hangar in it. It's Virgilian. The modern escape from the lead-weighted domestic tyranny of New Jersey.

Woolf's nerves are very steady, his instinct instructive and deep. His habit of living in abandoned structures is mythical, like the ghost cowboy. He stalks the grounds of state asylums, interviewing the sane. His early novella, *Hypocritic Days,* describes a Hollywood full of hope, not just another shabby suburb. Its central character is a brilliant cripple full of vicious adolescent energy which serves as a closely applied metaphor for the calculating self indulgence of the whole gaudy settlement.

In the widely comic survey Douglas Woolf did of the outback west, its arresting simplicities, its provocative dangers, its fearsomely selfish embarrassments, its desperate resistance to the regimented and poisonous cloud of acculturation lying on the horizon, we have a deposition which will stand in rebuke and correction to the boosteristic waves of development forever enveloping the great hemispheric far high west. From Alaska to Patagonia, nobody who likes thin air will ever forgive them.

Douglas Woolf's West was the Closed Frontier. The one Turner closed the books on. That didn't mean they stopped coming. It did mean it was never going to change, and it was a shack for some and tar paper for others. And thus they settled down to wait with the indians and the slaves, all programmed on arrival not to cooperate.

Bring out the playing cards, set up the whiskey—the Ghost Motel with its strip of art deco flapping in the Chinook, gas station crossroads, Jim Bridger recast as a grocer. Not an improvement. Fear and fright are built into the load and the load is distributed outward, the only place it's got to go. Woolf's Ice Cream Man/moral automata market right down the esophagus of your own street. It's a chilling reality for something so sweet. Junk mail will never replace it, there's no *telefonus interruptus* because nobody's calling. You had to keep a straight smile among those people. To Douglas Woolf, the whole struggling stratum was amusing, and his empiricist witness unerring—he is the nicest ironist since Swift.

"America" is a smug, hardhearted, unforgiving nation of jackals, which forever slaps itself on its back over how generous, selfless and idealistic it is. It is the most preposterous propaganda barrage since Goebbels ran an office, in bloodier and more interesting times.

You go to the window. You look out at the immense night. You see the plow, you see the dipper, you see the fish and you see the net. Every thing blood and bone ever needed is shown and displayed in the sky. You can hunker down and pay the mortgage, and save yourself a lot of trouble, or you can see the show. There actually isn't any other choice. For a mere traveller has no access to the haunts.

Woolf's west was underlaid with genetic proto-temps—the outwash of the Great Depression. Their offspring are the mutates of a system which has deliberately set out to create them for that function. I'm glad, if Douglas Woolf had to go, he escapes the horror of having to witness the perverse fulfillment of his most sympathetic projections.

Edward Dorn
5 July, 1993

HYPOCRITIC DAYS
&
OTHER TALES

Hypocritic Days

for Yvonne

O N E

HE STEPPED OUT the door into a cooling world. The sun was bright, but it was not so warm as it had been when he went inside, only its brightness seemed left to it. For years he had found comfort in knowing that if the sun were suddenly to go out its light would continue to reach the earth for eight minutes afterward, it had seemed a saving period of grace to him. But now he asked himself where the comfort lay, what if the sun were already out? What if it had gone out while he was with the old man inside, say at the instant the probing steel finger had found an exposed nerve in his wisdom tooth? Thinking back, retracing laboriously the spastic movements of the clock on the pink plaster wall, he calculated that it could not possibly have happened earlier than that. On his right the sun was large and perhaps still a little puffy with sleepiness, yet it had a calm, unworried stare. He looked ahead, to the top of the hill, telling himself that if he arrived up there before darkness fell everything would be all right. Thus it was as a man facing a crisis, whether of disaster or salvation he could not foresee, that he allowed the broken, inessential sidewalk to guide him home.

Earlier, pinioned there on his back in the leather chair he had wanted for some time to speak, but the old man had had both hands, the one of flesh and the other one, inside his mouth. He could not help but wonder at what point they had first thought of building men of steel, just how far they intended to go with it. Just how far, for that matter, had they gone at the present time? Already an old man could shove his shiny forefinger down your gullet and you either accepted it or lost your teeth. Equally they had done wonders with the eye, strapped it cleverly to the forehead, a bright bit of steel and glass whose stare you would no more return than you would the sun's. Black permanently wavy hair, patently borrowed from some nobler pate, they had glued realistically above that plump and hairless neck. As for the rest, how was he to know? The yellowing watermarks beneath the humid armpits certainly had the appearance of honest sweat, the breath pumped into his upturned face was hot and cleverly spiced with Doublemint. But because these would be minor refinements in so cunning an art he was not to be easily convinced by them, no more than he was convinced by the authentic-seeming vituperation which flooded him: "Pariah," enunciated the rather metallic voice, "spit out the blood."

His wish was to refuse the command, to dispose of his own blood as he saw fit. In the momentarily quiet room he stared defiantly up at the tall old man, not at the central eye but at the hairless cheeks, the continent, perfect smile, secretly fearing that he was the victim not only of the old man's anger but of a sinister metallurgical impregnation as well, that if he were to obey the command his spittle would show not blood but the pallid amber viscosity of machine oil. Only when the shiny forefinger jabbed its threat at him did he turn to spit, noisily, with eyes closed, into the porcelain receptacle at his elbow, and then upon opening his eyes to the small bubbles of blood, his own strong red blood, turned to face triumphantly the humiliated doctor.

"Don't look so damned proud," the old man said, shoving him roughly back in the chair. "Everybody has blood, and there's nothing so special about it either. There was a time when we thought our blood was something more than a fluid to keep us warm, we thought it was made after a secret formula which God concocted especially for each of us, for no one else. Well, it turns out that God isn't that ambitious a chemist, now we know that there are just four types of blood, A, B, AB, and O. Which doesn't make for much variety, does it? When you go into the army any ghoul will know what type of blood you've got, simply by glancing at your dogtag—'O', I should imagine, it's the most common—the thing he won't know is what type of genes you've got. Spit."

Staring up at the old man he chose instead to swallow his blood, and it tasted sweet to him. "All right, have it your way," the old man buzzed, "swallow it until you get the bellyache. It's your blood and your privilege to do what you want with it. Not so your genes, they belong to Humanity. You can't go around dripping a few into every begging cup, like some zealous missionary doling beans at Sixth and Main. You save them up for the proper time and place, and then you serve them up not with hymns and tambourines but with humility. God knows, they're the only thing of any value you'll ever have, your precious share in the currency of life, and you want to deposit them when and where they'll draw the highest interest rate. Our laws have made certain provisions in that regard—the age of consent is eighteen for the genetrix, you might like to know, short of that consent is not hers but the father's to give. At that, we compromise with lascivity. Humanity will continue to commit slow suicide until an age of consent has been set for either sex, preferably at thirty-five. Would you care to spit?

"No? Then stop squirming as though you couldn't stand it, because you could. God gave you two strong hands, didn't he, and one rather easily discouraged tool to use in them? I've yet to see the man who couldn't get along, if he cared to do, with such odds as those. I myself saved it until I was thirtynine, at the zenith of my strength, and I shouldn't have to describe to you the splendid dividends my patience earned. Or should I? Oh, I acknowledge you probably know the feel of her—to the fingertips, the tongue, and otherwise—better than I. To you she is a gainly bit of tender flesh, a dish of warm pudding shall we say, to be dipped into, tasted, devoured or cast aside. To her father she is something quite other than that. You'll understand when you have a daughter yourself, at the proper time, with the proper mate. Spit?"

This time he did tip up and squirt with careless violence at the porcelain bowl, not bothering to look for it, not even bothering afterward to bib the elastic spittle that dangled from his open mouth like a broken guywire on a marionette. The shiny forefinger threatened him, the good left hand shoved him back again.

"No, I'll do the talking. There's nothing you can say to me even if I permit you to. You think you love her, enough to ruin her. And it would ruin her, you know, just as surely as it would ruin me. Sixteen years of devoted labor aborted by a boy! No, I won't permit it. *Let me tell you something.* After this when you want to play with your marbles, don't do it with little girls; choose somebody old enough to make an interesting game of it. Does the analogy seem coarse to you? I'll use another one: two no's combine to make a yes and yet their usage is forbidden, the yes is invalid, not recognized. You ought to appreciate that, being a poet." The "poet" emerged from the same small contemptuous pout as the "Spit!" which shortly succeeded it.

"Do you follow me? I don't hardly think you do—at any rate, you do as much as you ever will. You poets are concerned only with the question mark, you don't mind what the question is. The question is Humanity, and you speak irrelevantly of love—a four-letter word which you employ to decorate your privy ignorance. Have you ever stopped to ask yourself what the issue might turn out to be? Ah, I know that you both appear to be healthy animals enough—a little pyorrhea perhaps, a tendency toward skinniness—but the seeds of betrayal are inside you both urging you toward genocide. Janice doesn't, happily, resemble me in the matter of hair, no more than you take after your father in stature. But these degenerate strains could as easily as not reassert themselves, combine, and what a pretty poem that would make! Spit."

Spitting, I'll thank you to leave my father out of this, he thought. I'd rather have hair any day than six-foot-four of chickenshit with a sucked egg blowing about on top. "So much for the question," the old man sighed, "the answer begs us now. We know—do we not?—that humankind is progressing toward ever greater longevity, thus it follows that proportionately the seventeen-year-old is younger than he was one hundred years ago. Today the seventeen-year-old has a life expectancy of some fifty additional years, far more than he formerly had at birth. Plenty of time, wouldn't you say, for him to enter the race? But no, unfortunately he hasn't learned how to pace himself in this the longest race the world will ever know, the human race, a relay race. Zoom, zow, he's off to overcome an imagined deficit, even before the stick has been passed to him. With what results? One, the judges call him back to the starting line, and two, he has so spent himself that he is incapable of performing creditably when his proper time comes round. A burned-out, useless old man with half his life ahead of him. Had he waited, saved himself, he might have contributed to his race something less inglorious. I like to think that this is what I have done: a subtly more delicate selection of genes, an added dash of thyroid, a precious overabundance of muscle tone. A masterpiece." The empty egghead hovered close, perilously close, to his, the burning eye stared critically into his gaping mouth, the shiny forefinger probed for a nerve, found it, probed again; the tears flooded his eyes, but he refused to cry.

"She is a masterpiece, you know and I won't have her defaced by a puling juvenile. It wouldn't do you good in the long run, anyway, she could never belong to you. Simply by being a male you outrage her in possessing the one quality which nature has withheld from her. There's a streak of stubbornness, of steel, in her that will never permit her to belong to any man, especially a little boy like you; the same stubbornness that enabled me to pull, I mean literally pull myself out of a dental laboratory into this snug office you find me in. Yes, the same steel reinforces both of us, Janice and me. If I am wrong, I'll answer for her myself. *Listen to me.* I'll answer for her, my young and winsome friend." The shiny forefinger jabbed once viciously at him, recoiled. "All right, I'm done with you. For now."

You would too, wouldn't you, he thought bending stiffly upward and watching the thin steel arm hung up to rest, imagining it impaling his throat there upon the sticky leather chair and turning then in an incestuous, abortive frenzy upon that other, secret throat of Janice's whose mysteries he himself had so lovingly explored. You'd do that, too, wouldn't you, old man?

But now the warm left hand lay upon his neck, showing him to the door. "About that wisdom tooth," the old man said, patting him almost playfully, "I'm afraid it arrived too soon. We'll probably have to yank it out."

"When?"

"What's this, the 30th? Shall we say the 15th of June?" The voice seemed to issue, threateningly, from an immense black calendar on the wall. "The situation should be quite clear, I think, by June 15th."

Nodding, turning dumbly to the door, he heard behind him the old man's unpleasant laugh, a toothbrush working a lather up. "Don't worry about it, Charles," the voice scratched after him. "You won't feel anything at all. I'm going to use gas on you."

The way home, no matter from which direction he approached, was always a difficult, uphill climb. Even when he was not running races with the failing sun, the road from the dentist's office, from Jan's house, was the most difficult one of all. His heavy feet struggled wearily with their enemy, gravity, and the more they fought the more firmly gravity clung to them. If he were walking on the sun, he knew, his body would weigh four thousand pounds, he would be instantly crushed by his own weight. What was more likely than that the earth beneath him was accumulating gravity too, a slow, slow process which one day would bring him to his knees, his hands, his face, before he finally crushed himself. But now tripping on a hidden crack in this ruin of a sidewalk he knew that he was almost home.

His destination, which he reached safely with the unpredictable sun shining calmly over him, was one summit of those low foothills cleaving the steel-blue smog of Los Angeles from the dusty yellow haze of San Fernando Valley to the north. Here he had lived for seventeen years in a vast green playyard which had once belonged to him. The castiron gate which he came to now had once been his to swing upon, jump perilously from one to another of the closing arms, heave outward again before rusty fingers locked themselves in a grip he was powerless to break, a contest which ended only when exhaustion forced him to permit defeat and turn home with the grim promise that by tomorrow someone would have opened his gate again. Today, one finger opened it, and hearing its vindictive slam behind his back he felt scarcely any resentfulness at all. The neatly plowed rows of orange trees which he now wandered through (following a certain devious course which he had chosen long ago) were as beautifully, as falsely green as they had ever been, but they too were no longer his. They, like the great gravel racetrack which led him in a circumspect oval around the House, had long since been stolen away from him. Nor could he tell when this cruel theft had taken place, any more than he could tell whom to lay the blame upon.

Surely not the old Corpse who once a month emerged from the House to make the cane-tap scouting trip, surely this stolen playground did not belong to him. As absurd to say that his own father Chick owned all this property, owned anything at all. Who then? Who owned it now that it had been taken away from him? One day soon the Corpse would be carried off in a gilt-edged box, his father Chick and he would move on to a lesser home, over some less grand garage, he himself in passing would point out this hilltop as having once belonged to him, and everyone, especially he, would look askance at such an improbability.

Behind the House he skirted the odorless incinerator, the gleaming antiseptic garbage pails, the stumpy grapevines pruned back like airedale puppy tails, and, finally the gloomy cavern over which he lived. But passing this last he did not so much as glance at the sombre brute which lurked in there, the ten-cylinder hippopotamus his father Chick, clambering over the fat squat back, had spent his morning currying. Slowly he climbed the outside stairs, the final steep ascent toward home. Inside at last, he gently closed the door, peered expectantly about the stuffed leather living-room like some amateur zoologist returning home, then softly called, "Say, are you home in there?" wondering how many years it was since he had been able to call his father Dad.

The kitchen door swung open and his father stepped nimbly into the frontroom, wearing that embarrassed, depreciatory smile which seemed to beg no compliments for having landed on both hind feet from some overhead trapeze. His father too peered questioningly here and there into the gloom. "Son?" at last.

"It's I," he unfairly corrected him.

Chick's hand went behind him to the wall, its intent as direct, premeditated as the switch it found, and the orange light which lit him up was a little uncanny too, like a jack-o'-lantern on Halloween. "Smile, Big Fella, smile for Dad."

Baring his teeth, he blinked off the quick rush of moisture that reached his eyes.

"Diamonds," his father said, moving sideways for other

views. "Like di-a-monds. What's the word, Big Fella?"

"No word," he said, standing there and following his father with his eyes. "He said he might have to pull my wisdom out—yank, I think he said."

"Ahhh." The light in Chick's face was snuffed quickly out, leaving it dark and moody with the pain he was suffering for his son, as he had always done. When now Chick extended a commiserating hand to him, he half-expected to see a bloody tooth in the palm of it. "He'll use gas?"

"Yes, he said he would."

"Well, that's something," his father said, with a poor counterfeit of encouragement, "something anyway. Soup's on. You're hungry now?"

"I'll wash—ablute, I mean." Quickly he marched past his father to the bathroom, fighting down the familiar, paralyzing sensation that if he were to offer any encouragement at all, a mere glance behind, his father would spring lovingly upon his shoulders and giddyap him expertly down the hall. For it was as a jockey that his father Chick had first been used by Milo Jones, and in all the years of his apparent domestication from jockey to second butler to privileged chauffeur he had clung as tenaciously to that first personality as he had to his whipcord riding clothes. Even on the monthly occasion of his guiding the Corpse about the grounds he displayed the sentimental air of a jockey leading some venerable racing horse to pasture, his respectful sideglances recalling the golden years, now forever lost, when that great sagging back had carried him in strength and glory before the multitudes. It was quite another look he cast upon his son, a raw young colt with untried potentialities.

In the bathroom he doused his face several times with the cold tap water as if to wash bad dreams away, and joining his father in the kitchen he was thankful to feel his hunger teased by the most tasteful odor in the world: "What's this," he asked, "have you been out quashing tortoises with the old man's Cadillac again?" and waited smiling for his father's pleased retort: "Hey now Big Fella, let's not mock Dad's turtle soup."

Before the advent of electrical refrigeration green turtles were used to feed the crews of sailing vessels, because the immense turtles could exist for weeks without food or water unable to roll over from their backs as they lay there on the afterdeck waiting impatiently to be eaten up. Seated watching his father from the breakfast-luncheon-dinner nook, he followed the meal's preparation with the interest such a turtle might have shown. His father expected it of him. At dinners, as at every meal, his father was head cook, maître d', and host. Everything he did he did with little, formalized flourishes of competence, as though the process of learning had been less easy for him than for others more naturally endowed. Or perhaps as though his every gesture aped some other, archetypal gesture he had once watched a man perform. Even while the soup dish settled unerringly between the faultless lines of silverware, the free left hand plucked up the white linen napkin and flicked out its folds for him. "You ought to operate a restaurant," he said, for perhaps the thousandth time.

"I do," came his father's pleased reply. "Chick's Exclusive Eatery, and you're my number-one customer."

Chick's number-one customer, he thought bending his face to the nourishing steam, I wonder what possible joy he finds in me. All the seventeen years of their shared loneliness, it seemed to him, had no more of permanence than this steaming dish of soup which he waited impatiently to spoon, all the meals and beds and games Chick had made with unwavering devotedness for him had been daily consumed, despoiled by his ungrateful appetite. Where then did Chick find his reward? At times it almost seemed to him that the key to his father's devotion lay not so much in love for him as for the sacred duty which Chick performed. How many fathers, Chick's attitude seemed at such moments to ask, have learned to become mothers as efficiently as I, how many have even tried? But then it invariably happened, as it now did, that his father smiled at him with the appearance of such genuine fondness that he was compelled to admit if any love at all were in this room it was he himself who at the moment aped it. "Won't you ever sit down?" he asked with lowered eyes.

"Ah, now there we are," his father said, and truly there they were, for with his father seated he could look over and smile almost easily at him. Seated the upper body had a certain deceptive heaviness that belied the weak, thin legs and hips the table hid. The head well-proportioned, almost dignified, the hairline high but dark and strong above the ample forehead, the prominent nose and lower jaw inclined ever so slightly in good humor to the left. Only the small, fixed smile which offered its subtle apology even in the deepest moments of facial repose suggested that everything was not altogether as it might have been, as it most certainly was not. One thing to look down at one's father at seventeen, quite another to have been retrieving his cap from closet hooks since one was ten. Unkind to expect that their invocation for God's blessing should be anything but a silent, bashful one.

Then, "You'll be going out with Jan this afternoon?" his father asked, raising his silver spoon delicately, and the daily forum had formally begun.

"She's at one of her meetings," he said, eating hungrily. "The Beverly Hills League for Future Women Sufferers or some such extraordinary thing."

"A real cheekful," Chick agreed, and grinned companionably. "I guess Maria won't be fixed in time for you to fetch Jan home?" his father added, superfluously, but his own greater restraint prevented his bothering to ask if he could borrow the Cadillac. It was one of the unexpected little hardnesses that his father carried like invisible, nonmalignant tumors inside of him.

"They'll have her ready tonight," he said.

"For the Brawl?"

"Yes, for the Brawl."

"Well then, Big Fella," his father said, hopping up, whisking their dishes away, "I guess you'll want to do a little homework this afternoon."

"I did it in study hour." He had his father at a disadvantage, standing up, and he used it practicedly: "I'll probably amble down and see how the car is getting along."

"Now you don't want to let those marks slip, Big Fella," his father cautioned from his unpaternal stance before the stove. "You don't want to let those little old marks go bad on you, you know."

"They won't," he answered glumly, "and if they do? Where's the catastrophe?"

"Hey now, Big Fella, hey now," his father said, brandishing his serving spoon as if it were a magic wand to wave bad thoughts away. "You don't want to talk like that, not even jokingly."

"No, I mean it, you give too much thought to marks, appearances. In the long run, it's the thing we hide that counts."

"The choice between college and the army isn't a question of appearances," his father said readily, but with a tactful lack of emphasis which took into account his son's fundamental criticism of him. "That's one sure difference your marks will make, Big Fella, isn't it?"

"The odds are a thousand to one it wouldn't kill me, the army I mean," he said. "I could die other deaths. Don't let's forget how often you've wished you had been old enough."

"Oh, me," his father said, his chuckle soft and hideous, "the only trouble with me was they had all the carrier pigeons they needed then."

"Dad, shut up!"

The chuckle weaker now, less sure. "You used to think that was a funny one. . . ."

"Never!" he cried. "I never did." The author of that remark, the recruiting sergeant whom he'd never seen, had been the first man he'd ever wanted to give his hate. He had named a pet kitten Sarge, and worried it to death. He tried once more, at this late date, to give his hate to him, but, muttering, it was almost as though he gave it to Chick instead: "It isn't funny, you know it's not."

"Well now, Big Fella," his father said, grinning pathetically in his distress, "you don't begrudge your Dad his little jokes, do you?"

He did not trouble to answer that, nor did his father expect him to as he placed his rabbit entree before him on the table, the food arranged so exactingly with one eye out for color and symmetry, the other for calories and vitamins. Feeling his father studying him, he looked up from the neat bald potatoes to his father's eyes. "Big Fella, who's worrying about appearances now?" his father asked tenderly of him. "I was old enough. You know I was."

He could not endure that look of his father's for very long, that look the insulted have when they pretend we flatter them. "If we were to try seriously," he said, looking down, "we might be able to discover something else to talk about."

"Right you are, Big Fella," his father said, winking from the stove his equivocal accord, "we'll talk about the army now. I didn't want the army any more than it wanted me, it was my pride that wanted it. You're different though. The army wants you to stay at home because it has other plans for you. You've got something more valuable than big arms and legs, Big Fella, you're 'an oasis in the desert' like your teacher said." (This with the belittling air that attempted to say, I'm merely using that crackpot to bolster my pride and my argument.) "You're special, boy."

"So was Christ," he said, reluctantly, for it was not this comparison his impatience singled out, it was the too painful comparison with his father Chick. Remembering that night, that electric night when Janice's secrets had first been his, completely his, he felt only discomfort at his father's words. Truly, special had been the word for him that night, he had had everything, everything Chick did not. Never had he felt himself so replete before, never his father so bereft. He had stood in joyous pity before his father in the livingroom, as though waiting to receive an invisible sword from him. He had stood there waiting expectantly, and Chick had smiled his amiable smile. "What's the good word tonight, Big Fella?" Chick had said, and even while he felt the joy gutted inside of him Chick had hurried off to fetch their traditional midnight snack. Nothing of his new honor was visible to Chick, he was still Dad's clever boy, Dad's joy, his specialness an inviolable thing which Chick himself had patented. Thus it was that he said now quietly, when his father was sitting down, "Perhaps my pride needs something too."

"Yours, Charles," his father asked, raising his heavy eyebrows in a dismay borrowed from some long-dead vaudevillian. "You're joking now. Just look at you, you've got everything."

"Look all you want," he said, "but nothing you see belongs to me."

Even as he spoke he knew the sick surprise of a hunter falling into the trap which he has set for a wilder game, whose waiting prey he now becomes. His father Chick stared across the table at him, chewing rapidly on the warped left side of his kindly face, holding his glum stare until ready to admonish him: "That's no way to talk, Charles, no way at all to talk to me. Hasn't Dad given you everything a boy could want?" Everything, he thought returning his father's injured look, everything except wanting to remain a boy for life. "You don't answer that," his father said, hurt or seeming so. "You're thinking I haven't given you a mother, boy."

And there it was, the secret weapon his father used against him in moments of direst stress, the guilt which somehow made him guilty too. "No, I'm not at all," he protested too loudly, as though he did not speak the truth. "You know I'm not."

"It pains my heart to hear you talk this way, Big Fella, it truly does. So angrily," his father said. "You, Big Fella, you've got everything a boy could want—brains, a physique, a handsome face . . . a father who loves you like a mother too . . ."

"I know that," he said, not quite gently. "I know all that."

"What's more, you've got important people who care what happens to you, boy. Doesn't that mean anything at all to you?"

"The Corpse?"

"Big Fella," severely now, "Mr. Jones is the best friend a man could have, I know that from experience. He thinks the world of you."

"His kind thoughts are not reciprocated and therefore not solicited," he said, enjoying chagrin at his own pomposity.

"We'll discuss it another time," his father said, preparing to do so now. "In a year or two you'll know how wrong you are, how wrong-headed. You'll thank me for putting in good words for you."

"Never," he said emphatically, "not if it were the only business in the world. And one day soon it will probably be just that—the last man will be a claims adjuster roaming the earth in quest of fraudulent beneficiaries. Finding none he'll lovingly cut his throat, being careful of course to leave a signed note behind: 'To whom it may concern: I did this by my own hand. My books are clean.' "

"Enough, enough," his father said. "We won't discuss it further now. We'll wait."

"Maybe when he hires me the Corpse will sell me a

comprehensive policy for my soul, loss thereof or partial hurt thereto. Do you suppose he would?"

"No, now, we'll wait and discuss it when you're more reasonable. . . ."

"How can you!" he said in sudden, belated passion. "How can you want me to do it! Your own son a blood-sucking usurer working for that fascistic Neanderthal? How can you endure to think of it?"

"What I think I think for you, I promise you!" Chick cried, wanting in his excitement to jump up but not daring to. "And after this when you discuss Mr. Jones I'll thank you not to call him a fascistic Neanderthal, I'll thank you to keep your voice down too."

"Why? He's deaf," he flung back at him, "deaf in every way! I think being his flunky for all these years has made you grow a little bit deaf yourself. You used to be able to hear the truth about men like him without its hurting you—you taught me to."

He waited for Chick to answer that, waited for him to retort angrily. But his father sat looking across the table at him in a stunned and vacant way, aware perhaps for the first time in his life that his son's rebelliousness had ceased seeking out generalities and turned on him exclusively. "If it's my politics we're discussing now," Chick said at last, and he chuckled distractedly, "I've told you many times that I voted Socialist that year because all the other levers were too high for me to reach. Now I wear boots on election day."

On his feet, himself now deaf, blind with a bitter, stinging unhappiness, he might have done something quite violent had his flying napkin not sent the glass saltcellar reeling across the table top for Chick to catch and quietly restore. "Dad," he asked from the last residue of his anger, "why must you do it? Why?"

Chick moved silently around him with sideways face to remove his dish. "Sit down, there, Big Fella," he said, "we still have our dessert."

Listless in his chair again, mashing with his fork the brown and emaciated twins upon his plate, he brooded pitilessly over the appropriateness of his father's preferring his bananas fried. In truth he might never have abandoned his foundling vision of himself, in which for years he had seen Chick discovering him outside the grounds of one or another of movieland's more voluptuous and immoral queens (her identity shifting constantly with his own lascivity), might never have conceded anything at all to Chick were it not for the small beribboned packet of certificates and documents which Chick preserved in the bottom of his sewing basket, to reassure himself and other skeptics of his probable authenticity. Here in yellow, crackling paper was preserved Chick's past, the brittle skins which he had briefly worn and shed: the highschool diploma which he had earned with less pride than humility, the ninetysix notices of races won, the certificate of marriage to Maria Annette Provost in 1935, the certificate of birth that December 20th of an unnamed male, the abbreviated adv. of Chick's formal bereavement on Christmas Eve. Everything of Chick was there save photographs; for some of us statistics have a kindlier sympathy. "How old were you," he asked his father, "when you married her?"

"Charles?"

Was Marie then his alone, did he reserve the privilege of restoring her? "How old were you?"

"Why, I was twentyfive, going on twentysix," his father said, and added as though in embarrassment: "Your mother was seventeen."

"I didn't ask you that," he said quite roughly. "I asked how old you were, that's all."

His father was watching him. "Why do you want to know?"

"I am interested."

"Charles," his father offered, with a look that wanted to penetrate, "is there something you have to tell your Dad?"

"Nothing."

Still his father studied him, but he was dreaming if he expected encouragement. "You and Jan, Big Fella," Chick said at last, "there's nothing between you two?"

Now he was laughing at his father openly, intending to. "Between us?"

"Nothing serious?"

"Nothing between us at all," he answered, somehow laughing still, holding his right hand up with two fingers intertwined. "Like this we are."

Across the table his father was grinning unhappily while he ate, which was more than Charles could do. Concealing the gluey fruit in a little mess beneath his fork, he stood up and put his napkin down. "I'd better hurry along," he said unreasonably, "they may have some question about the car."

"You told them to make the bearings one-twothousandth under?"

"They know all that."

"Well, try not to be too long, Big Fella," his father said, grudgingly releasing him. "Today it's ginger snaps and soda pop—black cherry, your favorite, boy."

Yes, it makes a first-rate douche, he wanted very much to say, but instead he grinned his phony pleasure and brushed his father's whipcord shoulder with his knuckles as he went by. "I'll make it just as early as I can."

"You've got money, Big Fella?"

Not looking back, "Enough," he said.

"O.K., then, boy."

T W O

Out the door into the light and down the narrow stairs, swiftly past the sleeping hippopotamus, the regimental garbage cans, he makes a cautious circuit of the House in which privacy is a health-food stored and sealed hermetically. Before the House, in the dead center of a theodolitic masterpiece of treeless lawn, the flagpole, man's rebuttal to foolish poets, perhaps even to God himself, stands aloof and cynical, casting no shade, no seed. Beside it an old man, as spare and barren as the pole, wraps himself in Old Glory and pours cheerful profanity into his own deaf ears. "Now, listen," he thunders, for as with all old men he is his own most difficult audience, "I wouldn't be caught wiping my arse with a rag like this. Sooner use my beard, come to that. My own beard, hear?" His beard, almost as venerated by movie-bred America as the flag itself, prominently displayed in ten Civil Wars, doused with tomato ketchup for two technicolor scalping scenes, tugged, tweeked, twisted painfully by most villains and heroines, has won him the sobriquet Uncle Sam. More recently, grown a little fuzzy upstairs, retired, he has been the hero of other more limited engagements, namely The Great Grape Arbor Fire, The Case of the Smashed Chandelier (Louis Quinze), The Man Who Locked the Upstairs Maid in the Downstairs Bath, until presently his only authorized functions around the place are to rake the gravel drive and raise and lower the flag on holidays. "Now look, boy," he remonstrates more quietly, for he has a new audience now, younger and more alert, "a flag like this would make Betsy Ross do push-ups in her grave. The moths have captured it, they're carrying it away with them."

"Uncle, how did the rope come down?"

"Boy?"

"How did that rope come down?"

"It's too old, boy, too horse-spit old to hold."

"It broke?"

"No, boy, it came untied. You can't tie a proper knot with it."

"Great," he said, taking the rope end from the old man's trembling hands: "Fine."

"Ladder's too short," the old man said now, and he peered up at the sky as if his old eyes saw something up there he might rest a ladder on were it long enough, "it wouldn't begin to reach."

"No, Uncle," he agreed, "I'm afraid you're right."

"We could lower the pole."

"Yes."

"We'd never get it up again."

"No." Here, all impossibilities eliminated, he felt his legs go weak. "I guess I'll have to shinny it."

Uncle Sam peered out at him through a hoary forest of eyelashes, furtively. "Mr. Jones will have our skins if he finds the flag's not up today."

"Don't worry, I'll get it up."

The eyes almost hidden now: "You think you can?"

"You don't?"

"You've never been all the way before."

"I've never been allowed."

"Here." Stooping stiffly, the old man picked up a length of rope. "I'll play it out to you."

"No, Uncle, thanks," he said, looping the clothesline loosely on his belt. "You stand back there and watch the pole, see that it doesn't break."

The first twenty feet were child's play, but even at that he took them almost timidly. Not that he was afraid he might hurt himself, he was simply reluctant to test his strength. Often enough he had started this climb confident that someone, Uncle Sam or Chick or anyone, would holler him down long before his strength gave out, and resting at half-mast today he listened briefly for an alarmed voice to call out to him. But glancing down over his back he saw Uncle Sam waving encouragement. "Better hurry it up, boy, before Mr. Jones looks out and sees."

"The hell with Mr. Jones. I'm not doing this for him, old man."

"Just because he's been half-dead these twenty years, don't think he doesn't know what day this is. Don't think he's forgotten our boys that sacrificed their lives for us. Our brave fighting men. Our silent heroes, boy. Our dead."

"For Christ's sake, give it a rest," he shouted through gasping breaths, for suddenly he was angry, angry at the old man's monotonous imbecilities, his stubborn refusal to admit the favors he so urgently required, angry too at the martial music which, reaching him faintly yet compellingly from the distant city which he dared not look down upon, seemed to shanghai his simple gesture of goodwill into a larger, civic ceremony, perhaps most angry of all at his own anger which drove him continually upward, beyond and beyond the willing limits of his strength. Probably if it had not been for this anger he would never have reached the top, for when he did arrive there it required the strength of all his limbs to prevent his sinking to the ground again; for seconds he clung there like a wounded bat while the old man bravoed and heckled him inanely from below: "Didn't I tell you you could make it, boy? Now just loop that rope around the wheel, just loop it around . . . What are you waiting on?"

What was he waiting on! With his hands numb on the rusty truck, the rope at his belt seemed an age away, unattainable. Slowly, as if parting with something as dear as life itself, he pried his left hand free—and found that the other held. Recklessly now he jerked the halyard from his belt, flung it up and over the truck in the desperate, graceless way of a man casting away a hand-grenade, and the old man cheered.

He had succeeded, but in the instant between success and his swift, searing return to the ground he imagined that he could not let go, that he must cling forever to that slender pole, his own memorial. Limp and breathless on the ground, he smiled sheepishly at Uncle Sam. "Well," and brushing flakes of rust from his wrinkled pants, "that's done."

"Good job, boy."

"Shall I knot the rope for you?"

"I'll knot it, I'll take care of everything. Just you run along now, boy."

Dismissed, not needed now, he got weakly to his feet and walked off down the gravel drive, nor did he turn to look behind until he knew for sure he was beyond the horizon of Uncle Sam's old, incurious eyes. "Uncle . . . !"

"Uncle!" He returned a step toward the old man and cupped his hands. "Uncle, you're hanging it upside down!" But lowering his hands, recalling only then that Uncle was deaf as well, he turned away, leaving all the reluctant heroes in the world dumb beneath the feet of one old, living man.

It is the easiest thing to hurry down a hill, so he hurried, leaving behind him the little bungalows withdrawn from him in cozy draws and crevices, the fenced-in watertank where as children he and Jan had risked contaminating the city's water with their naked innocence, the sanitarium, the country club, down to leveler ground where leveler people lived in more conventional bungalows. The dusty block where laborers and pensioners lived, the block of clerks and civil servants, the doctors' block, the block of car dealers and assorted criminals, then suddenly into the city itself where no one lived.

The parade had broken up. The little handfuls of people on the streets seemed caught in a breach of etiquette. On the corner the sight of a soldier making disconsolate love to himself, fondling his most tender parts. Out on the boulevard a pretty housetrailer cut ahead of a patrol car with a provocative flick of her mobile hips. Nearby a family-size parcel of tourists stared so expectantly at him that he gave them the Henry Fonda smile, waiting until he was a step beyond to raucously blow his nose.

And now the somehow military preparedness of a Chevron station waiting to service vehicles for tonight's attack, and he turned in there.

Mr. Hart waited until Charles was at his side before he looked up from the red pile of sawdust he was pushing with his broom, saving valueless seconds thus. He looked up shyly and shook his head. "This dirt," he said. "There's no end to it."

"Yes," Charles said.

Sweeping, "Billy's in the back, grinding your valves till I get done."

"Thanks, Mr. Hart."

Through the wide door he could see Maria tipped back on her ass with Billy hanging head-first into her gutted front; he walked up quietly and pressed the horn. Billy glanced over his shoulder in disgust, then grinned at him. "You and your horny valves," he said.

"Bad?"

Billy dipped into the car again. "I've seen worse," he said contentedly.

"Do you think she'll be ready for tonight?"

"You're planning on going to the Brawl this week, Charley?"

"Of course. Aren't you?"

"I'll have to come late," Billy said, with that odd contentment in his voice. "I'm racing this afternoon." Now Billy straightened up from whatever he was doing in there, and he stepped down off his toolbox to Charles's side. There was a wide smear of grease across Billy's face, but to Charles it seemed the same freckled face which four years before had won first prize in a local art show for one of Mr. Hart's steady customers. It was as though neither time nor experience had dared touch its unprotected, somehow American boyishness, nor ever would, as though that portrait had captured a rare innocence in Billy and preserved it permanently. For Billy there would be no conflicts, ever, no unplanned pregnancies, no homemade gas chambers, no emotion of any kind. For Billy there would be only robust, coplike Lois Bartlo and shiny racing cars. There would be speed. In this dimension alone one would measure Billy's maturity; every year, every race Billy would go a little faster than he had before.

"I need at least a third to pass out Dochousen on points," Billy said.

And, I, Charles thought, I need at least a whole new world, to live. "You'll get it easily," he said.

"Sure," was Billy's sure reply. Already he had an unprecedented sixth at Indianapolis.

"Good old Billy," Charles said, patting Billy's coveralled shoulder, "you've really got it figured, haven't you?"

"What, the race?"

"Yes," he said, "the race."

Billy shook his head. "There's no figuring ahead of time," he said with a thoughtful, teacher's emphasis. "All you can do is wait until you get in there and then do what seems best to you."

"You make it sound easy, Billy, but how do you find time to make up your mind when you're going so fast?"

"You don't have to make up your mind," Billy said, "not really. You just do whatever you can."

"I should think it would make you giddy."

"Giddy?"

"Going around in circles all the time."

Billy grinned. "Well, if it does," he said, "you're too busy to notice it."

"He's been giddy all his life anyway," Mr. Hart said, at Charles' side.

Grinning, Billy turned to the workbench and picked up one of Maria's valves. "Yeah, I'm a regular chip off the old block," he said.

"Now he's bragging," said Mr. Hart.

They watched Billy switch on the grindstone and lightly touch the valve to it. Sparks flew from Billy's hands but were quickly lost in the lighted room; they waited for the others that followed them. Billy too watched his working hands, but with polite curiosity, as though they belonged to someone else. Glancing sideways at Mr. Hart, Charles found it almost easier to believe the hands were his. He saw Billy pass the valve over his shoulder to his father, simultaneously switching the wheel off with the other hand, his own once more.

"Yes," Mr. Hart said, "that'll do it. We don't want any

blow noises in Charley's valves when he takes them home to Chick, not if we know what's good for us."

"Chick's pretty sharp," Billy said. "He would have made a first rate mechanic if he'd wanted to."

"Chick knows his automobiles," added Mr. Hart.

Charles fingered the valve Mr. Hart passed on to him. "Yeah, I guess he does, all right."

"I wish I had an ear like his."

"Yeah, so do . . . oh hell," he said in sudden despondency, "I'd better be shoving off."

Outside, people were emerging from the restaurants and Roland would be stationed at his theater now. Continuing west along the boulevard he walked with eyes cast down and sideways upon model livingrooms and gleaming, virgin toilet seats. Long ago he had learned not to look at people passing him on this busy street for fear that they might be celebrities, for fear that he might look at them hungrily. He did not want it really, celebrity, not at any rate in the physical way that Roland did. For his part, he wanted his name and the words he wrote to find a secret celebrity in the hearts of thoughtful men. He wanted this with a terrible sense of guilt, for his own heart questioned whether he had anything at all to say to them.

How could he have? He was the audience. In a world of busy talkers, it seemed to him that he was the only audience left. Everyone, everything had something to say to him, something he could not refuse to hear. How many times he had practiced deafness, only to listen days later to a frightening record of the voices he had stored spinning relentlessly its web of meanings inside his mind! How to be a talker when even now he had scarcely begun listening?

Now Roland was a talker on the other hand. Somewhere, somehow Roland had found the key, the switch, that transformed his personality, redirected his inner current from the cathode of receptiveness to the anode of garrulity. For Roland once had been an audience too. It was impossible to say when the change in Roland had taken place, but pausing just outside the glittering marquee, disconcertingly Roland's own advertisement, it was equally impossible to deny that change he had. One listened compulsively to Roland's studied English accents selling cheap dreams to a blonde in imitation mink. "Baby, it's cold outside," Roland said, in his new dark grey suit looking even more than yesterday like a revitalized leading man. "Just step inside and for all you know you may find yourself sitting behind Gregory Peck. An entire new life for a dollar-ten. Who knows. Van Johnson may be in the balcony, you save ten cents. Good girl, I knew you were a sport when I first set eyes on you."

The girl's own frank eyes said that as for her she would be satisfied with Roland Star, and watching her furclad, imitation rump Roland silently promised her that she would have a little bit of him before she left. "The personalized approach," Roland said, and Charles wanted to believe he saw a hint of apology in Roland's smile. "Since Television you've simply got to give them their money's worth, you understand."

"I do, yes," he said, his cynical smile illuminating his forbearance, "but Babette?"

"Babette's reasonable," Roland said, much too confidently. "I've got her up in the balcony, now that you mention it. I drop up from time to time, keep the oven warm till the show lets out."

In his annoyance he turned to study technicolor photographs. "Be careful that you don't fall up on your ass one of these days, old buck," but it wasn't at all what he wanted to say.

"Why, you pedagogical son of a bitch." Roland wandered off to fill some harassed family's empty day, his voice soothing, hypnotically British now. Bitterly, they succumbed.

"I'm sorry, Rollo," Charles apologized, unnecessarily for Roland had not been touched. "I guess I'm feeling a little horny today."

"No word from Jan, Charley?"

"Not yet."

"I thought you might have heard by now."

"I may tonight," he said. "She's at her meeting now."

"Well now, there you are. The very thing," Roland said comfortingly, "to scare it out of her."

"You think so, Rollo?" It was frightening to look at your only friend with a disgust that was almost hate.

"You do make her take precautions, don't you, Charley?" he heard Roland ask.

"Yes."

"She's so independent, I was wondering . . ."

"No."

"What kind does she use?"

"Cherry, Rollo. Cherry, of course."

Roland shook his head. "Pepsi," he said. "More bounce to the ounce."

"Well now," Charles said quietly, "maybe you could get them to sponsor you."

Roland grinned engagingly. "Christ, you've really got it bad tonight."

"Apparently," he said, turning away from Roland. "I'd better go somewhere and get rid of it."

"See you at the Brawl, Charley?"

"I guess so, yes."

"We'll be there, definitely. They were supposed to have a premiere tonight," Roland explained, "but fortunately for me they postponed it until tomorrow."

"You wouldn't want to miss that, would you, Rollo?"

Roland was serious. "I couldn't afford to, Charley."

"Oh? You'd better come early, then."

"I can't spend the rest of my life standing in front of this crummy theater, Charley," Roland said. "A man could grow old in a job like this."

"Yes."

"We're not getting any younger, Charley."

"No." To hide his unhappiness, his sense of loss, he turned away. But, "Charley," Roland called after him, "you haven't noticed the change in me!" and he turned back again.

"Your new grey suit, Rollo."

"No, Charley. Look again."

"I can't."

"My part, Charley, my part—I used to wear it on the left, you know that. I think it makes me look older, don't you, Charley?"

"Now that you mention it, I do," he said, walking rapidly toward the street. "See you tonight, Rollo?"

"Charley . . ." What actor's instinct for the opportune brought Roland across the outer lobby to pat his shoulder paternally?

"Tonight, kid."

Fleeing from Roland's patronizing hand, fleeing like the little boy Roland had blandly made of him, he was amazed, annoyed to realize that it had taken Roland of all people to first expose the fault beneath his surface personality. It was that he had lost the ability to dramatize himself. Most of us spend our lives retouching for ourselves the portraits we imagine others paint of us, yet tonight he made no corrections of any kind. More and more it was becoming true of him, he was content to let others misconstrue and hang him where they would. While five years ago his secret hand had brushed in the drooping mustaches of R. L. Stevenson, today he found it difficult to assume even the secret melancholy of Thomas Chatterton. He supposed that he was growing old, that he was preparing himself, as most dreamers must, for the role of average citizen.

And this of course was the biggest, the most precocious role he had attempted yet. And it was for Jan he attempted it. Jan who had once loved the Peter Pan in him, until he had left that other part of him in her. Wendy and her Peter Pan, she had called them once, but he had grown too old to play. Now I must offer her an entire new love, he thought hopelessly, or risk forever losing her. I must dress up my naked love in titles and certificates.

The three dollars he could manage; it was the three thousand a year that frightened him. Billy Hart, he knew, already was worth six thousand dollars. With Billy's money he could take Jan with him to New York and . . . and what, get a "job" and live happily afterward? No, he would need Roland's personality. With Roland's opportunistic personality and Billy's bank account he might, somehow, make a husband of himself. But Jan, what would she think of this combination plate? It was he she loved, and here he was offering substitutes; as easily offer her a substitute for him.

There was the army. A plan of his, his only plan, called for a kind of military exchange of prisoners in which he would trade his body for the freedom of his imprisoned ego, and Jan's. He who belonged to others, anyway, to society during the day, to Chick at night, could not fail to gain by such a trade. It would be like gambling with borrowed money, successfully; he could pay off his debts with interest and still have a nestegg for himself.

According to this vague and desperate plan of his he would sign up for a three-year tour of duty in Germany, where Jan would further her education under the disciples of Jung and Freud, and he, well, he had thought of being made n.c.o. in charge of inspecting generals. Surely others in this world were as curious as he to know who polished the general's shoes, their buttons, who shaved them, powdered them, zipped their flies? He felt that he could perform a high service to mankind by ferreting out these facts, reporting them to the people in biweekly communiques. In a world that was choosing new gods in place of old, moving their altars into the Pentagon, it was important that the people should see the human side of the men they chose to deify. Even the most popular gods of the fading era, the movie stars, were never above periodic inspection by the masses.

"Charles Ashton . . . Charles."

Charles Ashton, poet of the new era, turned on his public a ready smile. It was not the way of the movie stars, who invariably feigned an instant's astonishment before smiling gratefully, but acting after all was their career. In the future such dissimulation would be omitted, adulation would be expected now, required.

"I say . . . Charles."

Mr. Lippincott, looking in his vast tweed jacket and carefully wrinkled slacks like an overaged, overfed college boy, waved excitedly at Charles from a taproom door. There was about him too a collegiate air of impending miracles. His florid face glowed with some vague new enthusiasm which that last martini had hinted at, the next would clarify. "Charles, my lad."

Charles smiled yes again at Mr. Lippincott, who seemed to be using him as decoy to free himself from some less prosperous associate's hungry tentacles. Obligingly Charles stood his ground, forcing, allowing Mr. Lippincott to drag himself from his unwanted companion and, nodding, waving enthusiastic agreement with the other's importunate demands, join Charles at the curb. He greeted Charles with gestures which somehow succeeded in shaking his hand, patting his back without actually touching him. "Charles, lad, what extraordinary luck. Finding you here. You know?"

"How are you, Mr. Lippincott?"

"That bum," Roy Lippincott said, gesturing at the man he had been talking to. "Wants me to write a story for some genius polecat he represents. I suppose he does mean skunk?"

"I should imagine so, yes. In America we call them that. . . ."

"Screwy," Mr. Lippincott said, shaking his head. "Absolutely screwy. Can you imagine such a thing?"

"They're said to make fine eating," Charles said in Mr. Lippincott's rapid manner, feeling as he always did in Mr. Lippincott's presence that the only way to attract his attention was to imitate him outrageously. "Very sweet and tender . . ."

"Very interesting, Charles," Mr. Lippincott said, nodding. "Quite nauseating. Come, Charles, I want to talk to you. Time for a drink?"

"Well . . ."

"Splendid, lad." Whether Mr. Lippincott thought he was re-entering the taproom he had left but recently it was difficult to say, for his reception at the one next door must have given him the comforting sense of never having really been away. Like a man leading a stranger through his own darkened, cluttered livingroom he bounced gracefully among the tables and chairs to a table in the rear, from there waved enthusiastically at one or two half-known leading men, more cautiously at a red-headed model whose look at him promised she would do anything to get off her feet. Seated now with his back to all of them he stared in slight vexation at the table top, as though someone had thoughtlessly removed his drink. Only when the waiter had brought him a double martini, and in grudging compromise a single one for Charles, did Mr. Lippincott stop reacting to private stimuli and roughly pass a hand across his face in the way of a widowed man smoothing an unmade bed before turning in. "Charles, this is extraordinarily fortunate, meeting you like this. I've been wanting for some time to have a chat with you."

"Oh?" Charles said.

He was waiting to see if Mr. Lippincott would propose a toast, as Jan and he were apt to do, but Mr. Lippincott had no prayers to offer before he retired. He picked up his double martini and drank off one of them before putting the other down. "I had thought of cornering you tonight," he said more slowly now, his need to hurry temporarily arrested. "You will be over, won't you, Charles?"

"Oh, yes," he said, lifting his drink and sociably gulping a taste of it. "We'll all be there, Mr. Lippincott—everyone I've talked to anyway."

"I think I can get you a pre-release," Mr. Lippincott said persuasively. "I can't tell you just which one it'll be, but it'll be a feature attraction, I promise you."

"Great, Mr. Lippincott."

"There'll be plenty to drink. You know?"

Charles smiled. "We all know you give great parties, Mr. Lippincott."

"It gives me a bang, even a bigger bang than this," Mr. Lippincott said, indicating his drink and then finishing it. "Watching you kids cutting up, watching Lloyd. No, not *watching* him. Did you ever feel like you were seeing things through someone else's eyes? That's how I feel, on Saturday nights, as though I were lying there and watching you with Lloyd's eyes. Try to get the picture: as though I'd been blind a long time and he'd willed his eyes to me, like condemned men do."

"Lloyd is a wonderful person," he said, inadequately. "We all love him."

"Charles, he needs you kids."

"No, we need him."

Mr. Lippincott looked up from the fresh drink his fingertips caressed. "You sound like you mean that, Charles."

Under Mr. Lippincott's stare he blushed, yet he had no feeling of being compromised. "I do," he said.

Mr. Lippincott continued to look at Charles over his cocktail glass, covetously now, as though his newly-inherited eyes had discovered a precious intoxicant which some clumsy hand might spill. When he spoke his voice was steady with the precarious steadiness of a brimful glass of champagne offered in bridal toast. "Charles," he said, "you're the man I'm looking for."

"I?"

"I've read your poems, Charles," Mr. Lippincott announced without embarrassment. "In your little lit magazine at school. Lloyd has shown them to me."

"He has?" Charles said no more, for Mr. Lippincott

seemed to expect more of him and now he did feel compromised. It was as though Mr. Lippincott were presenting Charles's own poems to him and asking him to judge, if he had the time. Well, he declined, declined by even a look to pass sentence on the words he had so recently and with such difficulty divorced. Like a man awaiting his final papers, he clung to a husband's right to withhold incriminating testimony, while simultaneously refusing by jactitation to reclaim a dead relationship. Wanting not to seem present at all, really, he shifted slightly on his seat and turned his attention to pious proclamations of ill will above the bar. We reserve the privilege to refuse service to anyone; if you are under twenty one this means you. Well, he thought, we minor poets reserve our privileges too.

Meanwhile, "You have a nice choice of words, Charles," Mr. Lippincott was saying, as of an acrostic. "Very nice words."

So he had not read them, after all. A kick in the ass, alas, but it at least spared Charles the obligation to modify Mr. Lippincott's interpretations; or his own, as we must when others adapt our work to their own more extensive arguments.

"With words like these you could do just about anything. . . ."

"For the correct solution to today's acrostic kindly turn to page sixtynine," he wanted very much to say, but you did not say such a thing to a man who was paying for your drinks, whose house you were looking forward to visiting that night, whose son was the most extraordinary person you knew. No, you smiled in a self-depreciatory manner, and tried to shift the conversation to other vocabularies than your own. "We've been hoping to get some new stories from Lloyd," you said, and asked: "Has he had time to write any recently?"

"He's been frightfully busy with his other work," Mr. Lippincott said, a bit condescendingly but thankful too to be on the other ground. "We submitted 'The Cripple' to the studio as an original last week, last Tuesday. We heard from them today. I think they like it, Charles. I really think they do."

"Say, that's wonderful," he heard himself answering too readily. "Wonderful for Lloyd."

"That boy," Mr. Lippincott said. He shook his head. "He'll have a screen credit before his nineteenth birthday, you wait and see. Get the picture. It took me till thirtyfive. Why, Lloyd, he'll be a producer at thirtyfive. What's the gimmick, Charles? That's what I ask myself, what's the gimmick that made Lloyd turn out that way? You'll say the accident, of course. That's obvious. I used to think it was as simple as that myself. I'd ask myself what he'd be doing now if it hadn't happened, going to school all winter, working vacations as a messenger at the studio for fifty cents an hour? I wouldn't scratch my own crotch for fifty cents an hour. But wait. I'd scratch Rita Hayworth's for twentyfive. For nothing. So would you. Would Lloyd? Would he waste the time?"

"I doubt it," he said, and even as he smiled he felt that Mr. Lippincott's argument was not totally absurd.

"You know he wouldn't," Mr. Lippincott said, pausing to suck fresh enthusiasm from his cocktail glass. "You know he wouldn't, Charles. With Lloyd the gimmick lies deeper than meets the eye. Try to get the picture. You remember we were going to play his story for pathos, tears? Athletic boy faces living death after crippling accident, then gains worldly acclaim and spiritual fulfillment by writing inspiring book about his own life? A good straight-forward gimmick, nothing subtle, played for tears? Well, I wish I could tell you what Lloyd's done with it, Charles. I just wish I could. But the story's not mine anymore, it's Lloyd's. Go see him, Charles."

"Now?"

"Go see him, Charles," Mr. Lippincott said, on his feet. He was pitched a little crookedly toward the left, but even so he held out a guiding hand to Charles. "Go see him, lad."

"Right now?"

"Come back after you've talked with him." Mr. Lippincott's hands were urgent, like his voice. "He'll be reading now, or watching the television. He'll explain it all to you. Go see him, Charles. Go see Lloyd."

T H R E E

"I'll go."

Mr. Lippincott had given the signal, and the two martinis in his employ bounced Charles gently out of there. At the door he looked back enquiringly—to see Mr. Lippincott waving him enthusiastically on his way. But pausing just outside the bar he did not know at once what way that was. As if it were a secret he saved inside himself for moments of necessity, at other times did not presume to know. And even after he had started out, it was with no real confidence that he would arrive.

Perhaps because afterwards he was never able to believe that he had been. Not since that first Saturday night Brawl two years ago, when Roland had hustled him through the neon-lighted streets as to an uncensored movie which their parents would have forbidden them, and afterwards he had slunk home to Chick carrying this uneasiness in him that he could not admit. Especially not since that next week when he had taken Jan, who also wished to see the show, and she had analyzed his malaise for him.

It was that he could not pity Lloyd. Lloyd flat on his back, unable to help himself, was somehow more fortunate than any of them, a godlike *voyeur* of life's obscenities. A Saturday night God, had been Jan's phrase, who from his pillowed throne benignly shared a few hours of their frantic lives. While they, disporting themselves before him in their frenzied desire to please, were permitted a glimpse of his. Quite significant, Jan pointed out, that Lloyd had not gone to their school before his accident, that his former friends were never invited to the Brawl; they would have compared and pitied him. Not so these others. For Lloyd they vied to see who could drink the longest drink, hold the longest kiss, gesture the most extravagant gesture of inviolability, and when Lloyd cheered for them it was as though he somehow felt they needed cheering more than he. Even the girl who sat withdrawn from them at Lloyd's bedside, smoothing Lloyd's sheets, feeding his drinks to him, would next Saturday or the Saturday after be exhibiting herself with the rest of them (it had proven so) and another would have her place. And when finally it came time for them to leave, when excitement and drink had reduced Lloyd to a disordered, flapping mass upon his bed, they would tiptoe quietly away leaving Lloyd's girl to put their exhausted self-pity back to sleep.

Jan's analysis had seemed just to Charles, but did it explain why for two years they had returned to Lloyd's Brawl each Saturday night? Did it explain Charles's presence here today? Did it explain the cold funk he felt as he stood in the warm foyer waiting to press Lloyd's bell, and afterwards as he waited until the count of ten before speaking his name into the hollow brass tube that led to Lloyd? He did not, of course, expect any voice to answer his. Lloyd, who like God was always home, did not haggle with those who called on him. He either opened the door or left it closed.

But when presently the door did click, Charles resisted the impulse to put his toe to it; like a reluctant salesman, he gave it a moment's chance to close again. Inside the empty lobby the elevator as always awaited him, its one apparent purpose to deliver Lloyd his petitioners, then wait outside his door until he was done with them. For all that Charles had ever seen, Lloyd might have been the only tenant in this cubic acre of apartment house. Pressing the seventh-floor button, he half-expected to see Lloyd's name light up on the glass altimeter.

The elevator's climb was so slow, so hushed, that the body sensed no achievement of any kind, it was the mind that climbed toward Lloyd. Inside this stuffy, padded cage the mind seemed to splinter into tiny whirling particles of steel which were drawn relentlessly toward a powerful magnet somewhere above, while the body was repelled. And when the elevator door slid open of its own accord, it moved too slowly, the mind already was in the hall. Other doors were clicking now. Opening the first of these, Charles entered a corridor so dark that it hurt his eyes to look into it. A faint click ahead led him to another door, and when he opened this one and stepped inside it was as though he carried the darkness along with him.

"Lloyd?"

"Who else?"

It must have been Lloyd's electric voice which turned on the lamp, for when the darkness broke into a shimmering ultraviolet arc about Lloyd's bed he lay there quite firmly with his delicate, volitant hands grounded upon his lap, his handsome head resting in statuesque composure upon the pillows which flattered the deep, healthy tan of his skin. Lloyd's eyes did not turn to look at Charles, and standing outside the warm of Lloyd's inhospitable sun he wondered if they ever would. "Lloyd, were you asleep?"

"I was thinking." Lloyd did not say it apologetically, as we with more social obligations are inclined to do, but almost with pride. "Among other things, I was thinking what to say to you."

"There's always hello."

"The very thing." Lloyd lifted his head a few inches from the pillows and grinned at Charles. "Hello, fartface. You've been talking to my old man."

"Yes." Looking into Lloyd's large eyes, he felt himself momentarily shocked by their peacefulness. "He said you'd probably be reading or looking at television."

"Roy always says that." Lloyd's hands fluttered expressionless in the air, settled to his lap again. "It comforts him to pretend I waste my time that way, because he knows I live two days for every one of his, resents it terribly. He gave you a few drinks and sent you over here to keep me company."

"Well, yes . . ."

" 'Get the picture, lad. Lloyd will be watching television now, why don't you go over and bother him? Go on, Charles, go. Go see Lloyd.' "

"How on earth did you know?"

"I write his dialogue," Lloyd said, and somehow his cocky smile did not discredit him. "Besides, I was just talking to him on the telephone. He said you wanted to talk to me."

"He said the same of you. . . ."

"That's my old man," Lloyd said, grinning. "He likes to write dialogue too."

The telephone was ringing above Lloyd's head, and one would have reached exactly the count of ten before his restless hands discovered it. Lloyd listened only briefly, then returned the telephone to the over-sized cradle which some friendly grip had made for him. For a moment he lay staring at the ceiling while his hands fluttered to his lap again. "Gloria. She wanted to say hello." He grinned. "Have you ever heard her on the telephone? She always sounds like someone's putting it into her right then—really marvelous. But come, you haven't told me why you're here."

"No why. I came to see you, period."

"O.K. We'll run it your way, Charles. You'll be over tonight?"

"Yes."

"With Janice?"

"Of course."

"Marvelous. I always look forward to seeing Janice—more than anyone else but you."

"Thanks."

"You can relax though, Charles, this isn't Screw Your Buddy Week. Besides, she's not my type."

"She's not?" Charles asked. He had wanted to keep both relief and patronage out of his voice, but there was an over-articulation in his words that could have been put there by either one.

"No. Janice carries all her hormones in her head," Lloyd explained. "I prefer to have a whore moan between the legs, like Gloria." He paused to wince. "That was rather a bad one, wasn't it? After all that preparation, too. You grow fond of some real stinkers, lying here in bed."

"You don't have to apologize."

"Look," Lloyd said, and as he spoke the sunlamp went off. It went on again. Lloyd had not seemed to move.

"Marvelous."

"I do it with my good toe, Charles. Third toe, left foot—my mother ties a string to it. Poor Gloria, she's losing what wit she has trying to figure it out. Do you think I ought to take out a patent, Lloyd's Face-Saver for Sensitive Paralytics, Spastics and Idiots?"

"Positively."

"You like it, Charles?"

"Very much."

"I was sure you would," Lloyd said. "That's why I sent for you. No, there was another reason too. I want you to work for me."

"Work for you, Lloyd?"

Lloyd's dark tarantular hands wandered to the sides of his bed and back again, their motiveless delight under a terrible control. "I need someone to help me finish off 'The Cripple,' Charles. Naturally, I thought of you."

"I thought your father was helping you."

"But didn't Roy tell you—I fired him today." Lloyd frowned handsomely. "No, there must be a kinder way to put that. We simply decided this picture wasn't Roy's type. Perhaps when something more suitable comes along . . ."

"I suppose in a way he was telling me."

"I don't imagine he entirely believes it himself," Lloyd said. "It will take him a while to realize how wrong he was for 'The Cripple,' I mean psychically. He wanted to make a runny-nose picture out of it, play it for the Kleenex set? Roy can't seem to understand that that sort of picture went out with Hiroshima. People don't *cry* anymore, you know that."

"Truthfully, I never see movies except those your father shows us here. . . ."

"The hell with movies. You see the world, don't you, Charles? How long has it been since you saw anyone cry?"

Thinking of the people he had been with today, of Dr. Mattison and Chick, of Billy and Roland and Mr. Lippincott, of Lloyd, he did not know at once what answer to give. "Shall I answer you in years or in minutes?" he asked finally, seeing Lloyd smile at him. "There are lots of ways of crying, Lloyd."

"Exactly," Lloyd said, his smile even wider now. "And we're inventing new ones every day. I'll tell you why. When we are babies, what does our crying bring us—rattles and lollipops. Our crying becomes associated with our happiness, or at any rate with the pleasure we derive from indulging ourselves, possessing things. Later, when we are older and want to cry, we give ourselves double martinis and television sets, we go to a cat house or a movie show. But we don't ask them to make us cry, we express our sadness by simply being there."

"And you, Lloyd, do you cry too?"

"Of course," said Lloyd. "Just look at me."

Charles was looking at Lloyd when the lamp went out, and for seconds afterward the memory of Lloyd's smile seemed to dance in the darkness, miserably. But then the painted glass globe flashed on beside Lloyd's bed, its rotation immediate and perceptible, as distracting as a sudden recollection of the earth itself. Together they watched all the gaily-painted little continents pass once in review, and one minute of their lives was lost. "This is my world," Lloyd said, his face dimly reflecting it. "This is my glass world and I'm lying here watching a group of butter-fingered old men playing catch with it. (Would you believe that even in my dreams I lie flat on my back, not going anywhere at all? It's true.) I'm lying here watching this game the old men are playing, but I find it isn't a very friendly game of catch. They're tossing the globe among them, mixing hard fast throws with tricky little changes of pace designed to make a man fumble the ball. The object of the game, you see, is to find which old man will fumble first. Every now and then one of the old men juggles the globe with his stiff old fingers, almost drops it, but then just in time shoves it at another old man and laughs. I call out to them in warning, because suddenly it's my own head they're playing with. It's my head," Lloyd explained, and truly now Lloyd's head did seem to become the globe, revolving colorfully, "it's my head and every time an old man gives a toss I wait fearfully for someone to drop it. I can already feel it exploding against the floor. I call out to the old man, and he laughs at me. He laughs and flips it to another old man, and that old man laughs too. Now they're all laughing and throwing the ball faster and faster. I call out to them again and they laugh crazily at me. My hands reach for the phone, I want to call somebody. I don't know who it is I want to call—I want to call everyone. I want to get on the phone and call everyone in the world, you see. I want to call them all up and warn them about the old men, but I can't find the phone. The phone isn't where it's supposed to be, above my head. It isn't there anywhere. I hear the old men laughing and I know they've hidden it. They've hidden it under the covers, down by my feet, beyond the reach of my fingertips. I can feel it with my toes and I begin to move my feet, for the first time in three years I move my feet and I work the phone inch by inch up beneath the covers to my hand. Now I have the phone in my hand and I feel very happy, very powerful. Excitedly I place my first call—to a Mr. A. D. Marcus on La Brea. Eagerly I listen to it ring. I wait, listening to it ring and ring and ring. Mr. Marcus is not in."

Lloyd fell silent, and peering into the now predictable splashes of color that passed across Lloyd's face, waiting for Lloyd to go on, Charles knew that Lloyd was waiting too. "Lloyd, what do you do now?" he whispered, and it was as though Lloyd, whose dream this was, had given the words to him.

"I do what anyone would do," Lloyd said wearily. "I lie here and watch the old men play catch."

"You don't try to call again?"

"I want to, but I always wake up before I allow myself." Lloyd's laugh was loud and somewhat ugly, like the laughter of the deaf. "Charles, have I ever told you about my accident?"

"No, Lloyd."

"May I now?"

"Please, do."

"It was a little dog," Lloyd began in a dying voice, "a little grey dog with gummy fur and burrs in his ass. He was licking the remains of one of his buddies off the cement pavement ahead of me, on my side of the Pass, just where it skirts the studio. He must have been very hungry, because when I hit my horn he didn't move a hair, he gave me one annoyed glance and went on with his meal. There was a station wagon approaching fast in the other lane, so I had but two alternatives, the cur or the ditch along side the highway. Three seconds in which to make a decision which amounted to life's philosophy; naturally, I was unprepared.

"Well, when they dragged me out of the front seat, onto the grass, that filthy little mongrel came up and sniffed me with his bloody snout; they had to kick his ribs in to make him stay off of me. He moved back about five feet then and stood there licking his gums, reproachfully." Lloyd fell silent for a moment, but when he spoke his dying voice had discovered a new source of energy, and it was anger. "Well, I have plenty of time to make decisions, nowadays," he said, "and I haven't wasted a minute of it teaching mongrels the traffic code. No, I look out for myself first now, and I expect everyone else, man and beast, to do the same. I'm top shit now, Charles. I'm It."

"No," Charles whispered, so softly that he was not sure Lloyd could hear. "No, Lloyd." There are remarks which shock us by the ineptitude which we ourselves lend to them, our own most secret thoughts given voice by the very person we would least willingly confess them to, a child's calm reminder of his own mortality, an old man's accurate surmise of how our wife or lover performs in bed, vengeance promised by an invalid. Trapped, caught off our guard, we offer dissembling arguments: "You're trying to shock me, Lloyd."

"You don't approve of my philosophy?"

"This is no philosophy you're defining," Charles answered anxiously. "You're defining evil, Lloyd."

"Only as long as there are people left in the world who expect others to look after them, and people who are so busy looking after others that they destroy themselves. That's what makes me seem evil, Charles. The whole set-up is so phony it stinks. Look, our parents spend years making dependent imbeciles of us, and then when we reach a certain age they surrender themselves into our care. We are supposed to look after them now, even while rendering our own children as useless as ourselves. Everyone but me, that is. I've upset the entire scheme, Charles. I'm contrary to nature, you see. By being an invalid I abdicate my position in the vicious family circle our culture has enmeshed us in. I'm the broken link in the chain, no one depends on me. I'm free! I'm the only free man you know, you know I am. I'm my own man, Charles, and I'm under obligation to no one at all. No one!"

"No one, Lloyd," Charles said, "or everyone."

"Exactly!" Lloyd cheered. "You understand me perfectly. No one or everyone! There's no possibility of a compromise, no need. Everyone is related to me in the same way, and I treat everyone equally. I'm everyone's child! Don't you envy me?"

Nodding, when he had meant to shake his head, he knew his eyes would have made him out a liar, anyhow. "Perhaps, but I don't entirely agree with you. I prefer to picture you as a father, Lloyd."

"Thank you, Charles," Lloyd said with mocking formality, "but you honor me with a role which circumstance forces me to decline. No, you father the next generation, Charles, I'll be the child of the last." Lloyd's hands, in answer to a timid tapping on his door, wandered to the miniature switchboard beside his bed. "Speaking of poor devils, that will be Mother with my egg-nog now."

As the door clicked behind Charles's back, he turned to search the darkness which Mrs. Lippincott let in. He could not find her, but he heard her gasp. The miracles which just eluded Mr. Lippincott were performed momently before his wife. "Ah! Who . . . ?"

"It's only Charles, Mother, not Jesus Christ."

"It's Charles!" Mrs. Lippincott agreed, and clearly he was the more astonishing alternative. "I had no idea you had company, Lloyd. No idea at all!"

"Please don't apologize, Mother. Here, let me turn on the lamp so Charles can see what lovely eggnog you make."

One noticed at once Mrs. Lippincott's immense blue eyes, for everything else about her was colorless. Shoulder high, a little plump, she stood nervously before them pressing her corsage of beaten eggs against her unsupported breast. Her dress was a model of stylishness. Her face she left exposed in its nakedness, there was nothing for rouge to hide. Her shy smile said Mother, but nothing else. It was as though Lloyd had called casting and ordered her, sight unseen, for a walk-on part. "Charles, how handsome you've grown!" she cried, as a woman making too much of her opportunities. "How tall! You must be at least six feet."

Lloyd eyed him sardonically. "Charles and I measure our stature by the thoughts we think, don't we, Charles?"

"Lloyd . . ." Mrs. Lippincott stared at Lloyd, and her large blue eyes appeared to measure him, the entire length of him stretched limply on the bed, before she turned to Charles again. "How is your father, Charles?"

"Very well, thank you."

"Such a *sweet* man," Mrs. Lippincott said, her fluttering hand seeming to seek Chick's head to pat. She shook her own head lingeringly at Charles, as though deciding at last to disbelieve in miracles. Now she walked past Charles to Lloyd's bedside, freeing her unbecoming corsage and holding it out to him.

"Give it to Charles, Mother. He can make better use of it."

Mrs. Lippincott's smile acknowledged temptation, but her hands knew where duty lay, almost grudgingly they thrust the immense glass at Lloyd. "You need this, Lloyd."

"Why?"

"Don't argue, Lloyd."

"Yes, Mother," Lloyd said in a mock-meek voice, and winked at Charles. "Will you leave it on the bedtable, please? I'll drink it later, if you don't mind."

"Promise?"

"Yes, Mother."

"No spilling it by mistake?"

"No, Mother." Over her shoulder, he smirked at Charles. "Was there anything else, Mother?"

"No." But at the door she stopped. "Yes. Have you heard from your father recently?"

"Not for almost an hour, but Charles will be seeing him."

"Can I give him a message, Mrs. Lippincott?"

"If you will." Mrs. Lippincott's listless hand lay on the doorknob, and she did not turn to them. "You might remind him that he has a dinner engagement tonight. He'll want to shave before he leaves."

"I'll tell him."

"Thank you. . . ." Now Mrs. Lippincott did turn to Charles, and he saw her tender smile for just an instant before it was absorbed by the spongy darkness of the corridor. "Charles."

From the bed Lloyd leered at him. "If you ever feel the need of a slightly used mother, I think I can fix it up for you."

Charles smiled, feeling his own smile wan, like Mrs. Lippincott's. "Well, I'm off," he said.

"Charles, you'll start at a hundred a week."

His own hand lay limp on the doorknob now. "You're serious."

"Always. You'll think it over and let me know tonight?"

"Yes. Tonight."

FOUR

In the elevator, sinking slowly into himself once more, the greeting he received from the full-length mirror was anything but affectionate. His own once-friendly eyes looked beyond him, deliberately, and the hand he failed to grasp was as smooth and as cold, as evasive, as glass. When the elevator door opened behind his back, he watched himself smile with excessive cordiality at the girl who waited in the foyer, peering enviously in at him. He hurried to the door and opened it. "Well, hello!"

Gloria's fixed, bovine eyes stared up at him dolefully, and in fascination he stared back at her. Gloria was a woman you wanted to take in great handfuls, like modeling clay, refashion her after your own desire. She stood at least two feet away from him, but it was as though her heavy body were pressing him against the wall. He felt himself thin, breakable. "How are you, Gloria?"

"That saint," she cursed.

Holding the door, he arched his eyebrows questioningly.

"No," she said. "He'd be furious."

Shrugging, he allowed the door to close.

"Charley, have you been with him long?"

"A while."

"Did he say anything about me at all?"

He nodded, yes.

"What?"

"He likes to hear your voice on the telephone."

As she ducked away, her heavy lips writhed in a smile. He held the outer door for her, feeling the immense, somehow hysterical vitality of her as she passed by. "Are you going toward town?"

"No," and already she was loping away from him.

"Gloria, do you have any idea what time it is, Gloria?"

Gloria's answer was a laugh, unhappy yet meaningless. Nearby, perhaps a block away, some small stray band rang out with a brassy exuberance that frightened the living and mocked the dead. Pocketing his hands deeply to prevent their going to his ears, he hustled into town again. The clock above the bar said a quarter to four, but of course nobody heeded it; here, time is the measure of our capacity, just as money is the measure of our appetite. For Mr. Lippincott it was ten drinks past noon, five before the dinner hour. His smile for Charles said, "Feel better now? I've ordered you another one."

"Thanks, I won't have anything."

"You saw him, lad?"

"I did."

"Lloyd explained everything to you—our differences?"

"Not entirely. He said the two of you don't agree on what people want, that you still believe people cry."

"Exactly! Let me tell you what Lloyd has done with 'The Cripple,' Charles. Let me try. As Lloyd sees it, the boy hasn't met with a tragedy after all. Hasn't had to overcome handicaps of any kind. His accident merely serves to give him an earlier impetus in life, you know? Frees him from childhood's obligations, as Lloyd puts it, and sets him on the track of what he's always intended to do? No, in Lloyd's story it's not the boy who's the victim of tragedy —it's the father whose back is really broken, Charles. The boy loses control of his limbs, yes, but the father loses control of everything. A writer, he loses the ability to write anything but the most maudlin trash. A father, he loses his son, loses him over-night instead of gradually in the way most fathers do. A man, he loses the will to live. You see, it's the father who's the cripple, Charles. It's me, Charles, *me*." Mr.Lippincott's large face leaned toward Charles, and two small, bitter-looking tears, like martini drops, ran down his florid cheeks and fell at one time on the table top. "And do you know what, Charles? It's true, it's true!"

Charles, because he could find no nice words at all for this unhappy man, held his silence while Mr. Lippincott accepted the more spontaneous condolences the waiter brought. Together they watched the waiter's damp cloth soak up rings of moisture from the table top, but when the waiter had done only Charles appeared to notice that he had overlooked the two tear drops. Mr. Lippincott was collecting new tears in his brimming glass, a lachrymatory which he seemed to replenish as quickly as he drank from it. "That boy," Mr.Lippincott said in a sudden, wretched spasm of enthusiasm, "that boy of mine! What can one make of him?"

"I don't know," Charles said, and he saw Mr. Lippincott smile at the note of awe with which he spoke, "but just now I think I'd give almost anything to be in his . . ." He broke off in confusion, hearing the other's laugh.

"In his braces, Charles?" Mr. Lippincott suggested, laughing miserably. "So would I."

He wanted to look away, but he could not: the florid face continued to labor for several seconds after the sound of laughter died. Now they sat staring uneasily at one another, as though held in unwilling conspiracy by a subversive thought, which at last Mr. Lippincott pretended to disavow by sliding his half-empty glass away. "Don't you see, Charles, I'm through," Mr. Lippincott said, leaning close to him. "He's used me up, every drop of me. Get the picture, lad. My mind goes blank when he discusses his ideas with me. My heart is dead when I read the things he writes—there's no fluttering of any kind. Even my hands are numb when I try to copy his stuff for him. He needs a fresh mind, a strong heart, young hands. Charles. Charles, what do you say?"

Just now he said nothing. He looked at his thin young hands which he was being asked to give away. He listened to the strong beat of his heart, feeling a little guilty that even at this moment it should work so hard for him. He asked the question of his mind, and it made no comment of any kind.

But Mr. Lippincott was finding his answers in Charles' eyes. "You'd be more than an attendant, Charles. Far more. You'd be a collaborator, actually. You know?"

"I know," he said, nodding. "I know."

"You'd be well-paid, of course."

"There are other things . . ."

"Charles, what else?"

"There's Chick."

"Chick wouldn't approve?"

He laughed.

"Well, isn't that just what Lloyd's offering you?" Mr. Lippincott asked. "Isn't it? The choice between being a boy or a man?"

"Yes, I suppose in a way it is."

"My God, lad, you still have doubts?"

Again he laughed. "Wouldn't you?" he asked.

They were on their feet now, both laughing, their hands clasped not so much in parting as in sympathy. "Mrs. Lippincott asked me to remind you you have a dinner engagement."

"Jimmie Krako," he said, rather mournfully. "He may have a job for me."

"Well . . ."

"I won't keep you, Charles."

"Well."

"Until tonight."

"Yes."

Loneliness is like the common cold, a contagious disease which we catch in public places and suffer in privacy. We turn from a man's loneliness as instinctively as we turn from his sneeze, but his germ overtakes us easily. We carry it home and doctor it with old remedies, all patently useless: there is no known cure for loneliness. The best we can do is to give it to someone else. Just as soon as we observe our symptoms in another, our own become less severe. Now let him look for someone else to pass his to, for we have developed an immunity. In a week we'll be feeling fit again, and an old man will die of unknown cause in Buffalo.

Outside, the city lay around him like a bright thin circle of flame, and he felt himself a trapped animal who chooses his direction unthinkingly. Ahead the hills looked yellow, as if scorched by the heat he was fleeing from. To his left the sun hung low in the sky, a monstrous mirror of Los Angeles. He stopped on a neat square lawn picked and brushed with a dental thoroughness, hunted for a pebble without finding one. "All right, you meticulous old bastard," he muttered, "just for that I'll ring."

The chimes had scarcely begun to sound when the door opened noiselessly to Mrs. Mattison. For a second she looked at him almost affectionately, as though it were she he called upon. Now she spun like a graceful tackle leading his interference down the hall; he watched her broad shoulders take out two swinging doors, which he in turn straight-armed silently. In the kitchen's bright safety, she wheeled on him. "We'll hide in here," she whispered. "Doctor is preparing a lecture for the Society. 'Atavism vs. Americanism,' I believe it is."

Crossing to the stainless steel stepladder, he propped his elbows on the stainless steel table in front of him, and looked in surprise at her. "You mean he has to *prepare* those things?" he asked. But the question he meant really to ask was, is he Doctor when you're in bed with him?

Mrs. Mattison laughed roughly, drawing a sharp glance from him. "You have no, no respect, have you?" she asked, delightedly. "Doctor doesn't go to his study to write. He *stalks*, indignantly."

"I can picture it." Often he had observed that mothers flirted most strenuously with their daughters' favorite beaus, but he had never been able to decide whether they did it by way of challenge or mockery. "What's cooking, beautiful?" he said.

"Would Chick be furious if I were to offer you a piece of cake so close to dinner time?"

"What kind?"

"Pineapple upside-down."

"Chick would never know," he said.

"You children are all, all alike, aren't you?" She laughed not believing a word she said. "Janice never tells me anything. Never. This morning. If I didn't know her so well, I might never have known how sick she was."

"Sick?" Over the upside-down cake his eyes sought hers but she had spun away from him. "Sick?"

"When I spoke a little word of sympathy, she made herself another waffle, ate every bite of it. With gobs of that thick maple syrup you love so much. Ten minutes later I could hear her upstairs, wretchedly losing it. I didn't dare go up to her."

"Sick?" He was on his feet now, the great dripping slice of cake hanging unheeded at his side. Watching Mrs. Mattison's broad shoulders pivot to the whipping of some incongruous delicacy, breathing the uncomplementary yet piquant odors of pineapple and artichoke, he felt an emptiness in him that no rich food of hers could satisfy. "She's sick?"

"I did feel that I had to tell her, though, that I thought she ought to stay home today. She laughed at me, said not to worry if she was a little late. She said after the meeting she and one of the girls would probably go horseback riding."

"Horseback riding?" Sinking to his stainless stool, he licked a vein of brown sugar from his pulsing wrist. "Is it good for her?"

"What?"

"Is it good for her?"

"What!" Her shoulders were still moving, rhythmically, but he could see her hands dangling loose at her sides, and he listened appalled to the gurgling sound her laughter made. "Good for her?" she asked, turning her laughter upon him like a searchlight. "You ask that question of me? Of me?" She brought her laughter across the room to him, so close that involuntarily he raised a hand to rake cake crumbs from his lips. "You're quite a nice boy," she said, her sweet-breathed laughter flooding him, "but why couldn't you have been born in Gary, Indiana? There are lots of girls in Gary, Indiana, big girls with big hips and big busts for having babies. You would have had a fine time in Gary. Why couldn't you have been born in Gary?"

He pushed the rest of the gooey handful into his mouth, deliberately exaggerating now the callow figure her laughter made of him. "I love her," he said, quite messily.

"Ah!" She turned from him in disgust, as he had hoped she would, and he tried to feel some pleasure in his victory. Mrs. Mattison made it difficult. She was not a woman to slam pans and oven doors in moments of unhappiness, but under her forbearance the nerves flinched that much more painfully. "I'm also rather fond of you," he said.

"Why didn't you tell me years ago!" she cried, her good humor returning easily. "I would have adopted you. Do you suppose they have any cheap boarding schools in Gary?"

"I'll treat her well," he said.

Mrs. Mattison turned to look at him, and under her impersonal glance he might have been a clock, a small kitchen clock consulted in matters of mealtime gravity. "You'll kill her," she said quietly, turning the oven up.

"What crap!" he said, on his feet, across the room, confronting indignantly her athletic back. "What crap," he repeated, but knew that she would not look at him even if he were to take her by the scraggly hair and twist her head around. "Why?" he asked now, helplessly. It was the only way. All three Mattisons had an uncanny resistance to being bullied; it was some vitamin they took in the morning, and it stayed with them throughout the day. "Why?" he asked.

She would have answered him then, he knew, out of a deeply inbred sense of superiority if not of decency, had they not both at that moment heard the front door open and close, thunderously, heard her, Jan's, childishly clear and musical voice call "Dad?" through the shaken house, and turned in a kind of companionable jealousy to follow her slim dancing feet along the carpetless hall to his singsong. "In here, sweet."

"What crap," he muttered, slinking back to his stainless step ladder, taking himself furiously out of the way. He was etching it with a fingertip on the stainless steel table top, CRAP, when seconds later she pirouetted through the well-oiled swinging door, and he did not look up at her, not at her face.

"How nice!" Jan said, and furtively he watched her narrow feet dance over to the stove, furtively watched her impossibly narrow hips press against her mother's stalwart ones. Quickly he lowered his eyes again, for it embarrassed him to have undressed Jan, waist-down, in the presence of Mrs. Mattison. "Mom," she said, and her kiss sounded extravagantly loud to him.

Now he waited rubbing the tabletop with his sweater sleeve for her to acknowledge him, coolly he could be sure, for Jan particularly would resent being caught half-naked in the kitchen, and at the dinner hour. He imagined her hiding behind her mother, peering over her mother's shoulder at him. "Char," she said.

"Jan . . ." He could not help it, he looked up at her pleadingly. His eyes dug into her grey-blonde hair which she wore short and thick like kitten fur, and it felt almost unbearably soft to him. He looked into her large blue eyes; it was like seeking affection in two nuggets of blue vitriol. He had seen a lovely pair of brass knuckles in a pawn shop once, covered with velveteen.

"Did you have a nice ride, dear?" Mrs. Mattison spoke so quickly that she would have interrupted him, had he had anything at all to say.

"A nice long one. Pat and I ducked out of the meeting just as soon as those little idiots voted our motion down. We'll probably be blackballed now. I hope we are."

"Your motion, dear?"

"Resolved," said Jan, "to strenuously advocate and, when necessary, strenuously exercise the most modern principles of birth control. Little idiots!"

Mrs. Mattison, slicing a hard-boiled egg over a curry dish, laughed temperately. "How did the vote go, Jan?"

"Six idiotic nays to two yeas."

"Well now, perhaps some of those girls are Catholics?"

"Catholics!" Jan cried, her piercing laugh an unlovely,

somehow frightening thing. "Heathen virgins, every one of them!"

"Ah," Mrs. Mattison continued to slice her eggs; no one could have sliced eggs more noiselessly. "Are you hungry, dear?"

"For cake? I'm ravenous."

"No. It's too close to dinner time."

Without looking up, he knew her pout. "Char had some."

"I don't care. It's almost dinner time."

"But Char had some."

"How do you know Char did?"

"I can see it all over his beautiful mouth."

"Well, it makes no difference if he did or not. Charles is our guest."

He heard Jan laugh gaily on her way across the room to him, and he almost hated the little-girl role she performed so well. He wrote the word on the table top again, but feeling her cool finger on his neck he rubbed it out. Her voice was as gentle as her fingertips. "Char. Is Char our guest?" she purred.

Under cover of the table his hand took her almost roughly behind the knee. "I've got something to show you. Can we go outside?"

"Outside?"

"What could Charles possibly, possibly have that he can't show me?"

"It's outside," he muttered, furious at both of them.

"Well, I'm leaving anyway," said Mrs. Mattison, turning the oven down. "Jan, will you watch the dinner, see that it doesn't burn?" At the swinging door she turned, and like an eccentric old mare she neighed at Charles. "Jan hates to cook," she said.

He turned from the swinging door. Jan had extended her hands behind her, palms down, on the stainless steel drainboard, projecting her bust in the way of the movie stars. It was an unrewarding effort, but it was not a comical one. She eyed him bitterly as he walked up to her. "It didn't work," she hissed. "It didn't work! The goddam horse was afraid he might hurt me. He loped. He must have thought he was on a merry-go-round!"

He placed his hand on her taut shoulder, it was like caressing a billiard ball. "Don't worry about it," he said, straying to the soft, pulsing area beneath her chin. "It doesn't matter."

"It doesn't matter!"

Smiling, he shook his head. "I've got good news," he said. "A job. A hundred a week."

She laughed. "A hundred a week. What are you going to do, jump off Grauman's Chinese and leave your headprint in the patio?"

So he laughed too. "Even easier than that," he said. "I'm going to write movie scripts."

"Oh, no!" she said, cried. "Will you wear alligator sandals and purple slacks?"

"I'll be working for Lloyd."

"For Lloyd!" She was almost hysterical. "What are we coming to! What nonsense has Lloyd been feeding you?"

"No nonsense. He wants me to help him with 'The Cripple.' There will be others afterwards."

"Lloyd isn't in this world," she said to him in a voice almost too high to be audible. "How can you allow yourself to be duped this way? Lloyd has lost touch with our world, he's created himself an illusive one. His world is a bed! A bed! He's sick, and you're catching his disease from him!"

He pressed her arm, quieting her. "I think you're a little jealous," he said.

"Jealous! Of you!"

She was leaning so far backward that he could no longer reach her without seeming to molest her, so he withdrew his hand. "Well?" he said.

"Well, what?"

"Aren't you pleased?" he asked, feeling himself smile fatuously.

"Pleased!"

"With the way things are working out."

"Oh, My God!" she cried, staring at him as though he were a monstrous thing. "My God, I think you want it to happen. I think you *want* it to."

He met her blue vitriol eyes with a boldness he did not really have. Almost at once he looked away, unhappily, at the stove. "There could be worse things," he said, and it was as though he had stuck a frightfully sharp pin in her, deflating in one burst her anger, her pride, her hostility, everything. For several minutes he stood watching her helplessly sobbing, feeling superior and a little cruel. "The rice is boiling over," he said at last.

Pushing herself upright with her hands, she crossed stiffly to the stove and turned all the burners off. "I hate to cook," she said miserably.

He reached out and caught her round the waist from behind, spinning her fragile body into his arms. "I'll do the cooking," he said into the soft grey fur at her ear.

She laughed! She laughed, and burrowing her head beneath his chin begged like a kitten to have her backneck scratched. "My poor Char," she murmured. "My poor idiotic little boy."

"I'll see you tonight?"

"Yes."

"The usual meeting place?"

"Yes," she said.

He kissed her hurriedly but thoroughly on the lips, and, disentangling himself, ducked out the kitchen door without glancing back. He hadn't quite lost all his senses, yet.

Now it was all uphill again, and he stalked past citizens putting a nightcap on their holiday. Up and down the street, front lawns were being drowned, systematically, by stern-faced engineers. Front doors were being closed. Behind unshaded picture windows cocktail shakers rattled chillily, half-crocked old men, after dutifully instructing young children in old adages, turned up the television or the radio. In perspiring kitchens perspiring wives danced uncensored dances with half-frozen daiquiris, contemplated cozily the pleasures of domesticity and the prospects of being laid. Saturday night in the suburbs is a recurrent dream, not to be taken too seriously.

At the House he surprised the immense, preposterous sun trying to set dramatically, as in a travelogue. The sun's long rays made pink the descending flag which, tickled by small breezes, jerked and twisted evasively on its back, fell helplessly writhing on Uncle Sam. Charles paused to watch their silent struggle, from which Uncle Sam emerged at last victorious, whacking the flag into a square, talking some sense to it. He watched Uncle Sam march boldly to the House, and boldly enter it. Another day almost put away, and not one reprimand. Now to get through evening meal without spilling anything. Then privacy.

Tonight, by way of variety, Charles took the outside stairs

in double strides, entering the front room only seconds late, as the kitchen door whooshed closed. The implication was that Chick had spent his entire afternoon making a home for him, been surprised in the midst of it. The worn grey carpet was certainly clean, it bore the marks of the electrolux. Slatternly pillows became almost attractive in pregnancy. Disturbed dust was just now resettling on waxed surfaces. One lamp was lit. Only the shallow imprint in the leather easychair, the hasty alignment of the World Atlas and the World Almanac, attested that Chick had at the very last run out of small tasks to do.

"Say, are you home in there?" He needed quite urgently to go down the hall, but as always there were certain proprieties to be observed. "Hey!"

The door bounced open and Chick appeared, inaugurating the cocktail hour. The quart bottle of black cherry soda, corked, he had buried in a pail of broken ice, two champagne glasses sat on the tray beside gingersnaps. A clean white towel hung from his arm. With just a little flourish he slid the tray one-handed onto the cleared table between the couch and the easychair, stepped back a step. "What's the good word tonight, Big Fella?"

"No word."

He crossed over to the couch, and seated watched Chick revolve the bottle briskly between his palms. At last satisfied, Chick wrapped the bottle in the towel he had. He inserted the corkscrew carefully. Raising his eyebrows an apprehensive trace, lent force to it. The cork came out with a joyless pop, but Chick's anxious eyes went ceilingward, no stains were visible. Now Chick poured the champagne glasses full, rewound the towel, returned the bottle, corked, to the bucket of ice, tendered his glass in toast. "To our brave dead," he said.

"The dead are neither brave nor ours," and smiling they drank their black cherry chug-a-lug.

"Gingersnap?"

"Don't mind if I do."

Now it was time to repeat the ceremony, identically, the towel, the cork, the corkscrew, the anxious upswept glance exactly as before; Alfred Lunt could not have rehearsed his genius more lovingly. "Your turn, Big Fella, now."

"To Chick the Incomparable," he said, and drank off his glass while Chick flushed ecstasy.

"You saw Jan, Big Fella?"

"I saw her, yes."

"You'll be going out tonight?"

"Quite soon."

"Then I'll put dinner on."

Dinner was "on," of course, had been all afternoon. While Chick hurried into the kitchen to sniff at it, Charles went down the hall. How could he have guessed that one day he would wish he knew how to cook? In seventeen years of hobnobbing with a master chef, he had never got past a peeled potato, a crooked carrot stick. He never knew how hot the oven was. Always he had been the dinner guest, and his praise had been Chick's sustenance. In the kitchen he was delighted to find that it was Welsh rarebit tonight, but he only knew that there was cheese in it. "What kind of cheese do you use?" he asked, watching it stretch out from the pan to grilled tomatoes and golden toast.

"A good sharp cheese," Chick said.

"What do you do to make it taste so good?"

"I season it."

"What with?"

"Why, with condiments."

"What condiments?"

Chick shrugged. "Paprika and salt, mustard and Worcestershire, curry, red pepper, a cup of beer. Just about anything."

"Then what do you do with it?"

"Why, I cook it," Chick said.

Silenced, dunced, he slunk to his place in the dinner nook. If there had been a bib in the house he would have asked for it. "Marie, did she know how to cook?"

"Marie?" Chick was building a sturdy log cabin out of asparagus. "I never found out. We ate in the big house then. Marie was a chambermaid."

"I know that," he said, but regretted at once his snappishness. "It wouldn't have mattered, anyway," he said, watching Chick juggle condiment cans. "Whether she knew how, I mean."

"Not an iota, Big Fella." Chick came over to the tableside,

stood hopping there inconspicuously. "Sorry," Charles said: he had forgotten to pick up his napkin at Chick's approach. The Welsh rarebit dish looked blistering hot, but he felt that Chick would have held on to it all evening rather than hurry him. "Ah, what an aroma! If she were alive, do you think you'd be cooking now?"

"Marie?"

"Marie."

"Why, I have no idea," Chick said. "I've never given a thought." Seated now, he looked earnestly at Charles over his napkin-bib. "Why do you ask, Big Fella?"

"I was just thinking," Charles said, "how very lucky she'd be."

"If she had lived?"

"Yes."

"Yes, wouldn't she."

"No, no! I mean to have you as a husband, Chick."

Silence now. Marie was a battle ground, Chick a master of camouflage. His stubby fingers grouped shakers and silverware on the table cloth, illustrating his over-all strategy. We'll show no emotion before we reply. We'll smile with our eyes, because there are tears in them. "Big Fella, I was the unluckiest thing that ever happened to poor Marie."

"You?" Charles asked. He looked down at the havoc he'd wrought, and at that moment he felt he might have deserted to the other side had he not been so thoroughly disciplined. "I thought that distinction was reserved for me!"

Chick's laugh flashed around the room, as from some carefully concealed battery. "What foolishness, you were an unborn baby then!"

A direct hit, Charles thought, using his napkin violently. But because Chick made no conciliatory move of any kind: "D'you think she'd have lived, if I'd been born today?"

"Charles?" Now it was Chick's turn to be ready for rout. "Big Fella?"

"Childbirth is different, nowadays."

"Oh?" Chick was back in the fray. He was genuinely interested. "I didn't know they had found new ways."

"It's safer now. Doctors know more today."

"Doctors?" Chick lifted his eyes evasively. "I had the best that money could buy."

Pin-pointing Chick's eyes: "Then why did she die?"

"Why, she was small," Chick said, his arms flaying the air, disorganized. "And you were large, larger than anyone would ever have guessed."

"They would have known that, today."

Chick shook his head. "You were late, quite late, you see."

"Today they would have hurried me."

Chick's head shook violently. "I think Marie was afraid," He said. "I think she was afraid of you."

"Ah, now!" he said, lowering his eyes. "Ah, now!" He looked at the log cabin upon his plate, saw that it was leveled now. He looked at the rarebit; it had turned to cheese. He got to his feet, and his white napkin fluttered to the table cloth. He smiled with his eyes, because there were tears in them. Clicking his heels, he saluted Chick. "Your prisoner, Chick."

Chick was distracted in victory. "Your rarebit, Big Fella, your salad and apple pie?"

"I accepted pineapple upside-down from Mrs. Mattison at five," Charles said, "rather than seem impolite."

"Well, then," Chick said. He pushed his own dish away. "We'll finish when you get home."

"Yes, certainly. Now if you'll excuse me, I'll go in and bathe, ablute."

But in the bath he was so deeply chilled he could not get the water hot enough. He filled the immense tub with undiluted hot, yet the warmth succeeded only in pinking him, it did not penetrate. His heart was chattering. Too big and too late, he thought eyeing the entire stretch of himself, Marie was afraid of me. But watching the dissolute Moby Dick breaching and sounding by turns between his legs, he felt that you could not love anything without fearing it a little too. "You started it," he said aloud, chafing himself with a well-starched towel, "now I'll finish it." On a hundred a week he could buy a doctor of any price; two, in the event of twins. And entering the narrow library in which he slept he began to feel himself valuable for the first time in his life. It was a disturbing thing, feeling valuable. He put on a clean white suit tonight, thinking he would show up more clearly in the dark during his brief term as a pedestrian.

"Well, here I go."

"Ah . . ."

"You don't *have* to wait up for me, you know."

"I'll wait, Big Fella. I have nothing else to do."

"There's always sleep."

"I know. Maria will be ready, Big Fella?"

"Yes."

"You'll get it first?"

"Yes."

"Well, Big Fella, be careful. Try."

FIVE

"Too late for that."

Out the door into the night and down the narrow stairs, he made a vigilant circuit of the House where tiered and variegated window scenes bewildered the shopping curiosity as in a television store. High up, in the topmost set, Irene the House manageress peered chestily out at him from above her lowcut lounging robe, and his outraged glance shifted to the pantry where silent actors enacted in pantomime their serialized domestic tragedy, thence to a prolonged station break on the floor above, back, reluctantly, to Irene again. There had been a time when he had dreamed of a midnight sortie to that attic room, but tonight he consoled himself with knowing that this had been an excusable aberration in a boy too early weaned. He turned his back on the entire wretched display, deciding to wait until they had perfected it.

The stars were more beguiling. In the absence of the moon they sported merrily, while beneath him, the city mirrored their delight in a rather melancholy way. Yet it was into this faulty mirror that he looked, as a man shaving forsakes the mind's portrait to fondle the pimples on his chin, mistaking reality for truth. Not until he reached the rusty gate and opened it did he think to look up again, and then not at the heavens but at the plump dusty globe which stood sentry there, the hardy moths which buffeted it, the glistening blister beetle which basked in its yellow light on a nearby deodar. Why had he never quite got around to grinding one of those little buggers up to try its aphrodisiacal properties? Interesting to know what miracles might have transpired in a boy of ten, although now he felt he no longer had need of them.

A gentle wind sweeping down the hill kept telephone lines busy with singing messages. Front shades had long ago been drawn creating the illusion of privacy. From house to house influential sponsors skirmished valiantly with smug consumers who already had purchased two on the installment plan, while here and there he fancied he could detect the cataleptic click of poker chips, the tense whisper of canasta cards. In one small brown bungalow alone, which he knew to house a young diaper deliveryman, his crystal ears picked up the turning pages of a book. He moved with muted footsteps past this last, and he did not walk freely until the city's nightlight awakened him again to reality.

It was the early dinner hour. Yet people were running from everywhere, automobiles were slowing down. Anxious questions were in the air. The answer was a simple one: across the street a young housewife drew silver dollars from a laundry bag and scaled them at a traffic cop. One of the coins skipped along the pavement to Charles's feet, but he got rid of it in time to avoid being thrown to the sidewalk by two young boys in corduroy. He decided, out of a profound experience in illogic reasoning, it was something they were doing for radio.

Mr. Hart was busy pumping ethyl gas into a Duesenberg, but his attendant eyes watched Charles approach. He nodded stealthily over the conversation of his lady customer. An old lady with a short fur coat and polaroid bifocals on, she hopped energetically out of her Duesenberg. Her motions were quick and wasteful, like a highschool girl's. As she circled the little car, her saddleshoed hoof kicked at the skinny tires. The right rear tire she tested twice.

"Check it for you, Mrs. Fellows?" asked Mr. Hart.

"Please, Jack."

"You take thirty?"

"I think so, Jack."

"She's on the nose," said Mr. Hart.

Now Mrs. Fellows slid behind the steering wheel and, crouching low, leapt out onto the Boulevard, not looking anywhere. Mr. Hart and Charles watched her beat her first red light, and then they turned to sigh. Mr. Hart sighed noncommittally. "Charles, she's ready to go."

"Thanks, Mr. Hart." They stooped together under the hanging door. "Any news from Billy yet?"

"Lois called a while ago. He was a lap ahead on the fifty-ninth."

"Good old Billy. I knew he'd be."

"He's pretty fast, all right," said Mr. Hart.

In the greasy light of the garage Maria looked most painfully old, she bulged in all the wrong places, an old lady paying ungracefully for the dissolute youth she'd had. She had no makeup on. He never spent a penny on her face, only on internal surgery. Nevertheless, he loved her when she was running well.

"She may not want to start," said Mr. Hart.

"I'll try." He got in and stomped on her until she started up, unwillingly. Then he fooled around in there, allowing her a little throttle until she got warm. Under his fond touch Maria purred dreamily, although perhaps she dreamed of gayer men whom she had known. Cutting her throttle down, he felt that he knew what it would be like to love a jade too old for him to please. Nevertheless he loved her when she was running well. "She sounds wonderful."

"You'll want to run her easy for a while. You're not racing Dochousen."

"I know." Under Mr. Hart's unconfident watching he jockeyed Maria toward the exit door. "Mr. Hart, you can send the bill to me."

"To you?" Still not confident, as though the one way to make money were racing Dochousen.

"I'll have money in a week or two." Maria was anxious to be gone, so he waved at Mr. Hart and slipped into the sticky traffic. California drivers are the most gregarious in the world. Back your automobile into the Pacific Ocean, and in ten minutes you have opened a parking lot. They groped their way through three city blocks, Maria performing beautifully, and listening to her quiet idle when he stopped he decided it would no longer be necessary to park two streets away from the Matissons' on Friday nights.

On the corner ahead of him he saw Jan duck under a street-lamp with lowered head, as under a shower bath. She was wearing her "whore dress" tonight, a pale yellow thing made of some new material which required only a damp cloth to tidy up. It fit her with a contraceptive coziness, and opening the door for her he had a brief foreboding that it might break. Quite unexpectedly, she arched herself to reach his lips, and he gave her the brushing, tantalizing kiss she liked. "What does that mean?" he asked when he was done.

"If I knew," she said, "I would have found words for it instead. What have you done for Maria? She seems to have got over her pleurisy."

"After this I'll be able to park her on your old man's front lawn," he said. "Did you encounter any night patrols?"

"Dad, of course. I told him I was going to a movie show."

Putting Maria in gear, he said, "How accurately you lie, Mrs. Ashton."

"What . . . !"

"Excuse me," he said, glancing at the darkness where she sat withdrawn from him. "I was just trying it on for size."

"Well, it doesn't fit!" she said, and she stamped her foot almost noiselessly on the rubber floormat. "It doesn't anywhere nearly fit!"

"I'm shrugging my shoulders," he said, "and my voice is keyed low and pleasantly. Your mother said you weren't feeling very well this morning."

"It was nothing," she said sullenly. "It was just the quinine Dad got for me."

"Quinine?" He paused, saying nothing else, because the only other thing he could think to say was, "That son of a bitch will try anything, won't he?" and he did not feel they were being that honest tonight. They were in the busy blocks of town now, anyhow and there were lots of things for them to see. There were thousands of people moving in slow circles around each block, playing that never-ending game in which, each time the music stops, chairs are traded in theaters and restaurants. There was plenty of music too, it issued from very loud speakers outside most movie houses and all television stores. There was Rollo's movie house and, he noted, Rollo's substitute. "Rollo has his hair parted on the right today," he said. "I thought I'd better warn you ahead of time."

"I can't wait," Jan said.

They drove on in empty silence until she leaned suddenly foreward and ordered him to stop. Thinking she had seen someone they knew, he pulled over to the curb. But she turned to him instead. "Char, I *am* sorry."

"Sorry?" he said. He could just make out her pale grey head beside him in the dark, and it frightened him a little to find it almost angelic, ethereal. "For what?"

"For being so hatefully cruel," she said, curling her lips in a grotesque caricature of cruelty. "If any other girl were to treat you the way I do, I would hate her, Char. I think I hate myself."

He tried to peer at her. "That's a wasteful kind of hate," he said, and he felt chill.

"No, it's not myself," she said, grouping her words impatiently. "It's the things others have put into me."

"Oh?" He listened to his own distracted laugh.

"No, not that, Char, not what you've put into me!" she cried. "I love that. I think I always would love it if it weren't for all the awful, deadening things those others have put into me. *You* know who I mean, don't you, Char?" Her voice was thinly plaintive now. "Char?"

He felt that he did know, and his fists clenched ever so gently in the darkness, as though crushing egg shells, empty ones. He wanted badly to take Jan in his hands instead, but not gently, and not to crush. Yet it was the first such mutinous avowal he had ever heard her make, and he did not risk the appearance of exploiting it. He said, "Jan, everything will be all right."

It was only then that he knew, saw, despite the darkness, the miserable mistake he had made. Her offer had been to renounce sixteen years of intravenously injected loyalty, and his joyous encouragement had been, "Jan, everything will be all right"! She ducked her head as from an awkward blow, and once again she stamped in soundless fury on the rubber floor. He jolted

Maria into second gear, leapt off to Lloyd's apartment house.

The Rincon Apartments were entirely blacked out except for one grinning band of light on the seventh floor. It was as though Lloyd had ordered the rest of the building evacuated for the Brawl. Or perhaps it had not been necessary to order it: hot rods and motor cycles lined the curbs, it made one deaf to look at them.

"Charles Ashton," he said into the hollow tube, "and Jan." He put his toe against the crack, swung the door for Jan. The elevator, still in Lloyd's employ, sat yawning in the sleepy hall. Under the bright bulb inside he stood two feet away from Jan. "You look as though you were going to a funeral."

She turned her face away.

He took her tiny purse from her and opened it, drew her lipstick out. Uncapping it, he offered it to her. "Please."

"Oh!" Jan snatched the tube. Before the mirror she drew a bright scarlet smear across her face, extending it half an inch beyond the corners of her mouth. The effect was that she had tried to cut her throat and missed.

"Jan . . ." He had a facial tissue out, but at that moment the elevator stopped and its bright light thrust them together into the blind black hall. He shoved Jan's purse at her but aimed too low, and Jan laughed gratingly. Doors were clicking everywhere. He went ahead to lead the way. At the final door his hand lay motionless on the metal knob, and he felt Jan's soft hand find his. She was opening the door, and it was as though she were caressing him.

"Why, Charley!"

"Jan!"

"Hey, you two . . . !"

There were twenty active people in the room, yet a stranger would have seen only Lloyd. He sat dark and smiling on his white throne, basking in his private sun, benignly watching his company frolic in the shade. Tonight he wore a black velvet shirt with mother-of-pearl buttons and white string tie. (Requiring only half a wardrobe, Lloyd strove hard for variety.) His shirt hung loose and robelike about his narrow hips; Lloyd had no pants to tuck it in. Between whiskey sips he pulled on a curved cigar, while Gloria flicked for him. They smiled hello to Gloria as they walked up.

"You two are late," Lloyd scolded them. "Charles. Janice. How are you both?"

"We're fine. Great," they said.

"Almost everyone's here tonight," Lloyd said, looking around the room. "I think this will be a good one, don't you?"

"Marvelous, Lloyd."

"There's plenty to drink, of course."

"We see!"

"The old man says he's got a hit picture for us tonight." The movie projector was already set up on a coffee table near Lloyd's bed, facing a white screen across the room from Lloyd. "Stunning was the word he used."

"It sounds grand, Lloyd."

"Janice." Lloyd was smiling at Charles, his arms bound rigidly to his sides by thought control. "What do you think of your poet working on movie scripts?"

Jan smiled brilliantly, at Gloria. "I try not to think of it at all," she said, and left to join some couples at the bar.

Lloyd raised his eyebrows inquiringly, and now his anxious hands unleashed themselves. They frisked in zigzag paths at both his sides, tracking fugitive motives across the counterpane.

"I'm with you, Lloyd." Charles intervened. "Jan's a bit nervous tonight."

"Janice ought to associate more with Gloria," Lloyd said, his hands laying wreaths on her. "Gloria has no nerves. Have you, Gloria?"

Gloria raised Lloyd's whiskey glass to his lips, and tilted it for him. Between them they did not spill a drop. "No," she said.

"Charles," Lloyd said, drawing on his cigar, "I'm tremendously pleased you decided to go along with me. The old man ran into somebody else who wanted the job today. Sylvan Kirk, he used to write for the pulps before he came out to the Coast? Maybe you've heard of him. He's all ass-holes and elbows, anyway. I couldn't have worked with him. Now, we'll make a great team, you and I. A great one, won't we, Charles?" Lloyd's hands flapped passionately in the air, he wished to shake hands with Charles.

"I hope so, Lloyd," Charles said, and he captured Lloyd's left hand in his.

"Get yourself a drink," said Lloyd.

"Thanks, Lloyd, I will."

They weren't really late. No one was even close to squiffed, except perhaps those few the word party intoxicates. According to the custom of the house, everyone mixed his own drinks from the array of bottles on Mr. Lippincott's portable bar. There was a line three-deep there now. Other guests were huddled about the radio-television-phonograph. At the foot of Lloyd's bed a couple danced to slow music, rather awkwardly, with their hands cupped around each other's arched backsides. By the window Roland Star fondled Babette while chatting with a Nancy Somebody whose father had only recently turned movie producer after twentyfive years in the used car game. Charles was heading toward the bar and Jan, but Rollo's "Charley!" intercepted him. He stood waiting for Rollo to break away from Babette and come up to him.

"Charley, I've been talking with Lloyd!"

"Oh? How courteous of you, Rollo."

"Now, cut it out, Charley," Roland said, "I'm serious." He took Charles' arm in a serious grip. "We'll probably be working together pretty soon. Lloyd told me about the job he's giving you. You can help me, Charley."

"How, Rollo?"

"I'm trying to sell Lloyd on using me, Charley, I want to play The Cripple, see! Lloyd seemed impressed with the idea, really impressed. A word from you would cinch it, Charley."

"Oh," Charles said.

"Can't you see me in the part, Charley? It's a solid part. It's got real meat in it, real meat. It was *made* for me. With a part like that I won't be typed as a juvenile. Do you follow me, Charley?"

Charles peered at Rollo as though weighing what he had said. He frowned. "I'm not sure that I do, Rollo," he said.

"Watch this," Rollo said, glancing sideways at Lloyd's bed. Suddenly he went limp. His knees and shoulders sagged. His arms began to quiver a little bit. Pretty soon they were flapping frantically. His mouth hung open in a limp and utterly silly grin. His eyes revolved—counterwise to his revolving head. It was a wonderful imitation of an idiot, and Rollo kept it up until he thought to glance at Lloyd's bed again. "Well, Charley, what do you think?"

"Stunning," Charles said, backing hastily toward the bar. "Really stunning, Rollo."

At the far end of the bar Jan was talking animatedly with Mona Swan, but it was Mona who watched Charles approach. Mona was both editor of the yearbook and a pom-pom girl, and her attitude, her attire strove always to depict the ravages of a ceaseless civil war between sex and the intellect. Tonight she wore white nylon slacks and red high heels, two men's nylon handkerchiefs contained her breasts. As she reclined against the bar her white shoulders and her long, muscular back were rounded receptively, and her long white arms hung carelessly to her hips. One scarlet heel was hooked over the bar rail so that the knee jutted far to the side, displaying the tense, bulging muscle of her inner thigh. To represent intelligence she wore dark tortoise-shell glasses which she did not need. When he was a few feet away, Jan turned to him. "Have a good look," she said, handing him her untouched highball.

He smiled and raised the glass to them. "I was just wondering how Mona keeps her navel so pretty and pink."

"It takes some doing," Mona said in her slow voice. "Sometimes I have to call for help."

He examined his little fingernail. "What tool would you recommend?"

"Anything you've got handy," Mona said.

"All right, you two." Jan pretended to throw sharp looks at them. Often he had observed that she seemed to get pleasure out of the flirting they did. "Char, Mona is panting to hear about your new job."

"You make me sound perfectly degenerate, Jan," Mona moaned. "Only dogs *pant.*"

"Yes."

"Touché!" Mona said, smiling broadly. "Charles, I'm panting to hear about your new job."

"You've probably heard as much as I have, Mona."

"Well, from what little I have heard I'm thinking of offering myself as a private secretary to you two boys," Mona said. "I passed typing this year, you know."

He raised his eyebrows skeptically. "How's your shorthand, Mona?"

Mona's eyes went from him slowly down to the long white hands that hung slack at her sides. "I've never had any complaints," she said.

"Well, you'll have to take it up with Lloyd," Charles said. "He's doing all the hiring for this enterprise. I'm Lloyd's right hand, at best. If you'd like to be his left, well . . ." He was saying more than he had to say because Chub Farley was planning a maneuver behind Mona's back. Chub's right hand hovered close to the white pocket handkerchiefs which represented Mona's shirt, while his eyes studied the intricate knot she'd tied. Apparently it was too difficult, for Chub contented himself with simply grabbing the knot and twisting it. The knot held, and one of the handkerchiefs slipped sideways, off Mona's breast. Mona's white body flushed pink, but spinning she caught Chub's full nose with the back of her hand. Amid excited laughter she hastily remade herself. Now her lowered eyes sought the bar for a drink, and her hand jerked out to one. "Maybe I'll speak to Lloyd," she said.

Charles too was without a drink and pressing Jan's arm he went off to hustle another one. A new entertainment had taken the stage at the foot of Lloyd's bed: two boys were preparing a contest of chug-a-lug. They stood with glasses touching at shoulder height, awaiting a signal from Lloyd. Each glass contained four inches of whiskey, straight, and each boy eyed his glass with a look of severity. There was a little betting on the side, but most of the money was on the tall pimply one. No one in the room had ever known Walter when he did not have a flushed face and puffy, mottled mounds beneath his eyes. Although probably inherited, the appearance of debauchery was impressive and complete. The shorter boy looked too healthy, as though his only orgies had been at his mother's breast.

"Begin," said Lloyd.

At the signal the contestants touched glasses and tilted their heads back as far as they could. Carefully they tipped the glasses above gaping mouths. Their first gulps were audible in the silent room, then all sound was lost in a liquid quietude. Walter's Adam's apple could be seen pumping regularly over his unbuttoned shirt, but the other boy's seemed stuck. It protruded unpleasantly, and his face grew purple-red. Now one could see that the fresh whiskey he poured was not reaching his throat but running in two trickles down his cheeks and around the lobes of his ears. With what seemed an agony of effort he lifted his head erect. For seconds he held the great mouthful of whiskey in his swollen cheeks, then squirted it at Walter's feet. Walter, who had finished his own, grabbed what was left of his opponent's drink. Tilting, he finished it off to admiring gasps.

"The winner!" Lloyd cried.

Walter pivoted to acknowledge applause, but his body never quite completed the turn. He went down like a grounded flag, the lower half folding limply beneath the upper one. Seated cross-legged on the floor at the foot of Lloyd's bed, he belched once, politely, against the back of his hand. Two boys hauled him off to his car while everyone cheered, and especially Lloyd. But "Bravo! Bravo!" shouted one above everyone else.

Charles had not seen Mr. Lippincott enter the room. He must have used the back door leading to the toilet and the Lippincotts' room. He stood with his back to the wall, apart from the rest. His eyes, which had been watching the contest, moved now to Lloyd's bed, and they shone with a rapturous excitement that was close to malevolent. They said no one enjoys this as much as myself, just as a hymn shouter may say no one loves God as loudly as I. His entire body seemed to be aggressively glowing, as though he would prove his appreciation of fun a somehow worthier art than having it; such is the movie-man's argument. Under Mr. Lippincott's glow the actors grew tense, not camera shy but just a bit overstudied in the roles they were playing. They smiled too brightly, laughed too readily, gestured too emphatically, trying to have as much fun as Mr. Lippincott thought they were having. They did not react in this way to Lloyd, because Lloyd's watching was always there and they tolerated it as inevitable, much as we grow used to God's.

"Charles . . ." Mr. Lippincott, out of some ambiguous sense of propriety, would not come to the center of the stage. Rather than intrude among the actors, he would remain with his back to the wall and wait for Charles to come to him. Charles complied. "Charles? How's the Brawl going, lad?"

"It's a great one, Mr. Lippincott."

"Everyone seems to be having a good time."

"Oh, marvelous."

"Mix yourself a drink, Charles. There's plenty to drink, you know."

"Thanks, I'll have another one in a minute."

"Fine, fine." While he talked Mr. Lippincott looked over at Lloyd, but Lloyd was not watching them. He was watching a girl named Grace light a cigarette and swallow it. "That boy," Mr. Lippincott murmured, shaking his head, "that boy. Well, Charles," he said, turning his attention to Charles, "have you decided to work with him?" He looked almost bleakly at Charles, awaiting the word from him.

"I guess we're in business," Charles said.

"Splendid, lad. Splendid," said Mr. Lippincott, taking his hand. They shook hands in the way a resigning cabinet member and his successor might, each with his own dim view of the thing but saving it for his memoirs when he published them. "You two will get along famously."

Charles said nothing, it was the kind of remark that demanded an absolutely fatuous smile.

"Charles, I don't know whether I told you that I have a dinner engagement tonight?"

Again Charles smiled. "No, I don't believe you did, Mr. Lippincott."

"Well, I'd like you to operate the projector for me tonight, Charles. I've got it set up for you, ready to go. Will you do that for me, lad?"

"I'll be glad to, Mr. Lippincott."

"Here." Mr. Lippincott led Charles over to the projection machine. "This is the switch that turns it on," he said, flicking a switch. "All you have to do is push this switch, the machine will take care of the rest."

"I understand, Mr. Lippincott."

"Well . . ." Mr. Lippincott took one last rapt look around the room, then he waved his hand a little bit. "Have fun," he said.

A waiting silence watched Mr. Lippincott go out of the room. Now everyone turned to Charles, as though a comment were expected of him. "I guess we'd better get this thing started," he said.

"By all means," Lloyd said. "On with the show!"

Rollo was on the job. He sauntered back and forth in the center of the room, speaking pleasantly from the side of his mouth. "Hear, hear, hear, feature attraction starts in five minutes," he said. "Plenty of choice seats still available in the orchestra. One-armed sons-of-bitches to the balcony, please. . . ."

There was a race for the divan and the easy chairs. Those reaching them first kicked off attackers and howled for their mates. A last minute rush rocked the portable bar. Hands groping for glasses came away with bottles instead. The air was brittle with laughter and shattering glass. Out of a smoke-and-spilled-liquor fog Jan emerged beside Charles, her blue eyes sardonically appraising him. "How did you happen to get this job?"

"Prerogative." Sinking to the rug with Jan, he wondered if there weren't something more he should say to her. But words are for strangers, and friends; he took Jan's hand in his, and his free left hand touched the starter switch.

"Lights . . . Places . . . Camera!"

It started the way they always do, with a horn-rimmed career girl talking to her private secretary on the intercom. They were discussing a long trip she was going to take, in the course of which she would meet a tall dark man, handsome as hell. At first she would be revolted by him, but soon he would begin to discover things in her which she had never discovered herself. After a hundred minutes of teasing him she would at last give in, her only wish being to live in a house and have babies all over the place. Watching a romantic film is like reading a crystal ball, the imagination must be restrained and formalized.

In the darkness he at last spoke to Jan. His fingertips wandered over Jan's throat, her arms, her bare folded legs, conveying clandestine messages. There was that area at the nape of her neck where her hair became kitten fur, and his lips sang silent songs to it. He had other things to say, more urgent ones, but just now he could only hint at them. His hands put little questions to her, tentatively. Jan's body listened for a while, and then it began to answer him. Only the body can speak of love without hurting it.

Screenlife was proceeding according to an ancient plan. The girl on the intercom had met her tall man, and she had fled through three Pullmans and one dining car before they embraced. It had taken him some time to discover things in her she had never discovered herself, but now they had reached the point where he was taking her glasses off. At least he had started to, but a sigh in the room warned Charles that somewhere the story had jumped off its line, and he raised his eyes. He wished he had not.

At first his stunned mind wanted to believe the girl had merely ducked her head to nibble a banana, a large, ripe banana the man held in his fist. This was his first, wishful view of the thing, and he might have accepted it had he not seen that this girl was a different one. This was no movie queen. Her gaunt, ravaged cheeks had not been made up for the screen, her eyes were dark holes in her face. Her role was too well, too often rehearsed, her talent lasciviousness. And he heard their cries.

They were crying at him! "Turn it off, turn it off!" they were crying at him, and, "Turn on the lights, turn on the lights!"

He would have done so at once, but the switch was not there.

"Turn it off! Turn it off!"

The switch was not there.

"Will you turn it off!" Jan crouched between Charles and the screen, snarling at him, the projector's bright eye burning its obscenities into the flesh of her face. "Will you turn it off!" she hissed. "Will you, please."

How gladly he would, how joyfully! But the cursed switch was not to be found. He was clawing the machine when the lights came on. They came with the rude suddenness of a flash-bulb, discovering them white-faced, in guilty postures, blackmailed by their own innocence. Stooping to close the switch, so obvious now, it was as though he were turning life back on. In the stirring room Jan headed for a door, and he got to his feet to go after her. "No, stay here," she hissed, darting ahead of him, "just stay where you are."

He watched Jan slip out of the door. All over the room couples were disengaging uneasily. Girls were climbing off laps and straightening themselves. A few boys were smirking, but only Rollo could smile. He was waving at Charles. "Let's not stop now, Charley," Rollo called. "On with the show!"

"Sure: let's see how it ends," a boy seconded Rollo, but already he was following his girl to the door.

Rollo was hugely amused. "Hey, Sammy, where are you going so fast?"

"He's going home," Sammy's girl answered for him, shoving Sammy out of the door.

Now other girls began to move with white, stunned faces toward the door, their escorts following sheepishly. The boys turned back to wave at those who remained, or shrug, but the girls walked without looking behind. Soon the door was so crowded with departing guests that Billy and Lois had difficulty pushing themselves in. While Lois talked with some girls, Billy came over to Charles. Billy's hair was still wet from a bath. "How's it going, Charley?" Billy asked.

"Fine, Billy," Charles said. "How did you do?"

Billy grinned. "First, naturally."

"Good old Billy," Charles said, shaking his head. "You beat Dochousen."

Billy stopped grinning. "Dochousen flipped," he said.

"Ho." Charles looked at Billy's face. He thought he saw a trace of fear in it, but it passed away. "Well, I guess that takes care of Dochousen for a while, doesn't it, Billy?"

"Forever," Billy said.

Behind them Lois was leaving with a group of the girls, and she called Billy over to her.

"Hey," Billy said. "What the?" Lois made a brisk, coplike jerk with her thumb, and Billy shrugged. "I guess I'm leaving," he said.

"I guess so, Billy," Charles agreed.

"See you, Charley."

"See you, Billy."

By the time Billy Hart and Lois had gone, there was scarcely anyone left. Most of those who remained were close to the door, and they were herding one another toward it gradually.

"Charles, where's everyone going?"

It was Lloyd. Charles had forgotten about Lloyd, and turning now he saw that there was no one by Lloyd's bed except Gloria. Gloria sat at Lloyd's side, holding his hand and talking to him, but Lloyd was not listening to her. He was watching his guests leave the Brawl. "Where are they going?"

Charles went to the foot of Lloyd's bed, but he could think of nothing to say to him. Nor could he smile.

"Hey, come back!" Lloyd called past Charles, waving at his guests. "Come back, everyone! Come back to the Brawl. We haven't even started yet."

Lloyd's guests hesitated and turned to him. "Goodnight, Lloyd. See you soon, Lloyd," they said, and waved apologetically. Then they went out the door. Now only Charles and Rollo were left, Gloria and Lloyd.

"That God damned old man of mine," Lloyd said softly. "That God damned old man of mine!" he yelled. He flung Gloria's hand away and the bed bucked Charles's knees under the jolt of Lloyd's erecting himself. For an instant Lloyd sat up straight, straighter than Charles had ever seen him before. Then his body tipped forward, over his lap, so that his face ground into the bed at his knees. His arms thrashed the bed, to prevent his suffocating in the counterpane. Gloria grabbed hold of his shoulders, but cursing he flung her viciously off, and Gloria fled from the room. Now Lloyd somehow twisted to his side, and finding his legs with his hands he threw them from under him, one at a time. They landed on a pillow, and Lloyd lay there gasping and looking at them. He looked at them with disgust, as though he had never seen them before. Then he turned and saw that Charles was seeing them too. "That God damned old man of mine!" he yelled, heaving to his elbows. "I'll break the son of a bitch in two! I'll break him in two!" He was inching his way toward the bottom of the bed, the front half dragging the hind half along. He reached the footboard and, like a great black and white caterpillar, started to go over it. It was then that Charles and Rollo put their hands on him.

"I'll break him in two!" Lloyd yelled, flailing Charles and Rollo with the loose ends of his arms. "Break him in two! Break him in two!" They lifted him up and put him backwards onto his bed. Leaning on his arms, they tried to quiet him down. Lloyd was appallingly strong.

"Get off my back!" Lloyd cried, and he was sobbing now. "Get off my back!" He looked beyond them, craning his neck.

"Janice," he pleaded, "will you get these two parasites off my back?"

Jan stood in the doorway. She looked pale and ill, or rather she looked pale in the way of a person who has been ill but has recently gotten over it. Charles got off Lloyd's back and went across to her. "Are you all right, Jan?"

For answer Jan rose to her tiptoes and kissed his cheek. It was a gentle kiss, frighteningly chaste. "Char, I'll stay with Lloyd."

"Jan . . ."

"Mr. Lippincott will take me home when he gets back."

"Jan . . ."

"Goodnight, Char," said Jan.

So he said, "Goodnight," and walked out of the room. Babette was waiting in the elevator, and Rollo was following him.

"What a lousy break, Charley," Rollo said.

"Yes."

"Oh well," said Rollo, "who knows, maybe Lloyd will still love us when he comes to himself."

"Yes."

The elevator seemed crowded with the three of them. The full-length mirror, instead of lending an illusion of depth, made them a crowd of six. They followed Babette through the dimly lighted hall and out of the door. They paused for a moment on the steps, and Rollo and Babette said goodnight to him. In front of the apartment house, Lloyd's guests were breaking up into pairs and small groups to scatter themselves here and there over Los Angeles. They walked through the night like old men and old women who have been through it all before. And he, not following them, looked up to greet the full moon overhead. It was an anemic stand-in for the sun, and cold, but at least a man could bear to look at it.

—1955

The Pilgrimage

NOW HE COULD SEE the town ahead of them, but he could not feel the train slow down at all. For a minute he was sure it would rush right past the depot, as though it too had been brought here against its will. But the next he knew the conductor was pulling the signal cord, his mother was tugging at his arm, the black-lettered sign at the end of the platform was jerking to a halt outside their window. He looked down at the town stretched below them like a neat grey graveyard of granite monuments, and he imagined all the tiny people on its hilly streets had come to pay a visit to the dead.

As they climbed down from the day coach only the conductor and one stooped old man saw his mother's black-gloved fist dart out and rap the hand he held to her. Hastily he pocketed the offending hand, hoping that his thick tweed trousers would muffle the popping sound his knuckles made. All winter long his body had tingled with new and exciting currents, and this was the way he had found for releasing them. Just as soon as he had tried the nine possible joints of the right hand he brought it out and gave to it the heavy wicker lunch basket, freeing his left and pocketing it. But then in the nick of time he remembered that his mother's definition of a gentleman was a boy who did not use his pockets when walking with a lady.

He wanted to ask her how a gentleman behaved when walking with a ghost. He almost smiled at the thought of asking his mother such a thing, and then, glancing guilty aside at her, he did smile at the answer he imagined she would give. He imagined the thin black shoulders bracing themselves against his impudence, the black spidery glove with its roses reaching across her breast to grasp that gaudy astrology magazine which she had been reading before he joined her on the train, tuck it more safely beneath the black fold of her sleeve; and then, only then could he imagine the bleak white face fixing upon him a look both hurt and spiteful because she would have read so much more into his teasing question than he could possibly have meant. For his mother knew better than he that always, and especially today, they traveled in the company of a ghost, that it was only in such company that she was ever at her ease.

He tried to remember how many times they had made this pilgrimage before; eleven, twelve, thirteen? He had been three, almost to the day, the year his father died, and yet recently, since this anniversary had become for him a "holiday" from boarding school, the number of his annual visits to the grave, plus three, would somehow fail to add up to his present age. It was like an arithmetic problem at school which puzzled him more and more the longer he looked at it. "How many times does this make?" he asked, his eyes watching the uneven pavement beneath their feet. "Twelve?"

"For you, yes," his mother answered, not stopping to think at all. "For me, thirteen. I came alone the first year, the year after your father died. You had a cold that day."

I had a cold, he thought, and shuddered, for it seemed to him he had had a cold for thirteen years. It seemed to him that this place, this grave, they were visiting had become his own grave too. What gives life to her kills me, he thought, and for this he stared glumly at his mother. Why must we always look for him in death, he silently asked her, why not just once in life? But aloud he said: "Tell me what he was like, Mother—when he was alive, I mean."

"Like?" His mother was deep in thought, and she shook her head impatiently at him. "I never know what you mean by that."

"Was he the biggest man you've ever seen?" he asked, straightening his shoulders up. "Was he as strong as he was big?"

"Martin, really," she said, and sighed. "I've told you all that before again and again."

"No. When?"

"Shush," she said, and left him as usual to shuffle through his pitiful store of mementos and memories: the small gold watch, its monogram his own, which he would inherit when he was twenty-one, the great fur-collared Chesterfield which he could not tell yet whether he would inherit ever, the shelves of books in which his father's carefully written name proved that he had not known he would die so soon, the musty photo album in which his father's face lay dim and yellow among all the rest, the single photograph in which that face somehow beamed through the poor photography, eager, strong, alive, as though saying no to all the things his son would hear of him: that he did not go out with girls until he was nineteen, that he did not drive a car until he was twenty-one, that he liked, adored, carrots and string-beans, that he had learned not to scoff at astrology by the time he died. It was this bright photograph and not the other faded one in his mother's mind which caused Martin to grab her arm and ask, "Did he like to dance?"

"What?" his mother asked, deaf suddenly. "What? Your father? He danced." And then, as if her own words too were heard critically through a cupped black hand: "Ah, why must we always talk about your father in this way, his worldly follies? Why can't we try to accept him for what he's become, not what he was. He's dead, and there are no follies among the dead. Death purifies." She stared at him with anger and pity, and he knew the anger was for him, the pity for her who had him as a son.

"I'm sorry," he said, but in his mind he listened to her words again, and he couldn't believe in them because the follies of which his mother spoke were life itself, or all things which stood between man and the Soul, the Word, the One, that eternal magnificence in whose presence even God must blink his eyes. Life to her was a crowded horoscope in which ugly little crabs and rams tripped up the body as it ran in circles from the soul, and the soul had only one object, the body's death. Suddenly dizzy he took his mother's arm again. "I'll leave the basket here," he said, for they were at the edge of the graveyard now, staring at the rusty gate. Beyond, the cemetery lay neatly raked and pruned and dead. "It's heavy," he explained to her, but in reality he could not bring himself to rest their food on that cold gravedirt. "You go first."

His mother stood critically examining him, as though he were at this moment joining her on the train. "You're cracking your knuckles again," she said, and then, "I thought you would have worn your black suit today. You always have before."

Welcoming any delay, he laughed. "Have you seen it?" he asked, knowing that she had not since he left for school last fall. "It comes to here!" Stretching one large-boned wrist from its grey tweed sleeve he pointed to a distance far up on it where the black sleeve would have come. "When I move my arm it comes to here!"

"You don't have to exaggerate, Martin," his mother said. "You haven't grown so very much."

"Oh no?" he said proudly, extending his long arms sideways as far as they would go, feeling himself hover above his mother like some great grey hawk. "Look at these sleeves, just look at them. Is that where they're supposed to be?"

His mother lowered her eyes and shook her head. "Put your arms down at your sides," she said, "at once."

"Gladly," he answered her. "Gladly. But if you'd been at the dance the other night you'd have seen me dancing with my arms that way, down at my sides I mean. Like this." He held his arms down at his sides, a little stiffly, his large hands cupped inward to press his partner's hands, Jennie's, against his thighs. "That was so my sleeves wouldn't hitch up like this," he said, and laughed as he jerked them up again.

"Stop showing off, Martin," his mother said, passing through the gate. "What dance?"

"The dance! The dance!" he hooted after her. "The one I wrote you about. The one I took Jennie Roberts to."

"Oh? And who might Jennie Roberts be?"

He ran to catch up with her, pass her. "Who might Jennie Roberts be?" he repeated, wheeling to laugh in his mother's strained white face. "Don't tell me you don't know that? I thought everyone knew about Jennie Roberts— the Betty Grable of Pine-in-the-Woods? She's a year older than I am, of course, but she's a tiny little thing, a blonde."

His mother darted onto a path leading to the right, as though escaping him, and said, "Since when have the boys been allowed to invite their own girls to the dances? I thought the school did that."

"Not for the upper form, they don't," he said, speaking more patiently now, for this was a fine point and he did not wish to lose her interest. "It's written in the student constitution that way. In the upper form you get to invite whoever you want and you get to stay up after the dance is over. Your date does too."

"After the dance?"

"Till two."

"And what do you find to do till two!"

"Find to do!" he cried. He halted there in the path and muffled his cracking knuckles in a hearty laugh. "Come now, Mother, come down out of the clouds. What did you used to do?"

He was still laughing when his mother spun and leaped, not toward him but away; when her black fist lashed out at him with the frightened fury of a cornered cat. Like a great cat she crouched there before him in the path, alert to the gasping sound his dying laughter made, her eyes fixed on him with horror as though he had suddenly become an enemy. He raised his hand to his face and there was blood on it when he held it out to her. "What is it, Mother?" he asked, and took a cautious step in her direction. "What?"

His mother stared at his bloody hand. "It's nothing," she said. He watched her straighten up, still with her eyes on him, and smooth her coat. "You'll have to excuse me," she said. "I shouldn't have done that, Martin. I don't know what came over me. I must have thought I heard him again."

"Him?"

"Your father, yes."

"In me? . . . In me?" he asked incredulously, and then, with joy, exultantly, "Why yes, of course, of course in me!" Laughing he sprang toward his mother, lifted her up, high up above his head, let her down again, not heeding the blood he smeared on her, heeding nothing as he grabbed the crimson flowers from her hand. "Of *course* in me!" Past her he bounded and hurled the roses, not in a tight bunch as his mother would have done but in a grand profusion upon the grave. "There!" he said, whirling to her again. "That's how he likes them."

"Martin, Martin," his mother moaned, and he saw her shiver as she looked at him. "Have you no respect at all for the dead?"

"None!" he cried, throwing out his arms extravagantly. "None at all, I assure you."

She turned and fled from him among the graves, along the noisy gravel paths, through the rusty gate, and he laughed to see that in her mad rush from him she remembered to snatch up the lunch basket on her way. He laughed and, stopping, plucked a rose blossom from the grave, snapped its stem to fit his button hole, before he ran after her.

—1952

You Can't Get Another One

IT WAS RAINING again. The rain beat hurriedly on the high roof above the station platform and dropped from the leaves like tears at Daphne's feet. In a moment she would have to start smiling.

The sudden, arrogant blast of the engine's whistle made her jump. Ahead, Arthur strode forward to meet the approaching train. Daphne did not follow him at once, but stood staring at his broad back, repeating silently to herself, "Hello, Joan dear. Hello, Joan dear," and smiling.

As the train drew to a shrill halt, Joan was the first person Daphne saw. Joan was standing directly in front of her on the coach platform, wearing a little green raincoat and matching hat, and carrying the largest and most repulsive doll Daphne had ever seen.

"No!" The cry escaped from Daphne involuntarily, because the doll's hair was a vivid red. Not a soft auburn like Joan's (which perhaps had become a little redder in the six months Joan had been away), but a dyed, theatrical red like Nora's. The wide, full lips, painted a clashing purple, were Nora's too. Even the glassy eyes were Nora's. Daphne wished more than ever that Arthur had suggested she stay at home, but for the first time since her confinement he had forgotten to be concerned about her health.

Arthur reached up for Joan with his long arms and swung her down from the train. Then, after taking her suitcase from a portly conductor and dismissing him with a tip, he wrapped Joan, doll and all, in a wrestler-like hug. Daphne, a few feet behind them, felt that she had not even been noticed yet and she stood waiting to say her piece.

Arthur straightened up suddenly and turned to Daphne. "Say hello to Daphne," he said, prodding the child toward her. She had almost forgotten how happiness could soften the gaunt contours of his face.

"Hello, Joan dear," Daphne said, leaning down to kiss Joan's cheek. "Where did you get that lovely doll?"

Joan swung the doll quickly to one side, out of Daphne's reach. She said clearly, "Mother bought her for me."

Daphne felt the warmth running to her face. "What lovely hair," she said, and looked to Arthur. "What do you call her? . . . I'll bet I can guess."

"Bet you can't," Joan said, still holding the doll away. "Her name is Alice."

"You win," Daphne said. She hoped Arthur heard the irony in her voice. "I never would have guessed it."

Arthur glanced at his watch. "It's time Daddy went to the office," he said. He picked up Joan's suitcase in one hand and guided the child toward the car with the other. Daphne walked behind him, wondering if she trusted herself to say anything, even something innocent about how Joan had grown in the past six months.

"Hey, Artie!"

"Well, George! You are a stranger."

"Not by choice, Artie." Big George Oswald shook Arthur's hand and wheeled around to lift his hat to Daphne. "And Mrs. Hendricks." He rushed over the name, as though it embarrassed him to recognize such a frail, colorless woman as Nora Franklin's stand-in. Then he stood looking at her uncertainly, hat in one hand and briefcase in the other. Very deliberately, Daphne offered George her hand, forcing him to put his hat back on before he took it. "Hello, George," she said, smiling, making it almost a taunt.

George fumbled a moment before he took her hand. "Hey, hey!" he said, stepping back playfully to examine Daphne's figure. "What's this rumor I hear about you . . . ?"

Daphne caught her breath audibly and looked up in time to see the quick grimace of pain on Arthur's face. "That's an old rumor, George," she said, forcing herself to look at the big man. "It was dispelled a few weeks ago."

George's full-lipped mouth hung open. "I'm terribly sorry," he mumbled. "I've been away for quite . . ."

"Forget it, George," Arthur interrupted him, patting Joan's curly head. "You remember Joan?"

"Ah, little Joanie," George said, too loudly. "I saw her on the train. How are you, Joanie dear?"

Joan curtsied. "Fine, thank you."

"Good. Good." George gave her chin a chuck with his large hand, and reached down to do the same to Alice. Daphne waited for him to make some remark about the doll, but suddenly his eyes opened wide in recognition and he seemed to think better of it. "Well," he said, straightening up, "I'll be getting home before Maggie decides I slept through my stop again." He laughed, tipped his hat, and started moving away rather hurriedly.

"Give Marge our best, George," Arthur called after him.

"You bet, Artie. I will."

"The fool," Arthur said, jerking the car door open. "The poor damned fool!"

With four, including Alice, in the front seat of the club coupe, Daphne felt that she would suffocate. She tried to keep the doll's frizzy hair away from her face, but when Joan looked up and saw her doing it Daphne smiled and patted the doll's head. Joan scowled, and shifted Alice to the other side.

"She's from Saks Fifth Avenue," Joan said. "Mother had her reserved for me until this morning."

Arthur looked down at his daughter and grinned. "It's good having you back," he said, his voice soft now. "Daphne and I have missed you. Have you been having fun, darling?"

"I've been having a *glorious* time," Joan said, making Daphne wince. "Yesterday Mother took me to the circus. We saw every animal there is, even elephants. Elephants are the largest animals in the world, you know. They're gentle, too."

"They just seem gentle," Daphne couldn't resist saying. "They can be very mean at times. Besides, they have thick skins and don't feel little things that bother most animals."

"They're very gentle," Joan told her father.

For a while Daphne listened to Joan's well-coached recital

of all the things she had done in the last three days. Apparently Nora had sacrificed her own social life for three entire days.

"And how is Miss Framely?" Daphne asked when she could listen no longer. "Did you see her often, dear?"

"*Fram*ly," Joan corrected. "She stayed with me when Mother was acting at the theater. She's from England and she knows millions of children's stories. Mother says she knows more children's stories than anyone in the world."

Daphne, whose special love had always been folklore and nursery tales, looked quickly out the window.

Arthur wiped a cloth needlessly over the windshield and then returned it to the glove compartment. "How is your mother, Joan?"

Daphne closed her eyes and pressed her fingertips hard against the quivering eyelids.

Joan said, "She's going to be in a new play. She told me to send you her love."

Arthur swung the car around a corner and, glancing over at him, Daphne could see that he was smiling. She didn't look at him again until they pulled up in front of his office.

"I want to go in with you, Daddy," Joan demanded, pushing coaxingly against him.

"Well . . ." Arthur looked at his watch.

"Please, Daddy."

"For just a minute," Arthur said, opening the door and helping Joan out. "Daddy has an appointment in ten minutes."

Daphne took a deep breath and said, in a desperate attempt at casualness, "Don't you think you'd better leave Alice behind, Joan dear?"

"No, I want to take her with me."

"She'll get rained on." Daphne reached one hand out for the doll.

"I don't *care*! Besides, she's rainproof."

Arthur turned impatiently to Daphne. "Leave the child alone. After all, it's *her* doll." He held the door open. "Let's hurry, the rest of us aren't rainproof."

"I think I'll wait here," Daphne said, sinking back against the seat. "I'm a little tired."

Arthur's expression was instantly solicitous, almost,

Daphne thought, as though he were addressing one of his clients. "Are you sure you're all right?" he asked, bending over her. "Do you want me to drive you home?"

"No!" Daphne was unable to keep the exasperation out of her voice. "Go on inside. *Please*!"

Joan stamped her foot on the pavement, sending a small splash of water against Arthur's trouserleg. For just a second Arthur seemed undecided. Then he closed the car door and followed Joan into the building. He didn't even look back, Daphne thought, he didn't even wave.

But as soon as he was out of sight, she remembered the self-assured way in which he had opened the heavy glass doors, the jaunty pat he had given Joan's backside, the playful tousling of the doll's red hair, and she was filled with pity for him, and for herself. She wanted to run after Arthur. She wanted to ask him, beg him not to let anyone else see him with that horrid doll. She didn't move from the car though —and her very inability to help him seemed to her typical of their entire married life together. She felt that she would never know the joy of doing a single, tiny thing to help him. . . .

Much too soon, Daphne was startled by Joan and Alice pushing into the front seat beside her, their rain-spattered faces looking for all the world as though they had been crying too. She kept her own face averted as she slid over to the steering wheel, and she felt thankful that Arthur was on the other side of the car.

"You're sure you're all right, dear?" Arthur asked, poised to dash back through the rain.

"Yes," Daphne said. "Fine."

He peered doubtfully into the car. "Well, all right then," he said. "I'll try to be home early. By three o'clock at the latest. 'Bye, girls." He turned and dashed for the building, waving as he passed through the door.

Daphne backed the car away from the curb and started down the street in a heavy downpour. She glanced covertly at Joan and found her staring primly out of the window, her manner as unsociable as Alice's.

Daphne switched on the radio, getting a recorded program of dance music from the Wedgewood Room. She and Joan listened for a moment.

"I was there," Joan said, without turning her head away from the window. "With Mother."

"How nice, dear." Daphne restrained herself from asking how the dry martinis were this year. "Isn't this rain nasty?" she said.

"I like the rain."

They sat listening to it beat a frantic obbligato to the quiet dance music, neither of them speaking again until they reached home.

"You hurry in the front way with Alice, dear," Daphne said, helping Joan out, "while I put the car away." As soon as Joan was clear of the car Daphne drove into the garage. Then, carrying Joan's suitcase, she ran to the kitchen entrance. She walked through the kitchen and the diningroom, into the darkening hall. Her hand stopped half-way to the lightswitch and let the suitcase fall beside her.

Joan was standing just inside the hallway, staring incredulously at the floor. There, in the half-light, Alice lay amid a litter of china, the red wig thrown clear of her headless body. The doll's claw-like hands seemed to be clutching the air in a grotesque caricature of agony.

"Alice," Joan whispered. Her grief-stricken eyes lifted from the doll to Daphne, terrifying Daphne, sweeping her without warning back to that moment in the hospital when she herself had regained consciousness so suddenly that the doctor had not had time to veil the truth in his eyes. And it was as though she heard again his low voice telling her, much later, that she would never give birth to a living child, stifling with one phrase Daphne's dreams of making her marriage to Arthur a fertile, vital thing.

It seemed to Daphne that it took her forever to reach Joan's side, to kneel down and take her in her arms. She pressed Joan's frail body passionately against her, saying over and over, "My poor darling, my poor darling," and feeling the fresh tears spring from Joan's face beneath her kisses.

"Alice," Joan's small voice said between sobs, "it's my Alice."

"I'll get you another Alice, darling," Daphne said, smoothing the child's damp hair with unknown tenderness. "Just as soon as I can."

"You can't get another one," Joan sobbed.

"I can, darling."

Joan twisted in her arms. "I don't want another Alice, I want this one!"

Daphne drew back a little and said helplessly, "We'll buy another one just like her, darling. We'll go into Saks Fifth Avenue and buy her together."

Even as she said this she saw the grief in the child's face harden and become hatred, a hot, live hatred that seemed to dry her tears. Joan said quickly, "No, I don't want you to buy another one!"

"But Joan . . ."

"I don't *want* you to buy another one!" Joan's voice rose to a high scream. "I don't *want* you to buy another one! I don't *want* you . . ."

"Stop it!" Daphne yelled, shaking her. "Do you hear me! Stop it!"

"I don't *want* you to! I don't *want* you to!"

Daphne's hands gripped Joan fiercely, and she felt that she could shake every last bit of breath from her quivering body, but suddenly she released her and groped blindly at the floor. She caught Alice by her thin, composition legs, raised the doll high above her head, and smashed it with all her strength to the floor. Without pausing, she raised it and smashed it down again. She beat the doll again and again against the wood, feeling each crushing impact thrill like an electric shock through her body. She stopped when only the doll's shattered legs remained in her hand.

For a moment Daphne sat exhausted on the floor, staring stupidly at the debris scattered around her. She had a brief, detached picture of herself falling at the child's feet and pleading for her mercy, but it lost all meaning as soon as she looked up into Joan's wide, dry eyes. They were without grief or hatred now, emptied of everything but horror. Daphne dropped the doll's legs and stood up.

"Your father will be home in a few hours," she said, expressionlessly. Then she turned and walked past Joan's suitcase to the kitchen, to get the broom and dustpan. She wanted to clean up the mess on the floor before she left the house.

—1948

Note for an Autobituary

(a memoir)

THE SUN, WARMING, all-seeing, life-giving, terrible, rose forty or fifty years too early this summer morning. During a war it does that with everybody, but war had temporarily deserted North Africa and we had begun to live in the light again. We, a company of de Gaullists and I their ambulancier, had as much of the Mediterranean as we could use, more than enough of the Sahara, plus a few towns, to ourselves. The Germans had withdrawn to Italy, as had some of the Italians. The rest, left behind to cover the retreat, were gentle prisoners. In late months we had all come to know the darkness well and love it dearly, fear the moon, but nowadays the enemy seldom troubled to visit us even overhead. We had all that too, and spent our long days in it openly. The medical officer I was then attending could bully most of the demi-malades back on duty by nine in the morning, when we would drive in my ambulance to a nearby twenty-mile strip of beach that we seemed to have discovered alone. There we'd stay until lunchtime, dipping in the strong salt water now and then, but most of the time just lying there with our faces turned to the sun, greedily storing up. I think I've absorbed more sunlight, in Libya and Tunisia, California, Arizona, Florida, and on that tennis court at home, than you, any two of you, unless you've lived your lives in the lower latitudes and faced them better than most. The doctor was another like me. We met the slow passing days flat on our backs, conversing constantly—in his elegant English rather than my rude French. I would have preferred the French, after the frustration of dining with eight or ten slurring

Corsicans in the non-commissioned officers' tent, but he outranked me, as in abilities, length of service, age, had a derisive laugh, and planned someday to go to America. There on the sand he kept me talking as much as he could, he most often choosing the topic for the day, then a few days later running over it again: the war, the peace, America, American money, women, cities, jobs, the war, the peace, America, America, but when I insisted, a few words about the corporal who was going to die. This man had fatally knifed his sergeant, also Tunisian, in a drunken game of cards and had promptly been sentenced to death, now was waiting for various appeals to be made, denied, decent time to pass, justice to be meted out cold-bloodedly. Already enough time had passed to leave the sergeant a poorly remembered man, little more than an unlucky name to most of us. It was the corporal's ghost, powerfully muscled and with hot blood throbbing, they said visibly, in his veins, an 'example' to us they said, that brooded day and night over our company from the guardhouse. I never went over there, for one good reason because it was my ambulance that was scheduled to carry him back from the firing squad. I had volunteered. I offer no excuse—what would I say? Probably most people simply don't admit such things about the past, perhaps most don't have them to admit. Perhaps, though I don't know how, others accept finality more easily than I. I find it easier to admit terrible curiosity. Here was a man, full grown and in full health, who, they said, knew he was going to die, waited only to know the morning, the minute as positively as he knew what time the sun would rise. I couldn't believe it was true. This is my apology. I couldn't believe it: no man could know that much, in the face of such knowledge he would have to give up knowing anything, the sun would have to fall out of the sky, promptly at the appointed moment, inevitably according to some eternal plan. It seemed to me that I had to be there with this man, face the day with him, with my own eyes, in order to believe anything at all. Meanwhile the days passed by, the sun continued to arrive very regularly, all appeals were denied. It was on a bright day early in July that the doctor told me I would be awakened at four next morning, in time to pick him up; we were at the beach as usual, but no American English lesson that day. In fact I think we spoke in French, and we were back in camp too soon. For once I was glad I could not translate the Corsicans and did not try. I had a few duties to perform in the afternoon, after which, for want of anything else, I went to bed at dusk. Thronged, of course. I was still planning to get out and walk, as soon as the moon went down, when they came by to wake me up. I was already dressed, had as always to wait at the doctor's tent. He had been taken over the route, across open desert and through olive groves, the day before, but in the darkness he had difficulty making out the many turns, or pretended to. Still we arrived at the end of the track ahead of everyone else—if he was right. If not, we were lost and the execution would be postponed to another day, another ambulance. If it hadn't anyway been postponed, or canceled, after we'd left camp. Perhaps the corporal had escaped, or died. We stayed in the ambulance looking back at the lights of trucks approaching us, now running off, now coming on again. When they stopped behind us we got out and stood with the other men. I don't remember if the morning was warm or cool, nor what we did during that hour until the sun came up. I suppose we watched the track to the south, for lights, or watched the east. Finally we must have faced the east, for the sun came first, and I was surprised to find that it rose out of the sea. We were fifty yards from the edge of the sea cliff, yet I had heard no waves. Now I heard them, murmuring to the sun, and I must have been the last to turn and see the pale lights of a truck creeping to us from the south. How long it took: the sun was already warm on our cheeks by the time the truck crept past my ambulance, as far as it could, almost to the edge of the cliff. He was riding, standing, in the back with some other men. They helped him down, but then they left him to himself. Nothing held his arms or his legs. A stocky man of middle height, powerfully built, about the color of dark sand, curly-haired without a hat. Twenty-five or thirty, at most. He would not look at us. He was walking. He did it by looking down at the ground, just in front of him where the next patient boot had to take its turn. His companions on either side walked that way too, half a step behind. When they reached the post they took hold of him lightly, only because they knew where he should stand. His knees were shaking. His knees were *shaking* beneath his short khaki pants, and he looked up. He looked at the group of men standing in front of him about ten paces off, while his companions tied his hands together behind the post. It took them some time to make sure they had the knot tied just right. As they started to leave him he yelled out. It pierced us all, a terrifying, lavish sound. Now he fell silent too, listening too, only his knees flapping in front of the post. Someone spoke and the five men facing knelt in the sand. He yelled again—"*Pas les noirs*"—and his companions quickly tied a cloth over his eyes before they left him there. "*Pas les noirs!*" The five lowered their guns, but at a command they raised them again. At the click of their bolts he began to chant, in a new voice now, thin, soprano, sing-song and very fast. He could never have sung so fast before, yet it didn't seem that he was through by the time their bullets broke in on him.

Afterward, after the captain had administered the coup de gr⅓ace, wasted, into the dusty head from inches out, after the doctor had glanced at the ruined chest, and we had waited, outside the ambulance this time, for the chaplain to meet us at some desolate place, I went back. The Mediterranean lay just fifty yards away from the post, another forty or fifty down. A man who could break laws might have got to it. What could have prevented him? Not likely those blacks, those gentle Sudanese giants with their conical red hats. I came to know one of them later when he tended me in a dysentery isolation tent, where even the doctor (another) refused to come. I doubt if they would have thought to use their carbines; even if one had, that might have been the empty one. A white might have shot him then: as he asked. Did he hope to put death off with that? He refused to believe the truth, even in the face of it? Just as I thought my presence there must save him, he thought, his? Or, he knew, he *knew* at last, and seeing himself overwhelmed by life's cheapness had spat it back at us before he left? *Not the blacks* . . . I like to think I would have leaped that cliff. I almost think if I were there as ambulancier again I would leap, break the morning's spell, and perhaps take that damned apple along with me. Or would I have already scattered its seeds behind me, have I now?

—1961

Company

ARTHUR HALEY TOOK HIS finger off the doorbell and waited. Inside, there was a flutter of footsteps and he could imagine Mrs. Potter picking up magazines from the floor, fluffing the sofa pillows, telling Mr. Potter to hitch his trousers up to where his waist was supposed to be. Or was "Pop" still at the sheriff's office? No, he could hear him moving around heavily now as he pretended to help Mrs. Potter get ready for company. But Marcia, would she be there?

As soon as the door opened Arthur knew that the Potters were alone. He looked down at Mrs. Potter and then beyond her.

"I *must* be psychic," Mrs. Potter said, talking very fast, as though her words could revoke the momentary slackness that had come over her face when she first opened the door. "Just last night I was thinking about you, wondering what you were doing now. And now here you are. Arthur Haley, you were thinking about Brookhaven at the same time!"

Arthur laughed. "I guess I was," he said, as Mr. Potter took his topcoat. "It wouldn't have been at all unusual."

Mrs. Potter drew him back into the hallway. "Now, was I or wasn't I psychic, Henry?" she asked, turning only briefly to Mr. Potter. "Oh, but he'd never admit it!"

Mr. Potter winked at Arthur. "Welcome home, Lieutenant. Sorry—ex-Lieutenant. If you two'll settle yourselves in the living room," he said, "I'll get a couple of psychic highballs from the kitchen."

One of the first things Arthur saw when he followed Mrs.

Potter into the living room was the new picture of Marcia and her husband, and he noted with some surprise that Milton was bald. In that other picture Milton had been wearing his officer's cap, looking rather stiff and silly with the grommet left in it, and that was the way Arthur had always thought of him. During the five months Arthur had formerly lived in the house the portrait had stood on the bookcase in the corner, and it had been ever so slightly turned to the wall so that it was left partially in shadow. But this one was in plain sight on the piano. Arthur didn't look at it for long, because suddenly he saw that the thing Marcia was holding in her arms was a baby, quite a large baby.

"How exciting to see you again!" Mrs. Potter said, steering him to a chair. "Did you fly? Oh, but you couldn't have flown on a day like this, could you? So stormy."

He had forgotten Mrs. Potter's amusing-annoying habit of commenting on her own questions. It was not one of the things you remembered about her; you remembered the aura of charm that surrounded her, and you remembered how much like Marcia's her small, upturned nose was.

"No, my flying days are over," he said, as though she had asked him the question. "I came by train from New York. By bus from Tulsa."

"Well, you probably would have needed one of those what-is-it-they-call-thems—one of those hellish-copter things to land on the field anyway. They closed down the field last summer and they're just letting it go to rack-and-ruin. Nothing is left. No airplanes, no soldier boys parading around, nothing but weeds and broken windows."

"You make it sound sad," Arthur said.

"Well, it *is* sad. For old grandmothers like me anyhow, it's sad." She paused and Arthur saw her glance fleetingly at the picture on the piano. "For you young people I suppose everything to do with the war seems ugly now. To hear Milton talk—when he *does* talk about it—you would think England was a concentration camp. All you boys care about is going home and settling down with your families again." She looked at him uncertainly and then added, "But there's so much I want to hear about *you*."

Arthur was glad to see Mr. Potter returning from the

kitchen with three glasses on a tray. He stood up to help clear a place on the coffee table, but Mrs. Potter waved him back.

"Sit down, sit down," she said. "I should think you would be exhausted after your trip. Arthur has come all the way from New York, Henry."

"How's the big city?" Henry asked. "Bet you were glad to see it again, hey, Lieutenant?"

Arthur, remembering the things he used to tell them about New York, the big build-up he used to give it, smiled ironically. How could you tell them now that it was all talk, that you could live in New York most of your life and still think of "home" as a small town in Oklahoma where you had lived for only five months?

"It was good to get back there," Arthur said, sipping the cool drink and relaxing in the quiet of the Potters' neat living room. "But after two years of it, Brookhaven seems pretty nice."

"Well, Molly, will you listen to him!" Mr. Potter said. "From Milton I expect to hear that kind of talk; he's a damned hick like me. But coming from a New Yorker, that's news! You never met Milt, did you, Lieutenant?"

"No," Arthur said.

"That's right, you left before he came back. He was an ordnance major in England, you know, and he came back with some pretty unfriendly stories about the Limies; he lived with a family there. Makes Molly sore as hell."

Mrs. Potter seemed scarcely to hear her husband. She was staring intently at Arthur, her head tilted sideways a little, almost as though she were a doctor listening to his heart through a stethoscope.

Arthur tried to think of something that would make her stop looking at him that way. "Have they got any bookshelves in the public library yet?" he asked.

Mr. Potter laughed at the familiar joke. "Not yet," he said, affecting a yokel's accent, "but I reckon they ought to be here by Christmas."

Mrs. Potter smiled and leaned forward in her chair. "Now tell us everything you have been doing since we last saw you, Arthur," she said. "We got your card—the one saying you had been discharged from the Army. But that was more than two years ago." She looked at him reproachfully.

"I'm not much of a letter-writer, I guess," Arthur said, "but I haven't had much to write about really. Most of the time I've just been staying in New York and working. I couldn't get my old apartment back; so I had to live up in the Bronx and for awhile I had a job up there in an employment bureau, interviewing. Then a travel agency downtown. . . . And that's just about it."

"No flying?"

"No flying. Right now I probably couldn't land a Piper Cub."

Mr. Potter cleared his throat and said, "I've heard several people say you were the best instructor they ever had at the field. We sort of thought you'd keep at it."

Arthur shrugged. "I had more hours than most of them. More combat hours than all but one or two, I guess." He looked away from their sympathetic faces and finished the drink in his glass. "You get tired of it," he said. "You want to settle down to earth. Like . . . other people." He had almost said, "Like Milton."

"Here," Mr. Potter said, heaving himself to his feet. "Let me get you a refill."

"Thanks. Don't forget to look in the broom closet, Sheriff," Arthur said, remembering another of their jokes. Mr. Potter had a spectacular supply of liquor smuggled over the state line from Texas, and he liked to pretend that his deputies were on his trail, though actually they bought it from the same source. "I saw a couple of deputies lurking in the bushes when I came up."

Mr. Potter put a fat finger to his lips and stole noisily out of the room.

"Are you on vacation?" Mrs. Potter asked Arthur when they were alone. "Or you would call it 'leave,' wouldn't you?"

He laughed. "I guess you could call it that," he said. "I quit my job and gave up my apartment to a piccolo instructor with two kids. I'm not working."

Mrs. Potter was staring at him again. "What will you do now?"

Arthur hesitated only a second. "I'm on my way to the

Coast," he said, trying to imply that he had definite plans. "I've never been out. . ."

"Hey, Molly!" Mr. Potter called from the kitchen. "Give Marcia and Milt a ring. Tell them to come on over for the evening. We'll have a party."

Arthur looked at a row of books across the room, wondering foolishly if he could remember any of their names by their order in the bookcase. He heard Mrs. Potter say, "Why didn't I think of that, dim-brain that I am? We can have one of our famous bridge games." He waited for her to go on. How many evenings had they sat in this room drinking illegal Texas whiskey and playing bridge, he and Marcia paired against the Potters?

"Of course," Mrs. Potter said, "with Milton here we'll have to rotate." She laughed scratchily. "But the extra person will have his hands full keeping the baby quiet."

Arthur got up and walked across the room, past the piano, to the large bay window that overlooked the front lawn. It was getting darker outside now; heavy cumulus clouds were piling up in the north and soon they would let go and drench the dry leaves that seemed to be trembling apprehensively in the trees. He felt that Mrs. Potter was watching him. "Mum," he said, using Marcia's name for her for the first time since he had come back, "is the baby a boy or a girl?"

"A girl, Arthur," Mrs. Potter said behind him. "Susan will be two years old next week."

Arthur drew in his breath. "Thanks," he said, not turning away from the window yet. When he did turn back to her, he knew that she too had once calculated, and that whatever conclusion she had arrived at she had somehow managed to accept calmly, without theatrics.

"She has her grandfather's eyes," Mrs. Potter said rather loudly. "Only maybe a little less bloodshot."

Mr. Potter, coming in from the kitchen, grunted and popped his eyes humorously. "Have you called Marcia yet?" he asked.

Mrs. Potter looked over at Arthur, and he was glad now that he had thought to leave his suitcase at the bus station.

"I'm going to have to be a wet blanket," Arthur said, taking the drink Mr. Potter held out to him. "I'll have to be on my way pretty soon. There used to be a bus to Oklahoma City at 5:30."

"There still is, but hell, man . . ."

"I'm sorry, Pop, but you know how it is."

"You just got here . . ."

"Don't push, Henry," Mrs. Potter interrupted. "Arthur knows his plans better than we do."

"Well, it seems a damned shame to come all the way out there and then go away without seeing Marcia. He hasn't even seen Milt and Susan yet."

"Henry," Mrs. Potter said, "don't you think your wife deserves a second highball when there's company in the house? Don't be so stingy."

Arthur was thankful to her for keeping the conversation going while they sat there drinking their highballs and waiting until it was time for him to leave. Mr. Potter was still blustering a little when he got Arthur's coat from the closet, and he made Arthur promise to come back again.

"At least you'll let me drive you to the bus," Mr. Potter said.

"It's only a few feet," Arthur said, feeling himself smiling. "I wouldn't think of it."

In the doorway, Mrs. Potter stood up on tiptoe and kissed Arthur's cheek. "I wish you could have stayed, Arthur," she said.

It had started to rain and Arthur made a big thing out of turning up his coat collar. "I do too," he said. "I wish I could have."

When he was halfway down the path he heard the door close quietly behind him, and he could picture Mrs. Potter returning to the living room for the dirty glasses while Mr. Potter went into the kitchen to lock up the liquor closet.

—1947

Just the Three of Us

MR. CLIFFORD HAWKINS couldn't think of a venomous snake of five letters ending in t, and suddenly it occurred to him that he didn't give a damn. He folded the Bronxville *Press* neatly and placed it on the small mahogany table near the fireplace. Humming a tune from some half-heard radio program, he crossed the carpeted living room to the steps leading to the dining room and kitchen.

In the kitchen he found Mrs. Hawkins mixing a concoction which looked like the diluted Kem-Tone they had used on the garage, but would probably turn out to be a salad dressing. He stood for a moment in the doorway watching the quick, efficient movements of her hands. A slight glaze of moisture on her smooth, round face was the only indication that the work was not so easy as she made it seem.

"Darling," he said, standing near her and consciously restraining the impulse to pat her plump back, "we should have made Mabel stay in tonight. This is too much work for one person."

She turned her head long enough to give him a quick smile, but her hands didn't miss a beat. "Nonsense, Clifford," she said, "I'm having fun! Besides, I told Mabel weeks ago she could have this Saturday off. That club of hers is having a beauty contest."

Briefly, he pictured the dark, pinched face surrounded by bushy black hair, like much-used Brillo.

"What on earth," he said, "could Mabel possibly find to do at a beauty contest?"

Mrs. Hawkins laughed. "Cliff! I wish you wouldn't always make so much fun of Mabel. Just because she has her hair fixed unbecomingly."

"Good Lord!" he said. "Don't tell me she has that hair *fixed.*"

"Clifford!" Mrs. Hawkins was laughing so hard that her hands momentarily stopped beating.

"Well, in the absence of beauty," Clifford said, "what can I do to expedite the progress of this meal?"

"Not a thing," his wife said, still laughing. "I'm enjoying it. It'll keep me busy until the train comes. Look," she said, reaching into the refrigerator and drawing forth a fat avocado. "It's the first one I've seen in weeks. You know how he always liked them."

"I certainly do, Grace," Clifford said. He didn't remind her that, unlike John, he preferred his avocado with no dressing at all. This was to be John's night. Besides, she undoubtedly remembered.

"And look at this," Grace said. She brought a large, thick steak from the bottom of the refrigerator.

"Unbelievable," he said. "I'll bet John hasn't seen anything like that since he left. *I* haven't."

"I was lucky," Grace said, wrapping the steak carefully in the grease-spotted paper. "Everything worked out perfectly."

Clifford watched the care with which she placed the steak back in the refrigerator, almost as though she were tucking a baby in its crib. He wished he could think of some way he could contribute to the festivities too. John, he remembered, had just begun to acquire a taste for sherry before he left. The last of the pre-war stock was in the decanter now.

"I'll get the sherry," he said. "John might like a glass before dinner."

Grace seemed to be considering. Then she smiled. "Yes," she said, "I imagine he would enjoy that."

Clifford went to the closet in the dining room and took out the decanter with the chipped top. He handled it gently, fingering the clean lines of the cut glass. It had always been his favorite wedding present. He smiled a little, remembering that John had caused the chip years ago when he ran into the coffee table with his tricycle. Had anyone but John done it Clifford would have been very angry, but now the chip seemed a part of the perfection of the decanter.

He took the sherry and the three glasses into the kitchen, and washed the glasses in hot, soapy water. Then he dried them thoroughly with a clean dishtowel and placed them on a round wooden tray with the decanter. He stood looking for a moment at the triangular pattern he had made of the glasses. He was conscious of Grace standing beside him.

"Three glasses," she said musingly. "It's been a long time."

He glanced at her quickly, realizing that he had been feeling the same thing.

"Yes," he said. "I imagine it's seemed a long time to him too."

Grace's round face puckered in thought. "I suppose so," she said. "But he's had so much to divert him—new places, new people, new things to do."

"Yes," Clifford said. He thought of the fifteen months he had spent in France during the past war. Looking back, it seemed to him that, by and large, the time had passed very quickly. But there was a vague memory of a few dragging months, days even, that had seemed almost without end. He had been older than John, of course; he had been almost twenty-one when he went over.

"Clifford," Grace said suddenly. "Do you think I'm very selfish?"

"Selfish! Good Lord, what a thought!" He smiled at the earnest expression on her soft, scarcely lined face.

"I mean about Gertrude and Doris—should I have invited them over for dinner? Doris is so eager to see John again. Wasn't I selfish to want just the three of us tonight?"

"No, darling," Clifford said, putting his arm around her waist. "I'm sure this is the way John will want it too. Besides, you couldn't possibly have done any more work than you're doing now."

She took his hand and smiled at him sideways. "You know I could have, Clifford," she said. Then, "But John can call on them in the evening. I told Gertrude he'd be around about nine or nine-thirty."

"I'm sure he'll like it that way much better," Clifford said. "Besides, he has thirty days in which to see Doris."

"Thirty days," she repeated musingly. "It sounds like an awfully long time. Somehow I keep thinking of it as only tonight."

"Look," Clifford said, "you'd better finish up whatever you have to do. It's five-forty. We should leave in about fifteen minutes."

Grace sprang away from him and set to work transferring things from one pan to another, slicing carrots and celery, and seasoning everything in sight. "Thank goodness I thought to set the table this afternoon," she said.

Clifford smiled. He remembered that Grace had started straightening John's room up two weeks ago, when they'd first got word of the furlough. "I'll follow your good example," he said, "and get the car out of the garage."

In the garage, he pushed the sliding doors as far open as they would go, because he knew John would probably be driving back. Then he stopped suddenly and chuckled at himself. Among other things, John had been driving large trucks for the Air Corps over the icy roads of Alaska. He backed the car into the drive and went back for Grace.

They had twelve minutes to cover the mile to the station, but Clifford found himself driving faster than he usually did when he had half the time. And Grace didn't complain once. There was a slight smile on her face as though she were thinking of something pleasant.

"Now," she said when they were nearing the station, "at last we'll find out something about Alaska. It must be a wonderful place, but John's so much like you about letters. He's so vague."

Clifford laughed. "Most men are," he said. "But, darling, let's not ask him too many questions the first night. It'll all come out in time if we don't start in pumping him."

Grace frowned. "Clifford," she said, "I don't pump people."

"I know you don't, darling. I just meant, let's leave him alone as much as possible tonight—try to make him feel at ease."

"Of course I'll try to make him feel at ease," she said impatiently, "but I don't intend to sit like a bump on a log all evening. That's no way to make him feel at ease!"

Clifford reached over and patted her hand. "I'm sorry, darling," he said. "I guess I was just giving advice out loud to myself. I know you've been working for weeks to make this a success, and I know it will be."

She smiled and squeezed his arm. "Isn't it a wonderful night?" she said.

"Yes," Clifford said. "It's a wonderful night and we're seven minutes early."

They sat in the car, indulging in the fragmentary conversation that often accompanies the arrival and departure of trains. When at last they spotted a train coming around the distant bend, they left the car and stood waiting a few feet behind the yellow safety line on the platform. The local approached the station with what seemed unbearable lethargy and then at the last possible moment jolted to a wheezing stop. Immediately Mr. and Mrs. Hawkins were surrounded by shrill women and children returning from shopping and matinees, and men who somehow found something to do in New York on a Saturday afternoon. If there were people in the crowd they knew, they passed unnoticed. The train was only four coaches long and they watched each of them tensely as the four streams of people gradually thinned and ceased. When it seemed that the train was about to move on, they both spotted him on the steps of the leading car.

A conductor was helping him down the steps, and for a terrible second Clifford thought John had been hurt and they had not been told. He glanced at Grace, wondering if she had shared his melodramatic fear, and in shame hurried with her down the platform. When they reached the front car, John was standing on the platform and leaning slightly on the conductor. In one hand he carried the brown leather suitcase they had given him when he left, and in the other an almost empty whiskey bottle. He looked taller and heavier than Clifford.

As the train started up again, the conductor seemed about to say something, but then he half smiled in apology and sprang back onto the train. There was a loud clang as he let the coach platform drop back into place.

John didn't seem to see them at first, but when Clifford took his arm he turned bloodshot eyes to them. "Hello folks," he said thickly. "It's great . . . great to be home again . . . home, su-weet home."

He leaned over to kiss Grace and it required all Clifford's strength to keep him from falling. Grace took John's other arm and between them they led him over to the car and helped him into the back seat. Clifford noticed Grace's quick, furtive glance along the platform as she climbed in beside John.

"Here," John said, holding up a three-quarters-empty bottle. "A present for you. From Minneapolis. Carstairs . . . very special . . ."

Clifford took the bottle and placed it beside him on the front seat. "Thanks a lot, John," he said.

He started the car and pulled slowly away from the station, concentrating on the unpredictable train-time traffic.

"He's asleep," Grace said a moment later. Clifford glanced back and saw John sprawled across the seat, his head sagging on Grace's shoulder. His mouth was open slightly and there was a small, wet spot on Grace's dress. Clifford turned his eyes back to the road.

In the driveway he stopped the car and left the motor idling.

"Please, Clifford," Grace said. "Let's drive into the garage."

"We'll be pretty crowded." He looked back and saw Grace glancing over John's head through the rear window. "All right," he said. "We'll be able to manage."

He drove the car into the garage and got out. He opened the back door for Grace and then unlocked the door into the kitchen. Between them they managed to pull John out of the car.

"We'll leave the bag until later," Clifford said, sounding very practical.

They placed John's arms over their shoulders and almost lifted him into the house and up to his room. The room looked neat and comfortable in the fading evening light, and Clifford noticed that the bedcovers were already turned back. They were both breathing heavily when they eased John onto the bed. Clifford went over to the light switch.

"We won't need it," Grace said, raising a hand to stop him.

Clifford went back to the bed and helped her remove John's clothes. He seemed very heavy and it took them several minutes to undress him. His underclothes were damp with perspiration and hadn't been changed recently, but Grace folded the clean pajamas she had laid out on his bed that afternoon and placed them in a bureau drawer. She went to the bathroom and came back with a washcloth and towel. Carefully she washed his face and hands, patting them dry with the clean face towel. Then she swept the matted blond hair from his forehead and pulled the covers over him.

They stood for a moment looking down at John's large, relaxed body which seemed to dwarf the bed and the boyish room. His mouth had fallen open and his breath came in small, fitful snores. They closed the door quietly and walked with muffled steps down the stairs.

"I'll call Gertrude," Grace said. Clifford stood in the hallway outside the telephone booth, half listening to her call the number. Then she was talking quickly.

". . . Oh, he looks just fine," Clifford heard her say. "He's put on weight and his complexion has cleared up beautifully."

Clifford realized suddenly that it was true. The adolescent blotches were completely gone. That accounted largely for the change he had noticed in John's face.

". . . And my dear, wait until you see all the ribbons," Grace went on rapidly. "All red and yellow and blue. They're beautiful! I had no idea he'd have so . . ."

Clifford went into the kitchen. From the confusion of preparations on the table he took the sherry decanter and the three glasses and returned them to the dining-room closet. Then he filled a small bowl with ice cubes and another with peanuts. In the refrigerator he found an unopened bottle of club soda. He placed it on the round wooden tray with two highball glasses and a swizzle stick. Then he went to the garage and got the Carstairs from the front seat of the car. He placed that on the tray too.

Going past the telephone booth he heard Grace still talking. ". . . Not even a sleeper all the way," she was saying. "I don't know how he stood it as well as he did. . . . He'll call Doris as soon as he gets up tomorrow. . . ."

He stood in the living room waiting for her to finish. In a moment he heard the door open and she came down the steps. He took her in his arms and patted her shoulder. Her lips were quivering and she smiled apologetically.

"Look," he said, drawing her over to the coffee table, "I have a surprise." He placed three ice cubes in each of the glasses and divided the two inches of Carstairs evenly between them. Then he filled the glasses with soda and stirred them. He wondered suddenly why he hadn't done all that in the kitchen.

They sat near one another on the couch, holding their glasses before them and stared vaguely across the room.

Grace spoke quietly. "Alaska must be a horrid place," she said.

He could think of nothing at all to say to her. They sat for a while in silence, drinking their strong highballs rather rapidly. It was quite dark now, but it didn't occur to either of them to turn on a light.

—1944

The Kind of Life We've Planned

WHILE HE WAITED FOR HER at the first tee he took a few cuts with the old Atomic Driver, selecting for decapitation each time a particular dandelion blossom, enjoying the stunned look of it as it pitched a few feet in the air and landed, always a little askew, on the slope of the mound. After each swing he paused to look out over the fairway, far out toward the green, where the ball would have been. He did not need the ball out there to tell him when he had made a good shot, he did not need it because he had form and when you had that everything else took care of itself. Only duffers refused to believe that the golf ball was a precision-made instrument, like the bomb, made by experts to obey experts.

They would be out here in a few days, the duffers, now that summer school was over, hacking away at the course, making it look like a bridle path by the time he returned in the fall. They had done it last summer and the summer before that, they had even done it his freshman year when the course was first built, and still the University had not set the course off limits to townspeople. They simply sent some men out in the fall to patch it up, and again in the spring, until by the time summer school started they finally had a nice little golf course again, in time for the regional championships. And he would not, he reflected with sudden bitterness, ever see it looking like this again, for next spring he would be teeing off for the lord knew where and would not tell. He beheaded another dandelion, expertly, to remind himself that he was not a duffer, that he was Johnny Ryan.

He was really, in a way, doing the University a service, for school had been out only a day now and already the dandelions seemed to be crowding like duffers onto the course. They freckled the fairways in a very disconcerting manner, so that a golfer could not easily trace the roll of his ball unless it landed on the green. There were not, of course, any dandelions on the putting green. It made him a little ill to imagine a dandelion there, and he looked beyond the two-hundred yards of fairway to the distant square of green, to reassure himself that there were really none. Seeing the green, a small bright patch in the distance, he felt an almost physical sensation of pleasure. Heaven, he thought, would be a putting green at the end of a long fairway, far beyond the woods and the bunkers, a destination reserved exclusively for experts. Hell would be a bunker filled to the brim with yapping, shoving duffers. He was going to expand the metaphor and tell it to Margo when she came, but it occurred to him that Margo would not be interested in his philosophizing today, and at that moment he saw her walk around the corner of the clubhouse. She was wearing her hair up.

Leaning crookedly on the old Atomic Driver as though it were a crutch or an old man's walking stick, waiting a bit tensely for her, he tried to understand the significance of this, of her pinning her hair up today, for he was sure that in the two years he had known her he had never before seen it that way. It was a feminine trick, he decided, calculated to throw him off balance, and he knew that the first thing he must do was to get her hair down around her shoulders where his fingers could run through it, get them back on their old footing. Once they were back on their old footing, he knew he could not flub the ball.

Watching her walk quickly toward him through the dandelions, seeming so slim and virginal in her sleeveless sports dress, he felt for a moment that the last week was all a crazy nightmare from which he was emerging slowly now into the clear safe light of the golf course, and he wanted to call out to her his almost hysterical relief. But as she drew within a few steps of him he stared dumbly into her large eyes, her large green eyes which fear had made larger and deeper than he could possibly have imagined. He waited for her to speak first, knew that she must because she had stopped directly in front of him, just beyond his reach, where he could not under any circumstances have broken the spell of panic in which he found himself trapped. He waited, and Margo said, almost hissed, "Johnny, have you thought of something?" and he laughed.

He pointed to a certain large dandelion at his feet, drew the old Atomic Driver back in a half swing as though it were a niblick, let it drop in a short vicious arc. "Look," he said, "flying saucer."

The dandelion lobbed obediently in the air, fell precisely between Margo's dainty brown suede toes, and Margo jumped back as though stung.

"Relax, baby," he said, smiling at her. "That's the whole secret of the game. You've got to relax."

"I'm sorry," she said, but without smiling. "I guess I'm silly today, Johnny. But have you . . . ?"

"Hey, hey," he said, and he went over to her now and placed his hand on her shoulder, saw that two large pins held up her hair. "We'll walk. We'll walk and talk."

"All right. Anything," she said. "It's these damned dandelions. I don't like to look at them. They stare at you."

He laughed and patted her shoulder. "When *you* walk over them, they have something to stare at," he said, but it was no good, her smile for him was perfunctory, negative, and he adopted a matter-of-fact tone: "Somebody ought to invent a dandelion killer, something that would kill all the dandelions and leave only the grass. It's a damned crime, this course, the way it's going to pot."

"Yes." Walking beside him, she kicked at dandelions—kicked short little kicks which were, for her, almost vicious. "Everything has gone to pot," she said. "*Everything.*"

"I know," he said, wishing to sound humble and a little bit helpless. "I know it and I'm sorry."

"Sorry!" She turned on him now, abruptly, and as she turned her hair pins stayed in his hand while the hair fell unnoticed by her in a long plait over her shoulder. He had never thought he could be so attracted by a blonde, because he had read long ago that opposites attracted opposites and he had always cultivated brunettes. "I won't let you be sorry, Johnny. You said you would think of something, that you always could. I'm waiting for you to tell me what we're going to do."

He had her where he wanted her, he knew he had her, but he said: "I'm thinking of you, Margo. Isn't that enough?"

"To hell with me. Think of *us*."

"I am," he said truthfully. "When I think of you I think of myself too, and I think of all the fun we've had together and of how it's all stupidly spoiled now. I'm being very realistic."

"I *want* you to be realistic," Margo said. "We've both been unrealistic long enough and look at the mess it's gotten us in."

He knew that the moment had come to tell her what they could do, but he prolonged its excitement. "We could do what most people do," he said casually. "We could get married."

"And settle down in a little white house?"

He shrugged, looking unhappy in such an appealing way that she threw herself onto his chest. Her head fell back and he kissed her lips, in the painful way she liked, before he held her at arms-length and looked earnestly into her face. "I love you, Johnny," she said. "I do love you. *What are we going to do?*"

"We'll walk some more," he said, smiling, taking her arm. "Okay?"

She nodded, and they walked for a while in silence. He placed his hand on her shoulder, under her hair, and beside them the Atomic Driver hobbled like a bad foot in the grass. He watched it trip over a divot. "Pretty rough ground around here," he said.

"This is the fourth hole," Margo said.

"Yes."

"And there's the woods. Remember?"

"Of course I do."

"This is where you found the ball, isn't it?" she said. "Over here?"

They were near the edge of the woods now, in the rough, and he paused to locate the exact spot. He nodded his head. "Just about there."

She held up an arm to shade her eyes, waiting until then to screw up her face against the high sun which she could no longer see. "You were lucky that day," she said reproachfully. "Why couldn't you have been lucky about this mess too?"

He shrugged. "You can't be lucky all the time, I guess. Sometimes you have to play it smart instead."

"*Then what are we going to do?*"

He looked past her. "How much are you willing to do?"

"Anything."

"It won't be simple, a thing like this."

"*Anything.*"

"Anything?" he said, turning his wan smile on her. "Rape?"

"After all this time?" she said, her laugh skidding uncontrollably into a sob. "After five weeks?"

"No," he said. "I mean today. Right now." She had stopped sobbing even as she had begun, involuntarily, and one of her shoulders had pivoted away from his as though she would turn and run. "Forget it," he said, shoving his hands deep in his pockets to prevent their grabbing her. "It was just an idea, Margo."

"I guess I don't understand. I don't understand anything now," she said, taking a step toward him.

He said, "It was the only thing I could think of. Forget it."

"Explain it to me."

"I'd rather we didn't do anything at all to have you hate me, Margo."

"But Johnny . . ." She leaned back her head to look into his eyes and try to laugh again. "Wouldn't they have a doctor examine me?"

"Yes," he said slowly, "and he would find it was true."

"Oh . . ." she said, and he could hardly feel her pull back against his arms at all. "I see what you mean now," she said.

He spoke quickly. "The doctor would examine you and do whatever they do. Then he would pat you on the shoulder and send you home. After that it would be the law's responsibility, and they would be working overtime to avenge your honor. They might even call you in once or twice to identify a man, but you would say it definitely wasn't the right man. The case would begin to die out—until next month. Until you were past your time. Then you would go back to the doctor—or your own doctor—and they'd have to do something about it."

"But would they?"

"I don't know," he said. "I think they would. But even if they didn't, everything would work out for the best. Nobody would blame you for anything, they'd pity you. And when the baby came, if it did, they'd take it away from you."

She seemed to be staring at the twitching muscles of his neck, and for a long time she did not speak.

"Maybe by that time," he said, holding her, "by the time everything had quieted down, say in a couple of years, I'd be started well enough that we could get married and lead the kind of life we've planned."

"You'd be playing golf?"

"I should be in the big time, two years from now."

She said nothing else, and his arms were beginning to ache from holding her so tightly. "Well, Margo?" he asked.

She looked up at him, stared directly into his eyes now, for the first time. "This is the way you want it, Johnny?"

"It's the best I could think of."

"All right." She pushed a little against his chest, and he released her. He let her take his hand, and he allowed her to lead him through the grass, toward the woods. It seemed to him that they were almost running toward the woods.

He could feel the dampness seeping through his trousers now, up to his belt, and when occasionally a finger of sunshine found its way to them he could see in its cool light the beads of water glowing in Margo's long blonde hair. Stumbling after her, in the darkness, he surrendered wholly to the exhilarating sense of power it gave him to be led by the hand like this, among the trees, by a little wisp of a girl whom he had taught in this strange way to show her love for him. He felt her stop, suddenly, caught in an unseen net of underbrush, then drag him with her onto the damp bed of spongy moss. But afterwards it was almost as though the same force which had brought her there, now pushed him from her, and brought her quickly to her feet. He felt the moss sink beside him under her weight, and he grabbed her slender ankle. "Hey," he said. "Why so fast?"

"I've got to go to the police," she said. "Don't you remember?"

"You can wait a minute."

"No, I can't," she said. "Let me go."

"You know what you're going to say?"

"Yes. I know."

"What?"

"*This.*" Her foot jerked from his hand then, leaving him clutching her tiny shoe, and suddenly the forest was filled with her alarm: "Help . . . me . . . *help* . . . me . . ."

"Why you little . . ." On his knees, he groped for the old Atomic Driver, found it, lifted it with both hands to bring it down upon her head, but behind him the dense vines and branches held the club, permitting her escape. He lunged after her, thrashed wildly at the tangled darkness even though he knew that her first plunge had taken her beyond his reach.

"*Help* . . . me . . ."

He beat madly at the trees which stood between them now, he felt the Atomic Driver shatter from a violent blow, yet he did not stop. He carried its broken handle with him to the edge of the woods.

"*Get* . . . him . . . *get* . . . him . . ."

Margo stood on the fairway, among the dandelions, pointing to the spot where he emerged now from the woods, her flowing hair serving better than the tattered fragments of her clothing to hide her scratched and bleeding body.

"Margo, don't . . ."

Then he saw them, saw the duffers not more than fifteen feet away, three of them, bearing down on him from the fairway. They had dropped their golf bags there, and each one carried a club. "Don't listen to her," he shouted at them. "She's crazy. Do you hear me?"

They passed on each side of Margo, scarcely breaking their stride as they spoke some words to her, and they were coming straight toward him. He did not have time to turn and run.

"Didn't you hear me? I told you she's crazy. Crazy!"

But they did not hear him. They were almost on top of him now, and they did not stop. "I'm warning you, stay back, you duffers!" He brandished the broken handle of his driver. "Stay ba . . ."

It seemed to him that they all swung their clubs at the same time, that he could distinctly hear each separate club break at the same instant on a different part of his skull, and falling he shook his head. "You poor, poor duffers," he said. "I'm Johnny Ryan." But he did not think they heard that either, because he couldn't hear it himself.

—1954

The Cure

MR. AND MRS. HOBART STOOD WAITING beside the car while the little man with the tic put Mr. Hobart's suitcase in the trunk and locked the trunk door. It was the same little green-uniformed man who had carried Mr. Hobart's suitcase up the wide steps two weeks before. That day, following him at a short distance, Mrs. Hobart had leaned over and whispered to her husband, "See, a porter and everything. Didn't I tell you, darling? It's just like a hotel." Mr. Hobart had glanced at the man's back and at the sprawling wooden building with "Restview" in small, discreet letters above the door, but he hadn't answered. Instead, he had stooped down and placed his untouched glass of beer on one of the steps. They had climbed the rest of the way in silence.

Even when it had come time to kiss him good-bye and leave him in the lobby with that vague, deep-voiced Dr. Kramer, Mr. Hobart had had little to say. He had mumbled something about hoping Mrs. Hobart would have a nice time at her sister's, and his hands, brushing against her forearms, had felt as impersonal as the dry wings of moths. She had turned at the door, half-expecting him to call out to her, but he had been standing alone in the center of the lobby and staring at the only ornament on the high plaster walls, an enormous moose head with vacant eyes and an ugly, receding chin. Mrs. Hobart had hurried down the steps, toward the car, past the glass of beer which was certainly very flat now because he had carried it all the way from New Rochelle. Seeing it there, she had wondered if he could have left it as a sort of symbol, a pledge, for her to see on her way down the steps. I hope nobody kicks it over, she had thought, and she had cried all the way to her sister's house in Kingston.

Now the little man was through with his job, and he politely held the car keys out to Mr. Hobart. Mrs. Hobart reached over and took them, because she saw that her husband wasn't going to. "Do you want me to drive, darling?" she asked, hoping that his answer would be, no.

"If you like." Mr. Hobart stood looking at the car. The porter opened the door and Mrs. Hobart got in first and slid over to the driver's seat. After Mr. Hobart had got in beside her, the porter closed the door carefully and firmly with both hands and smiled with his gently twitching face. Mr. Hobart did not reach for his wallet, or even smile at the man, so Mrs. Hobart started the car quickly, a little too quickly, causing Mr. Hobart to lurch forward in the seat as they drove away.

They drove down the gravel drive, past the green lawn and the low white benches which were shaded by old, carefully-tended maples, and out onto the highway. Mrs. Hobart turned to her husband then, saw how he huddled in the corner with his coat collar sticking out awkwardly from his thin, almost old-looking neck, and it seemed to her that if she didn't speak at once they would drive all the way to New Rochelle in silence. "Well," she said lightly, "was that so bad?"

Mr. Hobart's eyes did not leave the road. "It was terrible," he said.

"But Dr. Kramer told me . . ."

"Dr. Kramer is a liar and a bore."

"But you *did* go for long walks, didn't you?"

"I did that to get away from Dr. Kramer and the rest of the bores," Mr. Hobart said, turning to her for the first time. "Good God, Janis, you know I never take *walks*."

"I know, darling. Didn't you make any nice friends?"

"None."

"There must at least have been some bridge players."

Mr. Hobart turned away from her. "If there were any, they probably played with deuces wild. I stayed in my room."

"Did you read? Did they have a good library?"

"I don't know," Mr. Hobart said. "I slept."

Mrs. Hobart winced, but then she thought of something

and smiled at her husband. "At least you didn't have any fleas in your bed, then," she said.

"Oh Lord, are we going to have to face *that* again?"

Mrs. Hobart laughed. "No more, darling. I left enough paradichlorobenzene in the house to kill every flea within miles."

"Where is that damned cat, anyway?" Mr. Hobart asked, hunching farther into the corner. "Have you got him with you?"

"Why, darling, don't you remember? We left him home. Junior Barton promised to come over every day and feed him on the porch. You remember, darling."

"No. I don't."

Mrs. Hobart looked over at her husband, realizing for the first time how nearly stupefied he must have been that day, and she had a sudden, terrifying picture of him waking up the next morning, alone, in an unknown room and in an unknown bed, not remembering clearly how he had got there but needing only the dry hot mouth and the wild craving for alcohol to remind him why. She reached out impulsively and put her hand on his. "Why didn't you call me, darling? Why didn't you call me and tell me to come take you home?"

"I didn't want to spoil your vacation," Mr. Hobart said, withdrawing his hand. "I didn't want to spoil the only chance you've had to get away from an old derelict like me.

"*Dave.* Don't talk that way, darling. You know there's nothing I want more than to be with you!"

Mr. Hobart laughed. "Didn't you have a nice time at your sister's?"

"Not very." Staring with blurred eyes at the road ahead, Mrs. Hobart thought of the two weeks with Jean and her husband Craig. She thought of the early morning golf, the swims, the evenings at the summer theater, the cocktails she had been able to drink without restraint for the first time in many years, and she knew, now, that she had been miserable every minute of the time. "It wasn't nice at all," she said.

"Well, there's always next year."

Mrs. Hobart's nails dug into the steering wheel and she did not speak again for many miles, not until they were more than halfway home. She slowed the car down then, and she said, "Dave?"

"What is it?"

"We won't be home until long past lunchtime. You must be feeling a bit peckish, darling."

"I'm not hungry," Mr. Hobart said.

"Well, I am." At the first restaurant they came to, Mrs. Hobart pulled off the highway and parked the car. She started to get out of the car, but she stopped with one foot on the running board. "I don't know whether I like the looks of this one or not," she said. "Shall we go a little further?"

"Why on earth should we?" Mr. Hobart peered out at the restaurant, and then he too saw the small neon cocktail glass above the door. He turned to Mrs. Hobart, and his lips trembled. "Good God, Janis, you don't really think I'm going to start drinking again," he asked, "after *that*?" He did not wait for her to answer but climbed out of the car and walked stiffly ahead of her to the restaurant.

A tall, beaming hostess met them at the door and led them to a table in the center of her room. When they were seated, she spread two menus before them and asked, "Will you wish to order from the bar before you eat?"

Mr. Hobart looked across the table at Mrs. Hobart. "I don't believe I'll have anything," he said, "but perhaps my wife will. Janis?"

"No!" Mrs. Hobart said, bowing her head to the menu. "No, thank you."

They ate without conversation, and without looking at one another or at the uninterrupted chain of cocktails which wound past their table. When at last the meal was over and they were once again outside, Mrs. Hobart paused hopefully in front of the car. But Mr. Hobart did not offer to drive the rest of the way; he settled himself on his side of the car and sat waiting to be taken home.

By driving as fast as she dared to, Mrs. Hobart reached New Rochelle at three o'clock. She did not stop at the A & P, as she had planned, but drove directly to the house. In the driveway, she shut the motor off, and smiled. "Well, here we are!"

Mr. Hobart held out his hand. "Give me the key to trunk," he said.

While Mr. Hobart got out the suitcases, Mrs. Hobart

walked through the small, trim yard to the front door. Junior Barton had cut the lawn, and he had even remembered to prune the privet hedge. The hollyhocks were blooming, and new pansies bordered the gravel walk. On the porch, the cat's empty dishes sat in a neat row beside the doormat. Randolph hadn't been there to say good-bye, and he was away someplace now. Mrs. Hobart did not call Randolph though, because Mr. Hobart was standing behind her, waiting for her to unlock the door.

"Ouph!" Mrs. Hobart said when she entered the hall. "Let's get some air in here before we do anything else!"

She walked into the livingroom, holding her breath against the oppressive air, and she felt as though she were moving at the bottom of a warm, stagnant pond. She did not let herself breathe again until she had opened the four livingroom windows, and then she stood for a minute breathing deeply and watching the green batiste curtains lap thirstily at the outside air. She turned to Mr. Hobart, who was still standing in the hall. "That should take care of the fleas," she said, and laughed. "Do you want to open the downstairs, darling, while I do the upstairs?"

"I'm going to take a nap," Mr. Hobart said. "I'll open the bedroom."

"But darling . . ." Mrs. Hobart started toward the hall.

"I'm tired," Mr. Hobart said. "I'm going to take a nap."

Mrs. Hobart watched his stooped shoulders disappear up the L-shaped staircase, and then she went into the diningroom and threw the windows open wide. She went from the kitchen to the pantry to the laundry, trying to make herself think of all the things she would have to do before she went to bed. When she returned to the hall, Mr. Hobart was coming down the stairs.

"Did you decide it was too stuffy for a nap, darling?" Mrs. Hobart asked.

"There's no glass in the bathroom," Mr. Hobart said. "I'm getting a glass."

Mrs. Hobart watched him go into the kitchen. "Shall I make some tea for you, darling?"

Mr. Hobart laughed. "Thank you," he said. "I'll drink water."

Mrs. Hobart went upstairs and opened the two windows in the study. She went to the guest bath and opened it up too.

She opened the door to the guestroom and she was stepping inside when something brushed lightly against her ankle. Mrs. Hobart looked down.

"Oh . . . no!"

Randolph took two steps past Mrs. Hobart, into the hall. He stood with his legs spread slightly apart on the hall rug, and his large, loose head weaved a little from side to side.

"*No,*" Mrs. Hobart cried, stooping to the wasted body. "*No.*" Randolph did not seem to see her, or even to know that she was there. He hung from her hands like an old, much-worn fur piece as she stumbled with him down the stairs.

"*Dave!*"

Mr. Hobart turned slowly from the sink. He started to walk past Mrs. Hobart, but he stopped.

"He was in the guestroom!" Mrs. Hobart cried. "He must have been sleeping when I put the paradichlorobenzene there! I called all through the house before we left, but he didn't even *cry.*"

Mr. Hobart stared at the cat, and then he stared at Mrs. Hobart. He stared at her for a long time. "Well," he said at last, softly, "I guess that takes care of the fleas."

"He could have *cried,* Dave!"

Mr. Hobart continued to look at her.

"He could have cried," Mrs. Hobart sobbed. She carried Randolph to the sink, murmuring it over and over: "He could have cried . . . He could have cried . . ."

Behind her, Mr. Hobart's voice was flat. "Maybe he doesn't know how," he said. "Maybe he's always left everything to you." He walked away from her, out of the kitchen.

Leaning against the sink, she watched a tear fall from her bowed head onto Randolph's back, sparkle there an instant before disappearing in the dry, matted fur. She looked after it almost in panic, almost as though it were her last tear.

—1951

Quadrangle

HE HAD TROUBLES OF HIS OWN, such as the constipated Texas lady bureau clerk who still after six hard months sat tight tight on the title to his car which he was finally ready to shed and depart from Arizona too if he could trade for a stronger one that might carry them somewhere high in the Rockies before it quit, yet he had eyes to see the stunned young wife sitting forsaken before Arthur Murray's in the parked new Olds convertible. She did not sit in the driver's seat. It looked, if a good man were to slide in there he could take her, on the rebound, without resistance, any place, and open up a world for her. She was slim, dark, pretty, all but unexplored, and it was not a pleasant thing to watch her die. Perhaps, he thought, basing this on six months of filling the Arthur Murray cigarette machine three times each week, here indeed was Romance's last retreat. Things at least sometimes happened here. He held in mind most vividly the old lady who took over the place many afternoons with a desperately beautiful whirl of skirts about her shapely thighs, as she danced with one or another of the slick-haired weak-chinned boys but always and above all with herself. There were mirrors on every wall.

He knew quite well the blonde who shared an intimate red leather couch with the owner of the Oldsmobile, even knew her well enough to feel the rub of jealousy. She was head hostess of this hall, but for him their acquaintance had begun long before. In fact he had seen her nude when she was five or six, as good as so when in her teens, and altogether in several cities after she left home: she was blonde as sunlight from head to toe. He had dreamed hard of asking her for one more look, but well he had a wife almost so fair and far more true, had what's more a daughter who at twelve was growing blonder with each new day . . . He had troubles of his own. Almost it could be enough to be asked in husky voice to put in king-size Chesterfields, "They sat-is-fy." Too, she had grown a little cold around the eyes, but ah he remembered far too well how warm her body was.

As for the husband, the lover, he was not new. A white shirt, a tie, a pampered waist. Clipped head. No doubt a boyish smile in kinder times. He felt only pity for the girl outside, frozen, stiff, apparently ready to die of what she thought she'd lost. After filling the machine, king-size Chesterfields all the way, he rested a moment quietly, to make it out himself.

"It's the baby," was what he heard, "if it wasn't for the baby everything would have worked out right. Then the car . . ."

"I understand all that," was said. "I'm sorry, but if I gave in to one I'd have to give in to all of you."

"Not even a month? You couldn't even give us a month?"

"No, you see, that way I'd be breaking my contract with the collectors too."

Outside he had to pass the Oldsmobile to reach his truck, but he did not loiter on his way. If a man were to slide in behind that steering wheel she would not know that he was there. She was rebounding from nothing, going no place. What she was looking so hard out the window at was a hundred dollar bill to be floating by, with that sexy portrait of Ben Franklin on his face. Baldness denotes virility. They say. He's scarcely met the man, himself.

—1962

The Imaginative Present

EXCEPT FOR PAY TOILETS and certain automatic elevators in small apartment buildings, Mrs. Weaver thought, the hall telephone closet is the only truly private place that many of us know in our public journey between the matrix and the grave. Here, for a quiet moment before we admit the grocer, the druggist, into our lives, and for that other moment after we have cut him out, we are alone. Here, in this unventilated hiding place, we need not smile, not even the wry smile which we reserve for our bedroom mirrors, and we need not listen to the secret, unsuspecting voices reaching us in muffled sentences from the living room. But we do listen, listen tensely with our teeth clamped unevenly together and our fingers resting with interrupted purpose upon the telephone.

"I can't show it to you, Gay," Mrs. Weaver heard her husband saying. "Not yet. You see, it's all wrapped up."

And Gay, his daughter, saying, "But surely you aren't going to *give* it to her, Dad. . . ."

"Not give it . . . ?"

"Not to *her,* Dad. To Mother once, perhaps. You must be thinking of Mother."

"Please, Gay . . ."

"Not to *her.*"

"Why not to her? She's always wanted one. . . ."

"But not now, surely, Dad." Gay's laugh was clear. "She's too big and grey!"

Mrs. Weaver's finger jabbed the five-hole of the telephone

dial as though it were an eye and she would put it out. Almost before the dial could purr back into place she jabbed again, the three this time, and then quickly the six, the three, the one, permitting no instant of silence in which to hear her husband's blending laughter, or even worse, his dutiful rebuke.

"Martin's Drugs."

"This is Mrs. Weaver, Mr. Martin. Will you please send over a quart of vanilla ice cream before seven this evening?"

"One quart of vanilla, Mrs. Weaver?"

"Yes, please. And some dinner mints too, Mr. Martin."

"A quart of vanilla and some dinner mints. Having a party, Mrs. Weaver?"

"Yes," Mrs. Weaver said. "It's my birthday."

After she had replaced the receiver, she did not immediately open the closet door. She stood listening, as though by an effort of the will she could restore her husband's censored words, the "Now, Gay, that isn't very kind to your stepmother, is it?" or the "Do you really think so, Gay?" which a moment ago she had deliberately refused to listen to. But there were no words now, no words for her to hear, though their unheard presence rested on her just as oppressively as the more tangible relics of her husband's past, the things which she saw about her daily, saw now, but which she did not and would never fully understand, the ancient warped golf clubs in their green-molding canvas bag which he and that other Gay, the original Gay, had shared for so many years, the suede windbreaker too, too small for him now, which had once kept those two warm on week-end hunting trips, the ragged plaid wool scarf which had been their banner on God knew what gay and carefree outings. She looked at these things, as she had so many times before when seeking a key, a meaning, for some nostalgic remark of his, or some unspoken thought which she had been made to sense, and as usual they told her nothing that she had not always known. And as usual she prepared her ready smile, her birthday smile today, and went forth to be her husband's wife.

She smiled going down the three low steps to the living-room, smiled graciously even though she knew that to the four terribly blue eyes waiting there she was but the monstrously padded caricature of a younger, slimmer woman who seven years before had had the incredible good fortune to die and remain forever a memory of loveliness. Down on their level now, her gracious entrance suddenly halted by the necessity of looking up into those waiting, watchful faces, she tried to think of something pleasant, something gay, to say. But it was Mr. Weaver who spoke, and he said the words which Mrs. Weaver might have predicted had she tried. "Well, there she is," he said, stepping forward. "How's my birthday girl?"

"Fine," she said, smiling between the two large hands placed awkwardly upon her shoulders. "Just fine."

"Can you stop your work long enough to sit down and have your birthday party now?"

"Oh, yes," she said. "I can hardly wait!" She allowed herself to be led to the sofa, to be gently lowered there, almost as though by sinking onto it all at once she might have broken it, and she smiled across the room toward the easy chair and Gay.

"Happy birthday, Hazel," Gay said, smiling too.

"Thank you, Gay."

They sat looking at one another while Mr. Weaver removed the glass stopper from the sherry decanter on the coffee table, filled the three sherry glasses on the way, ceremoniously passed two of them, first to Mrs. Weaver, then to Gay, and returned to the coffee table and picked up his own. He stood there, halfway between the two women, and raised the glass to a level with his eyes. Even now, after almost four years of witnessing this little rite, Mrs. Weaver was struck by the incongruity of the delicate glass in the heavy, hairy hand. She could think only of those stronger, more exciting drinks which once he and that other Gay had tracked in fabulous treasure hunts between Harlem and the Village, or ladled from a thousand bathtubs all the way from Greenwich to Baltimore, and which she knew he was thinking of too when he held his sherry glass that way.

"Well," Mr. Weaver said finally, "happy birthday, Hazel."

"Happy birthday, Hazel," Gay said.

"Thank you." She waited until they had touched the sherry glasses to their lips and lowered them again, and then she sipped her own obediently, despising it, not finding even his ironic condescending pleasure in it.

"Did you get everything done you wanted to?" Mr. Weaver

asked, sitting one cushion away from Mrs. Weaver on the couch. "All your little jobs?"

"Yes," Mrs. Weaver said. "Everything's all taken care of."

Gay smiled at Mrs. Weaver. "Did you order the vanilla ice cream?"

"Yes, Gay," Mrs. Weaver said.

"Bake the cake?"

"Yes," Mrs. Weaver said. "I baked it this morning."

"Gay thought," Mr. Weaver said, clearing his throat, "that it would be nice if we gave you your presents now, before dinner."

"Presents?" Mrs. Weaver said, turning to smile at her, and even at the moment of being appalled by her own fatuousness she went on, was swept on by the humiliating compulsion to behave stupidly in the presence of those who expected stupidity: "I can hardly wait," she said.

"I'm afraid my present isn't very imaginative," Gay said, "but you know I've never had any luck choosing presents for you, Hazel." She stood up then, and she walked over to the coffee table. Mrs. Weaver watched her pick up her patent leather pocket-book, open it, open the small black purse inside, and take her checkbook out. She managed to smile back at Gay as Gay drew out her pen and unscrewed the top, skillfully with one hand. "It isn't very much, I'm afraid," Gay said, bending to write on the coffee table. "But as they say, it's the spirit of the thing that counts." When she had finished she screwed the cap back on the pen with her left hand, and with her right she waved the check to dry it in the air. "Here," she said, handing the check across the coffee table to Mrs. Weaver. "I hope you'll be able to find something suitable for yourself. Something practical."

"Thank you, Gay," Mrs. Weaver said, and her eyes, lowered dutifully a moment to the loose extrovert handwriting, the lovely dollar sign, the too-large 25, rose quickly, hopelessly, to challenge Gay's. But Gay was looking at Mrs. Weaver's flushing cheeks.

Mr. Weaver cleared his throat. "Gay," he said, "perhaps you and Hazel can go shopping together one day this week—pick something out together."

"But we never agree on anything, Dad," Gay said. "We never really agree on anything, do we, Hazel?"

"No, not very often, Gay," Mrs. Weaver said.

"Well, you seem to agree on that at least," Mr. Weaver said, with a little laugh. He got to his feet slowly. "Now it's my turn," he announced.

Gay retired to her chair and Mr. Weaver took her place beside the coffee table. "My present," he said, reaching a long arm to the mantle and grasping the box propped there, "is imaginative and not at all practical." He smiled at Mrs. Weaver, seemed even to be trying to smile warmly with his cold blue eyes as he turned his back on Gay and held out the box. "I hope you'll like it, Hazel."

"I can hardly wait," Mrs. Weaver said. The box was light in her hands, and the note, slipped under the tight, store-tied cord, said, as she had known it would, "For Hazel (over)." Turning it over, she thought of all those other notes, the long series of "For Hazel (over)'s," going all the way back to the first one, the one that had hurt her most. He had written it early in the first year of their marriage, slipped stealthily off to the study one evening to compose it, and he had returned to hover restlessly with the unsure pride of the beginning author while she read the never-to-be-forgotten-words: "In the belief that a sound marriage is based as much on a thorough understanding of the past as on a dream of the future," it had read, in rather uneasy compromise between benevolent husband and successful corporation lawyer, "we will try at all times to speak out frankly and to hide no part of our past from one another. Much has happened to us in the past which has left a deep, indelible mark upon us, and without a full understanding of which neither can hope to know the other. If at times we seem to behave strangely, even coldly, toward one another, we will discuss our behavior candidly and we will see that it is not caused by any immediate, personal friction between us but by some unhealed wound of the past. By laying bare these wounds to the other's gaze we will prove that mutual sympathy and understanding can be as strong a bond between man and wife as love." At that time, read with contained, searing tears, the note had seemed a grotesque, lopsided irony to her, to her whose life had retained scarcely a scratch from the carefully planned sequence of girls' schools and the ten continent years as secretary to a happily married publisher. She had wondered then, as she almost never now did, that he did not see the irony too, or rather that he did not see that she saw it too. But she had managed to smile at him that day, dimly through the warm opaque shells of her eyes, and he had taken her hand and talked to her seriously of the past, his past. Now, as she placed his note before her on the coffee table and turned to smile at him, she did not have to try so hard to keep from crying. "Thank you," she said. "It's a lovely note, Paul."

He beamed, and Gay said, "Aren't you going to read it to us, Hazel?"

"Go ahead, Hazel," Mr. Weaver said. "Read it out loud."

She reached out, and her hand scarcely shook as she lifted the note. " 'To Hazel,' " she read, " 'whose patient and understanding companionship has been a solace and a help to me.' " She waited with eyes lowered to the note when she had finished, and there was silence.

"Why, that *is* nice," Gay said then. "You have such a clear, straightforward way of putting things, Dad."

"I'm afraid it sounds a little sentimental," Mr. Weaver said, beaming.

"Sentimental?" Gay said. "Realistic, rather. I wouldn't say it was sentimental, would you, Hazel?"

"No," Mrs. Weaver said, still not looking up, "I don't think so."

"Well," Mr. Weaver said, taking the note from Mrs. Weaver and folding it fastidiously into a square, "aren't you going to open your present, Hazel?"

She knew that he was beaming at her, and she said, gaily, "I certainly am! Right now."

"I can hardly wait," Gay said.

"I'll break the string for you," Mr. Weaver said.

The string popped under his thick hands and Mrs. Weaver watched her own trembling fingers crawl over the two sides of the box, pry the cover off, and she heard the tissue paper rustle restlessly, heard her own pulse beating, as she groped inside.

And then suddenly the room was deathly still.

"Well?" Mr. Weaver asked.

He doesn't mean it the way it seems, Mrs. Weaver told

herself, ducking her head to the terrible contents of the box: He just doesn't stop to think.

"Well?" he said again.

"It's lovely, Paul," Mrs. Weaver said, looking up at him, knowing that to him the tears in her eyes were tears of joy. "Lovely."

"You really like it?"

"Of course," she said. "Of course I do."

"Let me see, Hazel," Gay said. "I'm all agog."

"Yes," Mr. Weaver said. "Hold it up so we can see."

"All right," she said, and those were her fingers, her chapped and reddened fingers, raising the weightless, fragile bit of lace in front of her, holding it out for all to see. "Do you like it, Gay?"

"What *is* it?"

"It's a nightgown," Mrs. Weaver said. "A black lace nightgown."

Gay's eyes were wide. "My God," she said, "you can see right through it."

"Yes," Mrs. Weaver said. She slipped one arm inside the bodice, seeming already to fill it so full that its gossamer threads would break, and she could see every pore, every imperfection of her skin beneath. "See?" she said.

Mr. Weaver said, "You really like it, Hazel?"

"It's lovely, Paul," she said again.

"You can wear it tonight," Mr. Weaver said, sitting back and smiling at her.

"Well," Mrs. Weaver said, trying hard to laugh with Gay, "do you think I dare?"

Mr. Weaver looked from one to the other of the laughing women. "Dare?" he said.

"If it were a little larger, maybe . . ."

"What?" Mr. Weaver said. "I clearly remember asking the girl for the largest size she had."

Mrs. Weaver laughed again with Gay. "It looks terribly small nevertheless," she said, and, "Don't you think so, Gay?"

"Oh, not really *small,*" Gay said.

"Do you think it might fit you, Gay?" Mrs. Weaver asked, smiling over the nightgown.

"It's awfully hard to tell, just looking at it," Gay said.

"Would you like to try it on and see?"

"Oh, may I?" Gay jumped to her feet and came over to the coffee table. "May I really, Hazel?"

Mr. Weaver got to his feet too. "Gay," he said, "please . . . I bought that nightgown for Hazel."

"Oh, let her try it on, Paul," Mrs. Weaver said. "It might look lovely on her."

"But Hazel, I bought that . . ."

"You can get me something else," Mrs. Weaver said. "Something more practical."

She relinquished the nightgown to Gay, feeling the silky ribbons slipping from her fingers onto Gay's eagerly waiting ones. "There you are," she said.

"Thank you, Hazel," Gay cried. "Thank you!"

Mr. Weaver took a step toward Gay, and his hands were out. "Gay . . ." But Gay was already halfway across the living room, the nightgown floating behind her like a dainty, playful shadow. "Thank you, Hazel!" she said again.

"I hope it fits," Mrs. Weaver said.

They watched Gay dance up the three stairs from the livingroom and disappear into the hall, and then they turned to one another, for a moment silent with that constraint which solitude always seemed to force upon them. Mr. Weaver cleared his throat, and he reached for Mrs. Weaver's hand. "Hazel," he said, seating himself beside her on the sofa, "I just wish you hadn't let Gay do that. You know that I wanted you to have that nightgown."

Mrs. Weaver looked away from the serious face. "It will look so much nicer on Gay than on me," she said gently. "It was lovely, Paul, but it just wasn't meant for me."

"*I* think it was meant for you," Mr. Weaver said.

"No, Paul."

Mr. Weaver moved closer to her, and he pulled her arm a little toward him, silently demanding that she look at him. "Yes, Hazel, it was," he said. "I meant it to be for you. . . ." He paused, and she thought: Paul at a loss for words. She turned away. She couldn't look into those cold blue eyes, now, after all this time, and watch them try to speak to her, to her alone.

"You didn't have to do that, Paul," she said.

"I wanted to . . ."

"You didn't have to, Paul."

"Yes, I wanted . . ."

"Hello, everybody! Here I am."

They turned at the same time to Gay's excited voice, and Mrs. Weaver could hear her own breath catch. Gay did not descend into the living room but stood there slightly above them in the hall, her body, braced gracefully against the door to the telephone closet, revealed in startling profile against the wall beyond. Staring at her, at the pale skin beneath the transparent film of nightgown, the small taut breasts, the small hips, and the exquisitely rounded thighs which seemed designed for the gown as surely as the single band of black ribbon which defined the waist was defined for it, Mrs. Weaver felt for a shocked instant that now at last to this room had come the haunting image of Gay's mother. But then she heard the voice that too often had led her beyond the perfection of Gay's body to the meanness of her heart: "Well, what do you think, Hazel?"

"I think it's lovely, Gay."

Gay did not wait for Mr. Weaver's comment, did not even seem to expect one of him, but began to pirouette with slow, effortless abandon, as though hypnotized by her own heightened sensuality, not watching them as they watched her but glancing with lowered eyes at her slender, twirling body. She might have kept on this way, Mrs. Weaver thought, forever had not the front doorbell sounded its known deception from the kitchen. "I'll answer it," Gay called out and, whirling, even before Mr. Weaver could get to his feet and call to her, she was at the door, opening it, laughing at what she saw out there.

"Gay . . . !"

But they could hear her clear, exalted voice at the door, thanking Mr. Martin for the ice cream, paying for it, thanking him again. They couldn't hear Mr. Martin speak at all.

"Gay!" Mr. Weaver cried when the door had closed.

"Did you call, Dad?"

"Have you gone crazy, Gay?"

"I'll put the ice cream in the refrigerator, Hazel," Gay called. "I don't want you to have to bother with it."

Mr. Weaver turned back to Mrs. Weaver, stood looking at her for a moment, and then he sank heavily beside her on the couch. "What a foolish damn stunt to play," he said.

"She's young," Mrs. Weaver said gently, putting her hand in his, "and full of life. She doesn't mean anything wrong by it, Paul."

Mr. Weaver's baffled face was turned toward Mrs. Weaver, but he wasn't listening to her. "She's getting more like her mother all the time," he said.

"Paul . . . !"

"It's the truth," he said. "That's just the sort of foolish, vulgar thing her mother would have done."

"You don't mean that, Paul!" Don't say it, she thought, wanting to draw her hand away, please don't say it. Not now.

He pressed her hand. Now she did draw away from him, and she found herself staring back into those empty, bereft blue eyes, staring resentfully, bitterly, almost as though he had spoken disrespectfully of one she loved.

She said, "I'll go take up the dinner, Paul," and leaving him she felt that he had grown old, and big and grey.

—1951

Mr. Weatherwax and Psyche

WHEN A MAN REACHES FIFTY without having once been unfaithful to his wife, and in a deeper sense to his mother too, he begins to look closely at the paintings of nudes on the walls of his friends' gamerooms, and at the portrait of Psyche on the White Rock carbonated water bottle. Milton Weatherwax had no friends with gamerooms, but he had a steady little income which enabled him to buy all the scotch and White Rock he could use. He could use a good deal, for such a small man, and by nine o'clock in the evening he was usually on his second bottle of White Rock. This evening he was on his third.

"Mil-ton," Mrs. Weatherwax said from the center of the couch, "what are you looking at?"

"What's that, lover?" Mr. Weatherwax asked.

"I said," Mrs. Weatherwax said with energy, "what are you ogling that bottle about?"

"Was I, lover?"

"Oh, God," Mrs. Weatherwax said, and the grey, wild bun of her hair as she bent again to her sewing reminded Mr. Weatherwax of nothing more than a wren's nest in a high wind. Certainly it was not at all like Psyche's hair, which rose from behind her head in a smooth, firm coil, and which was beautifully yellow. Furthermore, Psyche was quite nude down to her diaphanous half-slip, and kneeling on the white rock peering into the still pool she leaned toward Mr. Weatherwax in an entirely titillating manner. *I wonder if she has a navel?* he thought.

"Did you say something, Mil-ton?" Mrs. Weatherwax asked.

"Did I say something, lover?"

"Oh, God," Mrs. Weatherwax said. "Have another drink."

"I will in a minute, lover," Mr. Weatherwax said. Watching the quick, impatient tempo of his wife's stitches, he knew that the time had come for him to inquire about her work. "What are you sewing, lover?" he asked.

"How many times must I tell you," Mrs. Weatherwax asked, "that I'm making a sampler?"

"What does it say?"

"If you must know," Mrs. Weatherwax said, "it says 'Home Is Where the Heart Is.' "

"Why, that's a nice thought," Mr. Weatherwax said.

"Oh, God," Mrs. Weatherwax said. "Aren't you ready for that drink yet?"

Mrs. Weatherwax was always tolerant of Mr. Weatherwax's drinking. She believed in the old-fashioned virtues, such as sewing samplers, preserving fruits, and putting your husband to bed in an inebriated condition. On the few occasions when Mr. Weatherwax was sober he made a periodic habit of throwing tantrums, and Mrs. Weatherwax had learned that, although these little exhibitions in no way fazed her, they somehow took the edge off her own. She liked to see Mr. Weatherwax drunk and docile.

"I think I'll have that drink now," Mr. Weatherwax said.

"Do."

"I think I will." Mr. Weatherwax stood up, but in doing so his relaxed right arm slapped the table, toppling his glass and the half-filled White Rock bottle onto the floor. He looked down at his shoes, which seemed much farther away from him than they actually were, and he saw Psyche floating toward him in a little stream of carbonated water. She was wet to the skin.

"Ahh," Mrs. Weatherwax cried. "*Now* you've done it." She was on her feet, glaring down at Mr. Weatherwax. "*Haven't* you?"

"Yes," said Mr. Weatherwax, "I have."

"I wonder how many things you've broken lately with your clumsiness!"

He tried to think of all the things he had broken lately, of the milk bottles, the Navajo salad bowl, the aspirin bottle, the polaroid sun glasses, the many drinking glasses, but he had difficulty keeping them all separate in his mind. "I don't know," he said. "How many?"

"Oh, God," Mrs. Weatherwax said. "Why don't you go to bed?"

"All right, lover," Mr. Weatherwax said. "I'll put the car away first."

"I don't think you'd better," Mrs. Weatherwax said.

"You don't?"

"Oh, go ahead," Mrs. Weatherwax said. "Maybe the fresh air will do you good."

"All right, lover."

Out in the warm night, Mr. Weatherwax paused on the porch and looked about him. He couldn't see anything, because it was dark. There was, however, a sense of enchantment, of tantalizing promise in the air, and his heart ticked off his quick little steps across the dewy lawn. The Chrysler loomed before him, a thing felt but not seen. He found the old chromium door handle and yanked it open.

"Hell-o, Mis-ter Weath-er-wax."

The voice, coming from within the car, was ardent, cloying, like the night. Mr. Weatherwax's trembling fingers sought the dashboard light and after a restless moment, found it. He saw then the bare, dripping shoulders, the bare midriff, dripping all over his Chrysler, the slender, yellow knot of hair, the diaphanous half-slip clinging to the slender thighs, and he said: "Oh."

"Hello . . . there."

"Haven't I seen you somewhere before?" Mr. Weatherwax asked.

"Often," said the warm voice. "Often and often."

"You're Psyche."

"Yes," she said. "And you're Mr. Weatherwax."

"Yes. How did you know?"

"I've been watching you," Psyche said, "for a long time. I always make a point of watching men who stare at White Rock bottles. I take a special interest in them."

"You do?"

"Yes," she said. "I wait for them to drop me on the floor, so that I can get off that damned label and pay a little call on them." She pouted. "I had to wait a long time for you to drop me."

"Well, I dropped just about everything el—"

"But not me. I've been waiting, watching you drop everything you got your hands on, for months, but you never once dropped me until tonight."

"I'm sorry," Mr. Weatherwax said.

They sat considering one another in the stuffy car, she leaning toward him a little, he leaning back, and he said, "Hadn't you better get home to your husband now?"

"Cupid?" she said, snorting. "That little playboy has forgotten where home is."

"Oh, I'm sorry. I didn't know."

"You have no idea how he neglects me, running around with his silly bows and arrows," Psyche said, sliding a little toward him on the car cushion. "That's why I'm so fond of unhappily married men. I sympathize with them."

"You do?"

"Yes," she said. He saw her moving toward him, felt the first damp touch of her skin against his hand, but he could shrink no farther into the corner. He pointed desperately at her midriff. "Why, you've got a—" He stopped, his hand trembling an inch from her pale white stomach.

She laughed. "A bellybutton? Why, of course. I used to be mortal until Cupid married me and made me immortal, the louse."

"I didn't think you'd have one," Mr. Weatherwax said.

"You should see Cupid," Psyche said with a slight disgust. "He's covered with them. Every time one of his love-matches results in a baby, he paints another bellybutton on his wings. The last time I saw him—not very recently, I must say—he had seven billion, seven hundred million, three thousand and twenty-one of them."

"He did!"

"Yes," she said softly. "But that's child's play." She was suddenly upon him now, and he could feel the firm encircling pressure of her arms, the passionate flutter of her wings against his perspiring neck, her soft lips smothering his weak efforts to resist.

It seemed minutes later that he managed to draw a breath and say, "I think I'd better put this car away."

"I'll take it the rest of the way," Psyche said. "You give me one more kiss and go back to Lover."

"Thank you," he said. He allowed her to kiss him once more, long and passionately, and then he patted her shoulder distractedly and slipped back out of the car. Walking back to the house, he could still feel the warm breeze of her breath upon his cheek, the delirious tremor of her wings fluttering against his neck, and his hands shook as he opened the door.

"Well," Mrs. Weatherwax said, "did you manage to put the car away without demolishing the garage?"

"Yes," Mr. Weatherwax said.

"Did you remember to pull the hand brake?"

"Yes, lover," Mr. Weatherwax said. Even as he spoke, from the direction of the garage came the rending sound of splintering wood, the whump of crumpling fenders, and the tiny tinkle of glass falling upon cement.

"Oh, God," Mrs. Weatherwax said. "What was *that*?"

Mr. Weatherwax just smiled.

—1950

Mr. Weatherwax Takes the Cure

MRS. WEATHERWAX WAS NOT BY NATURE a woman addicted to vanity, but periodically, usually around Easter time, she would look at herself in the bathroom mirror and decide that something had to be done. Most often her remodeling was in a minor key, a new brooch, a necklace, a bit of lace crocheted especially for her throat. But there came a time when she decided, quite rightly, that the source of her dissatisfaction was more fundamental than this. She decided that her hair was unbecoming, and becoming, as she grew older, constantly more so. Ever since being set on fire in Chicago by a permanent wave machine she had shied away from beauty parlors, but the thought occurred to her that the new Toni home permanent might be safe, even in the hands of Mr. Weatherwax.

"All you have to do is roll my hair around the little curlers," she told Mr. Weatherwax one evening, "and Toni will take care of the rest."

"All right, lover," Mr. Weatherwax said, eyeing her grey, rather distraught locks from his chair. "Do you mind if I have one more drink before we start?"

"Yes, I do mind," Mrs. Weatherwax said, eyeing him back. "I want my hair to be set in curls, not snakes."

"All right, lover." Mr. Weatherwax sat nursing the last inch of his Scotch and White Rock while Mrs. Weatherwax prepared herself in the kitchen. He could hear the gentle splashing of water, the scrape of her slippers upon the linoleum, her muttering, and when she called to him he got to his feet.

"Mil-ton!"

"Here I come, lover."

He found Mrs. Weatherwax doubled over the kitchen sink, dripping, and he stood on tiptoe to peer in at her. "Are you all right, lover?"

"Of course I'm all right," his wife sputtered. "If you'll shut up for a minute, I'll give you your instructions. Now, do you see that bottle there?"

"Bottle?" Mr. Weatherwax said.

"Not over *there.* Right here next to the sink."

Mr. Weatherwax returned from the liquor closet. "Right here?" he said.

"Oh, my God," Mrs. Weatherwax said, "not the glass. That's my Toni neutralizer. Now pick up that bottle!"

"Ah." Mr. Weatherwax picked up the bottle. He held it to his nose and sniffed it.

"That's my Toni wave lotion," Mrs. Weatherwax warned him. "All you have to do is daub it on my hair with that cotton. Do you think you're capable?"

"I think so, lover," Mr. Weatherwax said. "I've read all about this in the ads. I've seen the Toni Twins."

"Never you mind about the Toni Twins," said Mrs. Weatherwax. "Just start daubing."

Mr. Weatherwax started daubing, and when after several minutes he had smeared her hair to his satisfaction he stepped back to consider the effect. "It looks very nice, lover," he said.

"Oh, my God," Mrs. Weatherwax said. "You haven't even started yet. You have to do the curlers."

Mr. Weatherwax listened to his wife's instructions about the curlers. "You'll have to roll them good and tight," Mrs. Weatherwax concluded, "or they won't take."

"All right, lover."

Mr. Weatherwax rolled a nice tight curl, perhaps a little tighter than was absolutely necessary.

"I didn't say you had to pull the hair off my skull," Mrs. Weatherwax said, wincing.

"I'll try another one," Mr. Weatherwax said. He began rolling a series of curls, waiting each time until Mrs. Weatherwax said "Oh!" and then quickly clamping the curler down. When he had used up all the curlers, and all Mrs. Weatherwax's hair, he stopped and said, "There."

"All right," Mrs. Weatherwax said, "now why don't you mix yourself that drink?"

"Thank you, lover." Mr. Weatherwax picked up his glass, and finding that it was not empty he took a sip.

"Milton! Don't drink that!" Mrs. Weatherwax cried. "That's my Toni neutralizer."

"I'm sorry, lover," Mr. Weatherwax said. "I forgot."

"Oh, my God," Mrs. Weatherwax said. She took the glass from him and held it to the light. "Well, I guess there's enough left."

"I hope so, lover."

"From now on you drink your own poison," Mrs. Weatherwax said, starting to leave. "I'm going to my room to rest while these curls set."

Mr. Weatherwax watched Mrs. Weatherwax's rather naked-looking head disappear through the kitchen door. When she had gone, he went to the ice box for a piece of ice. He did not usually take ice in his highballs, because it seemed such a lot of trouble, but just now his stomach felt a little uneasy and he wanted to allow it a moment to rest. He managed to hit the ice with the ice pick, and the cake split in two. He hit again, and this time one of the halves broke into quarters. He hit one several times more and by the time he stopped all the ice pieces were reduced to just about the right size for a highball. He selected one at random.

It was when he turned back to the sink that he saw them there. They were bent side-by-side over the sink, their heads hidden, their twin satin-clad posteriors whispering unknown secrets to one another in the quiet room. Mr. Weatherwax did not say anything, but he dropped his ice.

"Hello, Mr. Weatherwax," they said in chorus, turning as one to face him. "Here we are."

"Then there really are two of you," Mr. Weatherwax said with relief. "I was afraid for a minute that I was seeing double."

"Of course there are two of us," they said, curtseying. "We're the Toni Twins."

"Yes, I know," Mr. Weatherwax said. "But what are you doing here in my ki . . . in my wife's kitchen?"

"We've come to give you your reward," they said.

"My reward?"

"For being the first man to drink Toni home permanent neutralizer, of course."

"Oh, I see."

The Twins leaned forward a little until they were down on Mr. Weatherwax's level, and he could see that they were breathing ardently. "Well, aren't you going to claim your reward?"

"Yes, I guess I am," Mr. Weatherwax said. He tried not to giggle. "I don't know just where to begin."

"That's the catch," the Twins said, smiling mischievously.

"The catch?"

"Yes. First you have to guess which one of us has the Toni."

"Oh," Mr. Weatherwax said. He could feel his jaw dropping, and it seemed as though his whole body were stooping to pick it up.

"It's not so hard," the Twins encouraged him. "There are only two of us."

"I know. But I'm not much good at these games," Mr. Weatherwax said.

"Try. You'll be well rewarded," they said softly.

He looked from one to the other of them, at their lovely blonde hair, their long slender bodies voluptuously encased in satin, their soft lascivious lips, their yearning eyes. "I don't dare," he said. "I might guess wrong."

"You can only try," they said, and as though with a single thought they lifted the left straps of their gowns and slid them off their bare white shoulders. "Try."

"Well . . ."

"Mil-ton!"

"*Now* look," the Twins said, glancing toward the door. "You've taken so long that you'll have Lover in on us in a minute."

"Milton, what's going *on* in there?"

The Twins tittered.

"Nothing's going on, lover," Mr. Weatherwax called.

"Hurry!" the Twins whispered.

"Well . . ."

"Hurry!"

"All right." Closing his eyes, Mr. Weatherwax stumbled blindly forward. "I choose . . . this one."

His hands groped until they touched flesh, and he drew it to him. But the body in his arms was not the warm, pliant form which he had expected, the lips were not soft, not passionate. The breath was not sweet. After a moment he opened his eyes, and he blinked. "Oh!"

"Now, what was that for?" Mrs. Weatherwax asked.

Mr. Weatherwax made himself look up at Mrs. Weatherwax's face, which was glowering at him beneath her Toni. "Nothing, lover," he said. "Just a little reward."

—1950

The Contest

GERALD BLAKE WAS NOT a familiar type. He was married, had two children, one boy and one girl, in the fourth and sixth grades, two automobiles, a house in what is called the residential section of town, worked for a large company, had a hobby, and a television, but he had not been tranquilized yet. He was in love, rapt, with his wife's body. There are many men like him, but they are uncommon. They are obsessed, with those shoulders, those receptive arms and breasts, those soft and agile thighs, that firm belly, that hair, that tenderness. It must be unbearable to them, as it was to him, to watch the body coarsening, the shoulders sagging, the breasts sagging, the skin drying and flaking, soon even the thighs withering, turning spongy and blue, over the little bunches of hard muscle, all so slowly and so perceptibly, and to know that there is nothing for it. With all that can be said about the beauty of old age, it comes late, at best, and there is still a long time in a passionate man's life when he is not ready to see it, not in his wife, as Gerald wasn't. In Julia he found something far more precious to him than wisdom, character, dignity, self-possession. Voluptuousness. He wanted to preserve it and, in some way, share it.

His hobby was photography, but he was not a fanatic. He enjoyed taking pictures, and was competent, but it could not keep him long away from his wife. His greatest pleasure with it was to practice in her presence, with Julia as model. He took untold quantities of pictures of her in every conceivable kind of dress, undress, mood, setting, light, activity, posture, some very wild ones. Julia enjoyed it too, though the posing perhaps more than the viewing. Still she was always ready to sit down and go through the albums, with him, in the evenings especially, preparatory to another session. This despite the fact that they had been at it for almost eight years now, since shortly after the last child was born, and were getting no wilder. For all those years they had kept it a private pleasure, between themselves, the albums, costumes, props, not hidden, but not in evidence. They were thus content until the night Gerald conceived an especially beautiful view of Julia, seen in an oval mirror, on her back, groping for the bedcovers. It turned out to be a fine photograph. He sent it to a photography magazine, whose editors saw its beauty too, awarding it first prize for adult subjects in a nationwide contest.

When complimentary copies of the magazine arrived Gerald welcomed them with an exquisite pleasure, an ecstasy of gratification, which Julia shared as well as she could. For him it was the same pleasure he always felt in Julia's presence, but now intensified by the acknowledgment of others, whose excitement was new, detached, not biased by fifteen years' intimacy with the source. He found himself tremendously uplifted by this sharing, however impersonal, and for a while felt no urge to include any of those close about him—until a few very good friends, finally, whom he felt he could count on for appreciation, and usually after some drinking. The word soon spread through town, of course, and the magazine. Gerald was first aware of a new camaraderie, among casual acquaintances, a new smatter of laughter around him in response to jests he was supposed to be in on. Then the winks, backslaps, innuendoes. They made Julia aware, males and females of every age, with their staring. Whenever they looked at her Julia felt they were not seeing her at all, nor even that picture of her, but various shrinking unloved things of their own. Gerald knew this too, and it was terrible to him. That the Blakes had children and these were school days did not help either. Within a week the whole family was frantic, no one could speak to anyone, nor look, even among themselves. In June they sold their house and moved to a new town, but by then Gerald was so broken in spirit that he was impossible to live with, and Julia had to sue for divorce. The decree became final on her thirtyeighth birthday.

—1959

The Third Doorman

EVERYONE WAS SMILING EXCEPT the man in the Cadillac. Pete the new Second Doorman was smiling as he swung open the car's backdoor, doubled at the waist, cried, "Good morning, sir. Welcome to the Miami-Ritz!" The four bellhops were smiling too as they trotted out to vie for the three pieces of luggage the chauffeur had unloaded from the trunk of the Cadillac.

"Good morning, sir! Welcome to the Miami-Ritz!"

"Welcome to the Miami-Ritz, sir!"

"WelcometaMiamiRitsuh!"

"Welcome . . ."

"Screw, hey. Red and I saw him first."

"You say so."

And of course Tony the Superintendent of Service was smiling too, that indecent exposure of teeth that became even more shameful when one realized the teeth were his own. "Good morning, Mr. Stuyvesant! Welcome to the Miami-Ritz!" he cried, and the bellhops pouncing on the name chorused, "Good morning, Mr. Stevenson . . . Good morning Mr. Stevens . . . Goodmorning MrStun . . ."

The man, too tall and angular ever to have been a child, emerged from the Cadillac ponderously as though from a great black mechanical womb, the newness of his attire and of the Cadillac's somberly gleaming doors lending credence to one's sense of witnessing the fruition of a modern immaculate conception. There was even an awful dignity in the way he tripped at the lobby entrance and fell flat on his face.

But the bellhops scurrying to tilt him upright failed to borrow any of his dignity, their fingers, ostensibly dusting him off, lapped thirstily like little pink tongues at his jingling pockets, and their eyes sought his solicitously. Mr. Dalrymple gliding forward to meet the new arrival stopped short with one limp hand raised in disjointed alarm, and Saul the Window Washer, from his high position on top of a ladder, expected to hear Mr. Dalrymple cry "Hark!" But Mr. Dalrymple stood speechless, as though waiting for someone to retract a tactless remark.

It was Tony the Superintendent of Service who spoke first. By covering his teeth he assumed an instantaneous appearance of grin, almost threatening concern as he said, "Mr. Stuyvesant, are you sure you're all right?"

The tall man flicked at his lapels and although he did not touch the bellhops the effect was almost as though he had brushed them off onto the floor. They stood there at his feet, facing him in a little half-circle with Tony the Superintendent of Service ever so slightly above them, awaiting his answer. "Awkward of me," the man said over their heads.

This statement, openly absolving the hotel from blame, was all that was required to set the Miami-Ritz service in motion again. Mr. Dalrymple glided forward with his unpredictable hands held tightly behind him for safe-keeping, stopped when his prominent nose was only an inch below his guest's. He wet his lips and some of the spittle became a fine spray as he spoke. "And a good good-morning to you, Mr. Stuyvesant," he said. "Welcome back to the Miami-Ritz."

The tall man looked at Mr. Dalrymple, at the tense little ring of bellhops, and finally at the scattered audience of curious guests, and for a brief moment it seemed to Saul the Window Washer as though everyone in the lobby had fallen flat on his face except this tall ugly man who stood patiently waiting for them to pull themselves together. "Hello, Dalrymple," the man said, and his high, narrow shoulders seemed frozen in a perpetual shrug as he stepped stiffly around Mr. Dalrymple and went to the reception desk. From his ladder Saul could see the girl's lips outlining the words, "Good morning, Mr. Stuyvesant, welcome to the Miami-Ritz," but he could not see that the tall man's lips moved at all.

"I can't find what the trouble is," Tony said. The Superintendent of Service was passing in and out of the lobby, approaching the low entrance step from various angles and at varying speeds. At each entrance he painstakingly tripped over the step, first with his left foot and then with his right, as though to find out whether it was possible to fall. Once or twice he did seem on the verge of toppling but by using his arms he managed to right himself in time. "I don't see how they do it," he said, shaking his head.

Mr. Dalrymple assumed a stance directly in Tony's path. "The step is too shallow," he said, speaking generally to the little group that had assembled at the lobby entrance. He held up one beautifully manicured hand with tapering thumb and forefinger extending horizontally and ever so slightly apart. "The step is not high enough," he said.

"I guess they couldn't make it higher, could they?" suggested a bellhop.

Mr. Dalrymple shook his head slowly. "I don't think that would be practical," he said.

Everyone studied the step.

"Maybe if you put up a sign," a bellhop said. "WATCH YOUR STEP or something like that."

Mr. Dalrymple smiled gently at the bellhop and shook his head. "One doesn't put a sign in a hotel doorway asking guests to watch their step," he said. "Not in a first-class hotel."

The bellhop received this instruction with a series of thoughtful little nods of his head, and for a moment nobody spoke.

Mr. Dalrymple said, "I think I'll do it with flowers."

"Flowers!" Tony's large head swung towards Mr. Dalrymple.

"Yes, with flowers. A long window-box of flowers extending at a forty-five degree angle from each side of the step. It will have the effect of a kind of path leading to the entrance, and I hope it will make people more careful about where they step."

"I can't see it," Tony the Superintendent of Service said. "I can't see what good it will do cluttering up the place with more of your flowers. You've got the place looking like the leaning gardens of Pisa already with your flowers."

There was some truth in Tony's words, floral decoration did seem to be Mr. Dalrymple's special domain. He had had the entire lobby framed, at the height of about fifteen feet, by slender boxes of hanging ivy and various nondescript plants which he liked to describe to guests as "tropical importations." On every table he caused to be placed, each morning without fail, a large vase of flowers of strikingly unassimilated color and size. One never saw Mr. Albriton the Manager or Mr. Cox the other Assistant Manager, or even Mr. Fowler the Steward, paying any heed to flowers at all, but one of Saul's first Miami-Ritz memories, on his very first day at work, was of Mr. Dalrymple standing at the foot of a ladder directing with expressive hands a houseman's attempt to water a box of ivy without spilling water on the freshly painted pink-tinted walls. And the scene had been repeated almost daily thereafter.

"Flowers can be functional as well as beautiful," Mr. Dalrymple said, hiding his annoyance behind a smile.

"You said a mouthful," Tony said.

"What's this conflagration about?" Mr. Cox, who had recently attended a summer session at the Cornell School of Hotel Management, joined the group. "Somebody making book?"

Mr. Dalrymple spoke to Mr. Cox. "It's this step. Mr. Stuyvesant tripped on this step."

"Who's Mr. Stuyvesant?"

"Mr. Stuyvesant," Mr. Dalrymple said, "is one of our guests." He wet his lips more eagerly than usual, as though in anticipation of his next remark. "Last year he took the Penthouse."

"Ohhhh," Mr. Cox said, with a note of awe that must have satisfied Mr. Dalrymple. "Ohhhh, I see. You say he tripped?"

Mr. Dalrymple's forefinger, pointing directly downward at the step, extended a full two inches below his knee.

"Something will have to be done about that step," Mr. Cox said.

"I think we'll do it with flowers," Mr. Dalrymple said. "A window-box of flowers extending at a forty-five degree . . ."

But at that moment the door to the Manager's office opened and Mr. Albriton stood in the doorway. Almost before Mr. Albriton beckoned, the two assistant managers were on their way across the lobby to make their report. The little group broke up busily. A bellhop said "Watch your step, please," to a Guest leaving the hotel, but by then the door to the Manager's Office had closed.

"They could carry them over."

Saul, whose mind had been preoccupied with less succinct thoughts, smiled down at the little man who stood at the foot of his ladder examining the step. "In a flower box maybe," Saul said.

The houseman nodded. Dressed in a black bow tie, starched white porter's jacket that was too long, and black trousers that were inches too short, he looked like an aged and dessicated zootsuiter. But his sharp dark face with the greying moustache was that of a preacher, and his tongue had a preacher's eloquence. "You can scrape more chewing gum off these marble floors," he said, scraping at a wad of gum with his long-handled dustpan, "than you could off the boardwalk at Atlantic City, New Jersey."

"Are you from around there?"

"Naturally."

They worked in silence, the houseman sweeping cigarette butts and chewing gum wrappers into his dustpan, Saul sloshing fresh water on the windows he had neglected since the tall man's trip.

"Those windows get mighty dirty in this sea air," the little man said.

"They get dirty faster than I can clean them," Saul said.

"I know a colored boy, about your height, who could clean all the windows in this lobby in half an hour. Quicker than other people can clean that one window you're working on."

"You do?"

"He's studied the window-washing business, made it his regular profession. But would this hotel pay him the kind of wages he needs? No, they wouldn't pay him."

Saul shook his head. "They don't realize how much a man like that could save them in the long run," he said.

This sudden capitulation left the diminutive houseman wordless for a moment, but when he spoke his manner was warmer. "What do you use on them?" he asked.

"Use?"

"In your water."

"I use vinegar," Saul said.

"Vinegar," the man repeated, nodding. "This boy I mentioned to you a minute ago uses ammonia."

"Oh, does he?"

"Ammonia gives the glass a real bright sparkle. I wouldn't presume to give anybody advice on how to do his trade, any more than I'd want anybody to tell me how to do mine, but this boy I was telling you about says ammonia gives a window a real bright shine. . . ."

"Harry . . ." Mr. Dalrymple was emerging from the Manager's Office, and the little houseman stopped his work respectfully and stood with his small hands folded around the long handle of his dustpan, waiting for Mr. Dalrymple to come up to him. "Harry, have you watered the plants yet this morning?"

"No sir, Mr. Sir, but I'm going to get around to it just as soon as I finish up my tidying."

"Well, I hope you won't . . ."

"There's just one little thing that's bothering me, Mr. Sir. I wonder if you could straighten me out on one thing."

"What's the trouble, Harry?"

"I just want to make sure whose supervision I'm under, you or that other Mr. Sir with the black hair."

"You mean Mr. Cox," Mr. Dalrymple said cautiously.

"That's the man, Mr. Sir," Harry said. "Now I'm wondering whose supervision I'm under, yours or the other Mr. Sir's. That man has a mighty hard time keeping his mind made up about what he wants done and when he wants it done. Is he going to be supervising me, Mr. Sir, or are you?"

Mr. Dalrymple was evasive. "Well, Mr. Cox is going to be working at night a good deal of the time. For a while anyway."

"I see. I just wanted to make sure whose supervision I was going to be under. That man has a mighty hard time making up his mind and keeping it made up."

"Well, I don't have a hard time making my mind up," Mr. Dalrymple said hopefully. "Will you water those plants soon, Harry?"

"Just as soon as I finish up my tidying, Mr. Sir," Harry said, moving off with his dustpan.

Mr. Dalrymple smiled up at Saul and Saul hoped there was a minimum of conspiracy in his own smile. There was an oppressive silence as he continued to work and Mr. Dalrymple tried to think of something to say. He decided on something and cleared his throat. "Your main job is keeping these windows clean, I guess," he said.

Saul wanted to let the remark pass quietly unnoticed, but he was aware of Mr. Dalrymple standing there unashamedly waiting for his reply. He dropped his sponge into his bucket and looked down at Mr. Dalrymple. "I'm the window washer," he said.

"Yes," Mr. Dalrymple said, and then his eyes lighted up. "These windows get terribly dirty, don't they?"

"Yes, they do," Saul said. "The sea air does it."

He had stolen Mr. Dalrymple's next line and there was a long moment of silence. Then Mr. Dalrymple sniffed. "What do you use?" he asked.

"Vinegar."

"Is that about the best thing for cleaning windows?"

"No, a lot of people seem to think ammonia is better."

"Oh."

"Mr. Dalrymple," the reception clerk called.

"Coming," Mr. Dalrymple said, and with a little wave of his hand, whether or departure or arrival Saul could not be sure, he swept across the lobby. Saul climbed down to move his ladder over to the last section of the high windows, and then he climbed slowly up again, watching Pete the Second Doorman hurry off to do a chore for a lady guest.

"You'll find the keys in the car," the lady called after Pete.

Running, Pete tipped his hat to the lady to show that he had heard. He found the keys to the Buick convertible and unlocked the trunk. For a moment the upper half of his body was hidden in the trunk and then he straightened up with two leather cases in his hands. He turned them over slowly, one at a time, studying them.

"Just the movie camera," the lady called. "Nothing else."

Pete put down one of the cases and pried open the lid of the other, peering into it. He looked at it for quite a while. Then he replaced the cover and set it down, picking up the other case.

He peered into that one too. His face was growing red, almost as red as his large, heavy-wristed hands, and he turned his back to the terrace and the lady who stood there patiently waiting.

"Just my movie camera," the lady called again.

Pete said nothing.

"What's the other thing?" the lady called. "A radio?"

Pete still did not answer. He peered from one to the other of the two cases, and then suddenly he flipped the top back on one of them and placed it quickly inside the trunk, as though afraid that he might change his mind. He locked the trunk, replaced the key in the ignition, and trotted hastily back to the terrace. "Here you are, Ma'am," he said, smiling and tipping his case.

The lady took the leather case and slipped a quarter into Pete's hand. "What's your name?" she asked.

Turning on the steps, Pete touched his cap. "Pete," he said.

"Thank you, Pete."

Pete's smile followed her, like a pet poodle, across the terrace and into the hotel. Then, as she passed from sight, it turned crookedly up to Saul and became a cynical grin. "Don't work too hard," Pete said.

"Don't worry."

Mr. Dalrymple seemed to be having a bit of trouble with two of his Guests. "We'd *like* to go over to the Normandy and ask them to stop working entirely," he was saying, "but unfortunately we cannot."

"We don't ask you to do that," the Guest said. "All we ask is that you move us up a little bit higher, away from the noise. Every morning they wake us up with their hammers and their yells."

"We wish we could accommodate you, Mr. Swartz," Mr. Dalrymple said, licking his lips, "but we have a limited number of rooms at our disposal and the hotel is already filling up, as you can see. Rooms on the upper floors have been reserved by Guests for as much as a year in advance." He paused, adding with emphasis, "The hotel has certain obligations to its steady Guests."

Mr. Swartz and his wife, with uncanny co-ordination, turned together toward the elevator. "I see, Mr. Dalrymple," Mr. Swartz said. "Thank you."

"Yes, *thanks,*" Mrs. Swartz said.

"If there's anything else at all we can do to be of service to you," Mr. Dalrymple said, spreading his limp hands to express the wide range of services the Hotel wished to perform, "please call on us." When the Swartzes were safely tucked away in the elevator, he glided over to the desk, where Mr. Cox had been waiting to lend his assistance if needed. "I do wish," Mr. Dalrymple said, fanning himself gently with his pocket handkerchief, "that sixth-floor people wouldn't be so pushy. Will you believe it, that pair wanted to move to the *twelfth* floor."

"Sociable climbers," Mr. Cox said.

"One would think they had been visiting us for the past ten years." Mr. Dalrymple said "ten years" as though he were speaking of generations. "This is only their second year, and last year—last year they stayed only one week! . . . 'We heard there were some vacant rooms on the twelfth floor,' " he mimicked, " 'and we want to move up there.' In the future we'll have to have a strict understanding among the chambermaids that there will be no discussion of vacancies during duty hours. Soon *anyone* will want to be upstairs, if we don't put our foot down while the putting is good. It's a little like training a dog, a matter of precedent."

"You're right," Mr. Cox said. "It's a matter of precedent."

"And furthermore, it isn't good business to allow a sixth-floor person to move into a forty-dollar room. They stay a short enough time when they're only paying *thirty* dollars a day."

"You're right," Mr. Cox said. "You're entirely right."

"Harry . . ." Mr. Dalrymple called, and he hurried to catch the little houseman on his way out of the lobby.

The lady with the camera was back. She stood at the iron railing which divided the parking lot from the pool and cabanas, and she called out to Pete. "Pete," she said, and she held out the leather case to him. "This isn't my movie camera. It's my binoculars."

Pete came running over to her and, tipping his cap, he took the leather case. Once again he went through the ritual of taking the key from the ignition, opening the Buick's trunk, and peering inside. He exchanged the case, and trotted back to the lady. "I hope that's your movie camera this time," he said, handing her the case.

"It must be," she said. "My husband says we haven't got a radio in the trunk. Just the camera and the binoculars. So this must be my camera." She smiled at Pete and pushed a quarter into his hand. "Thank you, Pete."

Pete tipped his hat and smiled after her. He winked at Saul as Saul came down the ladder.

"Don't work too hard," Saul said.

There was a clicking noise as Pete slipped the quarter into his pocket. "Don't worry," he said.

"Tony," Saul said to Tony the Superintendent of Service, "I'll bet you could use another good doorman out here. A Third Doorman."

"You want to be a doorman?"

"That's right."

"I could sure use one," Tony said, "but you'll have to speak to the Steward about that. The Steward does all the hiring and firing here."

"Thanks, Tony." Saul stepped off the ladder. Leaving his pail and shammy to mark his progress along the window, he went around the hotel and through the Service entrance to the Male Employees' Washroom in the basement. Abram the Potato Peeler, a little man with a grey, shaved head and a grey shirt and grey trousers, was washing his hands in the only basin, so Saul leaned against the wall and waited for him to finish. The grey-clad man, hunched round-shouldered over the sink, was scrubbing his hands with what seemed unnatural intentness, and as he worked he made small moaning sounds through his nose. The two waiters reclining on canvas deckchairs next to the urinal were watching the little man too. The bald one winked at Saul and jerked his head at the potato peeler. "Abram is a famous skin specialist," he explained. "He's sterilizing his hands for an important operation he's going to perform this afternoon, aren't you, Abram?"

Abram said nothing.

"He's an eye doctor," the other waiter said. "He's going to remove about a thousand eyes this afternoon, aren't you, Abram?"

Abram spoke without turning his head. "When we handle

the food we must wash our hands," He said in a hoarse, heavily accented voice. "When we work in the kitchen we must be clean so when the people eat the food they don't get sick. We must wash our hands." He was finished with his ablutions now, and he dried his hands on the paper towels with the same fastidiousness that he had washed them. Then his stooped body turned sharply toward the door and, his eyes looking neither to left nor right, he hurried out of the washroom.

"What's eating him?" Saul asked.

"That's Abram the Potato Peeler," the bald waiter said with a laugh. "Abram spent the war in one of Hitler's rest camps."

"He had a due bill there," the other waiter said.

"If you think he's batty now, you should have seen him last year," said the bald waiter. "He wouldn't answer when you spoke to him last year. He wouldn't even let you call him Abram—he said his name was Heinrich!"

"He still does," the thin one said.

Saul turned on the water in the basin. "I thought the war was over five years ago," he said. "What's he afraid of now?"

"Who knows?" the bald waiter said. "Maybe he thinks the Turkish bath upstairs is a gas chamber, who knows?"

"Maybe he thinks Mr. Fowler is Hermann Goering," the thin one said, standing up. "And what the hell are you making yourself so pretty for?"

"I'm going in to see Mr. Fowler," Saul said. "When we handle the boss, we must wash our hands."

He left them enjoying a good laugh and threaded his way through dimly-lighted passages to an unventilated cubicle in the center of the basement. He entered the door which announced STEWARD'S OFFICE in large grey letters. "Mr. Fowler?"

"You want something?" The beefy man behind the desk glanced briefly at Saul, flicked the ash off his cigar.

"Tony suggested I speak to you, Mr. Fowler," Saul said, stepping up to the desk and looking down at Mr. Fowler. He concentrated on the curly grey eyebrows above the heavy face. "Tony's looking for a good Third Doorman."

"Meaning you?"

"Yes, Mr. Fowler."

Mr. Fowler's stubby forefinger tamped his cigar. "What was your name again?"

"Greenbaum," Saul said. "Saul Greenbaum."

Mr. Fowler looked up at Saul, and it seemed to Saul that only Mr. Fowler's gums were smiling. "Saul Greenbaum," he repeated. "Jesus, kid, couldn't you have found a better name than that?"

"Is there something wrong with my name, Mr. Fowler?" Saul asked.

"There's nothing wrong with it, Saul," Mr. Fowler said, and shrugged. 'But with a name like that, you want to wait on the public?"

Saul leaned toward Mr. Fowler, over the desk. "I've never had any complaints before."

"Before you go flying off the handle, Saul," Mr. Fowler said, raising his cigar in caution, "let me ask you a question. How do you think I became Steward at the second largest hotel on Miami Beach?"

"You tell me, Mr. Fowler," Saul said. "I can't imagine."

"All right, Saul," Mr. Fowler said, inhaling. "I'll tell you. One day I sat down and picked up the Miami telephone directory, and I thumbed through it until I found me a nice cleancut-sounding name. A nice cleancut-sounding name that would appeal to a Guest's ear, like Bob Fowler. Robert Fowler."

Saul took his hands off Mr. Fowler's desk. "What's so special about these Guests," he asked Mr. Fowler, "that we have to go around appealing to their ears?"

"There you go again, Saul," Mr. Fowler said, shaking his head. "Always leaping at the throat of an innocent party. You want to know what's so special about these Guests? What's so special about them is that this hotel and the other hotels on the beach are about the only resort hotels where they're welcome. And we try to give them the same atmosphere they'd have in any other hotel. . . ." The phone rang and Mr. Fowler turned to answer it. "Yes?—Yes?—Yeah?—Oh, he did?—Mr. Stuyvesant? Too bad—Tough luck—Sure, sure—I'll send someone right up." Mr. Fowler replaced the phone. "That's a good job for you, Saul," he said.

"For me?"

"One of the Guests tripped on the front step," Mr. Fowler said. "Mr. Dalrymple wants a hand to carry some flowers out there, or some screwy thing. Like the job?"

"Delighted, Mr. Fowler," Saul said, turning away. "Thanks."

"And Saul," Mr. Fowler said to Saul's back. "You know who that Guest was, tripped on the front step?"

"Sure, Mr. Fowler," Saul said, "that was Mr. Stuyvesant. He took the Penthouse last year."

Mr. Fowler shook his head. "Wrong again, Saul," he said, grinning. "That was Morrie Silverman, P.S. 22, class of nineteen-eleven. I should know, I was there myself."

"Were you?" Saul said, turning again at the door. "I bet you two boys graduated at the head of your class."

Upstairs, Mr. Dalrymple was making final calculations before executing his floral design. He stood in the center of the lobby, one bony elbow upheld by one slender hand, his glance roving slowly over the flower boxes on the walls. "I think we can spare that one," he said to Saul, pointing boldly at a corner box, ". . . and that one."

"All right, Mr. Dalrymple," Saul said. "I'll get my ladder."

He got his ladder from the terrace, and he brought down the two boxes Mr. Dalrymple had selected. He carried them to the front step, where he placed them, at a forty-five degree angle, in line with Mr. Dalrymple's neat, pointed toe. "Is that all right, Mr. Dalrymple?"

"That's very good, Saul. Very good," Mr. Dalrymple said. ". . . Well, well, Mr. Stuyvesant!"

Mr. Stuyvesant loomed in the doorway. "Fixing up that step, Dalrymple?"

"Yes, Mr. Stuyvesant," said Mr. Dalrymple. "We're doing it with flowers."

"At a forty-five degree angle," Saul said.

"And you're helping him, boy?"

"That's right, Mr. Stuyvesant," Saul said, smiling up at Mr. Stuyvesant. "I'm getting in a little practice with doors, so maybe Mr. Dalrymple will want to make a Third Doorman out of me."

"What are you now?"

"I'm the window washer, Mr. Stuyvesant."

"What's your name, boy?"

"Cecil, Mr. Stuyvesant. Cecil A. Smith."

For just a moment he thought Mr. Stuyvesant would pat his head. But Mr. Stuyvesant's hand reached into a pocket, and it brought out a quarter. "Well, Cecil," he said, handing him the quarter, "I know you'll make Mr. Dalrymple a fine doorman. A fine one."

Cecil turned to face Mr. Dalrymple, and beyond Mr. Dalrymple he could see his ladder, standing tall and aloof at the edge of the terrace. Suddenly he wished with all his heart that he were on top of it now, looking down, but he knew by Mr. Dalrymple's welcoming smile that he would never be up there again.

—1954

The Ice Cream Man

TO BEGIN WITH, I don't know what they mean when they release a boy into his parent's custody. What on earth could they mean? That somebody else is to blame, that they have delivered my son out of the hands of a pernicious society, into mine? (I try to leave Alice out of this because with the little girls following one two three I've come to feel that Bobby somehow belongs to me, and yet in all honesty I should point out that that ratio, three to one, had in the past fairly represented our overall involvement in the home.) But if they do mean that after seven years I am to consider this my first chance with the boy, that as far as the two of us are concerned there is no past, they are being altogether too kind, for such kindness is really stupidity. Of course I am aware that there are other influences, school, church, community and so on, but if I admit that Bobby belongs to any of these more than to me I admit that his love does too, and I refuse.

Or could they be this subtle: meaning really to say that I am the guilty one, that in a lifetime of seeking my boy's salvation I shall find my own just punishment? If this is it, if they are willfully casting us upon ourselves in this way, it is cruelty. For surely they must know that the only person who could have saved either of us, the only person who in fact ever tried to save us, was the ice cream man himself.

Here I have a frightful observation to make, but I believe that a secret poll of our neighborhood would find that a majority of the adults living in it are pleased. I say *pleased,* at what happened. I will go further: I believe that if it had all occurred under different circumstances, say two houses down the street or, better yet, on another block, I too would find myself pleased. I believe that at five-thirty each evening (for almost a year the invariable hour of my first grimly discerning the ice cream man's approach) I would look at my watch and, instead of shuddering as I do now, smile at the silence.

Parents used to ask him how he could stand the goddam noise, and he would wince a little, as though at the music. You get used to anything, he would say, or, it's all part of the business. These were lies. I know that he loved that tinny rendition of "Happy Days Are Here Again," loved it for its childish philosophy and for the wave of ecstasy that it carried before it as it cut irresistibly into the smug quiet of our neighborhood. I used occasionally to glimpse that ecstasy on my son's face, before he learned through some terrible wisdom to hide it from me, and I would try to imagine how it would be to see it openly, a thousand times a day, on a thousand faces. It was the look children are supposed to have when daddy comes home at night, and until a week ago every child in our neighborhood had the same daddy. Without so much as a glance at our wives, he was the great big thieving daddy of our children.

I have it in little pieces, like this from six months ago:

"Mr. Ice Cream Man?"

"What is it, Bobby?"

"Are you really made of ice cream, Mr. Ice Cream Man?"

"Yes. Butter pecan."

"I love butter pecan."

Please, it wasn't just funny, it was the conversation of love. Perhaps Bobby has a sense of congruity which I have lost, for the maddening thing, to me, was that his words suddenly gave point to the odd, icecreamcone-khakis that the ice cream man habitually wore. For the first time, I saw that he had purposely chosen them to support that huge scoop of a head. Of no remarkable height, he was the kind of man one naturally measures in girth, all two-hundred-odd pounds of him distributed impartially from the great tan sneakers to the great bald, butter pecan head—"packed solid from the bottom," as the gaudy advertisements on his truck professed. And his smile, that smile which seemed to split the face wide open, appeared to me at that time a planned fault intended to reveal all the solid goodness inside.

"You must be about the most popular man in town."

"I hope I am."

"I know my son won't come in the house at night until you've been by."

"Bobby's a fine kid, Mr. Knight."

"I suppose you go all over town?"

"Just this section, here."

"That's funny. Have you ever thought of spreading out, hitting every block in town once or twice a week like the vegetable man and the egg man do?"

"No, that's all right for them, but I think I do better coming every day."

"Why so?"

"Well, I deal in more perishable commodities."

"That's true enough . . ."

"Pleasure, love."

The smile then broke a little narrowly, clearly not for me, not for any of us. We tried, some of us, stocking our freezers with store-bought popsicles, allowing our children to make only token purchases from the ice cream man. No need to say he met our challenge, just as in combating television he had begun selling certain bars at a loss on nights when the good shows were on. Cheerfully he sacrificed everything except his powerful position in our neighborhood.

"Bobby, I think I told you you couldn't buy ice cream tonight."

"I didn't buy. This is the smashed ice cream the ice cream man promised me."

"Promised, when?"

"Yesterday. He said if I'd give Amy her dollar back he'd give me the next smashed ice cream he had."

"What were you doing with Amy's dollar?"

"She let me have it. She said I could buy ice cream with it."

"Bobby, don't you know that you shouldn't take money from other people, especially from little babies like Amy?"

"Yes. The ice cream man already told me that."

From a dark corner of the living room I liked in those days to watch the ice cream man drive by our house, smiling, waving, slowing at first expectantly, and Bobby's answering wave seemed to me not so much forlorn as superior. To me it said that he had grown out of the ice cream world of childhood, into ours, and for a while, only a little while, I tried to imagine that it said this to the ice cream man too.

"How've you been, Bobby?"

"My daddy says I can't buy your ice cream anymore."

"Never?"

"Yes."

"Why does he say that, Bobby?"

"He says it's bad for me."

"Yes. So is inflexibility."

The ice cream man never stopped waving and smiling; Bobby did. Although I try, I cannot forget the delight I felt the evening Bobby answered the ice cream man's wave by throwing a stone at him. Actually it was thrown with fine, fine accuracy at the side of the truck. The ice cream man looked back at the stone lying in the street and shook his head reproachfully, but he did not stop to examine the red and white paint for scars. Nor can I forget the shame I felt when Alice came upon me as I watched him wave and drive away.

"I want to apologize for my son throwing that stone at your truck last night. I've punished him."

"I don't believe you can call them bad. The little boys are thoughtless sometimes, yes, but I don't believe they are old enough to be called good or bad."

"In any case, I want to pay you for whatever damage was done."

"No damage."

"Well . . . While I'm here I guess I could use a quart of vanilla. I guess you'd better make it two."

Now with no money of their own to spend, Bobby and some of the other children liked to disaffect what customers the ice cream man still had left. Although I no longer watched, I know exactly how it went, how they persuaded the younger children to set their hearts on flavors he usually ran out of by five or six o'clock. The ice cream man soon stopped running out, but he could not and probably did not wish to spoil their fun. It seems they had discovered which unpopular bars he stored farthest back in the ice cream box, and it was their game to promote a demand for these. There was delight in watching the ice cream man squeeze inside, thrash about in there, wriggle out, gasping but always smiling, with the little ice cream bar clutched in his hand.

"I guess we'll take another boysenberry."

"Sure, Bobby wants one too."

"No, I think if Bobby's father wanted him to have ice cream he'd have given him money to buy it with."

"He's got money."

"I'll tell you what, Bobby, you ask your daddy tonight. If he gives you money tomorrow, I'll let you have two bars for the price of one."

"Don't let him kid you, Bobby."

"Give him his boysenberry. He ordered it."

"I'm a customer. You can't treat a customer that way."

"Get in there."

"Ah! There he goes again!"

The thing was that he had outgrown the ice cream box. When he had first built it a few years before, he had been able to slip the upper half of his body through the waist-high door and still leave enough light around the edges for him to see by. Perhaps it was all the ice cream he ate, perhaps the months of holding his breath against the suffocating dry ice fumes while he groped in there: lately he could reach the back of the box only by folding in, L-wise, until his backside filled the doorway like a huge cork and his tan sneakers dangled loosely six inches from the ground.

"What are you doing in there, Ice Cream Man?"

"He's trying to climb inside."

"He wants to cool off. It's hot out here."

"Sure, he's sweating. Look at his pants."

"Do you want some help, Mr. Ice Cream Man?"

"I think I heard him he say he did."

"O.K., Mr. Ice Cream Man."

"Whatever you say, Mr. Ice Cream Man."

"Get his other foot!"

"You lift, I'll push!"

"That's it!"

"There!"

"Close the door!"

They say they could hear him call, but his voice was muffled and the only word they could make out was boys. And they could hear him thump. But my guess is that he did not struggle with much hope, that after a few minutes he decided the thoughtless little boys had become ashamed to face him and had run away. If he decided this he was right. For by that time Bobby was with me in the house crying out in terror, or more like rage, at what I told him he had done.

—1959–1965

Stand Still

UP AND SEATED IN THE KITCHEN, watching Helen work, Stuart Toll found himself a less promising man than he had been in this room and chair last night. He asked her if he had talked too much, and her answer was that she had enjoyed their evening. Although he yawned and cleaned his eyes, he could not fairly lay his comedown to sleepiness. He was in fact one of those who wake up more easily than most, at the slightest sound or touch or change of air shrug sleep aside as though ashamed of it. This did him little good, already he had surrendered some small part, seemingly essential, of himself. His days he spent regaining it. He thought that if he could begin just one day where he'd left off, he might be capable of anything. Even the roaches had managed to move the cats' aluminum dish two and a half inches, overnight. He knew because he had drawn a chalkline on the floor, a starting line, and certainly he had heard them at it long enough. He did not speak of this. For some reason Helen assumed the problem to be entirely hers (she could shriek "You crapping roaches!") even though it was he they kept awake, and it pleased him not to taunt her with their vagaries. If she was curious, she knew the line was there. On her part she showed as much restraint toward his own problem, also real: he could see time crawl by. It was not the roaches, not even last night's excess, that had him sitting his chair uneasily, ready yet motionless.

The celebration had been mostly his, but here he sat half-enchaired, watching Helen scrape together the clotted droppings of their evening, waving his hand from time to time as though to say, "Leave all that. I'll do that." His gestures were ignored, of course. Not that he lacked willingness, or was in pain, he simply felt the need to wait. Here was a morning when he could wish he had a taste for coffee, or still smoked. Sliding the glass ashtray close he hefted the cold butt of a lone cigar, half-serious concession to their irresolutions of the three-weeks-old new year. He sniffed and dropped it back again, for partly that was what they had celebrated, abstinence. Last night it had all sounded very high to him, a fine shedding of needless and degrading appendages in search of self, but today some questions troubled him. For one, how to prevent any such program becoming merely an exercise in restraint, a glorification of things given up rather than whatever might be revealed—in short, if this was strength, why celebrate? And two, what if a man did conscientiously deplume himself, only to find that his seat was oversized? Better to fatten up those lung tumors, embalm them well, than fall victim to man's most pernicious possession, health? He had taken tranquilizers for two days once, stopped short when Helen complained of being bored. So. He fondled their cigar again, wondering if he should propose that they retrieve tobacco from their list, trade it in on alcohol. But he recalled their pledge to go on the wagon too, at least until he found a new job or some other good way to use his time. His view last night had been that it was too late to undertake anything serious, unless it were done fanatically. Now he winced to think what compromising new postures this might lead them to, a sudden partiality to tonics, cough syrups, all-day-sucking lollipops, for he was aware that their immense cigar had looked just as unrealistic in his thin face as hers. "Leave that, Helen, I'll do that."

But Helen swept the ashtray up and spilled its surfy contents into the refuse bag. "You have enough to do today."

"I!"

"You," she said, and she too was nervous, her full lips were almost thin on her coffee cup. "Last night you said you were going to your room all day and think."

He had, but said, "I've been thinking that perhaps we're carrying this asceticism a little too far. I mean, maybe I should keep my job at least."

"Why don't you change your mind?" she asked. "Tonight we can celebrate."

He laughed, and wondered if she knew she smiled less easily without her lipstick on. "You don't like me today," he said.

She did not say.

"Well, we won't talk about me now. We still have a week to decide."

"Stuart, I don't care what you do!" she said, slapping cup to saucer dangerously. "Sit there all day." She crossed to the stove for his bacon and egg, and the disdainful way she ladled them up suggested they weren't ready yet. She left the milk for him to pour.

Eating he asked, "Wasn't there anything else I had in mind to do today?"

"You said you were going to dispose of cats."

He remembered that. "What did I plan to do," he tried to ask angrily, "cut off their heads with the carving knife?"

"I think you were going to drown them in the garbage can."

"Well, good for me," he said. He pushed his plate aside. "Was there nothing else, nothing possible?"

"You said you had twentynine books to read and one to write."

"What else?"

"I don't know. Yes I do," she said, and he looked up. She was facing him, leaning back against the sink with her hands deep in the pockets of her white quilted robe which camouflaged her exquisite body too successfully, making it appear almost robust. One hand came out palm-up, bearing the front door key, but she did not look at it. "You said you were going to have a duplicate made."

"Ah." He had told her about the key club. This was a social club got up by certain Dutch army officers in Indonesia, married ones who brought their wives to weekly parties at which each man tossed his latchkey into a hat and at the end of the evening they passed the hat around. He looked away, for he wanted to remember her face as it had looked then, as he told her of this, feel again his really heavy smile as he detailed for her what the motives and emotions might be, of those involved. "Did you find it an interesting story?"

She was busy again, scraping things. "A little hard to believe," she said.

"It was?" Did she think he had entirely lost his memory? "Last night you seemed more convinced than this."

"You told it well."

"No, I mean finally . . ."

But she was on him now, locking his head between her arms, kissing the stiff smile on his lips, over and over, and softening it. "Only because I knew it was you."

"Liar," he said.

"I told you, all I want is you!"

"Oh, is that all?"

"No, it's everything.

"But that's not enough."

"For me it is."

"Yes?" He reached inside her robe to pat her thigh. "Remember me, I'm Cary Grant? I borrowed your key from Frankie boy . . ." But she drew off calling threats toward the livingroom: Have you brushed your teeth. Yes. Carefully? Yes. Your hair. Yes. Made your bed? Everything! He turned in his chair to face the door, to see Joan dance in. She did, and for a moment he could too. When she stopped just beyond his reach, her face was sodden with sympathy.

"Poor Daddy doesn't get to go to school today."

"You're luckier."

"Why doesn't he?"

"It's his winter solstice," Helen said.

"What's *that*?"

He was not sure. He believed he had used the metaphor at first simply to describe the mid-year break, refining it as he went on to suggest his present view, his distance out, but above all his determination to start back. "It's something the high school principal decreed," he said. "It gives his baton twullers a chance to practice for the championship, and it gives his teachers a chance to look for other work."

"Does he want them to?"

"Yes."

"Will you, will Daddy look? What is Daddy going to be?" It amused her to address him in this indirect way; this was her morning mode, by evening she would talk to him personally. As for her question, he could not think about it.

"Have you fed your cats?"

"Not inside!" Helen begged, too late. Joan opened the door and they filed in, Mother, George, Bright Eyes, Santa Claus, he did not know them all. They were common cats, hopelessly large. She went to the refrigerator for their can, rooted in the kitchenware for their fork, not hurrying. She liked to have them cry at her and rub her legs. Before feeding them she returned their dish to the starting line. "How far did it move last night?"

"Two and a half inches."

"Is that a new record?"

"Almost," he said, and he could hear Helen murmuring.

Joan filled the plate sluggishly, bite by bite, and they sat hunched over it in a ring, all except one skinny one who sat slightly apart watching them. "That black one will probably die," he said.

"No, he won't."

"I think he's going to die today."

"You don't know," she said. He let it go at that, for she was right.

Helen told Joan to get her brush, and she followed her into the livingroom. He sat listening to their half-hearted war, Joan's cries for mercy at first ignored, finally a grudging truce. When she danced back, drawing up within reach this time, she had blond cobwebs about her head. "All set?" he asked.

"I hope Daddy has a nice day today."

"Have fun," he said, "and play."

"All right."

"Talk all the time, you won't have to listen then."

She nodded.

"Don't read, it hurts the eyes."

She would remember that.

"Don't pay attention to your teachers. They don't know."

At his pause she studied him with big-eyed solemnity. "I'd better stay home, with you," she said. He laughed, and she reached up to haul in his head gently, press his cheek, then spun away, ducked low, and broke fast for open field. He heard her break stride to kiss Helen goodbye. "The baton is the thing," he called, but she was gone.

Helen came to the door and looked at him. He smiled but knew she did not see. "I have to get dressed," she said.

"Oh, not again today!"

"I have to be at the Market Bag by nine."

"What are you going to hand out this time, cigars?"

"Pickles, they said."

"Sweet or sour?"

"Sweet."

"How will you serve them, whole or sliced?"

"Sliced . . . oh shut up," she said.

He stood up grinning and kissed her cheek, but then he took her in his arms and kissed her pouting lips. "Have fun," he said when she had relaxed.

She frowned. "At least you'll have the house to yourself all day."

"Don't worry about me, you have your career," he said, as they broke apart. "I'll see if I can get the garbage out ahead of the garbage men."

He took up the refuse bag and, cradling it in an arm, gathered the cans and bottles awkwardly into another bag. The cats were anxious to go out, but they changed their minds when they found he would hold the door for them. He shoved them with his foot. The day was fair, and even for Arizona warm. He stood still just outside the door, as though he had stepped into a pocket of pure oxygen and was afraid he might walk out of it. Listening he could hear no voices, the merest suggestion of radio. The only certain activity was one block north, where a strangely insipid bulldozer scraped over the already level desert, helping their fat city stretch. Farther east there was hammering. Although he tried, he could not object. Even the telephone poles and wires had been set with stunning artistry against the sky. Empty carports looked almost interesting. A ladies' day, he thought of it, languid, round, the sort of day he had always hated to pass up. What had he thought he would do with it? What would he do? He had his cans to dump, though not the cats. What else? It pained him to think that he would spend this perfect day fiercely trying to decide how to spend it well.

In general, everyone seemed to keep busy enough. His neighbor to the east had some of those empty golf balls that won't go anywhere, plus some child-sized clubs, and he'd laid out a little golf course around his house. On weekends and summer evenings one could see the whole family out there, teeing up, swatting those golf balls with all their strength and crying "fore" as though their hearts would break. Once they had even asked the Tolls over for a game, but by that time they were too far advanced to make it interesting. They should worry though, they had set themselves a seemingly impossible par for their nine holes, *twentyeight.* To the west was the duke of the barbeque, easily the most carnivorous man he had met. Three nights a week he could be viewed out there, bent at the waist, pumping his bellows and puffing his pipe. Just before dark his family would join him around the pit, stand gorging themselves with meat while assuring him it was his tenderest yet. He would keep busy as long as the cows held out. These were good neighbors both, he would not have traded either for anything. Down the street there was this friend of his whose pleasure it was to study girls' behinds, classing them according to breadth, cleavage, and bounciness. He preferred the little rigid ones. Calling attention with a discreetly arched eyebrow or nod, never a nudge, he would say, "Look at the ass on that one," although with him it was more like "aas." Well, lately he had this feeling that he was needed somewhere for something too, he had no idea where or what.

Almost he could envy the garbage men, who by their chosen profession had their own view. Not a total view, but pure, unspoiled by I'm-fine-how-are-you-today. He wondered how much they did observe. For example, would they begin to notice that he was drinking less? Would they be surprised, disgruntled, pleased? Or would they only note that his can was lighter than before? This last he doubted, for he on his side had noted the appraising glance they gave a collection as they shook it into the truck. They would have dumped rapidly and blindly, if weight were all. He had seen their nice discrimination in choosing articles to be set aside, their preference for shoes and hats, and their devotion to the printed word. Nor did he often hear them complain, about anything. They almost seemed satisfied. One of them was up there now on his overflowing truck, bent over a very large doll head with bright red lips and long blond hair that fell loosely over the pillow he had laid it on. He had fashioned shoulders of plaster and porcelain, something as white, like a hopper lid, only briefly visible above the black velvet sheath that appeared to cover her lower parts. Far down at the other end big shoes stuck up, gold, high-heeled of course. He himself wore a romantic black felt hat, and on the hand that fondled her bare shoulder he wore a white kid glove. His other hand held a beer can, which he placed on a nearby table whenever he desired a kiss. An uprooted paloverde tree leaned overhead, affording him a little shade.

The man on the ground put down Stuart's garbage can to step back for a fuller view. Encouraged by his audience, the lover bent to his pleasure more passionately. Holding her lips with his, he let his hands dwell on the ample mounds of her breasts, whole grapefruit size. Slowly his hand slipped under the sheath to touch her hidden parts, and black velvet seemed almost to palpitate. The man on the ground gave a happy cry and leaped onto the truck. He scrambled easily up the hill to the lover's side, tapped his shoulder several times urgently, but the lover seemed oblivious to almost everything. Now the invader laid both hands on his shoulders and spun him around. For a minute they hung there grappling, king-of-the-mountain style, then rolled together down the hill and over the tail of the truck, falling together onto the ground. There was a yell and one jumped to his feet, but the other remained lying there. His felt hat lay nearby, and his left arm was folded beneath his bare head, not comfortably.

"What's happening!"

The lady next east stood in her robe just inside her kitchen door. At her shout the driver got out of the truck and ran back to investigate, bend over the fallen man.

"What is happening there!"

"Nothing, ma'am," the driver called. "Just a little accident." He and the other man lifted the injured lover by his shoulders and feet, heaved him quickly together up on the truck, beside his love. His partner joined him there while the driver ran back to the cab. He had left the motor running and within seconds they were roaring down the alley, cans and papers flying high.

The lady next door came forward now. Helen too was

approaching, already dressed, and the neighbor on the other side. Helen observed their full garbage can.

"What is all this?"

He began to explain to them what had happened, as he had seen it. At first they stood listening open-mouthed, exclaiming from time to time. They were genuinely pleased to be sharing this drama with him. But as he went on, describing the scene and action as accurately as he could, they began to glance at one another and they clutched their lapels more tightly in front of them, those with robes. They seemed anxious to get back to their homes: nothing like this had happened before. They looked at their full garbage cans when he was through. One wondered if the truck would return, another spoke of these garbage men, but they asked no questions of any kind. Perhaps because there were three of them, he thought, perhaps because he belonged to one. Perhaps because they sensed his capacity was unlimited. About this last he could not say, for sure. As they turned away he could have raised the point with each of them, round robin, but he let it rest.

—1960

Fair-Weather-Wise

SATURDAY NIGHT, when they had had a fair Saturday and when had they not, was a time of keen joy for all in the little frame cottage at 8001 South "S." He himself, eager to be the most joyful of three, by midafternoon could no longer wait. Already how many times he had bent to their southside window, peered out past their curtains at a deep blue sky stunningly laced with streamers of immaculate white. How many tens of times he had approached their eastside window, later their west, only to feel through those curtains themselves the faint unquenchable glow of the winterly sun. How countless many times he had parted in turn the curtains at their two other windows to examine from every possible view a small shoddy brown cloud to the north, which did not, could not, and *would not* grow, it was all smog today. Thus his aching impatience, to gather his family about him before the stove, draw the kitchen curtains tight, dial the radio to bearable, get soused and fling his joyous jeers at the few lone liners left up there who would try but could not break his night.

They had rented on a foggy day, with $40 preserved for escape from the Odem Hotel Apartments House. It had taken him five roundtrips to transfer their goods, five round happy ones, bedding, foodstuff, tricycle, panda bear had never been so light, streets and highways never so still, he had long legs and we were made to walk. Home for the final time, tucked snug in their nest by the motherly fog, plenty of chairs, fire in the stove, refrigerated beers, he had announced his resolve to wrest a day-off from the boss. He had to get them settled right, patch up their roof, hinge their door, replace their windows before the storms set in: he meant not just someday, but Monday, tomorrow for once. Monday morning, breaking fair and wild, bore many a surprise for all. The boss told Judith oh yes sure, he was sorry to hear about that, hoped it was nothing serious. Judith, already breathless with running home from the phone, had to shout Howard his message several times over before he could make any sense at all of her words amid the bellow of the blowbirds assailing their sky. "What, he said *what*?" Soon grown hoarse, finding him deaf, she wrote out his message in capital letters. He, who had received the baptism of shit years ago on Attu, slunk outside to fulfill his commitments, while the shaken girls remained indoor with loud radio. He could hear it himself, through their shambles of shingles, if ever the blowbirds laid off for a moment catching their breath.

That was about the last of the fog. Oh yes sure there were clouds, but most often high ones, soft white and weakly, polite, they hated to rain, hurricane, even tornado, God forbid it should snow in the winter, visibility audibility terribility unlimited. He himself still had his job, had in fact more job than ever now that the boss could not do without him; by the time Howard got home today's invasion was usually over. Judith and Janice were not so lucky. Oh it wasn't so bad today Judith would tell him, her voice hoarse but still shouting, just wait until Saturday. For Howard did not work, the boss liked a long weekend. Then, even more if the week had been partially cloudy, all heaven finally broke loose, the regular blowbirds were joined by the reserve blowbirds for a massive offense that began before sunup and did not end till they downed it. What could he do but prowl his frame rooms and catch through his curtains terrible glimpses of brilliant blue sky, was he to smile at his family huddled there in the kitchen, lead them back to the Odem Hotel Apartments House, ask the boss for a bonus? He could not save them, not for months, nor was there any way in this house he could soothe them. They had a radio. Meanwhile the landlord lowered the rent $5 in return for Howard's services, and was good about furnishing window glass as it was needed.

He did his chores Sunday, when many of the blowboys

and most of the reserve blowboys were hung up at church. He himself did not attend, though he understood some were soundproof, all had loud organs; he slept, with luck, under both pillows, till ten. From ten to noon he ate breakfast and loafed about the house in trenchcoat and sneakers, attending to whatever indoor chores needed doing. Twelve to one, while the boys were donning their gear and racing past to the fields, found Howard outdoors. Sunday afternoon wasn't so bad, a good radio time, they could turn it all the way up in the oven and make believe they had stereo. No, Saturday was the cruel one, concerts were only half-hearted, people were shouting, Judith did have to cook sometime.

"Are you ready to go!"

"How, I told you, I've hardly started! Why don't you just take Janice today. Do you mind?"

"What! No!" he cried. "May I wake, may I get her?"

"Oh go ahead," she said, mumbled, "she's been in there an hour."

He entered the bedroom on tiptoe, a habit not easily dropped. Another man looking at the bed would not have guessed Janice was there, but he, patting, probing the bedding, soon found and revealed her staring out from under the panda bear. "There she is! Are you ready to go now?" When she smiled for him he picked her up and carried her to the kitchen, a habit he clung to though she had been walking for nearly a year. Judith had her clothes piled high on a chair by the stove, where she stood waiting to bundle her.

"Well, there she is! Do you want to go for a nice long walk with Daddy?"

"Yes."

"Come here and let Mommy dress you . . ."

But he held her through the concussions of a dive aiming toward them, hitting them head-on with savage insistence, strafing them a thousand times over through their shuddering windows while Judith stood smiling. Now as the air settled back into place, mumbling to their windows obscenities picked up from the blowbirds, he handed over the rigid little body. Judith went quickly to work pounding Janice's shoes on, double-tying her laces, buttoning her sweaters all the way up, buttoning her coat all the way, tugging her hat down over her ears, tugging her gloves, patting her solid back when she was done and kissing her cheeks, all that was left of her, the maternal instinct still eternal. He himself put on his sweater, his brown canvas walking shoes in place of his sneakers.

"Goodbye, we'll see you!"

"When?"

"Right after dark!"

They took off on the run, after a short laugh at the mailbox, with heads down and eyes studying the road shoulder. It was their way of travel on "S," better known as Route 9 to the tourists and truck drivers, and it loosened their muscles. At the first turnoff they turned, looking back, waving bye-bye to Judith, before they trotted over to "R" and turned north, beginning their walk. Last week it had been "T," he recalled, but they liked variety. In fact he himself made a point of checking the other neighborhoods, to hear if there were any better. On the move he could not say positively—they never stopped—but it did seem true and struck him hard that blowbirds seldom passed them overhead out on their walks. They came on, took aim, dove hard, but almost always on edge and sliding toward a more vital target somewhere else. He, walking backward, could see them fall on it, behind some trees. He could hear the shiver of window glass four blocks away, and facing north he tried to close his ears to Judith's "Farts!" He had never seen a blowboy on the ground, never knowingly. How and when had they made their choice? Perhaps they had spotted him entering or emerging from the basement at the carpet shop, found him a little too reserved to suit their taste? Or had grown tired of passing him to-and-from, a pedestrian on Route 9 who did not look? Yet once indoor jeered lustily enough for all to hear on Saturday night? No, at times he thought he took life too personally, as Judith said, blowbirds did not really have it in for him. Perhaps the mailman had simply made out a list for them, an impartial list of prospects who never heard from anyone. More likely still, blowboys selected their victims from the air: how could they pass up a little place with one lone tricycle abandoned in the drive out front, no telephone wire or antenna on the roof, a wife handships at the door quoting things they could not hear? For all he knew the sons-of-vultures could even see his shingles shake.

She could have come—what farting difference did it make that she didn't "like" to walk, he would have crawled. Thus how it delighted him to see the walker Janice was, fast, steady, straight-toed, indistractable. She might never learn to ride a tricycle, but she could walk. Now she wanted him to take her coat, for it was growing quieter, and he could see how straight her legs were, how hard they pumped. She *liked* these walks of theirs, and tossing her coat onto his shoulder, stepping out with both arms swinging free, he showed her how much he did too. She laughed and side-by-side they strode, sharing their happiness, leaving the fields behind, leaving another week. Now it pained him less to look at her. He could almost say: such a week was a valuable childhood experience which he himself had missed. She would grow up to appreciate peace no less than he, yet would be ready when they drafted her.

"Daddy, see a birdy?"

"Yes!"

A friend, acquaintance of his down at the shop had asked the family over to the apartment once, three flights above the Bolamor. Apologies had been made for "noise," scarcely more than a distant rumble of mortar guns, which it seemed reached them through the radiators. The Howards had gone home almost relaxed, by their entire evening not just their walk. Next week they had returned the invitation, without apology, for they knew only a few lone liners would be left up there and they wished to see what others thought. Man, wife, and child had gone to the door at nine, in shock. That was the last they saw of them, except of course down at the shop, which seemed to be too true of life these days. No one knew anyone. Only blowboys wagged their wings, or engaged in a moment's playful dogfight before they blew off, secure in their ability to elude not only their own but one another's barks. Or were there truly any living things left up there? At times he doubted it, even from the roof he had never seen anything resembling a head in one, far less a waving arm or claw. All blew over impersonally, hollow and humorless things: misguided rockets, capsules, saucers, bombs, if not anti-mail missiles the Post Office had launched. Walking backward Howard waved at one, got no reply. He could not honestly see it as a bird, more like a stingray, skate, or horseshoe crab, too sodden and cold-blooded to take to air, though one thousand times loud enough.

But not quite so loud from here, for they were inside the city limits now, still walking well. Here no blowfish dared pursue, yet they held to their brisk pace. He mentioned offhand the quietness, but Janice had a horsy for him to see. However, a moment later she gave up her hat. He let her think she led the way. This city route was familiar to both of them, for they followed it every week. It led them past at least half a dozen parks which they only eyed askance, they had a favorite one.

"Daddy, see!"

"Good work!"

Theirs was a fullsize corner lot of long-loved dirt not yet claimed by apartment house or church, well worth the added walk. What they themselves particularly loved about it was a fine crooked path that led around a rugged mountain, past a fort, a cave, a trench, over a drawbridge, over a moat, past the skeleton of a hut, ancient sites wrought all by hand, passed down by countless fathers to countless sons and, in good times, improved upon. There was a hollow in the north end of the trench so deep that a small boy could crouch in there and look up at nothing at all but sky and earth; someone had left a piece of rug in it. Nor had the fresh dirt from this excavation been just tossed aside, the mountain was a little higher now. Here and there were evidences that grown men too returned at times to this boyhood haunt, a circle of five scorched rocks, a charred plank torn from the side of the hut, empty bottles, cans, sacks, all the usual ammunition men hurl at night. A few grown girls had accompanied them. Cats and dogs leave no traces of their loves and wars. The lot was a toilet for everyone. Janice handed over her gloves, and Howard sat down on the fort to watch her play. She had a discriminative sense that would see her through anything.

"Watch out for the hole," he called.

She would.

"Have fun—we can't stay long."

"Why?"

"We promised Mommy we'd be home by dark."

He was much too loud. It was quiet now, quiet enough

to hear airbrakes, backfires, the rough gears of trucks. Every now and then a voice broke through, very young or old, and once he believed he heard a laugh. Somewhere, he could have sworn, a lady wore high heels. He looked to the sidewalk, there she was! Above, the sky was blue, pure blue. Only around the edges was it laced with fine threads of white, where blowfish frolicked in the sun, silent, graceful, indigenous. Up on the mountain top Janice was singing, a quiet song, "Baby, Baby, Baby, See!" When she saw him watching she broke off to pat some dirt, but soon she started up again. He didn't have the will to tell her they would have to go. He let her sing another forty verses of her song, then climbed up to her. He sat down, and she gave one of her sweaters up. "What's that you've made?"

"A house." She patted hard, it wasn't finished yet.

"That's a nice house. It's nice in here, isn't it?"

More roof.

"Let's come again next week."

More *roof*.

"Maybe Mommy will come too."

"Mommy too?"

"I hope she will. We'll ask her when we get home. You know we promised her we'd be home by dark."

"Is it dark?"

"No, but it will be soon."

In fact some lights were blinking on, they seemed to startle those that had blinked all day. Now those others quickly took heart from them, glad of the company, glad to be earning their keep again, proud to be outlasting the sun once more. Blood of all colors pulsed with excitement at the approach of dark, and grew richer with every pulse while the sun looked on in pastel funk. Its time was near. Soon all blowfish would converge on it, snare it in their net, haul it back out to sea. Night! Bundling Janice's things beneath an arm, applauding her roof, he took her hand for the first fast block, that there might not be too many afterthoughts. She went along with him willingly enough, even when he let go, but it was clear that today their park was the point of no return. Still he let her go on as long as possible, until he saw her stagger in the 6400 Block. She took warm possession of his arms, blinked up at him. "Is it dark?"

"Not yet," he said. He could see her plainly too. The streetlights had just come on, casting their stupid impatient glare upon the street. They were much too early, the sun hadn't quit, nothing, ever, was left in peace! Walking fast he looked to either side for darker streets, but there were none. He knew it would be no darker when they reached home, lighter if anything. There three streetlights waited in a row, marking the bend where So. "S" bore toward the fields, burning brighter and brighter the later it got. Oh yes sure they could hang their blankets up, be kept awake by the cold instead. In summertime they could suffocate. He vowed they'd be long gone by spring. "I'll tell you what!" he said. "Some Saturday we'll go the other way, out to the country and seek the dark."

"Mommy too?"

"Yes! We'll go on a foggy night, it doesn't have to be Saturday, just any night. We'll take some supplies along. We'll want weenies, potato chips, marshmallows, anything else? A case of soda pop! We'll take our blankets too and camp overnight, out in the dark! In the morning we'll wake up early and have bacon and eggs, more soda pop. We'll break camp when the sun comes up. We won't have much to carry home: we'll burn our refuse, wrap our empty bottles in our blankets, I'll pack our bedroll on my back. How about it, old pal, is that a date for the first foggy night?"

She nodded yes, but when a few minutes later he announced their house she was smiling at him in her sleep. He kissed her before he hurried to the open door where Judith stood waiting in high heels and silk, two frosty ones and an orange one on the kitchen table at her back, chairs drawn up, candles mellow against curtained outside light, radio low down in the oven ready to give lone liners hell.

—1960

Bank Day

DURING THE NIGHT HE DREAMT that someone gave him $15, not for anything he had done but for the sport, and now he tried in various ways to relive the ecstasy of his acceptance. He could not do it, because awake he knew too much, as that nobody ever got anything for it is better to a giver be. One thing he did not know was what time it was, yet he had himself so placed that he did not have to listen to the clock tick off its superior knowledge in the dark. He lay with his head, and his impatience, buried beneath the cover, waiting for the alarm (which did not know it was set) to sound. Oh, he might easily have imagined that he lay thus fortified against Martha's soft respiration, or against the shocking knowledge that a wife of his could on this day be so tranquilly asleep, but he tried not to permit her innocent failings to make of him a bully or a nag. Neither could he admit the intolerable truth, that what had kept him so long alert was pain. Being a lesser kind of realist he had proposed that everything, even a brutal alarm clock, must one day break down, and being by press of circumstances a pessimist had decided it would choose to break down today. Thus when at last it did sound off he was already halfway over Martha, halfway over her incredible baby which even as late as last week they had both imagined to be a persistent gas, and Martha was grunting quietly. Thank God I love you, he thought, kissing her somewhere as he passed by.

Now steadying himself on the slippery linoleum he had himself working fairly well, alarm going off, lights going on, almost at once, and in the long-desired morning saw that the clock's amputated hands approximated his own opinion of the time. In fact he knew so well their vagaries that he corrected them, aiming the silver stub straight up toward twelve, the other, Wild Pink as Martha's nails, toward five. Whenever possible he liked to do two things simultaneously, and turning freed the cat from the bathroom with his left hand while scratching a kitchen match with the thumbnail of his right. "Pret-ty Kit-ty, Pret-ty Kit-ty." Stopping stiffly he stroked her supple back while lighting the burner under the coffee pot. But now he had to remain there squatting, watching the cat spring onto the bed to knead Martha's uneasy mountains with her paws. And somehow he did not cry aloud as he lunged with grinding vertebrae into the bathroom to comb his hair and brush his teeth. (He had shaved the night before, while reading the help wanted ads for the final futile time.) Back in the room again, he cleverly combined a proper kiss on Martha's cheek with stopping for his polished shoes. What stunned him was how, on such a diet, anyone could smell so sweet. "Martha, Martha," he softly called. "Bank day today."

"Un?" Frowning she partly opened her blue eyes, and rolled sidewise onto the sleeping cat. He kissed her on the other cheek, at the same time groping cautiously.

"John?"

He held up the ruffled, delighted cat.

"Oh, did I quash Pretty Kitty!" Smiling ruefully, she enfolded it. "Aren't I a Humpty Dumpty though?" she asked.

He kissed her mouth this time. "You're a damn beauty, but it's becoming unsafe to sleep with you . . . I'm sorry, I didn't mean that," he said, and wincing erected himself again. He turned his tight-skinned face from her. "Why don't you get up," he snapped.

Now he imagined Martha's smooth white forehead inventing pain, for both of them. "You get back in bed," she said.

"I'd love to—we might get hungry around supper time."

"I don't care," she said, but at the same time she was quaking the bed, rolling out of it onto her hands and knees, muzzily cursing the slipper which eluded her and which he at last shied toward her with his toe. "Oh, *there.* What did you mean you didn't mean just now?"

"Nothing," he said. The coffee water was boiling, and he shook coffee in, set out coffee cups.

"Tell me. You always mean something, John," she begged, but suddenly heaved to her slippered feet, confronting him all humpty-dumptyish in white. "Ah, you oughtn't to have said that, John."

"I apologized long ago."

"Still, you're right," she said, and sighed. "You're so right, you know."

"I'll sleep in the cat's room from now on," he said, seeing her start for it. They still had the radio, and passing she flicked it on. He leaped after, furling the sudden flag music that threatened to smother him. Soon music stopped, and a man's voice announced that MUZ was on the air again. This man asked all his friends to leave for work five minutes early today, as a light frost on their windshields might hamper visibility. "Turn it down, Martha, turn it down," he implored, on her return.

Martha did so without complaint, but placing their toast on the burner, spreading oleo, he heard how unhappily she opened the catfood can. And she looked unhappily aside as she handed the can to him. "We should never have kept that cat."

"I know," he said, spooning only a modest portion for Pretty Kitty, for himself a giant one. He selected several condiments from their large supply, basil, savory, sage, shallot, added them freely with flourishes. That was their extravagance, whenever they had pennies to spare they bought a seasoning.

"Tonight I'll barbecue you some frankfurters," he said, cracking the egg she passed to him and dropping it one-handed onto the meat in the frying pan. "A pound of them."

"With refried beans," she said.

"And beer?"

She nodded a festive yes, but, "I still wish you wouldn't go," she said.

"You've lost your appetite?"

"Let me go instead. Now that we know I'm not really sick."

"You? They wouldn't take you like that."

Looking down, "I'll tell them I've been eating well."

"Aha." It was not that he thought her incapable; in fact he fancied she would make the sacrifice with a certain swagger which he himself could not pretend. Certainly he detected no deficiency of blood in her! What he cowered from was the picture of her standing in the dark in that ghoulish line, listening to those sanguinary jokes, and then competing meanly for that frightful prize. "No, what is it they say? I still have some pride," he said.

"Let me go with you then."

"What is it they say again?"

"Think of the extra money though."

"No," he said. All dripping sounds made him feel weak, and he crossed to bang the leaky sink. "Will I get enough for us to pay up my insurance and live until my check arrives?"

She nodded, "Just."

"Then that's enough."

"If they take you, yes."

"Oh, they'll take me," he mumbled, giddily watching her pour tomato juice: "Please, Martha, not today."

"It's good for you."

"*Not today.*"

Now that he had their breakfast ready, he stood aside and allowed her the pleasure of serving it. He did not sit down until she told him to, and then only because he knew how it distressed her to see him prowl the floor while snatching mouthfuls from the ice box top. Doubling up, he wondered if having a baby was like sidling cramp-backed into a breakfast nook. At least she did not watch, but looked at the calendar above his head.

"Gene Autry was born today."

"Thank God!" he said, swilling coffee before he ate.

"I wonder if anyone was born on my birthday. Shall I see?"

"Maybe some other great man," he said fiercely through clenching teeth. "Maybe he left $15 to every female born that day, out of sentiment. Whimsical, he stipulated in his will that no one was to get her inheritance until she turned thirty-five. All pregnant women get a double share, of course."

But she sank sighing opposite. "Battle of the Alamo."

"Ah, then I should have been an insurance agent after all," he admitted readily, "now retired on the policies I'd sold myself, buying new ones with my dividends. Or I would have made a fine shattered disk jockey," he proposed, and glared at the whispering radio. "Right now I could be lying in bed warning all my friends of light frosts on their way to work, warning them to buy new windshields on their way back again." Briefly he paused, washing down his cat pourri with a third or fourth cup of black coffee sloshed from the tremendous pot. "What I really should have done," he said, "was re-enlist in the army for forty years. That way they'd have had to invest in a new back for me, instead of leaving me to subsist on thirty-five a month and pain. Well, thank God anyway I was carrying that ice cream freezer in the line of duty, rather than throwing it at some dyspeptic officer." He paused to laugh. "What is it they say, an army is only as good as its bloody cook? I'll never forget that big one I worked with in India. Neither will you, I've told you about him often enough. Babu? He used to sit cross-legged on a huge table, Buddha-esque, supervising his two dozen native cooks. They'd bring him a taste of each dish they cooked, if they left out one of their twenty or thirty curries he'd know and remonstrate. Needless to say, he thrived. Three hundred forty pounds of him, and never moved from his table for twelve hours a day except to leak. Now there's the job for me. The only difference would be that I would lie down on my table, my cooks would specialize in sauteed snails and bouillabaisse. I myself would never lift anything heavier than a very young squab, plucked of course." He paused to glance at her, then quickly away again. "I know what you're going to say," he said, "I should have been born to the baronetcy of Upper-Aultby-by-the-Sea or Sweet-Sweet-Puke, but the answer is no—let's be practical."

She did not laugh or smile at any of this, but did shake her head occasionally as he in order not to howl aloud explained on and on to her his views. That he had spent half his life cooking for men who despised his dishes but greedily devoured them. That the sense of gratitude, like his food, was a passing thing. That if he could lay his hands on any one of several men there would be no frankfurters for dinner tonight, roast pig au jus instead. That the ugliest man in the world was an unused cook, was he, was him. At last he could endure it no longer but straightened cursing to his feet to stride the floor, lift their miserable frying pan and slam it on their miserable stove. He wheeled to her, asking, "Well, aren't you going to make me up," appalled.

She mumbled some mild apology, squeezing past him to the bureau top. He followed her, but by the time she had her rouge uncapped he was pacing the room again. "Stand still," she ordered, cornering him, and under her soft fingertips his nerves did quiet a little bit. He closed his eyes and pretended that she was caressing him. In truth she was, of course, and he wished that she would never stop. Yet a moment later he broke roughly away from her. "Well, how do I look?"

Martha stretched to look at him closely, too closely, and it seemed to him that her considered judgment was, "You look, you look."

"What!" Very ugly indeed, he thought, when your wife speaks to you of love and only the nerves respond.

"Come here," she said.

"I can't understand a word you say," he said, stooping to receive her kiss. "How do I look?"

"You're a damn beauty," she said. "Have you everything? Here's your shopping list, your firewood, your matches and cigarettes."

"Thanks, thanks, thanks," he said, taking everything at once.

"I gave you both the cigarettes."

"You'll need one."

"Not as much as you will two."

But he, flinging the cigarette onto the bed, denied her any sacrifice. He strode sharply to the door, which she unlocked for him. "I'm a son-of-a-bitch," he said.

"Don't tell me your troubles," she said, and as he passed by she turned his jacket collar up.

Groping down the narrow passage between the two facing rows of cabins, he believed that he had never seen the world so dark before. It was not until he reached the sidewalk that he glanced up at their palm tree and realized their neon sign was out. This vastly pleased him, for he could stare back at the darkness he had left and almost imagine a home was there, a well-tended little home that drew milkmen, ministers and paperboys. Well, he was on his way to work, and unseen he swung out his piece of wood almost jauntily: for the first time today his thoughts did not twinge with pain. Walking did this for his back, almost made a citizen of him. And almost he returned to leave Martha a gentle word, but knew too well that by the time she had nervously unlocked the door he would have thought of something else. Thus he contented himself with remarking to a passing car, "Oh, *aren't* I one?"

Now he wished he had that second cigarette. More strongly he wished he had four miles to walk, instead of blocks. He wished he were a mailman, with a full-time watchman's job at night. But already he was approaching a lighted street, where the jobholders did not appear to be allowing frosty windshields to slow them much. He felt anger rise again, for each one carried a box of kleenex on the rear window ledge, and he could always be sure the skinny queen up front would stare out at him from her limp embrace to ask, "Hey mister, don't you wish you had me?" Thus he became sensitive about his piece of wood, tucked it under his right arm now, away from the street. Cold though he was, he turned his collar down. "Well now, ma'am," was his reply.

So it did not displease him to be turning the final corner into blackness now, even though it meant that he was almost there. In fact he could already see their puny fire, see the boys bent over it like thin frozen fingers over a glowing ember held in the palm, Winston shorter and broader and a little apart, like a stubby thumb. If at first he only imagined Winston's fast anxious gabble coming through to him over the receding traffic noise, a step or two later he could hear nothing else. Surely it was the most comical sound in the world, being at this distance wholly unintelligible, yet somehow he could not smile. For $15 he would have turned around and toted an ice cream freezer the four long blocks that he had come. Receiving no offers of any kind he approached the fire in a circumspect way, on grass. Winston, however, was not surprised.

"Hey, Johnny! Johnny! (It's Johnny.) Hey, you're late, Johnny," he cried.

John bowed stiffly to the group, extended his hands with the others over the fire. "Gentlemen." He looked from one to another of the boys, and some returned his look. Oliver alone did not face the fire, nor mingle his hands with theirs. He watched the darkness warily, but glanced back just long enough to grin at John. John looked at Winston last. "Winston, it takes a while for the three of me to get ready a morning, you understand."

"Ah ah ah!" Winston shouted laughter down, leaned close to peer at John. "What are you going to make, a deposit or a withdrawal today, Johnny?"

"I thought I'd cash in a few frozen assets today," John said, blinking faster than Winston could.

"Ah ah ah! Come on up to the fire then, Johnny. We'll warm those assets up for you, Johnny. We'll warm them up," Winston cried, his thick hands like bracelets on John's thin arms. "Anyway, I see you brought your firewood, Johnny. We'll use that one any minute now. That's a nice one, Johnny. Here, give it here, I'll put it on the pile here. We'll need plenty of wood before we're through." Winston reached into his loose pants for a large gold watch he had, bent to read it at the fire. A flame was licking at his hands, and like scientists they watched while Winston appeared to read the number of seconds it took him to feel the burn. Hearing laughter, he pocketed his watch, kicked the barrel wrathfully with his big black boot. "It's those goddam palm fronds, they snap at you. You ever notice that, Johnny? You notice the gutter when you came up, how neat it was? They like that, don't they Johnny, the way I clean it up for them? And it helps us too. They have a clean gutter and it keeps us warm. That way everyone wins. Johnny, am I right?"

"Winnie, why don't you stop whinnying," the carpenter said. Whenever he spoke to anyone he cocked his head and screwed up one eye, his left, as though aligning nails, and his voice had a metallic ring: "Why don't you save your strength, you'll need it in a little while."

"Ah ah ah," Winston warned, moving to the carpenter's side. He clenched a fist and held up a hard arm to him. "By any chance what you're looking for?"

The carpenter ignored the arm, but reached behind Winston to rap the wooden brace instead. "Hell, I could make a better man than you out of knotty pine."

Winston hearing their laughter smiled. He stood nodding and blinking at the carpenter. "Ah you you," he said.

"Man offered me a job yesterday," the carpenter said over Winston's head to John. "He called it a little Sunday job. Ten bucks for the day, hanging doors. Bastard would have had to pay three times that much to any man with a card. I told him I'd wait and let them bleed me here, it don't take so long."

John nodded. "It leaves no scab," he said. He enjoyed watching the carpenter rolling one, for he tucked the brown paper into the creases of his fingerless hand as though this were some sort of new-fangled machine he had. He sprinkled the tobacco casually, used a patented twist and a lick, and when he was done he put his machine away. "Carpenter, why don't you give up and go back home?"

Lighting up, the carpenter cocked his head at John. A spark was feeding on his thin grey sweater, already pocked with tobacco burns. "Maybe I will in a gallon or two."

Winston, tiptupping around the barrel, leaned close to John. "I had muscular spasmatisms, Johnny," he said. He paused to throw in a stick. Then he nudged John toward the barrel, looking up at him. "The wife is sick this weekend, Johnny. Figure it out for yourself: the weekend is the only time you can sell ice cream, the kids are home. That's a sure twenty I lost right there. Then I had to give her twenty-five Friday for the license plates. The state tax was seventeen. Figure it out for yourself, that took care of the bank account. I had $1100 in the bank before I got sick, after I sold the store. You've seen my bankbook, haven't you, Johnny?"

"I've seen it, yes."

Winston's hand came out of his pocket, clamped John again. "I guess you'd be surprised if the wife kicked me out one of these days, wouldn't you, Johnny?" he asked. "Well, I wouldn't be surprised, Johnny. I'm ready for her, Johnny." He looked down at his shoes. "I have to have my shoes made special, Johnny. Look at that arch. Look at that toe, Johnny. Steel." Winston gave the barrel a ringing kick. "Dr. Bastard, you better take me today, you son-of-a-bitch. I was first man here."

"What time you get here, Winston?" Oliver was guarding the darkness still.

"Winnie spends his nights here," the carpenter said. "Then around midnight his wife drives by and gives him an ice cream bar."

The little man with the cruddy vest opened his eyes. His

name was Henry or Hank, Herman perhaps. "You should tell your wife to carry beer on her truck, I'll come over and keep you company."

"Hell, Howard, are you here?" Oliver wanted to know. "What were you last time they tested you, about ninety proof?"

"Sure, straight Kentucky bourbon. They pay me extra for that. That's a hell of a lot better than a puking 3.2."

"Don't worry about me, I'm a sarsaparilla man."

Howard grinned redly at Oliver's back. "I always noticed you coons had queer names for that bathtub poison you like to make."

"Easy boy, Howard," Oliver said, and his voice was soft. "I'm liable to split your skull and light a match, we'll all blow up."

"Ah ah ah! Howie, you going to let him get away with that? Hey, Howie?"

Howard nodded a goodnatured yes.

"Hey, Larry! (There's Larry.) Hey, Larry! You've got your helmet on today."

"Larry forgot to take it off when he got up this morning," John said, turning his back to bake.

"Not hardly," grinning Larry said.

"We thought you went back East last week."

Larry shook his aluminum head. "Too goddam cold back there. They got twelve inches of snow at El Paso Friday night. Three feet in the drifts. Hell, I'm waiting for spring. A climate like this, a man's blood gets thin."

"You can say that again," the carpenter, spitting, said.

"Ah ah ah!"

"Amen."

"Hey, look at the size of that one," Winston whispered loudly, and they turned to look. "Look at that chest, look at that asseroo. Look at that tourist crease in the pants. What does the bastard do, sell it by the goddam barrel?"

The newcomer stepped among them now, spread great hands to the fire. He did look as though he could get rich fast. "How do they pay here?" he asked. "Cash on the line?"

Looking askance, they nodded yes.

"I lost my wallet to a floozy last night, papers and everything. I need gas to get out of here."

"Gas." Everyone looked everywhere else, the carpenter whispering obscenities.

Flushing the big man drew in his hands, stepped back a step. "What time does the show start, anyway?"

He had to wait a minute for their reluctant "Eight."

"We better line up," said the carpenter, moving toward the bank, "Before some tourist tries to bull in ahead of us. Oliver, you go first. I'll come after Winnie—after Winnie anyone looks good, ah ah ah!" But he turned to look closely at John, as Martha had. "On second thoughts, maybe you better follow him."

"Thanks."

Even such a line as theirs, now started, grew, as though aimless passers-by tagged on out of curiosity. Yet there was a kind of sardonic knowledge on every face, wary eyes were large, and the sickly dawn showed complexions blue. The sense of watchful apathy survived bad jokes and expletives. It almost seemed that Winston himself had found a mood. He moved from line to fire, back again, without announcements of any kind, confronted John with unblinking eyes. "Dr. Bastard has it in for me, Johnny. You notice that? He'll try anything to pass me by."

"Winnie, why don't you give up?" the carpenter wished to know. "Last time they took you they were pumping it into your right arm faster than they could squeeze it out your left."

"I was sick that day."

"Hell, they couldn't get a pint out of you if they cut your throat, you know that."

"Ah ah ah, out of you, you mean."

"Me, I'm a red-blooded American boy."

"The carpenter has it made," Oliver said. "He sells it Mondays—then Tuesdays his old lady comes down and gets it back."

"So?"

Winston gripped John and the carpenter: "Dr. Bastard goes for the black ones, you ever notice that? Johnny, you ever see him turn a black one down? What is he, a comminist?"

"Ah ah ah," the carpenter said.

"So maybe your old lady's half full of the dark stuff now, you ever think of that?"

"Easy boy, Winnie," Oliver's calm voice said. "You're

liable to lose that blood without getting paid for it."

But now small noises were made inside the bank—a thud, a word or grunt, the squeal of sliding furniture, a peevish laugh, a politic one—the line tensed forward to interpret them.

"Dr. Bastard must be knocking off a piece."

"They're finishing Winnie's coffin up."

"They're playing darts with our needles, men."

Here a blind was raised. They blinked, surprised to find that the sun was out, it lit up Marie's bright smile for them. She waved her fingers pluckily. Some smiled but no one waved at her, for she was too pink, too plump, too newly starched. Under present circumstances they would have preferred one of the little hairy ones. When a draught carried Winston's stinking smoke to them, they were glad at the chance to flail their arms and cough and curse. Why doesn't somebody pee on it, we'll use Winston's ass to plug it up, ah ah ah, there goes the lock.

"Hey, Marie. Marie! Is Dr. Bastard our doctor today?"

Marie nodded her head, reprovingly. "You boys know the rules, just six at a time," she said.

Dr. Baxter did not look at them. He sat on the edge of his desk, his long thin legs crossed and braided intricately, his long thin fingers shuffling papers which his deep-set eyes seemed not to read. When Marie motioned to Oliver, Oliver glided forward to the doctor's desk. The deep grey eyes swept intimately over him, like smoke, the slender head jerked almost imperceptibly. "Thank you, doctor," Oliver said, but Dr. Baxter seemed not to hear. He waited for Marie to lead Oliver out.

The eyes had withdrawn again. The rustling papers seemed to converse with the little sounds of Winston's nervousness, the gaspish breaths, the twitching lids, the clenching and unclenching fists. Winston was sickened by what he heard: he looked wildly to John, for help.

"Winston," Dr. Baxter said in his soft grieving voice, "do you remember what I said to you last week?"

"Doctor?"

"I said I did not want to see you here again."

"Doctor!"

"I want you to go home, Winston, please."

"Doctor, you didn't even look at me!"

"Nor am I going to look at you."

"Doctor, doctor . . ."

The doctor prepared to rise, and all stood watching him untwine his legs like sometimes useful things. Winston jerked forward now. "Dr. Bastard, Dr. Bastard!" he cried, grasping Dr. Baxter's arm.

Dr. Baxter shrugged Winston off, quickly closed a door on him. Winston stood shaking in front of it. John and the carpenter tried to hold onto the jerking arms, but just now Winston was too strong for them. "You've got to help me, you bastards," he cried. "Johnny, what will you do for me? What will you do?"

"Maybe we can get Marie to take a little from the rest of us."

"Sure, just two ounces apiece from eight of us."

They turned to the opening door.

"Ask her, Johnny. Ask Marie!"

But Marie came out shaking her pretty head. "Don't bother to ask," she said.

Winston tore loose, stepped toward Marie. "Marie! Johnny!" he cried, turning back to him. "What will you do for me?"

John did not answer him. He watched Dr. Baxter in the doorway now, watched Winston jerk to the quiet voice. "Winston, I thought I asked you to get out of here?"

Turning Winston glared at the boys, nodding his head, jerking his jaw at them. He moved to the door in this convulsive way. He looked hard at the boys as he went out, but instantly was in again to point a finger at the watching doctor across the room. "You you you!" he cried and the door slammed closed.

When Dr. Baxter was seated on his desk again, tightly screwed, he laughed, and Marie called out to John. John pinched his cheeks. Stepping smartly to the desk he fixed his eyes on the mournful face, willing, look at me, Dr. Bastard, look at me. But Dr. Baxter stubbornly spared himself. "John," he said softly, "I thought we agreed you would skip a week."

"Next week, doctor. You remember, I get my check next week." He felt the eyes sweep lightly over him, now briskly back and forth across his cheeks, while he stared back horrified. "*Doctor!*"

Looking away, the doctor almost laughed again. "Marie."

"Thank you, doctor," John said, following Marie out of the room. He paused at the foot of Oliver's bed. Oliver nodded at his bottle, already half full, and smirking he winked at John. "I'll wait for you."

"Do."

Removing his jacket, John stepped into his cubicle and lay down on his clean bed. He smiled at Marie when she came in. Her fingers were warm as she puckered him. "You better stay home next week, you heard what the doctor said."

"Don't worry, Marie."

"Eat lots of red meat."

"Yes, nurse," John said.

As soon as she had gone, he opened his eyes. He fired up his cigarette and lay deeply inhaling it, watching his bottle fill. He was glad that Oliver would wait for him; he would need Oliver's steadiness on the long walk to the grocery store, and he knew Winston would be out there reviling them. He did not blame Winston at all. Yet he did not allow himself to brood long on tomorrow's uncertainties, but centered all his failing attention on the warm, smug feeling of the man who knows that for today at least he still has it, made.

—1960

The Flyman

WHEN THE MOVING MEN HAD SHOVED and strapped the last piece, the last slippery convenience, inside the moving van, George Nader looked about him with very little sense of loss, for everything that remained, the flypaper, the swatters, and he believed the turtle bowl, was his. Had Zoe been divorcing him, and taking along her legal property as dowry to another man, the division of goods would have been exactly this, except of course that she would then have been leaving George himself behind to enjoy the pure, seeming inconvenience of the house. He would never know what time it was: only sit at the back-door and watch the cactus shadows on the sand outside, perhaps noting whether the sun or the moon was moving them. With the hours thus confused there would be no prompt, rude guests to demand his silent presence in the livingroom; their polished mahogany cage would be gone, not to mention their electricity. He would look without commitment at the mirrorless walls, for the loathsome electric razor would be buzzing the fuzz on some other cheek or the stubble underneath Zoe's arms. He would sleep, night or day, in the built-in bathtub, and survive on grapefruit and oranges and the neighbors' eggs. Delighted with such pictures, smiling upon Zoe's swollen rear, he took up a handy swatter and brandished it enchantingly until the men returned.

What he liked about the moving men was their pride in being watched. They spoke in low rough voices, cursing only humorously when his flypaper caught them up, pausing occasionally in their work to compliment Zoe upon this piece or that but once outside tossing her furniture quite insultingly among them as though it were simply so much stuff which they alone knew the real value of. At the very first, when they had stood in the livingroom wondering where to begin, he had said, "Take everything with faces, or legs," and had settled in a chair to watch how nicely it worked out that way, with the exception of a few planters of ivy and the pasteboard boxes of odds and ends, until they had taken the chair itself from under him. "Easy now," he had standing said, and when they smiled expectantly as though hoping he had found some failure in their work: "Everything but me, that is." And now he stood grinning as they shoved respectfully past Zoe at the door, where she hoped her presence would urge them to use a little more care, less skill, in their wild slippery sprint to the van, but as the van door cracked shut he sobered his face for her turn to him.

"Looks different, doesn't it?" he quickly said, not in sympathy or even sincerity but only wanting to take the words from her pursing mouth. "Bleak?"

"It does, it does," she agreed, forced to it, but hastily regained herself: "We filled two-thirds of a van, you know."

"Big baby too," he shot.

"It was," said Zoe.

He looked fiercely away from her fuzzy head, to the grey, permanent shadow of the departed television-radio. What had she expected of him once, that he had not given her? He supposed that at first it had been children, although as a struggling, wild-eyed veteran his reasons had been entirely economic, plausible, and she had agreed with him. Only in time, as he progressed, had the question become less economic than eugenic, and she had agreed again. How could she not. For it had grown increasingly clear that no child of his could have the common view, or chance. Today the question was no longer asked, yet he felt that secretly, in whatever depths she had, Zoe would have welcomed the pleasures of an abortion, the living proof that in fact she could create. Few men would help her prove it now, he and time had taken care of that. So they had settled on an easier enmity, as less harrowing, more mentionable, her loss of the housewife's sweet dependence which he had so easily usurped for himself. Deprived of her empty days, Zoe had filled her nights with appliances. Looked at in this way the unwieldy procession which he had just witnessed could not be said to betoken Zoe's unfathered children so much as a bitter, accurate accounting of Zoe's paychecks, and this cynical view of it made him able to turn to her again. "Wait until we get up north," Zoe said.

"Oh, wait." He followed her zigzag course toward the kitchen, even he finding it oddly difficult to avoid the flypaper strips with the furniture no longer there to inhibit him, and he fancied he heard soft curses among Zoe's fat breaths. Watching her unwind from a gummy strip, he felt himself struck by a change in her appearance, the first he could recall in years. It was as though the moving men had carted off not only her movables but her very makeup itself, that pink, almost livid glaze with which she regularly hid from him and all the world the face he had loved twelve, maybe fifteen years before. And seeing in this abrupt way how dry and sucked of life she was, finally justifying her endeavor to look like anyone else but Zoe, he felt a sudden terror of time and reached his hand to her. "Zoe."

Zoe took his hand.

"I'm sorry, Zoe."

She patted it, and now he watched her puffy fingers drape gummed paper along the soft, freckled flesh of his outstretched arm until it clung to the hairs there securely enough for her to draw free of it. Looking up from dead and drying flies, he saw her bright black eyes twinkle with something between defiance and disgust. "Why this?"

"Because," she said. "It's yours, isn't it?"

"Ah." His hand shot sidewise for a buzzing fly, caught it effortlessly in mid-flight and tossed it stunned to the floor for his ready foot to quash. There had been a time when Zoe would have watched this exhibition with genuine admiration, but today she turned sharply off as though he had belched or gassed the place. Well, as the doctor said, some men hate Mexicans and Republicans, some beat their wives.

"George, promise you'll have it all cleared out when I get back?"

"Back?"

"From the market, George."

He suddenly smiled, at the picture of them following that

two-thirds van of conveniences through eighteen hundred miles of ice and snow and stopping from time to time to eat cold canned goods beside the road. Certainly he would not build a fire, and he could not imagine heat from a fire of Zoe's. This was not a new thought, but he added to it now the one that Zoe would surely have packed the can opener away in the kitchen appliance box, and he spoke hurriedly lest she too might think of it. "You hurry right along," he said. "I'll take care of everything."

"Well . . ." He followed once more as she zagged through the kitchen, the front room, the hall, somehow this time escaping entanglement but turning finally at the front door to seek her purse. With all the furniture gone, there was nowhere for Zoe to hunt. Even at best, things had been, as he thought, fuzzy around their home. For Zoe's talents were almost purely operative, or rather her affinities: she was a superlative driver of automobiles, unhampered by any comprehension of what made them run; she could twirl painful clarity from television sets, just so long as their extension cords and socket plugs were good; and of course over both their lives loomed that cryptically initialed machine, monstrously dialed, with which she made airplane parts whose names and places she did not know. Otherwise there was that fuzziness, that flapping, searching, beseeching, wasted fuss which made him grind his teeth and wince. But we do not hate people, he recalled, not even for enduring us, and grinned a wistful grin at Zoe before turning his attention to his papered arm. "Look on the mantel piece," he said, and imagining Zoe's bleak glare of thanks waved his swatter graciously.

He felt her departure in much the same way that he felt the flypaper tear free of his hair and flesh, as a paradox of pain, relief. He tensed to the chattering porch, to the car's whamming doors, to the pitiable whine of a young motor overtaxed, and finally to the smothering cloud of dust that seeped through the fine-meshed screens, yet he was glad. When he turned it was almost as though Zoe had really left, scattering her own ashes behind her over the neighborhood; in twenty minutes, he knew, she would be back to stir them up again.

Meanwhile he did not mind too much what he had to do. It was the thought alone that had almost paralyzed him, when the furniture and Zoe had still been there, the thought of tearing down all his ingenious, tactically flawless stations without the possibility or necessity of ever replacing them. But now in the empty house his defenses hung like so much random paper, forlornly grouped, disorganized. What he did, quickly, was start at the front door and work his way in as nearly a straight line as possible along the south wall, yanking flypapers as he came to them and draping them in careless yet attractive disarray over the handle of the swatter which he still held. Then quickly back along the other wall and crisscross here and there about the room. When he had filled his swatter he reached for another, presently a third, but half a fourth finished the livingroom. The bedroom and kitchen yielded two swattersful apiece, one each for the bathroom, pantry, hall. Back in the livingroom he stuck his entire collection upended in the empty turtle bowl. Gathering the remaining, unused swatters, he added them one by one with flourishes to his bouquet, stood back to pass on it.

He was glad to have found some use for the turtle bowl. It had not worked at all. Despite weeks of enthusiastic experimentation, under the most favorable conditions he could devise, George had never known a turtle to catch a fly. Place twelve flies with two hungry turtles overnight in a covered bowl, and in the morning twelve unmolested flies emerge. Put syrup on a turtle's nose, a fly may eat his sweets in peace. It did not work! Only if you dropped a fly into a turtle's water would it partake, and George refused to offer such sacrifices, dead or alive, simply that a turtle might stuff himself. He donated his turtles to the neighborhood and turned his attention to new pursuits. Chronologically the gyrotraps had come next after the turtle failure, and it was these he would attend to as soon as he had disposed of the mess in the turtle bowl.

Most weekends he did not go outside, except very briefly at lizard rotation times, for these were George Ingersoll's days at home. Not that he disliked the other George, he simply did not like the sense of driving him indoors. There had been a time when their weekends had been quite otherwise, they had become almost more than neighbors, finding several dependable interests in common such as their handicaps (mostly physical for the other George), their memories of beautiful, terrible northern winters which in past years they had somehow both survived, and more particularly their memory of North Africa and its big, blood-sucking flies which a man could look down upon, whether feeding on his own sores or on a corpse of whatever nationality, and say this is Evil, it isn't the Jerries after all. They had of course also had their common dismay at finding themselves banished by doctors to another Africa, a New World Sahara, their sense of loneliness and exile in this wasted land and their exasperated fascination with its flora, fauna and insect life. Weekends they had fought the desert together side by side in their backyards, tearing up its cactus and tumbleweed, coupling their two hoses to lay its dust, attacking its blackwidows, scorpions, flies with lethal insecticides, all the while offering bitter, gasping encouragement to one another across the fence. But soon it had become clear that their intensities were not the same, that one could be satisfied with a mere surface tidiness that the other fiercely disdained. George Ingersoll spent more and more time resting on his canvas chairs, now looking contentedly at his swept backyard, now at George, his occasional shouted encouragement grown amused, polite. A certain restraint had grown between them as nowadays it so easily did (people no longer visited the Naders, they came in small explorative groups instead) and it ended with their reverting to a neighborly distrustfulness. George understood. The other still had the so-called job, was employable, while George himself had long ago lost the benign effects of the six-day purge. He understood, yet it surely hurt him that his neighbor no longer showed sympathy for what he was trying to do, neither took time to enquire about his experiments nor looked at them. Thus he was surprised, or a little angry, to find George on this last day lingering outside, hanging on the fence above the rubbish cans which they had found it easiest to continue sharing stealthily. "Morning George . . . Ah morning George." They performed this ceremony solemnly, each glancing sidewise to see if the other still smiled at it. Neither did, though with George Ingersoll it was hard to say, for pain and the desert sun had long ago combined to draw back the brittle skin around his mouth into a permanent grimace. Whenever George looked up at him he was unpleasantly aware of his own soft juiciness. "Hello, George," he said again, and falsely coughed. "How have you been?"

"Oh fine, fine," George Ingersoll said, and now he did appear to smile at a ghastly joke. "And you?"

George also smiled. "Haven't seen you around much, George," he said, at the last minute muffling the "for a year or two."

"Yes, been busy inside," was said. There was a pause, while George tugged at the stubborn garbage lid. "Well, Zoe's transfer came through at last?"

"Yes, it came through," George said, banging the lid with his free fist.

"Give it one on the other side," George Ingersoll advised, and George gave it a brutal one. "No, one on the side of the top," and George belabored it everywhere. He put down the turtle bowl, grasped the lid handle with both big hands and lifted the entire barrel off the ground, shaking it furiously from side to side. But we do not take out our anger on inanimate objects, and cursing he let the whole thing drop. The lid bounced off. "Ah," he said, swatters clattering in.

"I wouldn't mind having that bowl, if you're done with it."

George passed the bowl over his shoulder, over the fence. "It's no good," he said, wiping his hands of it.

"Looks just like the thing for Miriam's fish."

"Oh fish—I never did try fish."

George Ingersoll patted the bowl. "I don't suppose you'll need any of this, up north?"

"No, none of it."

Still patting, George Ingersoll glanced at his neighbor's yard, then shamefully away again. "What about your lizards, George?"

George, who had stooped for the garbage lid, straightened quickly to the sidewise face. "You'd like them, George?"

"No no no, just curious."

"Ah." George came down hard, jamming the lid back on for George.

"I don't suppose they'd live through the winter there, even if you needed them?"

George shook his head, and it was almost as though he were shivering.

George Ingersoll too looked cold. "George, what does the doctor say?"

"The doctor? Not much—it might be good for me." Probably what the doctor had said to Zoe was that anything, even painful death, could be considered a benefice. But the doctor was no medical man, George had long ago passed them. "They say there's work up there, you know."

"I certainly hope so, George." When they looked briefly at one another now, it was almost in their old way, with common memories. George Ingersoll put out his hand. "I certainly hope the change of climate is good for you."

"Well, thanks, George," he said, taking the knotty hand reluctantly in his own soft freckled one. What he would like to have known before he took it was whether his eyes blurred at the sympathy of a friend or at the certain euphemisms of a hypocrite.

"We'll certainly miss you, George."

"Oh, well now," George said, and it almost blinded him, his dubious sentiment. He yanked free his hand to wheel away. "Well now, George."

"I certainly . . ." Fortunately some of the Ingersoll children were fighting now, and hugging the turtle bowl George moved to disentangle them. "I'll see you, George."

Oh oh oh, will you now, George thought, stalking quickly along the fence to the garage, the shop. He emptied the wheelbarrow of rusty tools and dragged it wickedly to the shop's locked door. He had the key, had it at all times on a string looped around his belt. Quickly inside, he swung the door on howling Ingersolls. Two years ago he had papered the ceiling and walls with flypaper (no paste, no waste, the flies make their own design) but now in the broken light of the one narrow window he noted how the ceiling curled and peeled, the walls writhed disgustingly, their glue had dried. The place smelled greyly of dust and wings, nor did the 200-watt ceiling lamp do much to clear the atmosphere. As it turned out, he would not have to redecorate.

His inventions lay everywhere, on the benches and shelves, and on the floor. These were mostly the gyrotraps, tiny razorblade fans which he had connected in series to a motor salvaged from a Lionel train. Each fan was designed to fit snugly into a

No. 2 can liberally coated with marmalade. (These had worked, although their blades required daily honing and from time to time their shafts would gum.) Then too there was the syrup door: a delicate device which the weight of three inverted flies could trip, slamming them against a red brick wall. (There were only three of these, for he had been unable to make them react to the weight of a single fly, and it had tormented him to think how many strays escaped.) There were several examples of the Infallible Fly Bath, simply a solution of molasses and hydrochloric acid (which he made himself by combining sulphuric acid with common table salt) in small glass tubes. These had worked very satisfactorily indeed, until neighbors began to understand what was happening to the noses of their cats. So it did not bother him very much to dump everything in a box and wheel it out for the garbage man. He did at the last minute leave one example of each behind, on the slim chance that some future scientist might find them a starting point, a useful groundwork for further exploration in the field. Not that this possibility greatly moved him either, for in his heart he knew that with the lizards he had come as close to a final answer to the problem as any man could, or would.

Here at last was what did hurt, having to gather his beer bottles now at the very time when he had finally perfected a formula for their rotation, a formula based on the observed frequency of flies at a given location at a given hour of a given day, as modified by such known variables as temperature, cloud covering, wind, humidity, and taking into account too such intangibles as the probable traumatic effects upon flies of his increasingly devastating war against their kind. Yet if the rotation formula was a marvel of deviousness, the trap itself was almost casual in its simplicity. Squeeze a small, vaselined lizard into an empty beer bottle, feed him just enough flies to prevent his escape; now coat the bottle mouth with almost anything at all, and wait. (No electricity, no mechanical parts, after a few days at large a lizard may be used again.) He gathered the bottles quickly but gently, arranging them in neat tiers in the wheelbarrow, and he wheeled them smoothly out over the desert to a rock he knew. There he cracked each of the forty-eight bottles with deft little taps, being careful that the lizards were not cut by the broken glass. Even at that, and despite his practice of selecting his lizards for healthiness, one lizard had succumbed. Impossible to say how many flies he had taken first, although in death he did look well-satisfied. George buried him. Now he stood for a while watching the others stagger over the desert, their bloated bodies unwieldy on their stiff short legs. Facing his wheelbarrow toward the house, he steered with care among his glutted friends. Ahead Zoe's dust was in the air, and Zoe herself waited at the kitchen door for him. "You did a nice job," she said.

"Thanks, Zoe."

"All ready now?"

Silently he looked about his experimental yard, a desert once again. He raised his eyes to an evilly buzzing fly, too high for him, and he did not move or speak until it came back again. He did not snare it at once but watched it cautiously circle his head, allowing it this last time the appearance of teasing him. When it finally settled on a freckled arm, he picked it off and held it out to view. "When you are, Zoe."

"Oh, why don't you get in the car," she said, and she followed him.

"You've remembered everything?"

"Yes."

It almost seemed she had. The canned goods lay boxed in the front seat, a shiny new opener visible. He knew their bags had been in the trunk for several days, and climbing into the car, into the back, he could smell the sweet insecticide. Despite the noonday temperature, all windows were tightly shut. He smiled at how narrowly Zoe opened the driver's door, how nearly flat she squeezed, how quickly she slammed once she was in.

"Mind if I open a window, Zoe?"

"Please, let's not."

"It's hot in here."

"It's hot everywhere."

"It smells."

"Let's wait until we're underway, at least," as the motor howled.

"Ah." Outside, George Ingersoll was leading his wife

forward to see them off, and Zoe stopped the car to point the friendly neighbors out to George. All arms were raised; with the windows up the pantomimic mouths could have said anything, oh-oh-oh perhaps. Now the saving children must have yelled, for the Ingersolls turned their wagging heads and ran. Releasing brakes, Zoe gaily blotted out the farewell scene.

"Now?"

"Wait until we're on the highway, George."

So he sat waiting, his eyes closed to the dusty light, his breath almost closed off too, until he felt the car spring free of sand and heard the tires take up their gleeful howl on a highway paved with kitten fur. "Now, Zoe?"

"Oh, *wait.*"

But he leaned forward anyway, not toward the window but toward the driver's seat, his hand going up. He might have slapped down on her then and there, had Zoe not caught the movement in her overhead looking glass. He hung there rigidly.

"Did you see one, George?"

"No."

"Well, please remember our frontseat rule."

"Sorry, Zoe." Leaning back again, tilting his head to rest, he continued to look at Zoe. But from the lower edges of his sight he could see his great short-sleeved spotty arms, folded across his chest, and from the fuzzy edges of his consciousness could hear his big hands slapping quietly.

"What now?" Zoe wanted to know.

"Don't worry, Zoe." He watched her shaking head. "You're happy, Zoe."

"Well?"

"No, I'm glad for you," he said. His hands were working harder now, moving rhythmically and conscientiously from freckle to freckle over his juicy arms, as Zoe turned round to him. Slap slap slap, he answered her. "I'm really glad for you."

"The temperature in St. Paul last night was two below."

"Oh, was it? Below?"

"Snow is probably falling now."

"It *is*?"

In her looking glass she smiled at him. "They say the winters are nine months long."

"That's all right," he said, and also smiled, for he would have lots to do.

—1958

The Love Letter

THE SCENE IS A NEIGHBORHOOD BRANCH of the Post Office Service. A façade dividing the public from the working area is far downstage, giving a closed-in feeling, and allowing little room in front for any except crosswise action. The clerks behind the façade seem to have all the room and light. On the right are post office boxes, rather outsized, remindful also of a honeycomb, catacombs, or a punchboard, depending on who you are and where standing. You are waiting in one of several lines, waiting to approach your own post office box perhaps, or one of the three service windows visible from where you stand. (All seats are tied back with brown cord. No one will be seated until after the play unless in a wheelchair.) While you wait, you watch luckier people in front squeeze forward, or dart in from right, go to their boxes or, those with packages to send or receive, to the Stamps—Sales & Service window, the first and largest of the windows, just left of center stage. Few go on to the other two windows, the Money Order—Real Estate window, or the Counsel window at far left stage, although clerks stand behind each of these windows too. Offstage right a heavy swinging door creaks and whooshes each time a client enters or departs. You feel drafts, and restlessness. You have time to notice the people in front of you, that they are well-dressed, the men wear felt hats, overcoats, scarves, carry briefcases. There are some well-dressed young women, but men, all ages, are in the majority. Nobody talks, or not so you can hear. You begin to observe, since the more interesting activity is to the right, that all clients go to boxes of their own height, seven-footers to boxes of the top row, six-footers a row lower, and so on down to the big drawers at the bottom which are collected by little office boys in new leather jackets, carrying new leather bags with gold initials on them, A.I.T, C.G. & Co., P.S., etc., etc. The drawers contain a great deal of mail, which the boys stuff into their bags quickly and efficiently. In fact everyone collects a lot of mail, efficiently, with almost a safecracker's touch of the dial, a fine fast pluck, a sharp slam, on the run, for it is almost closing time on a cold winter evening (December 31, if you can believe the calendar in the working area, and you can of course). That's why the lights in the working area are on, and why you are standing in a gloom that constantly increases as darkness falls outside. The clock beside the calendar read 17:17 when you came in, and whatever it says now is correct. Meanwhile the tempo of business too has kept a steady pace, with clients emptying boxes, it seems, almost as fast as the clerk on the other side can reload. He is a marvel, his hands fly almost faster than you can see, the sharp sleeves of his uniform flash like propellor blades, while his green eyeshade points always straight forward from a perfectly motionless head. You observe this whenever a box of the centermost horizontal row is briefly emptied of its mail, but almost immediately he loads that box again, except the one farthest to the right through which you cannot see him anyhow. This box is always empty, and has been so all along, the only empty one. You are increasingly aware of it, because the greater the gloom around you, the brighter the light shines through that box from the working area behind. It begins to take on a red-orange glow. You may guess it to be vacant, until a man who has been standing quietly near you all this time, steps forward, walks slowly up to it. His head is at just the right height to black out that glowing emptiness as he leans forward to peer inside. Although you may not have noticed him before, you notice now, for he is dressed differently enough from everyone else to be conspicuous. He wears a nondescript grey cap, a heavy nondescript sweater, nondescript pants which are not threadbare or patched but are finally losing their ability to keep a good sharp crease. Too, it takes him a little above average to work his dials. A little bottleneck develops. Clients hover impatiently beside him, eyeing him, as you do. His nondescript shoes aren't new, but their shine is if anything brighter than anyone else's. And his handkerchief is definitely new, is in fact so sharp-edged and white that you may briefly have mistaken it for a letter when first he whipped it out of the righthand, door-side pocket of his pants. But you soon come to know what he has there as you watch him flick, efficiently, first the two walls, then the floor of his glowing box. You see him quickly return handkerchief to pocket without shaking dust. He slams, turns left, works his way in what seems slow-motion along the busy clients slicing left and right. Seen in profile he is somewhat less conspicuous, for his sweater is faced with a darker, smoother material, almost coatlike, to the waist at least, with narrow lapels, buttons, even a white scarf at neck, or perhaps it is another new handkerchief serving part-time duty as cravat. It turns out he has a briefcase too, clasped against his chest by his left arm. His cap is of felt in front, with a narrow snapbrim. His front pants creases, as far as you can see, are sharp.

Nonetheless he does still stand out somewhat, for he wears very little cosmetic on his weathered, homely face, while his cap entirely hides whatever hair he has. He looks older than the smooth smiling pink old men with silver ducktails, and younger than the grinning pink young men with heads shaved all but bald beneath their hats. If he would smile or grin, doff his cap, you might be able to put him in his place, but he will not. He is nervous though, gives himself away by the two quick tugs he gives his snapbrim as he ducks suddenly past Stamps—Sales & Service, slices toward Money Orders—Real Estate. The clerk behind Money Orders—Real Estate is of about the client's height, thus you see little of him while they converse. You can hear him clearly though, because business is slacking off just a little (it's 17:22) and because he has a hearty, friendly voice.

Clerk: Hello!

Client: (*a little too loudly and gaily*) Hello! Hello!

Clerk: Well, another big one almost ready for the record books, hey?

Client: Almost! Almost!

Clerk: They seem to crawl by a little faster every time.

Client: They do! They do!

Clerk: And what can we try our level best to do for you?

Client: Just like to renew this lease here, if I may. That's Prebble, Arnold A., Box 420-0560.

Clerk: Yes, sir. That's what we're here for, like they say. (*and after a minute, from somewhere left*) That was Arnold A.?

Client: Right! Arnold A.

Clerk: 05, that was?

Client: Correct! 0560. (*A longish pause, during which Client shifts weight uneasily, tugs sweater down in back, you sense he tugs snapbrim, tucks scarf, pats briefcase up in front.*)

Clerk: (*at window again, compassionately*) Your IBM is tagged.

Client: Oho! (*and with really forced gaiety, underbreath*) Red, white, or blue?

Clerk: I'm sorry: Blue.

Client: (*looking quickly left*) How's he been doing today?

Clerk: (*looks too*) Fair. His a.m. was busy, but p.m. has been a little slack.

Client: Ah. (*Leans right to peer past Clerk to clock: 1725. Straightens shoulders, summoning new determination, old gaiety*) I'll be back! There's time! There's time!

Clerk: (*with gaiety to match*) Of course, of course!

Client: (*starts left, ducks back, beseechingly, underbreath*) Try to hold it for me, will you, please?

Clerk: You bet, Mr. Prebble, sure will.

Client: Thanks. Thanks very much.

Clerk: Good luck, Mr. Prebble.

Client: (*slicing left*) Thanks! Thanks!

(*Clerk leans forward in window to watch Client go, hand half-raised in farewell encouragement. A pleasant-looking, unsmiling man of medium build, he seems to have less than average cosmetic on, and wears his hair not shaved but rather long, grey not silver-white. Wears the uniform almost casually too, top button unfastened, creases soft. By contrast, Counselor is a brilliant figure in white white shirt and luminous hand-painted tie, above which shines his great cheerful hand-painted smile. A slender eight-footer, similarly windowed, the more impressive part of him is still clearly visible after Client's approach. You would see even more of him if he were counseling an office boy, for his window starts low down near the floor, like a baggage window, though it has a sliding panel in front which he adjusts quickly for a client to lean up on comfortably. Client immediately does.*)

Counselor: Greetings!

Client: (*head tipped back so far that you can see his snap-brim jerk*) Greetings! Greetings!

Counselor: Last one through the slot! Last-minute rush!

Client: (*gaily presenting his IBM*) Yes! Yes!

Counselor: (*lifting card to omnivorous smile*) Ho, having a little trouble with your volume?

Client: No no, just . . .

Counselor: Just a little too much winter for you this year? Couldn't mush over here three times a day?

Client: No! I have!

Counselor: Have to update your mailing list, weed out the dead letterheads?

Client: Well . . .

Counselor: Well, Arnold, let's just see what your IBM has to say. (*There is a humming noise as he inserts card in machine to his left, studies it.*) Oh-oh. (*Presses button.*) Oh-oh. (*Presses another.*) Oh-oh. (*Another.*) Well, Arnold, your net weight, outgoing, isn't bad. Four pounds-two—that's fair. But your postage, outgoing—(*shakes head*) one pound-twelve. Your postage, incoming—oh-oh. (*Shakes sadly now.*) What seems to be the trouble, Arnold? Been studying your Lessee's Guidebook lately?

Client: Oh yes!

Counselor: Been following Uncle Po's helpful hints? (*The eversmiling face wags knowingly.*) Not lately, eh? You should. It pays. Uncle Po says these are changing times, you know.

Client: I know! I know!

Counselor: (*wags head, looks toward clock*) Well now, I guess we have time for a brief review. Arnold, can you see the IBM calendar all right?

Client: (*not very gaily*) Yes.

(*You can too, high on the rear wall of the working area, above the barbwire-topped façade, next to the clock. It's the same one that gave you the date, by means of a bright red light in square 31. Counselor presses a button and this light goes out. Now all squares are white. When he places a card in his machine, many squares are replaced by solid blue, some by diagonal red lines, while a very few remain blank white.*)

Counselor: (*taking extra-long, light pointer from beside window*) Let's first examine an average IBM. (*Wags pointer a few times over workers' heads, preparatory to leveling at calendar*) Arnold, this is your average family man, resides with five-six kids, mushes over here an average of six-seven times a day, at least twice on Sundays, has a new-model typewriter, a good briefcase, an outgoing personality. Now: (*pointer poised for pointing*) Note how he starts right out with a good strong volume—*one, two, three, four—solid, solid, solid, solid.* Five is a little weak: that was a Sunday. He bounces back: *Six, seven—solid, solid.* Eight, nine, ten, eleven—these are weak. He's mailed his overseas packages and is resting. *Now: twelve, thirteen, fourteen—solid—* he's mailing his Christmas cards. Fifteen weak, but bam! *sixteen solid, seventeen solid, eighteen solid, nineteen sol*—a little weak but almost solid, *twenty solid.* Twenty-one weak—he's received the bulk of his Christmas mail, he's followed Uncle Po's helpful hint and knows his correspondents, he's weeded old odd-balls annually and double-checked each new replacement, now he's past his peak and resting. *Twenty*-two weak, twenty-three weak. Twenty-four—a little flurry, he receives a few last-minute greetings and odd-ball packages. Now: Twenty-five white—he's at home, opening, sorting, counting, studying his Guide and resting. *Now, twenty-six solid*—he's sending his thankyou notes—*twenty-seven solid, twenty-eight solid, twenty-nine solid, thirty solid—thanks, thanks, thanks, thanks.* Thirty-one isn't in yet—we'll have it any minute. Meanwhile let's take a good look at what we have here, Arnold. First, *sequences, horizontal* (*pointing fast*): *One, two, three, four*—a sequence of four. *Now,* a sequence of two, a sequence of two, a sequence of three, a sequence of *four. Vertical*: a sequence of four, a sequence of two, no sequence, no sequence, a sequence of three if you count that flurry on twenty-four, no sequence, no sequence but *almost* a sequence of *three.* Now, *diagonals*: a diagonal three, a diagonal two, a diagonal two (*catch that one, inclining right?*), another diagonal two, a diagonal two, a *diagonal four,* once again if you count that twenty-four. Begin to get the picture, Arnold? (*Client nods head, looks toward clock, nods hard again. It's*

17:30. Business suddenly stops, Stamps—Sales & Service window slams. Client looks frantically toward Money Orders—Real Estate: still open. Although Client can't see, Clerk is looking his way anxiously. Counselor meanwhile is watching calendar.) Ah, here's thirty-one! *Solid,* Arnold! What does that give us now? A horizontal sequence of *five.* A vertical sequence of three if you count the twenty-four. A new diagonal *two* inclining right. Arnold, get the total picture now? (*Client nods hard, hard.*) Now then, with all our returns in let's take a quick look at a model lessee's card. (*Still pointing at calendar, with free hand places new card in machine.*) Now: (*chanting, pointing, fast, fast*) One is solid, *two is solid, three is solid, four solid, five solid, solid, solid, solid, solid,* all the way through twenty-three. Twenty-four is almost white—few last-minute greetings and odd-ball packages. Twenty-five is *white*—he's home and opening, sorting, counting, studying his Guide and resting. *Here* he goes—twenty-six *solid,* twenty-seven *solid,* twenty-eight *solid,* twenty-nine *solid,* thirty *solid,* thirty-one SOLID. (*Pauses briefly for breath and admiration.*) Now: *sequences, horizontal*—a *five,* a *seven,* a *seven,* a four, a *five. Verticals*—a four a four a five a five, a three a three a four. *Diagonals*—(*ecstatically*) a three a four a five a five, a five a two inclining right. A two a three a four, a four, a two a three a four a three a two inclining left! (*Overwhelmed, all but exhausted, lets pointer dip toward floor. Softly.*) Arnold?

Client: Sir?

Counselor: Lovely?

Client: Yes! Yes!

(*Counselor reluctantly removes card from machine, inserts another. Now the* IBM *calendar looks much as it did when empty. Counselor and Client examine it in silence for a moment, as do you. On closer examination, a few diagonal streaks are discernible.*)

Counselor: (*raises pointer wearily*) Recognize this one, Arnold?

Client: Sir?

Counselor: (*pointing, droning wearily*) Here you go—one is void, two is void, three is void, four is void. (*Lets pointer fall, turns to Client slowly.*) What happened, Arnold?

Client: (*hanging head*) I was waiting for my check.

Counselor: Ah yes. Here it is on five (*a hairline, which he traces with his pointer*). Six—a flurry. Your overseas packages, Arnold?

Client: (*recovering a little*) Yes, my Guidebook says . . .

Counselor: (*wearily intoning*) Seven is void, eight is void, nine void, void, void, void, thirteen a flurry, fourteen a flurry—your domestic mailing?

Client: Uncle Po . . .

Counselor: (*ever more wearily*) Fifteen void, sixteen void, seventeen void, void, void, void, void, void, void, twenty-four a flurry—last-minute greetings and odd-ball packages?

Client: No no, a love letter!

Counselor: (*visibly starting, pointer jumping*) Outgoing or incoming?

Client: Incoming!

Counselor: Registered?

Client: (*hanging*) No.

Counselor: (*letting pointer droop and turning forward slowly, not with weariness now but with severity*) Your Lessee's Guidebook warns. . . .

Client: (*quickly*) I know, I know.

Counselor: (*looks down hard at him, though smiling. Then returns to calendar*) Now then, where were we—twenty-four a flurry—*last-minute greetings and odd-ball packages.* Twenty . . . What's this, Arnold? *Twenty-five* a flurry, almost solid? (*Client, head hanging, nods.*) Well, Arnold? More last-minute greetings and odd-ball packages?

Client: (*weakly shaking head*) Postcards mostly.

Counselor: Postcards! Outgoing or incoming?

Client: Incoming.

Counselor: (*sarcastically*) Did they have love on them?

Client: Well . . . a little bit.

Counselor: (*with increasing sarcasm*) *All* of them?

Client: No no—one or two.

Counselor: Ah? Registered?

Client: (*groping*) Well, not love really. They promised it in letters following.

Counselor: In letters following? Did you receive them Arnold? (*Client hangs, unanswering. Counselor scans calendar rapidly.*) No you didn't receive them, Arnold, not if they were properly registered. Where's your solid? *If* you'd received a properly registered love letter, you'd have an automatic solid, would you not? Where is it? I don't see it. Where is it, Arnold? (*No comment of any kind. Counselor bears down hard with his big smile.*) Well, how long did you intend to wait, Arnold? How long did you expect your clerks to wait? (*Casts arm toward working area, which is empty of workers now, except for Clerk still waiting at his open window.*) Arnold?

Client: (*glances into working area, hangs head again*) I made my final mush after 1700, as Uncle Po suggests. I hoped—

Counselor: (*with great excitement, working up towards frenzy*) Hoped, Arnold! Your Post Office doesn't lease boxes on hope, Arnold! Hope's no collateral, Arnold! Hope won't pay the postage! Hope won't make the cancellation! (*Grabs up pointer, jabs it at calendar viciously.*) Look at all that mushing hope! *Twenty-six hope, twenty-seven hope, twenty-eight hope, twenty-nine hope, thirty*—what in Heaven is *that* (*a fine diagonal hairline which you cannot see, though Counselor traces it. Client slowly raises head to look, but quickly ducks down again. Counselor raps thirty furiously, breaking pointer.*) *What* is that, Arnold?

Client: (*hanging*) A solitaire.

Counselor: (*staring, big-eyed, subdued by astonishment and fractured pointer*) Arnold, Arnold. You tried to plug all that empty hope with a solitaire? Arnold, what does your Guidebook give you for a solitaire?

Client: (*hanging farther*) Half-credit.

Counselor: Right—double handling. No, Arnold, I'm afraid you wrote your own separation when you self-addressed that solitaire. I think we'll let your carrier carry your mail until you . . .

Client: (*head back and crying*) Please! No! Please! I'm outgoing! You can see that. Look at me! Look at me!

Counselor: (*shaking head, holding a very long paper up*) Arnold, have you seen our waiting list—all waiting for a doorside box? You yourself will be happier. This way you'll have full time to build your volume up, instead of all the time mushing over here with nothing save mushing hope. You'll learn not to waste your time hoping for love letters that never come . . .

Client: They'll come! They'll come!

Counselor: (*nodding impatiently*) Sure they will, Arnold, sure they will. Your lovers are only waiting to publish first, take advantage of our book rate.

Client: No! No! (*Looks wildly everywhere for help. Cannot see Clerk, who is very busy, writing, stamping, canceling, etc.*)

Counselor: Yes, Arnold, you'll have more time this way to study your Guidebook, catch up on your Uncle Po. You'll have time to know your correspondents, weed old odd-balls out, drop dead letterheads, double-check each replacement, bolster your volume up. You'll learn when to ante a money order, when to raise with an air mail, when to call with a card, when to bluff with a telegram. You'll get you on some steady dunning lists, get all dirty pictures forwarded to the General in time for posting on the wall. You'll have time to clean your typewriter, earn extra points for neatness—more time to use it too, thus expedite delivery and support the value of your handscript. And here's a little trick of mine, a little time-saver I worked out myself: for ready calculation, think of your slots not as Air Mail, Out of Town, Local, Newspapers, think of them as *points: 8, 5, 4, 2,* then multiply by weight in ounces, not forgetting your fractionals. You'll be surprised how much time that saves, how fast your volume mounts. Before you know it, in a year or two, you'll be back at this window with a big outgoing smile, ready to renegotiate!

Client: No! (*But Counselor is already moving off. Clerk can be seen ducking ahead of him, licking envelope, soon his hand can be seen at Client's gaping box.*)

Counselor: (*calling*) We'll just white-tag your box, Arnold, then you can sign your release and be on the mush. (*From box, in which a letter is visible*): You should dust your own box, you know.

Client: I do! I do!

Counselor: (*removing letter*) Arnold? What's this?

Client: Sir? (*Stands on tiptoe, leans as far as possible through window watching Counselor return.*)

Counselor: (*at window, a little withdrawn from it, examining letter closely, both sides and every corner. At last—*) It claims to have some.

Client: (*tensely*) Love? (*Counselor nods.*)

Client: Registered? (*Counselor nods.*)

Client: To me?

Counselor: (*nodding, studying*) It's not a solitaire. (*Hands letter to Client, who takes it almost reluctantly as though unwilling to believe. Counselor clears his throat, fusses behind counter.*) We'll have that calendar checked out, over the Holiday (*and, fussing*) I'm giving you an extension, Arnold. Your lease is probationary, you understand. If in a month's time your volume warrants, we'll discuss a contract then. You understand?

(*Client nods, nods, taking the* IBM *the Counselor offers him.*)

Counselor: (*sliding panel up*) Better hurry now! We've already put in fourteen minutes overtime!

(*Client moves nonetheless slowly, letter in one hand and* IBM *in other, to Money Orders—Real Estate where Clerk awaits him. Hands* IBM *slowly through window, as in a trance.*)

Clerk: Yes, *sir,* Mr. Prebble.

Client: (*removing nondescript wallet from hip pocket, extracting bills and handing them to clerk, softly*) Thank you.

Clerk: (*handing receipt, which Client tucks carefully in wallet*) Thank *you,* Mr. Prebble.

Client: (*remains at window fussing with wallet, pocketing it, pocketing letter, taking letter out again. Finally, once more*) Thank you (*and turns away*).

Clerk: (*underbreath*) Happy New Year, Mr. Prebble!

Client: (*same*) Happy New Year, Mr. Grey! (*Walks from window with a dazed-happy half-smile on his face. Seen head-on, he almost seems to wear a regular coat, for his sweater-jacket has a little apron or loincloth in the front. Suddenly realizes where he is heading, slices rightstage now with a steady outgoing gait. You hear the creak and whoosh of door for the last time. Clerk quietly closes window down. Lights in working area go out, except one night light. The four slots at left centerstage are thin cracks of light and, rightstage, Box 420-0560 is a dimly blinking, throbbing glow. Soon you come to realize that the lights will not go on again, your neighborhood branch has gone to sleep. You can find your way out in the dark.*)

—1963

Juncos and Jokers Wild

FIRST IT WAS THE JUNCOS. Our girls had lived only in the Southwest, where any bird seemed to have good brains enough to nest off the ground, if not in a Giant Saguaro at least in a creosote bush. Then to be taken to the dense, sky-high forests of northern Idaho and find there little birds living down on the ground, what to think of that? I too found it odd and exciting, as though in a bird heaven the juncos chose to be mice. At times I can almost see their point, in a man's heaven I myself might rather be a coyote, but in that forest I felt for the first time in my life entirely content with what I was. Dim grey ugly Cabin No. 3 is the nearest thing to a home of my own I have ever had. I don't mean the Northwest, put me out on a desert and I can form an easier attachment to any motel room, car, truck, bush or hole in the ground available, but that cabin and as far as you could see around it through the dark, lush jungle of evergreens and creeping vines, is the Place I love best. If it ever began to feel too close inside, I had only to walk through the backdoor of my forest for a few hundred yards to the huckleberry field and the space to be seen from there. And there was always time, any time. I hesitate to say such a thing, but it wrenches my heart, is wrenching it now, remembering all this. Of course I know now, if I tried to forget then, that such perfect isolation can never last. Within three months, things outside began to fall apart, the weekly trips to town became daily ones, to pick up the special delivery letters and the telegrams, make the long-distance phonecalls, soon the long-distance trips. Death, not satisfied with its own tragedy, left behind a tragic illness that extended a few months' suffering over years, gathering new victims along the way. What's worse, there seemed to be almost nothing working on the other side. Everything started in all that time has turned bitterly sour by now. But those are my problems, not the girls', not the forest's, not Cabin 3's, and not what I wanted to tell about. I often write to Mrs. Sam and she always answers me, mentioning that our cabin is available. If we ever get back up to Wallace, finally, I wonder if a new family of juncos will have settled in that abandoned nest. It was used for only two or three months, our first summer there.

We were in the habit of stopping on the path, a few feet from the nest, to peer into the greenery on our way by. God knows how many times a day the girls went that way. They knew when the first egg was laid, and the second, the third, and the fourth, and knew when three of them were hatched. We were taken out to look each time, though we usually had to take the girls' word for the news, what with the mother always sitting on top. Then one day the mother was gone and three huge baby juncos were in her nest crying for her. We watched her fly back in a hurry, sit all over their squirming heads. After that, once seen, their progress seemed all too slow. I by now deep in a novel, forgot about them for days at a time. It was only because the windowless storeroom where I wrote was apart from the rest of the cabin and nearest the nest, that one afternoon I was first to be aware of an unusual fuss. By the time I reached the path my wife and the girls had heard too. It was hard to tell what the trouble was. As though all three of the babies had suddenly at the same time learned how to fly and now with the parents were going, for juncos, wild. But then I realized there were only two birds in the air, the babies were here and there on the ground. Two were in the greenery near the nest, but the third was flopping toward the woodshed some thirty feet away. The frenzied parents were dividing their utterly distracted attention between the nest and the fleeing bird, crying him back to the nest, or so I thought. I wanted to help. After a short chase I had him in hand, held him cupped in darkness until he lay still. I placed him as gently as possible back in the nest, but almost as soon as I opened my hands he was flopping wildly away again. By now the noise and activity on the ground and in the air, had become almost unbearable. We ourselves stood paralyzed, wondering what to do. Not until minutes later did we see the snake, sliding off into the forest with a fluttering bird in his mouth. Amid the screaming outrage that followed I beat the snake to death with a stick, too late to save the bird. Nor were the other juncos reassured, they were more frantic than ever if possible. The two remaining babies were staggering in opposite directions through the underbrush, while the diving, shrieking parents followed them, driving them not toward the nest but fast, fast away from it. The girls tried to call them back. For a while we all followed at a distance, unable to think of any way to help. Then we went back to bury the snake, and the bird, trying to believe that was not the one I had put back in the nest. In the evening we could still hear one of the babies peeping far off in the woods, halfway to the huckleberry field, and in the dark it seemed that a hundred tired juncos were still crying in the trees.

In the quiet of the morning our youngest girl picked up all the feathers she could find around the nest, put them in a kitchen matchbox. That was the start of her first collection, though at the time she did not think of it as such. For a few days that seemed enough, but then she began picking other feathers off the ground and bushes, plucking her bed pillow, and following birds around. Now that the juncos were gone, bluejays were her favorites. She could not get as close to them, of course, but they were big and bright and she liked to watch them hop from branch to branch screaming at everything. And their feathers were easy to find. When she asked me if I thought feathers made a good collection, I with an eye to the cartrunk since we move around too much decided they made a lovely one. We all began to help, and she was using a shoebox soon. That was all right—my big mistake was mentioning her collection to a few people outside who I thought might find it interesting. By air mail came the painted turkey feathers from circuses and football games, which a little bending made shoebox-size, but then from the cities flew the peacock feathers and ostrich plumes. Too much, too much. Overnight, the whole collection went under the bed, behind the toys; a bluejay could drop his feathers now without causing a stir of any kind. One morning I picked up a particularly lovely one, but Lorraine said she was not collecting feathers anymore.

She planned to let them go, was only waiting for a windy day. She took them with her, as it turned out, when a few days later we were called down from breathless heaven by telegram.

It was in Wallace that Gale first tried collecting too, the next summer, when we finally returned in late July. She had accumulated a few postcards over the years, but it was a French postcard, family-style, that started her collecting seriously. Old and brown, it was the handsomest card I'd ever seen myself, quite aside from the flattery it bore. From an enthusiastic editor requesting a story for his imminent new magazine, it was sent to me in care of another editor, who took care of it for me a few months until he had time to write me one of his own. A fine start for Gale. She made herself a paper filing case, with compartments for half a dozen groups of states and that many continents, a lesson in geography. To hurry things up she began writing out, letters for cards, and I began to help. They began to come in, one by one at first, often with little notes on back. It didn't matter that most of them were aimed at Dad; Gale cherished them and packed them carefully each time we moved, finally in Pueblo bought herself a regular metal filing box, with twenty partitions and room for two hundred cards. When her French postcard friend sent her a whole parcel of those, plus twenty or thirty early American antiques, the modern collection went into Lorraine's shoebox overnight. The antiques enthralled us all, with the stories they told. Several were to and from a lively teenager named Geneva Powell, offering tantalizing glimpses of the life she led from about 1905–1910. Gale gave a section to her, but soon Geneva seemed to want the entire file for herself. The collection was by now excitingly out of control, when suddenly came another batch, this time carrying stamps advertised as already valuable up to 10¢ apiece, much more if the world should burn up and only Pueblo be left. A stunning new thought. What did it mean, what did it *mean*? What about bird feathers? What about hair? What about us? Overnight, not to the winds this time, but under the bed. The girls began to make their own postcards, hand painted and printed, with appropriate titles, and sent a few out. Where to send the rest? Where to look for something more than silence, a backhanded note to Your Dad, or a loaded batch? I find myself less and less able to advise them anymore. Should

I tell them: Don't collect, Don't ask, Go it alone, Travel light, Help less? I may have been on the track once years ago. At twelve I was collecting autographs of people I esteemed, but on a pack of playing cards, just fiftytwo cards and two jokers, in a little box.

—1963

Slayer of the Alien Gods

Now Slayer of the Alien Gods I hear him.
Sky through from one I hear him.
His voice sounds in every direction.
His voice sounds holy, divine.

FROM A NAVAJO SONG

HE TROTTED AS HE DID EVERYTHING ELSE, expertly: on the balls of the feet, the plump khaki thighs moving out evenly and rhythmically, out and out, out and out, like that, the arms relaxed, the wrists relaxed, even the fingers relaxed although they held the rolled map, held the firehat too swinging easily. But on his head the other hat, the round Indian Service hat, official, sat straight and firm and sweatless. A real Indian trot, anyone would say, he thought. The funny thing was that he had perfected all this in college, on an indoor wooden track.

Now the people were watching him out of their white wooden houses freshly painted, out of their bright new Ford pickup trucks, over their lovely white laundry so clean you could count the gnats on it, and to himself he did not deny that he had known they would watch, that he had wanted them to, that on leaving the radio room he had snatched up the firehat unnecessarily and purposefully. The trotting alone would not have been enough, though he did not often trot these days without good reason. So trotting he carried the firehat, easily, and to their questions he gave brief affirmative nods, for he was still breathing through his nose and he did not wish to spoil it. He wished to reach the house without panting. Yes, he nodded, yes, yes, yes.

He made it very nicely.

Inside he slammed the door, for effect and for Nancy, and removing his hat sank onto the Montgomery Ward chair. Now while he waited he mopped with a clean white handkerchief the drops of sweat forming, forming on his brow and on the nape of his neck. He took out another white handkerchief and polished his glasses against the light of the front window. Then he sat back and waited for his heart to quiet: he was altogether relaxed, yet his heart was still trotting. This was the only part of himself over which he had not perfect control. Oh, he could light a supervisor's cigarette in the wind without scorching it, he could look a ranger in the eyes and tell him a white lie without blinking, he could help a lady out of a pickup and she wouldn't look as though he were breaking her arm; only his heart denied him, thump, thump, thump, thump. Wild. Sometimes he could almost scream.

But now hearing Nancy he had no time to indulge a weakness, no wish to. When Nancy came to the kitchen door he was on his feet with his hat on straight, the other and the map ready in his hands, and he waited standing stiffly, officially almost, for her quick, disproportionate worry which would come not as an expression of the eyes but of all the body, all the taut, nervous body he loved. He waited for her worry, wanted it, but as soon as it appeared it enraged him, for it made her look almost old, "Sure, some of them are okay when they're young, but Jesus . . ." How many times he had overheard them express their opinion, how very hard he had tried to prove them wrong, giving her everything, the automatic washers, the nylon hairbrushes, the nightcreams, everything the others had. (How carefully in fact he had studied her smallboned slimness, her fine taut face, before he married.) And now even so at this moment she looked ten years older than she had any reason to look, she looked easily forty. Tonight she would use her nightcream if he had to hold her down on the bed and apply it himself, all bottles of it. "Relax," he said, and he saw her involuntarily tighten.

They stood thus for several seconds, she taut in her slimness, he in his stoutness, for it was in this way that they succeeded in communicating most deeply. For all the words they had, in the two languages, this was still the way they decided things: *You're not going, George . . . Nancy, oh yes I am.* So. All the rest was mere reconciliation. But it was all very necessary too, and he braced himself as she prepared to speak.

"What have you got that silly hat for?" she asked.

He did not look down at the firehat in his hand. He said, "Nat just radioed me."

"Ranger Duffy?"

"Yes, Nat," he said. "The Salitre Mesa fire is coming up. Nat wants a radio at Bluewater."

"He wants a radio at Bluewater!" As with all usually tolerant people, there was something almost childlike in her scorn. "That isn't any of our business, Bluewater. Why can't the Forest Service look after its own fires?"

"Nat called me, Nancy," he said when she had stopped. "Maybe someday I'll want to call him."

"You?"

He nodded.

"You call him?" she said, pretending to laugh. "He'd laugh."

He did not comment at once. He took off his glasses and held them six inches in front of his face, against the light of the window, studying them. "Why?" he asked.

"I'm sorry," she said, and she had come a step or two toward him, bringing herself too into his new perspective. "I'm sorry, but why does he always call you? He doesn't have to always call you."

He replaced his glasses, blinking slightly as he adjusted them.

"Do he, George? Do he?"

"*Does he.*" He did not try to keep the fury from his voice, never could. She had been to school, had even taught school, she knew better, yet she perversely reverted to these illiteracies in moments of excitement. He hated it in any of the people, but he hated it most in her because she was his wife and she knew better. "Does he what?" he asked more gently.

"Does he have to call you all the time?" Nancy asked. A little of the enthusiasm had gone out of Nancy's voice too. "Can't he call one of the supervisors once in a while?"

"I told you Nat wants a good radioman," he said, now

very weary of it and wanting to be gone, perhaps conserving himself a little too because he did not wish to be exhausted before he even began. "Nobody can understand supervisors on the radio, not even other supervisors."

"I remember the last time he wanted you to be a radioman," Nancy said. "You chopped trees."

He did not allow himself to wince at the memory of that day and night, but she knew. "My radio broke down that time," he said, adding a bit stiffly, "It won't happen again. I'm taking two radios."

"I don't want you to go," she said.

"All right." He tossed the firehat onto the Montgomery Ward chair. "You know what they say about us over there anyway," he said tossing the map down too. "They say we have to do everything in pairs. They say we even go to the . . ."

Nancy said, "George!" and ordinarily he would have smiled.

"They say we even go to the telephone in pairs," he said. "One to hold the receiver and the other to do the talking. It keeps us busy and it conserves our strength, they say."

He knew now that she would insist that he go, now that her function was served. Long ago they had found this the only way to deal with the others, the rangers and the supervisors, to look at everything together from both sides, at the same time. "Go on, then," she said, and he smiled. "Go on then."

Stopping to pick up his equipment he did it without flourish, for he did not really wish to upset her, not any more. "Estsanatlehi," he said softly. "Changing Woman."

She looked at him with a somewhat forced sullenness. It still disturbed her a little when he used the holy people in this way. Estsanatlehi above all, but it pleased her too because she knew that at such times he was pleased with himself, and with her. He smiled at her. "But you are," he said. And she was—for him at any rate—the holy one, the good wife and somehow, although not tiresomely, the good mother too, infinitely kind, infinitely patient . . . eternally beautiful. Yes, tonight there would be nightcream. "You really are," he said to her. "Goodbye." But at the door he turned quickly and came back to her, stooping to kiss her and at the same time pat her backside. It always surprised her just a little, so she giggled. It was a good custom.

Outside where the people were watching him he resumed at once his trotting as though he had only momentarily broken his stride. And now, briefly, he could answer their many questions because he did not have so far to run this time, to the pickup only, and after that there would be fifty miles of restful driving, and after that the radio. Yes, it was a forest fire. Yes, it was the lightning. Yes, it was the chain lightning. Yes, it was the wind, yes. No, it was over on Salitre Mesa, over by Mt. Taylor, over by Bluewater, over there. Yes, he and Jimmie Charlie were going over there. Yes, they had called for him, yes. Some of the people seemed disappointed; he could hear them mutter, feel them lose interest. Would they prefer to have the fire on the reservation? "Fire is fire," he said trotting. "It burns everybody, like the sun." Some of them nodded.

There around the pickup the people were gathered watching Jimmie fasten down the tarpaulin and smooth it with his hands carefully, as though this were a picnic they were going on and they did not wish to lose the wienies. He trotted up to Jimmie and the people made way for him. He threw the map and the firehat into the cab. He was fine, he was scarcely panting at all. "Jimmie, have we got everything? The pack radio, the canteens, the field glasses, the sleeping rolls?"

"You know it," Jimmie said. "And the chow."

"Good. Let's go." He jumped into the cab of the pickup and started the motor, gunning it a little while the radio warmed up. Then he picked up the radio speaker. He held the button down for precisely three seconds before checking the radio, both channels, with Manuel in the tower. He gunned the motor again and into the clear space ahead shot the pickup forward past the warehouse, past the radio tower, past the bright white houses and the clean rows of laundry, onto the road in high. The people were all watching and he was glad that he could not see Nancy watching him from the front window of their house. This way he did not have to wave goodbye to her like a little boy going off to school on the school bus.

He took the back road, the dirt road that led past Hosta Butte to the valley—already before him he could see the two sacred mountains aligned, Mt. Taylor, the blue mountain, looming in the distance, Hosta Butte, round-thing-sitting-on-another-round-thing, squatting in the foreground, one beautiful, one grotesque, both sacred—he took this way because it was shorter in miles and because on the way to a fire there was no good sense in getting caught in a traffic of tourists. The road had not been scraped since the spring thaw, it was fretted with deep, sun-baked ruts in some places, loamy in others; but this only called for more skill in driving, and he had ample of that. The pickup was of course performing beautifully, like everything he used, like himself. Through the windshield the low sun lay like a blanket on his chest, warming his blood, while from the south a fresh breeze passed through the open windows of the cab; together they comforted him. "It's a good day for a fire," he said.

"Good for a fire," Jimmie agreed. "What about fire fighters?"

"Don't worry about that," he said. "We'll be on the radio." He was glad to have Jimmie with him today. He usually was glad to have Jimmie with him, although he did not like to look at Jimmie any more than he had to. For in appearance Jimmie was almost a smaller replica of himself, with the same stoutness, the same stockiness, the same official clothes of course, even the same steelrimmed glasses, except that with Jimmie the glasses always seemed to reflect light, as did somehow Jimmie's face itself. He did not think that his own glasses reflected light, yet he was aware that others saw them in this way, as brothers, somewhat comical brothers, twins big and little. So he did not look at Jimmie as he said, "What they need over there is a good radioman, Nat said."

"You're getting famous," Jimmie said. "Maybe they'll make you a supervisor for this."

"Sure, in thirty or forty years," he said. "They give us that posthumously. It's cheaper that way."

"Just like the goddam army."

"That's right," he said, "just like the goddam army."

He always spoke of the army in this way to Jimmie, but

actually he thought of the army with almost a fondness, a fondness that increased steadily in proportion to his frustration in the Service. Quite aside from the college education, the radio training, the life insurance, the bonuses, the army had given him that intimate knowledge of the others which he needed in order to compete with them on their own terms, and which with his natural ability had enabled him to surpass them at their own talents. Secretly, very secretly, he wished that he had remained in the army, for in his present position he found himself stupidly thwarted. By now he should be a supervisor, like those others who had been in no longer than he, or at any rate a G-9 or 10 rather than still a G-4. In the army he might be a major by now: Major George Whiterock. To him it was the sweetest sound in the world, sweeter than supervisor. Whenever he thought of himself leaving the army he blamed it on his heart, although the army doctors had never been able to find anything at all the matter with his heart. They had called it his nerves. He did not like to think of himself as having nerves, and he laughed. "I feel fine," he said, and now he did not turn to look at Jimmie, for the pickup was stopped waiting for sheep. "Really fine."

"That's nice," Jimmie said, reflecting light.

At least he had got more out of it all than Jimmie, far more. Jimmie had come home from the army with nothing but the separation pay and the glib army talk, and he had gone right into the Service. He was still a G-3, and with his education he probably always would be. The answer to Jimmie was that he had no ambition, or at any rate what ambition he had was a false one, to be measured only by the Geiger counter which he carried at all times, even now, at his waist. Or where was it now? George had to raise his voice over the noise of the sheep: "What the hell are you doing with that thing?"

"Just testing," Jimmie said, leaning far out of the cab.

"You can't use it that way, squarehead," George said. "The steel in the truck throws it off."

"Who knows?" Jimmie said.

"I do."

Shrugging, Jimmie drew in his counter, slid it like some priceless fish into the case at his belt. "When I open my uranium company I'll hire you for radioman," he said. "I'll make you a G-10."

"Thanks." The sheep had passed, and now he did not have to look at Jimmie any more. He had his own idea about the uranium. It was the entrails of the first of the alien gods, the giant Yeitso, slain by the holy brothers, the two war gods, children of Changing Woman and of the Sun, slain while he drank from the lake, in this same valley they were going to now. Just as Cabezon Peak was Yeitso's head (tossed over Mt. Taylor by the elder brother, they say), just as the lava bed flowing southeast of Bluewater Lake was his blood, so the uranium found everywhere in this neighborhood was his entrails. But with a difference too. While his head was now dead and sightless, his blood long dry, the entrails were still alive, still wicked. Left to themselves the people would probably never have found them, yet today they spent half of their time testing the earth with their picks and their Geiger counters. The appalling thing to him was that they, who were so superstitious about so many more trivial things, should so casually take part in the most sinister sacrilege man had yet devised. For this, the secret fruit of his own imagination, was more sacred to him than the entire sacred legend itself. He had often thought of telling it to others. Yet he knew that it would do no good to tell it to the people. He knew that it was the others who ought to be told, but nobody ever listened to him except on the radio.

Ahead now to the left Hosta Butte squatted like a giant anthill scraped off at the top, and he looked for smoke toward Mt. Taylor but could see none: only the brooding sun, watching. Big fires were rare in this country, almost unheard of, but it could happen, it could happen. The forest was tinder dry, there was plenty of slash left on Salitre Mesa from past timber sales, there was the wind, there was the sun. Oh yes, it could happen, and if it was a good radioman they needed to get everyone working together, to co-ordinate the attack, they had him, he was ready. George pressed the accelerator pedal; it was already down to the floor. "When he stooped down to drink from the lake, one hand rested on Mt. Taylor and the other rested on Mt. Sedgwick, they say. His feet stretched as far as a man can walk between sunrise and noon, they say."

Jimmie turned from his window. "The fire is Yeitso?"

"In the morning the brothers went to the valley and waited for the giant to come and drink, they say."

Jimmie slapped George on the back. "You're Slayer of the Alien Gods," he said generously. "I'm Child of the Water."

"All right, younger brother."

"We've run away from Changing Woman to visit our father the Sun."

"Yes, brother."

"He gave us the armor and the lightning arrows, brother, and he shot us down to Mt. Taylor on a streak of lightning."

"You've got it, brother."

Jimmie leaned out the window, pointing ahead. "There it is, brother!" he shouted. "Do you see it now?"

"I see it, brother. I do see it." For rising over the crest of a hill they could see the smoke everywhere ahead now, black, burning in timber and slash, burning the air and making the morning suddenly hot, making the wind hot too, making the wind suddenly the fire's own hot breath. Shooting down into the valley, past Casamero, past Smith Lake, past Thoreau, toward Bluewater Lake, he knew that everywhere along the way the people were watching him from their hogans, from their houses, from their wagons and their battered trucks, but he did not look at them, he looked always ahead, joyfully. But when they reached the edge of the lake there was no longer anything to look ahead to, it was everywhere around them now, over them, in them, of them, and for perhaps the first time in his life he found himself breathing deeply and joyfully, for it seemed to him that this at last was the kind of air that he had been born to breathe.

He felt extraordinarily calm as he asked Jimmie to get out the pack set and hang out a good antenna in the event that any of the lookout were difficult to reach. His hands were not trembling at all as he spread the map out on the hood of the pickup, carefully weighted its rolled corners down. His heart was behaving beautifully. "Everything set, Jimmie?"

"All set, brother."

"Before he came down to drink he showed himself four

times on the mountains, they say," he said. "First he showed his head over the high hill in the east, they say," he said. Now he spoke calmly into the microphone: "Mt. Sedgwick, 833. Mt. Sedgwick, 833."

"Read you clearly, 833. Read you clearly."

Of course you do, George thought smiling, of course, of course you do. Quickly, expertly, he got Mt. Sedgwick's fire bearing, recorded it on the map, thanked Mt. Sedgwick, and signed off.

"Then he showed his head and chest over a hill in the south, they say," he said. He called El Morro and recorded the El Morro reading on the map as well. "Then he displayed his entire upper body over a hill in the west, they say," he said, and he called Mt. Powell.

It was not Mt. Powell that answered him. Already he had recognized the slow, tired voice of Ranger Duffy. It came again now, slowly.

"George, where the hell are you?"

"I'm at Bluewater Lake, Nat," George said as slowly but more distinctly. "Range 10 West, Township 12 North, Section 33, northeast corner. Everything is all set up here. I'm getting fine reception from all lookouts . . ."

"Look George, skip all that," Nat broke in. "Skip all that."

"Will you repeat that message? Will you please repeat that message? Over."

"I think everything's under control, George," Nat said, and his voice was quite distinct now. "We're backfiring the south line, that's what most of the smoke's about. I think everything will be okay, if the wind doesn't shift. We could sure use some more help on the line though—my men are about bushed. We could sure use you boys, George. Over."

George held the button down about five seconds, longer than necessary. "You won't need the radio at all then, Nat?"

"Not the way things look now, George. But leave the pickup there just in case. You can make it in to the line from there in about twenty minutes. If we need a radio we'll know where it is."

This time George let Ranger Duffy wait almost a minute before he spoke. "833, 10-7," he said. Then he turned the radio off and folded the map and returned it to the pickup. When he returned to Jimmie, Jimmie was winding the antenna into a coil. "And the fourth time," George said quietly, "Yeitso showed himself all the way down to the knees over Mt. Taylor in the north, they say. And then he descended the mountain and came over the lake where the brothers stood trembling, they say."

Jimmie was stowing the pack set carefully into the back of the pickup, but now he stopped and peered at George. His glasses reflected a bright and somehow hideous light. "The fire is Yeitso?" he asked.

George did not answer that. Instead he took a shovel from the back of the pickup and handed it to Jimmie. "Then the younger brother cut off the giant's scalp and took it home to Changing Woman, they say," he said. "Thereafter he was known as He Who Cuts Round, they say," he said.

He took another shovel out of the pickup. "Then to stop the flow of Yeitso's blood Slayer of the Alien Gods cut deep lines across the valley, they say," he said. "He did this so that Yeitso might not return to life," he said, "they say."

Clicking his heels Jimmie shouldered his shovel like a gun. George did the same with his; it clanked dully against his firehat. They marched away from the pickup in single file, in step, Jimmie in front, George a few steps behind. As Jimmie broke into a trot the leather case flapped at his waist uneasily, and trotting after him George imagined the needle inside secretly palpitating, like his own heart, to unspeakable terrors beneath and upon this earth.

—1955

The Spring of the Lamb

to you alone

ONE

It was wild the way she had turned him out of the warm and dark into the cold and grey. She had not, he could tell, tried at all to wait awhile. There were better times than this out here. He could tell that much. What about yesterday, when she had been jumping all over the sky. Had she ever paused for a moment to think of him? No, she had waited for this coldest night, then pushed him out.

Welcome, honey, to a bed of slush. Have some fresh frozen snow on top. Here, I'll add my big cold nose to that. Dimly he could make out her looming bulk amid the savage flakes. Now he could feel her slapping tongue, right in his face. Cold nose, warm tongue . . . but *rough.* Ah, now she relented a little bit, nuzzling his cheek with her brow or woolly upper nose. One might almost say she was being gentle with him. Perhaps she thought he was dying or dead, still born, was it? He tried to go limp—no st-i-f-f. He got butted in the balls for that. One could say she was mad at him. Oh well now—she had her big head under his belly now, was tossing him. She wanted him to stand up, and walk!

He who had never even used his legs except to kick her a little when she went too high in the sky. No doubt she remembered that. Well, she could forget it now, for he had no legs. He judged she had broken them yesterday leaping some silly wall or fence. They would not work—oh yes they would, a little bit. Enough to hold him up. It was true she never scraped even her wildest wall, or belly-flopped. What got you inside was her landing jolt. Little wonder he was weaving so much. His whole sense of equilibrium was shot, he hardly knew which end was up. Little wonder he sank down in a heap, after an upbringing like this.

He lay peering at her looming bulk. There now, old sport, what do you say about this? She did seem to peer back. Luxuriously he let his lids droop, and imagined himself home in the warm and the dark—at night. She wasn't a bad old thing when she stopped. She was built just about right. What! She was at him again, flipping him all over the slush. What, was she playing with him? What did she take him for, a frolicsome kid? He folded his front legs at the knees, landing on those when he could. Make sport out of that. She did—oomph—with the hard top of her crazy old head. He had had more than enough. This time he landed on all feet, took two steps away from her before he tripped over himself, skidded stiff-bellied in slush. When he looked back, she was rolling all over the place. With laughter, was that? No, what rolled were his eyes. She was coming at him again, probably straight. He got to his feet, stood watching her with rolling eyes in a weaving head. Hit that.

She caught him by surprise again. Bending over him, she let her tongue gently blot the snow and tears from his face. He closed his eyes, not just to protect them but to relish her licks. She nuzzled his cheek and his neck, and he nuzzled back. He could have sunk to his knees in the pure joy of her warmth. B-a-a-h!—she butted the face she had licked. M-a-a! he cried out. She hit him again. B-a-a-h! She hit his rear end. She wanted to go for a run!

No she didn't—she wanted to leap over a wall with him. He could see her looming nearby. No, it was not she but looming all right. She shied off from his side. He tried half-heartedly to follow, even as the long front legs, hands, lifted him up. B-a-a-h! M-a-a! he cried, twisting and kicking to get himself loose. The warm arms cradled him gently but firmly. He began to relax. The smooth face rubbed his cheek, the cool nose dug his neck. He nuzzled back. B-a-a-h! Maa, he murmured in sleep.

He awoke in a blanket in a box in a house. Bright light

burned his eyes. A big bare hand patted the blanket further over his face, dividing the light. The big smooth one loomed nearby on a box. M-a-a! B-a-a! she called back from just outside the white wall. A soft hand stroked the blanket on top of his head. B-a-a-h! Maa, he sighed back. He awoke high in the air and went stiff. The long arms held him safe, while the head burrowed into his neck. Uhn, uhn, uhn! went the mouth. Bbbbk! He relaxed under the warm kiss of the lips, looking up. The top of the head had some wool, but all tipped to one side. It might fall off! He studied the face. Those were interesting eyes, so full. He looked in as deep as he could. An arm did something behind him and cold sky hit his back. He tried to cuddle in deep. Bbbbk! kissed the lips, but the hands put him down in the slush. B-a-a-h! M-a-a! He turned, weaving, to watch her approach.

She didn't hit him for once. Circling, she sniffed. Now she nudged his rear end, and he looked up at the smiling face in the house. An arm waved at him. With his tail he flicked back, and staggered under a blow to the ribs. They were playing hard-head again. He took two steps toward the house, and she knocked him back six. This time he took three or four through the slush, and she only nudged. The slush burned bright white. The savage flakes lay in peace. The sky was all blue like those eyes, but not full. She herself was grey-white, rather brown at the tail. Together they "walked" all over the world in search of a wall.

She found one in sun, with a hump in its back. From here one could not see the house, only the sky and the slush. Ah, she lay down. At least they wouldn't be trying to jump over that wall for a while. He lay down at her side, looking up. She had a thin face. Why was she always moving her jaws so much? She looked very pleased with herself. Maybe she thought this was better than a house with a box. Welcome to a nice wall with a hump. Make yourself a nice little bed in the slush. Go blind in the bright. At least it did feel warm on the head and the back; the old girl gave off real heat at the side. It even seemed to be turning to warm water underneath. He looked up for a smile, or a look. She was too busy looking over the world, still quite pleased with herself. It seemed she had lots of jawing to do. He felt his lids droop. Let *her* look out. He let them droop shut, awaited a whack in the ribs. Maa? Baa. Ah, it seemed she was content to lay off for a bit. Let the little kid have some sleep. . . . What did she think he had been doing in that house? Maybe she thought he'd been up kissing all night.

T W O

He had dreamed of jumping, as usual, all over the sky. For most of the days since he had entered the light, the world had been half slush. Thus he jumped highest in sleep. Today the turf looked just right, mostly green, except near some of the walls. Hm, she knew about that whenever she chose where they would bed. She herself was already at work. Munch, munch. Up on his feet, he thought to have breakfast before he tried his first jump. On his way he only pranced, and dove under from some distance out. He wagged his wild thanks as she lowered herself. Oh, it was good, almost like the warm and the dark! For a little while they were almost that close. Then, whack, right in the ribs. She shook him off and moved away a few steps. Munch, munch. The old girl sure was chary of her milk. He measured her distance, but decided against. She sure liked her vegetables a lot. If she weren't so busy all the time, she might happen to note how the other mothers gave it out. M-a-a, look at that sport. Even that old mother of twins shows more patience than you. M-a-a, *look* at those tails! Aren't they thankful for the mother they've got! M-a-a! B-a-a-h! she said munching off.

He leapt, up, up! Look, ma. *Look.* He jolted down, and looked: another kiddo was in the sky, up, up, up, higher than anyone, hung there gracefully, gracefully—landed gracefully. On the feet. Maaa! He dove underneath, into the warm and the dim. She let him wag a minute before she whacked—ow, she sure made him pay for each drop. At least they weren't playing hardhead so much these days, unless he started it. He measured her, decided not. She was rubbing her back against a wall with a convenient jut. Wasn't she an itchy one though. Scratch, scratch. Munch, munch. He jumped up—up, hung almost gracefully and knew that she watched. He landed hard but on his feet. Maaa? She was too busy scratching her twisted old neck. Mm, ver-y in-ter-es-ting rock. Maybe one could see what was inside of it, if one looked close and hard enough. He looked hard at her rump, decided not just yet.

He turned to the banging door of the house, saw the tallness stand out. Up, up he leapt, up, and could feel himself watched. Hang gracefully, gracefully, and slowly drop. Now, near the house, the kiddo sailed, up, up, up . . . gracefully hung, slowly, slowly dropped to graceful feet while tallness watched. Over by the wall, the old girl studied rock. Keep looking, ma, I'll help you scratch. Lowering his head he aimed for her woolly ass, not stumbling once on the excellent turf. Whack! Didn't I land her one, he thought bouncing off. Quickly he scrambled up as she turned on him, and dashed ten feet away before she sent him flying in the sky, not so gracefully but higher than even the kiddo had been. And landed on his feet! Had the tallness seen that? The house was bare. Maaa? Munch, munch. Cough, cough. It seemed he had taken her mind off that itch.

He pranced and hopped a little bit, then wandered off. At the other end, the kiddo was wandering off. They met her in the middle and sniffed. The kiddo was bigger an ear or so, had a smiling face. Probably his mother had stopped to think of him one sunny day when his own old girl had been flying in sky. The kiddo leapt—up, up, up, while both mothers watched. He too leapt, hung almost beside the kiddo for an instant before the kiddo dropped. Now he too dropped, gracefully at the kiddo's side. Together they looked left and right: the one was watching while the other one munched. Together they pranced and leapt, their bodies wriggling higher and higher, their trails screwing them deeper and deeper into the sky, the kiddo above by no more than an ear. Now they were less graceful when they dropped; they ran wild circles to cover that up.

Others joined. They leapt up up up, he and the kiddo higher than all. Landing they ran wild circles, butted, pranced, leapt again wriggling into the sky, to the great excitement of barkers on the far side of the wall. Landing they raced, flew to the other end of the field and flew back. Then one last leap, up up up. Bark bark bark. Landing one by one, they pranced to a stop. He and the kiddo stopped in a head-to-head butt. In a far corner some others were jumping now, but all together and not quite so high. They did not wriggle their bodies so much or screw up their tails. They seemed to take care to land square on their feet. Up up—thump. The kiddo made a little square jump and everyone smiled. He did it again, holding his tail very stiff like a stick. Thump. Everyone shook with laughter inside. He did it again, crossing his eyes. Everyone rolled on the turf, and the kiddo pranced off.

Many mothers had watched. Even the old girl had stopped in mid-munch. Staggering to his feet he trotted over to her, dove underneath. She let him wag for a while before she shook off. Well, he did have to pee quite a lot. Was that milk? No, that was not. He went to a warm wall, flopped there eyeing up. The old girl was *loaded* with milk. Well, let her munch. Rest a while, dream up new jumps . . . He awoke dreaming of lunch. Yawning he noted she had not taken it far. He was on his feet taking aim when the kiddo pranced up. Together they raced and dove one on each side. Whack! The kiddo flew off. Hmm. He himself dove again, wagging: Nice Shot. She let him stay somewhat longer than usual before she shook free. Nearby, the kiddo was making spectacular leaps. The old girl paid him no heed. In fact she was wandering off. Under these interesting circumstances, was she good for a drop of dessert? Probably not. Well then, ma, let's jump. He ran at her and leapt high, high high—over her back. *Look,* ma. He came down almost gracefully on her far side. Maa? She acknowledged with a flick of her tail. The kiddo, nearby, acknowledged with a grin and a wink.

They pranced off, leaping spectacular leaps. Others joined in. It was starting all over again, even more than before. There were some newcomers this time. One was a high one whose prance was somehow more elegant, sedate. He went around sniffing, and they sniffed up at his half-smiling face. Suddenly with a toss of his head he pranced off, and they pranced to catch up. What, what? They followed him the length of the field in rather elegant style. From a corner this morning's square-jumpers watched. He tossed his head and they too joined in. All together they circled the field in a great prancing pack. They almost ran down an indignant old girl with two feet all tied up in a rope. Lurch, lurch. They grinned at one another as she hobbled all lop-footed off. The tall prancing one shook his head, but now the kiddo lurched off in lop-footed pursuit. Lurch, lurch, he went, prance, prance, lurch, lurch. She turned to look back and he lurched into her rump. Lowering her head, she took out after him all enraged and askew, would quickly have caught him if his own feet had been tied with real rope. As it was, whenever she drew near, he would prance, glancing at his audience cross-eyed. Some rolled on the turf, others stomped with their hoofs. The tall elegant one stood shaking his head; the square-jumpers trotted away in a group. Hey, kiddo, watch this. While the actor played lop-foot with the old thing, he himself sprang over her lopsided back.

Y-a-a-a-y! he heard, and soft hands clapped. A bare face smiled through a gate. Not really tall but quite straight, she reached a hand out to him. It held something round, which he sniffed. It didn't smell very good, but when her little pink mouth kissed the air he came close. She offered him the little red ball on the stick. Behind her a wagging barker drooled yes; he himself flicked his ears no. Putting her head through the gate, she offered her lips. He kissed, looking up. She had dreaming blue eyes, above a tiny white nose. Soft yellow grass hung over her head. Her bare hand patted his cheek. Whack! He was heading for a wall, wriggling hard to meet it with feet. Not quite. Thump. B-a-a-a-h! called the old girl, and turned away to munch. Ohhhh! A little hand went to its mouth at the gate. He flicked his tail reassuringly before he pranced off.

He followed the old girl, but forebore to sup. Flopping near a wall with a hump, he looked out, chin resting on feet. The old girl sure had a rough wool, did she not. It hung from her in long tatters and shreds. It was grey, except near her ass. She stared at him with a sour look on her face. Maybe she had eaten a bad grass, alas. Maybe she still thought of him as her little kid. Well, those days had pranced, let her mull over that . . . Hm, he had not well chosen his wall: it grew a very fast shade. He scrambled up and away, but a glance told she had seen. Well, it was late. He was now ready to sup, and he dove. Three wags later he lay with his surprised chin on the turf, watching the old girl munching off. She sure was one for a grudge. What, did she want him to hang on to her tatters for the rest of his life? Did she think he was too young to smooch with the girls? Well, think twice. . . . He sniffed a young grass near his mouth. Very fresh, and a beautiful green. He nibbled it off with his teeth. Soft. Sweet and sour at once. Its juice in his mouth tasted a little like milk. Up on his feet he nibbled another young one nearby. Same thing. He stood chewing the two, sucking their juice. Same. Very like milk. Hm, it seemed the old girl wasn't the only one in the world. Had she seen? Tucking the little wad in his cheek he aimed, fast and uphill, for one last leap over her back.

T H R E E

He awoke in some heat. It seemed the old girl had chosen a wrong wall last night. Well, no, she had chosen aright, if one did not oversleep. One had to remember that the world grew earlier and warmer each day. She herself was already up and eating, in shade. He trotted over to eat by her side, which she acknowledged with a flick of her ear. In shade the grass was still wet with night, though rather too thoroughly worked. More and more one had the sense of nibbling sloppy seconds or thirds. It began to seem there were more mouths than blades in this world. No doubt that was why they all mulled over so much, their faces turning loose-jawed and blank. He himself liked to chomp, suck juices, and prance. Sometimes he still dove, when the angle was just right.

She let him have a few drops before she shrugged off. Now the grass looked even less choice. Tatters and shreds. The world itself seemed over-heated and stale. Off in a corner stood the troops, munching in u-ni-son. Even some of his friends had gone slack. The elegant secretary still pranced regular rounds, but only he himself and the actor still leapt, and not very much. Right now the actor was up on a wall—nibbling a lone blade of grass! Cross-eyed of course. Now here came a little one, one he could never well remember for being one half of two twins. At least he still pranced like some kid. Together they pranced out in the sun, amongst the mulling mothers and young, past the square-munching troops, to the house. The twin wagged at the open door until tallness stepped out. Now the twin wagged happily and he himself flicked. Two bare hands patted their heads. They both wagged their thanks. B-a-a-a-h! Wheeling he fled, leaving the twin.

The old girl must have missed. When he turned to look, she was busy scratching her back on a wall with no jut. Good luck, enjoy your smooth rock, polish it up. He pranced among solemn munchers all intent on their work, ignored dirty looks. If he was breaking their grass, they were eating his turf. Still, he soon jumped onto a wall, leaving a few blades for lunch. Now the actor jumped up. Carefully they pranced on the rocks, met head-on in a soft butt. Staggering, all knock-kneed and cross-eyed, the actor thrashed air. He made a complete thrashing somersault before landing lightly on turf. Hey, kiddo, watch this! He jumped up from the wall and flipped twice, landed next to the actor with a four-legged jolt. Together they wheeled and jumped onto the wall, bowed to one another in a slow-motion butt.

B-a-a-a-h! The old girl wanted to get into the act. He turned just in time to evade her and fly off the far side. She plunged after, landed aloud on the hard-feeling place. Maa! They were playing in earnest today, he realized up in the air, and saw the actor jump in. She met the actor head-on before he hit ground, sent him so fast it was impossible to tell whether he had remembered to go cross-eyed or not. The actor hit the wall with a thump. She never liked any of his friends. Now here she came back. Maa! he yelped, scurrying up the black strip. She was close on his tail, all resolute and hard-nosed. Clomp, clomp. Whack! She tossed him to the wall as a little green house rushed by. Here came a big roaring yellow one all covered with doors. He was thrashing halfway up the wall, but she butted him down.

She had gone out of her mind. She liked this narrow black strip where the houses had sheared off all the grass. When he balked, she hard-nosed him on. Shriek, shriek, two little red ones sliced by. Up ahead, the green one was stopped next to a tree. Something was up in that tree, swinging on the straight wire branches with birds but no leaves. The birds flew away . . . He turned to fly too, but she butted him on. They clomped by there fast! Now she was ahead, clomping hard toward a hole in a wall on the other side of the strip. Through there he saw grass.

Inside, or outside, they jogged to a stop. She gave him a

quick glance before she started to munch. What, was she proud of this grass? It looked rather dry. No doubt she had a liking for brown. He sniffed some hay at her side and then dove. For a wonder, she let him hang on awhile. He wagged extreme thanks. In fact he was beginning to tire by the time she moved off. She seemed to know where they were going. They were hiking uphill on a well-beaten path. They were grazing its sides, not munching in circles as they did down below in the green. (There were a few young blades under the brown.) She seemed to know every hole in the walls. When there were none, she led the way over the top, sometimes over a fence, leaving great tatters of wool in the wires. At least they would be able to find their way back.

There were others grazing around, but somehow her way never led near them. She tended towards insects and birds. The birds up here were less friendly, flew away sooner, not in alarm but in mild surprise. They made him feel like a stranger—down below he had thought they were homeless. The flies here seemed thinner and faster, the butterflies no different at all. Maybe butterflies had no need for food and drink. Their heads were so small it was hard to tell what they were doing. What heads? Where were their bodies? Perhaps they were only big dizzy flowers. There were plenty of sober ones up here, growing very close to the ground. Somehow the little white ones made him thirsty. Maa? She had sunk down in the shade of a wall, mulling something she had probably brought with her. He had brought nothing. Flopping down beside her, he nibbled a grey hay not far from her nostrils. Maybe next time she would give him fair warning. . . .

He awoke to see her up on her feet, hitting the trail. The trail was becoming less clear, and less easy. Climbing was a little like climbing a wall, it was almost that steep and rocky. The kiddo would have been stumbling all over the place, crossing his eyes half in earnest. Up ahead was nothing but brightest blue sky. Was that the top, which they were aiming to jump over? Maybe this trail had been made by the birds. He himself could no longer distinguish it. Still the old girl plunged on as though making sense of a rockpile. She didn't slow down when they passed a lovely heap of white wool, washed by the sun and the rain. Nor take note of another, grey, rotten, buzzing with dissatisfied flies. She had big clomping plans of her own. Follow me, honey! This way, dear! And she clomped over the top, out of sight.

He expected to catch a glimpse of her on the far side, clomping down through the sky. Thus his pleased surprise at finding her almost level, munching green grass in the shade of a tree. A gentle breeze stirred her tatters. She glanced over at him, one brow somewhat arched. Sinking down beside her he flicked an ear in acknowledgment. She had after all known where she was going. From where he lay, the fresh grass stood at eye-level. In a world without walls, it spread out forever. The trees too were more free. They stood just where they wanted amid their used limbs and discarded tatters. The grass left them alone, there was room here for everyone. Flowers were fewer, but more themselves. Only the butterflies seemed no different. Perhaps some day he would understand those.

But never the old girl. She was off again, hustling through free grass in quest of some obstacle. Maybe somewhere ahead was another nice mountain all covered with hay, topped by a rockpile. He followed rather languidly, pausing often to browse the young blades. Look, ma, you missed one. You'll want some of those to mull on the way. But she had plans of her own, involving stunted trees and thorned vines in a thicket. No doubt she liked to scratch her back on a wild rose, but who could enjoy being snapped in the eye by a testy limp tip? It would have seemed prudent to leave the trees and the vines to fight it out among themselves, yet he plunged blindly after her—into cool belly-deep water, rushing by.

What was its hurry? It ran all over itself wanting to go somewhere. Where else was better? Dipping their heads they drank freely. This was brand-new water: cool, clear, and not woolly. He dipped again so deeply that it laughed in his eyes. Slow down, foolish water! With his nose he splashed some onto a rock, where it rested. He would have enjoyed this contest a while longer, but the old girl was splashing up onto the far bank, legs wet to the bone, tatters dripping. He splashed after her. At least on this side there was less thicket—great spreading trees overhead prevented. The old girl signalled a halt. They stood in an island of sunshine, shaking themselves. Suddenly she went stiff, and he began shaking in earnest.

It was something shaggy in the deep shade of a tree. The old girl took a step forward on one skinny leg, and he followed closely. Now he could see that it had two long, curved bones on the top of a head tilted high and backward, nostrils sniffing. The old girl took more dainty steps toward the motionless creature, and he followed beneath her. They stopped at the edge of its shade, but not in it. Still the hard-boned one made no move, except in the nostrils. Kiddo would not have looked cross-eyed at that one. His watchful face was unsmiling. His body was thick and sturdy like a tree trunk. His shaggy wool was the color of deep shade. They stood peering in at him for what seemed, in the circumstances, far too long. In fact the shade was beginning to grow over them. He nudged the old girl's belly, and for once she heeded him. Together they stepped back into the sun and moved away from there, slowly.

None too soon, it looked, either. By the time they had hiked a couple of miles to some lonely grass, night was beginning to fall. She looked back over her shoulder into the dimness they had come from. Munching he glanced at her with one brow arched high. She feigned not to see. Soon she stretched out along the side of a very old and resting tree without limbs, without skin. He sank down at her side. She lay her head near on the grass and he cuddled in close. The stars were resting nearby above, though not on their sides. Maybe those were sleeping butterflies. This looked like a promising place to study such things.

F O U R

Most often these days he was up before the old girl. Here in the open on the top, it was seldom too warm, she could sleep late in her wool. She no longer woke them up with her cough. He himself was up to seek sun. Too, the night made him hungry. Eating made him hungry. Of course, there wasn't a great deal else to do, unless play with the water. If he were down below with his friends, there might still be some prancing and leaping. The old girl was no good at all in that way, once having jumped up her mountain. Certainly old hard-horn wasn't much sport.

He never moved, if you chanced to catch sight of him. Not counting nostrils. It could give you the shivers. He always seemed to be studying something serious. It could make you feel bad, when you stopped to think how little headway you had made with your own studies.

The old girl was up now and munching, which was comforting. Grass was beautiful, not just necessary. Together they studied it in big munching circles. It seemed they could eat forever without once repeating. No one else liked it except the rabbits. The birds only looked in it. It was hard to say about the ants. Grass liked sun but not water. It made its own juice. Well, it did like a little water on a cool morning like this. Hm. Odd that it didn't like water in the heat. Let old hard-thinker mull that for a while. Grass was beautiful. Mull that.

They did have one thing they did. Around midday, after a dip in the water, they went back to the edge of the top. There they lay down in the sun, in good grass for nibbling without standing up. They didn't lie on the very edge itself, but far enough back that they could see only sky. Thus they considered their world. The occasional noise from below, the rumble or pound, was softened by sky. Somehow it made their world turn even quieter than before. Those below did have one way of carrying their noise up through the sky, in big houses with wings that beat on the ears. There was no good in running from such a noise, for it was already going away fast. Soon quiet absorbed it, the sky sealed it up. Loud as it had been, it was a forgettable noise. The fact was that sound never stayed long unless the sky itself chose so. Sometimes it rained, and twice it hailed. Hail hurt not only the ears but the head and the eyes. Hm, could that be what those hard horns were for?

Thinking of the thinker, there he loomed now. He was wagging his tail in the sun! No, he was thrashing it, high and stiff. *Good Lord,* did he want to play hardhead? They got to their feet, hopefully not for that purpose. He nudged the old girl's side, made ready to run, but froze at the low baaa of an authoritative voice. Quietly answering, the old girl moved away a few steps. She was showing good sense, doing exactly what he had meant to suggest by his nudge. But now as he looked to follow, she hit him a terrible blow in the ribs. He landed on his back looking up at that thrashing tail overhead, and squirmed out from under. Crouching low to the ground, he turned in time to see the old girl fly over the edge. He quickly looked back. Jerking his head toward the woods, hard-horn took off fast through the shade of a tree. He himself paused for hardly an instant before he jumped over the edge. Barking was the nearest sound in the air, coming up. Ah, her way was not down but around the side of the steep, and he followed her rattling path through the rocks. Stumbling and leaping by turns, he was able to keep her in sight. Barking was still coming up. He plunged on, hoping to keep enough sky behind him to swallow that hysterical noise.

What finally made him despair was knowing by the desperation of her own stumbling and leaping that she too could hear barking, that far ahead of him. He knew equally well that as long as she continued to run he would never catch up with her. His dry lungs were burning, his heart throbbing. He would have given two days of grass for one dip in the water. Barking was nearer. Now she was beginning to admit the hopelessness too. Veering uphill, she drove hard for a point of rock jutting out. There she stopped and looked back. With mixed fear and relief he followed her on. Here sky dropped straight down on three sides, a jumpy breeze whipped around them. He found his head weaving as it had that first day on earth. Standing at her side in the center, as close as possible without pushing, he concentrated his attention on the oncoming barker. Closing in, the barker was frantic. He leapt to within breath of their faces, his open jaws drooling. It was a clear choice he gave them. They could jump over the edge or stand there forever listening to his hysterical yapping. Probably the old girl would have held out longer but for the barker's foul-smelling mouth. At this dizzy height on the top of a rock one could not bear it.

She plunged forward, he beside her, the barker close on their heels. At least the barker was quieter, only spurring them on with an occasional yipping reminder. Three days of grass for one good fart, but he could not muster it. They were descending that same imaginary trail through the rockpile. There to one side lay two little heaps of white wool, washed by the sun and the rain. Now down below they could see dabs of grey-white on the move, urged by a different barker, who was himself urged by the tall one. Soft baas of complaint rolled uphill. The old girl slowed, while he himself pushed forward. She had never liked any of his friends, had she. They soon joined the crowd, with the encouragement of their barker, and he himself dashed ahead of the old girl the last hundred yards. Guess who was the first one he spotted. Trust the actor to be caught capering in the most far-out fields! Seeing him, the actor reversed direction, staggered uphill all knock-kneed and lopsided. Where ya been, pal, he was asking: been looking everywhere for ya, cross-eyed of course. They met in a head-on butt that made up for some missed ones. The tall one took notice. Staggering to their feet they pranced to the head of the line. Just like old times. Here joined some others. Up ahead were the twins, still smaller than anyone, and still prancing. Soon they were all running together.

It was like old times, only better. The twins promised plenty of action, while the actor promised parties. There was a new kind of grass the twins had uncovered; the actor had discovered something new you did with the girls. You could do it with the boys too, his manner suggested. In fact he became quite persistent. Easy there, kiddo, let's stick to hardhead. Behind them some engineers discussed a road they were building, two-laned, divided. Not far from home they were joined by the troops, square-marching in unison. In the narrow strip the little green house was parked, something was up climbing in the wire-limbed tree. At the gate the elegant secretary waited to welcome them.

Ducking past the half-smiling face, he and the actor trotted about looking things over. Home had not changed much. The grass had grown back well in general. The walls had grown only in places. Home had grown smaller. The birds seemed rather less friendly, as though surprised by this visit. Come to think of it, those up on top had grown gracious. As for the water, thirsty as he was he could not look at it while drinking. Even the actor crossed his eyes and spat woolly. He must have enjoyed their water up near the top, while it was still hurrying. Thinking of the top, where had the old girl gone off to. For the most part, mothers and young still stuck together. He didn't even remember what the actor's mother looked like, if he had one. Motherless both, they trotted together like lifelong buddies in search of some fun. Aha, cats can be chased.

Now the actor staggered forward all knock-kneed and twisted, attracting an audience. He was imitating a lop-footed old thing with her legs all tied up in a rope. Lurch, lurch she went. Lurch, lurch, prance, went the actor, looking cross-eyed back over his shoulder for laughter. Just like old times. Watch this, kiddo, he called, but did not dash forward. It was the old girl herself who lurched to a high corner, stood very straight looking down at them. Some winked and giggled, while the actor lurched back and forth in front of her. Ignoring them, she began to chomp grass voraciously. When she needed a new patch, she did not lurch but jumped to it. Hm, was she saving up for something? He too started eating, just in case, and not to seem to be standing around not enjoying the action. Soon the audience scattered. They ate on alone together. When darkness fell, she let herself flop to the ground in a bundle of tatters and legs. He did not smile, but he slept well clear of her tie-strings.

F I V E

It seemed the actor too had acquired the habit of awakening early. Their munching paths met soon after daybreak. In little or no time they were joined by one of the twin agents, who wanted them to meet someone. Imagine their disappointment when it turned out to be only the secretary. They pranced around a little before parting. Don't worry, gang, plenty of action later, promised the agent trotting off. They stopped to watch the troops practice square-meal, or munch-by-the-numbers. In the very center of the field the engineers discussed a freeway they were planning, with limited access. Should they use the wire-limbed tree or go underground? They already had technicians calculating the placement of signs. Prancing high, he and the actor traced a zigzag path for the cross-eyed. Girls eyed them while eating. They eyed the actor especially, but a few eyed himself longer, more thoughtfully. Where were their mothers?

Even the old girl had been awake rather early, munching from a half-lying position. Now, no sign of her. It would have been hard to miss her with her tie-strings. Over behind the house was mixed baaing. The near gate stood open. Soon a pair of odd ones came through, all red, white and naked, one running, one lurching. Even the actor stood momentarily frozen in wonder. Then he glanced rather stark-eyed over his shoulder before he lurched forward reeling. The old girl paid him no attention, but that did not prevent his audience. Whose audience? Here I am, son! Wait for me, honey! All eyes were on her as she lurched toward him. There wasn't so much to her, once rid of her tatters. He felt quite bulky by comparison. It was the smear of red paint on her ass that made her really outstanding. Someone had thought to cover all that brown for her. Someone had put a new tag in her right ear, all perky and freshly numbered. Really this was becoming more than a little too much. Did he himself ask for these kinds of problems, special attentions?

Hm, others were coming through the machine now, stripped, smeared, and numbered, and not just the old ladies. They were also marking the girls. Was that the only way they knew for telling the girls from the boys? Oddly, they did not strip the girls, who now began to look bigger than their mothers. In fact they looked as though they were tending the victims of pernicious anaemia, some with their legs tied together for support. . . .

The old girl had had it. Lowering her head, she made a lurching charge at a wall. He thought at first she intended to hard-head it, but at the last minute she lurched up its side. Hanging there, she let her two free legs scratch for purchase. Now she lurched upward a rock farther. Again her feet scratched, catching hold just in time to save her from sliding all the way down. This time she lurched up to the edge of the top, hung there for a moment like a bug trying to decide whether to roll backward or forward. What she did was fling herself up onto her back and flip sidewise, and over. Her marveling audience paid her hushed tribute. Baaah! she replied, clomping on pavement. Leaping high he followed her over.

Charging side by side they almost made it to the end of the black strip before being caught by a barker. But for her rope they might have been well up that high wall to the sky. As it was, the barker divided them. For a wonder, it was not the old girl he was after this time. Maa? Heading downhill he could feel snapping teeth at his heels. The gate was closed—he flew over the wall. Almost as soon as he hit the ground tallness was on him, a rope in his hands. Soft hands tied fast, brushed themselves off with what looked like small claps. As tallness moved away he lurched to his feet. He still had two free ones if he could figure them out. That one—that one and not that one—not that one but that one. . . .

It did no good to leap! Every prance turned into a lurch. He was hopelessly lopfooted. His ass wandered sidewise. Entirely his was the audience. Some were not smiling, he noted, and none very broadly. Even the actor eyed him almost soberly, one might almost say compassionately, though he did surely stagger a little as he prance-pranced away. Over by the gate, tallness was offering a little treat of rye or alfalfa. There stood all the troops and the groups wagging in unison. One of the twins was baaing him to join them. Paying no heed, he munched grass in a corner.

Baaa?

Maaa! He looked up at the wall her low voice had come over. Baaa, she said softly. Lowering his head he made a lurching rush at the wall, at the last moment sprang up it. There he hung on its side, all feet scratching. Which were the free ones? Ah, he found one, thrust it deep in a crack just in time to prevent himself sliding down again. Baaa, she encouraged. He hung there a moment before kicking, with the one foot, all his body one rock further up. Again all feet scratched, seeking everywhere for purchase. None could find it! He could not move upward, nor hang scratching forever. Maaaa! he cried out sliding backward.

Baaaa! she called back almost angrily. He sprang at the wall again, but this time he was too near it. Lurching back a few feet, he lowered his head. Even as he did so, a detail of troops moved in from behind him. Taking positions between himself and the wall, two of them gently but firmly nudged him backward. Baaah! Maaaa? he called out to her, and heard her clomping lopfooted away on the pavement. Under the prodding of the troops he sank to the ground, to avoid them. They soon trotted off. Now here came that same twin with a stranger who wanted to meet him. This was the manager himself, the twin's manner implied. Big and hard-horned, he glanced down judiciously. Ah, roped are you. He nodded reassuringly, and he and the twin trotted off busily. Lots of people to see today!

Over at the gate stood the little straight yellow one, with a wagging barker beside her. He thought to go over there but gave up after a lurch or two. He did lie looking up at her for a long time though, returning, or trying to return, the look that she offered him. Her interesting eyes were as blue as the sky, and full now, so full that sad water flowed out of them.

S I X

They spent the night on the two sides of a wall, from time to time calling over to one another. He himself did not call with much hope, mainly for comfort. But with morning the old girl grew more insistent. Finally he clambered to his feet and lurched at that wall again. He sprang hard, he did try to. Stiff and sore from lying all cross-legged, he did not gain even yesterday's rock. On his side at the foot of the wall, he sighed over to her. She seemed to understand, for she called back almost softly. Now at the gate was an unusual activity. Was that another little treat they were getting?

It was the same agent who came for him. The little fellow trotted patiently beside him, not to aggravate his lurching. If this was another treat the barkers were in on it. Ah, it was the boys they were wanting; they were separating and aligning them. The red-backed girls stood aside eyeing them curiously. The red-backed mothers called nervously. The troops fell smartly into formation. The engineers huddled together planning a way to get into the alfalfa larder. The secretary sniffed the scene with one lifted eyebrow before trotting red-backed away toward the mothers.

Now the gate was open and they were all marching ("marching"!) through it. They were moving around the house to another house, where stood the tallness. He had something bright in his hands, which were covered with leather. That was a thin bottle with a nail on the end of it. Maybe now they would get their red spots and numbers. No, they were getting jabbed in the back but not spotted. Jabbed they leapt forward all stiff-legged, then stumbled here and there rather loosely. Was that the agent receiving his reprieve now? No, that was his sister—he was leaping away from her in rigid surprise to land with the others, loose-legged and tipsy. Even the actor seemed to be moving very slowly, and the salesmen. And the redacteurs. The steady technicians were discussing how best to spread the alfalfa once the engineers had got it. Nearby stood the manager making sure that each got his fair share of the jabbing. Would he remember his promise? What promise? Say that you dig it, the manager urged. He shook his head No. Lurching past the producer, nudged on by the lawyers, he put his last hope in the tallness. He sprang away from the jabbing so stiffly that his knees crossed in his tie-strings, landing him awry on his back in the milling.

Pinned there he peered up through the staggering legs and the tails. The sky was pure blue and empty—except for someone high in a tree with wire branches, looking down watching. He hung by a strap so that he could lean over backward. The boys were entering the house one at a time now. Though they approached the door in double file, they entered in a single line. Maybe they were finally to get their red spots and numbers. No, a shrieked maaing said otherwise. The sound seemed to stick to the foul-smelling air. He tried to get to his feet but was unable. A butterfly flitted over him dizzily. Try to pin that down! Stunned boys were peeing. Good Lord, there went the actor! His cry stunned the air.

Now for the poet, he heard, and leather hands threw him into the house. Grey wool with legs was piled high in a corner. A smaller pile lay in another. The sickening air was unbreathable. The tallness held a long blade in his hands, high over. Stiff on the floor he stared up at it. Was this the end of everything then? No more leaping, no more prancing, no more wagging? Maa . . . ?

Wasn't there next year? Maybe, but the old girl wouldn't be climbing her mountain forever. They were getting on to her ways. Maaaa! High high high high went the head!

—1970–1971

HAD

To the Sun

IT WAS A GOOD JOB. He had made it of clover grass, interlaced with violet, a formula of his own. He had lined it well with down. No string. She had helped of course. Had. Over the years they had developed a way of aerating the down which he had not seen used before, though no doubt by now some others were copying. It was accomplished by collecting the down in a leeward place, fluttering it with the wings. Then they hung it on a rosebush for several days. They transferred it to the tree house on a sunny afternoon, piece by piece. Had, all had. He had always thought to show the children exactly how it was done, so that the way would not be lost or misconstrued, but the children were always gone so soon. He was shivering.

He had built the house, as always, in a position to receive the early sun, when it was free. It was not today. It would have shown directly on him, where he was now; he knew that by years of memory of the house with the viewpoint of his nook. This was mere pastime, for the sun was busy reading cloud today. Sun read backwards; otherwise cloud would have moved east to west. Hm, down south it often did. That meant sun could read frontwards and backwards too. Come to think of it, so could he. It only depended on where he was. It was going to rain.

He had not regained strength enough yet to fly. Oh, he could flap a little, like some poor chicken, but he still had his shivering pride. He preferred not to try the air unless he could dive and skim and wheel and glide. Besides, it hurt. Thus he was not eating well. How she would have been after him! Guiltily he stretched his neck to look after his nook. This was an important outpost for ants, quite luckily, though he favored a wingèd fare. Occasionally a careless one did present itself to him. Yesterday there had been a wasp: his twittering stomach remembered that. Surely he had not fed it so many seeds since his first year. His childhood had been an unusual one. His parents had died young, in a cat—he'd been "brought up" by a daffodil. He still went back to visit now and then, in season. Not this year, not this year.

Usually he built within view of one. How to account for this year's oversight? Ah, now he remembered, last year there had been three of them, right over there. The people in the people house had scraped that earth, a great swath of it, and now they were watering it, in the rain. He could see the first big cloud drops bouncing off those noisy, spitting ones. He could see the laughing, flashing parts of them as they broke, splashing earth. He was thirsty. Well, he could hop. Hopping he tried to catch a cloud drop, on the fly, but missed. Thirstily he pecked one of the spitted ones, from a tulip leaf. Thank you, little drop.

What a commotion he must have caused in *that* universe! He looked around at the many others before he chose. Some were larger than our own, he guessed, others not, but all quite large enough. Not everyone understood. It was a matter of perspective mainly, and dimension. Down and up are separate dimensions, in balance: up too big for down to see, down too big for up. The beings in those other universes were, from their perspective, as large as we. Some of them were probably even of people size, and elephant. Hell, 83′ wouldn't surprise him much. From their viewpoint they had almost infinite space, though like us they probably tended to crowd some parts of it. Was there, in that one, say, a world as beautiful as ours? Had been. Well, yes, perhaps, to them. On the other hand, quite possibly we had been given the most beautiful one. He always thought to point this out to the children when they grew up. *Had.*

He pecked a few more before he hopped back. Now he was shivering totally. Around the edges of his blinking eyes he could see his feathers dance. It was not only the cold and wet. That one had come back again. It sat hunched on a branch above his house, jabbering with that wife. One would think it owned the place. Ah, a person from the house had noticed too. He had come out to douse his water. He could not reach the tree house, but he tossed a stick toward it. Cursing, that one took off, leaving that wife gleaming evilly down on them. These people had good hearts, even if they weren't around when you needed them. That had been very early, of course, even he had scarcely begun his bout with morning. They had shown up, finally, in time to give them a proper burial. Had. Most of them. Here one came now with her fingersful of seed again. That was nice. He made a show of pecking a few for her. Didn't they know about wasps? Perhaps they were vegetarians, like the finch. Or, he had heard the robin complain that they were digging up his worms. He would have to remember to ask the chickens about that. They knew them best.

When she had gone, he ate an ant. Now his shivers turned into a coughing fit. In his house he would have been all right. Violet is for the chest, and he had always had a touch of weakness there. It also calmed the nerves, and sharpened the wit. White clover is for Promise. Had, had. With that one scared off awhile, he took this opportunity to explore the battlefield. It was better than just sitting around all day with shivers and coughs. He set them hopping toward the tree, under that wife's steely glint. It did not take him long to find whom he was looking for, in a clump of grass people were too high and straight to see beneath. Although this was one of the unwounded ones, he was already beginning to disappear. His bare skin was grey and sere. The hardest part was, he could hear him cheeping still. He was too young to understand. He wanted to come back and eat. It's all right, you can go now, he called to it, you can go now . . . No, he could not understand.

Nor in truth could he, on his side. Had it been a squirrel to blame, it would have been easier. Or a cat. Yes, even a cat. Cats were an inherited evil, in him at least. Squirrels were squirrels. Sometimes he could almost smile to see them frisk. But these other monstrosities, he had heard of their happening, of course, and seen, but somehow he had always relegated them to nightmare that one could awaken from. Had. He shivered slowly back toward his nook, beyond sound of cheeps.

En route he spied a daffodil. Two or three of them.

Perhaps now he remembered seeing them there, before. The people had moved them to the other side of their house. It was a thing they liked to do. They wished to offer the daffodil a better view? In that case, all those trees they felled were intended to improve the view of those left standing? They cut them up into naked strips in order to give those others a lesson in anatomy? Not very likely. No, they used the flowers and trees, just as he used the grasses and wasps. The important variance was in the realm of quantity.

These were lovely wilting ones, like his "old man." He had seldom seen them young, even though he was an early bird. Had been. Too early for once. Had he been a little later, that one and wife might have chosen another house. He remembered after he had repelled their first attack they had checked out the older housing, but they had returned when they found that everyplace else was in need of work. There was no such thing as patent anymore: they steal it out from under you while it's pending. No more property rights. Ask any daffodil.

They did in fact have a lovely view, of sky, and hill, and "his" tree house. He found it comforting to sit with them awhile. He seemed to shiver less. Perhaps it was all the arms they had that steadied him. Daffodils seemed so certain of themselves, as though even in the rain they were reflecting sun. Perhaps they were directly related to the sun, perhaps only in the way that he himself was related to them. Finally he had to admit that he was getting soaking wet. The old feathers weren't as warm as they once had been. He felt a ball of coldness in his chest, only his head was warm, or fever hot. I hope you don't mind if I head back to the nook, he said. They smiled, and he hopped back.

It wasn't until he had returned that he understood what they had said. The world is a subdivision of the sun. It was their job to keep an eye on things in springtime, when so much was happening. Once everything was well along, they could sleep. That was their view at least. Meanwhile that one was back. He had brought some crazyseed with him, was sharing it with that wife. He could tell by the heightened pitch of their gibberish. Meanwhile the blood was pounding in his head. His head rolled in such dizzy waves that he could scarcely keep his feet. He steadied himself by concentrating on the seeds the person had given him. If that was down, then this was up. Everything else was poppling. Soon he had himself well enough under control that he could pick up a seed without pecking his feet. The eating helped. Had the person known barley was good for dizziness? Now his gently weaving head could concentrate on a fly nearby. Fly, come in out of the rain in me. This fly was a friendly one, and wet. Tasty too, though hardly wasp.

He had dropped in just in time. The rain was letting up, or rather the sun was letting the rain stay up. Poking for an ant, he came upon an unusual thing, to him. It had one straight, sharp leg, and a tiny head. Probably a people thing, a smaller model of that spoke they used to hang the finch house up. He placed it on a little ledge he had. Now nook was house. Those others were having a brawl in that other one. Something about "family" life. Now that one took off, probably in quest of more crazyseed. It did not dive nor wheel nor glide, but shot. A wingèd ass hole was what it was. What colored wings? Glint? The dark feathers became only a glint of the real light, nothing was their own. Bleck. The black, the white, the blue, the yellow, yes, the black and white and blue and green and violet, like himself, but not the bleck.

A person came out to turn that water on again. Now he could watch the last cloud drops break up on it, as he had the first. The person did not have to toss a stick, but she did come back with fingersful for him again. He had scarcely made a dent in her earlier heap. He pecked but once. Maybe she would get the idea to save some of her seeds for a later month. She had nice toe nails, shiny pink. Could sing well too, her red lips pursed up, sing better than that other one. That one quawked. Not now at least. The sun came out.

When she had gone, he hopped into its light, to feel its warmth. He tried to fluff his drooping feathers out, and turned his wounded wing to warm. It really hurt. The sun felt love. Did it feel love for that one, who could stab a lovely lady in the breast, then eat her eyes? Could murder six helpless babies, feed half of them to that wife? Then proudly quawk! He had done his best. He really had. Even flopping like a chicken on one wing he had fought and fought, had fought until the people came out to throw their sticks. Then he had reeled out to his wife beneath the tree, had done what he could to comfort her while he watched their burial. *Had.*

He was reeling now, in the sun. He tried to tell himself that he had slipped. Not good signs, in either case. How she would have scolded him! The next morning he had watched her burial from his nook, with no one to comfort now. No one ever again. All had. Now there was only he and the sun. His feathers drank of it, while they could, for it was hurrying on its way. It had work to do, clouds to read on the other side. It had family everywhere. A chill wind moved in to take up the space left behind by sun's departing warmth. Wind fanned his fevered head deliciously, fanned too the ball of cold he carried in his chest, increasing it. It was that ball that he reeled around. He "hopped" back to his nook.

That one was back, and he and that wife were having fits. Grass is one thing, poppy quite another. He could not make their raving gibberish out, except that it was foul. He called the people, just for the hell of it. They always came out promptly in the afternoon. This time they both threw sticks, and one of them hit that wife on the glinty head, right on the lethal yellow beak. He knew it did not hurt her—those ones were made of steel, or snake—but did she quawk! That one too! Together they flew raving, quawking off.

Sweet silence replaced their quawks. The people stood for a minute drinking it too. Then they spoke comfortingly to him and turned their water off. When they had gone inside, he felt quite refreshed. A wild impulse had come to him. He tested his wounded wing. It did flap, askew. Wouldn't she have been angry with him! He flapped both wings and they lifted him. Flopping back to his nook, he prepared himself for a running start. He was off like a fart. He had never imagined air could hurt so much. He seemed to be tearing his way through it, inch by inch. It was like clawing his way through a net, but he did. With one last flapping, flopping lunge he was seated on the edge of "his" house.

He had done a good job of it, now befouled. After catching his breath he tried to brush some of the garbage out, with little success. She had six eggs. He did not touch them, but drove the little spike in among them, head end first. Turning around, he dove, tumbled, back to his nook.

He was *reeling* now, and bleeding. Was he having a fit, himself? His shivers were having a fit. Dark was falling. The first stars were out, and reeling too. His head revolved with them. He took one last peck of seed, while he could see. Soon he would be pecking star seeds . . . "One world at a time." Suicide is pointless—time cares for itself. Let's see what comes next. What may be, what *might* have been—the past tense now is almost lost. It was time to get a fix on the universe. The suns were surrogates. God stationed them out there to look after us. He couldn't be everywhere at once. Have you any idea how many universes there are out here! He did check his suns out from time to time, made sure they were doing the job. If one slipped up he was retired at once. Watch it there, old Sun-daddy! His spinning head could picture them huddled around the fireplace in the Old Suns Home. He had to smile. Above, in the spinning dark, a clean star smiled too. He knew, he knew. Now closer to home there was a piercing quawk. That wife had reached the end of her quawking patience; she cursed that one most vilely. He had to laugh. Above, that star laughed too. He knew. What was a little space between friends? (Save The Ozone, It's Your Roadside) He was shivering convulsively now. The worlds are ends. Lovely roads. This one had been so. He had really enjoyed the view. Now let me out

—1977

Market Research

SHE WAS SETTING THERE, or he was, the pigeon, nested in the snow warmed and already receded from whatever body heat still felt. The surprisingly large black eyes looked up at me in their own surprise, not, I felt, surprise at me, at surprise itself. Pigeons take to fear not easily. I paused, having never seen this on a city street before, on my way to work. I had a quota to fill, 8 more Pepsi Light ladies to interview, on the Sunday after Christmas '81, if you can believe it, anyone. I did pause quite a while, and talked to her, not most quietly amid the falling snow, but almost; the noise of the passing cars on this her last, this busy one way street, seemed to quiet too. She could still raise her head, and peck at air a little bit, to habit, not effect; her body was forever there, we knew—or until tomorrow's snowplow slapped softly through. University Avenue.

Her feathers on her back seemed like split apart, left and right, by the icy atmosphere, or no, by death itself, we felt. I could have walked back three blocks, after twenty three, to the Red Owl store, and bought her what, some cereal? Post Toasties? A final gesture her huge frozen eyes might still have been just clear enough to see? I could have. I was on my way to find 8 Pepsi ladies on this very Sunday of a holiday, and they believed in that, oh did they not. Sugar free. Non fattening. Lemony. My bosslady termed it an emergency. New York had called to remonstrate: one of her interviewers had got his quota not door-to-door but by telephone! They had double checked on that. Well, hello, here's a Kleenex for your nose, I bet it's cold out there. One offered coffee too, with banana bread, fresh homemade and warmly caloried. I enjoyed it, I must note.

—1982

"A Story I Wasn't Supposed to Tell"

IT WAS A CRYSTAL DAY, late afternoon. I was coming from the south side. They boarded in dead center town, from all the leaning loafers therearound. He got on first, to ask the driver. Yes, the driver said; so he beckoned her encouragement. She pushed up off the squalid concrete bench, with real difficulty it seemed to me, and gained the bus without his hesitating help. They sat on the sidewise-facing seat, on the left side, close behind the driver. I was seated just two seats back, on the right, from where I could see them entirely, so entirely clearly. She was thin and tall, about five feet nine or ten, still red-haired and fading freckled, in flowered dress and long-worn leather sandals. He was the same height, in boots, his hair still full and black, to match his trim mustache and sideburns. He had placed her travelling bag on the floor beside her, on her right side, so that they could sit close together. She was laughing. The driver was half outside his bus and leaning forward, banging his picture window with the one hand, cranking his reluctant destination with the other. Finally the thing came unstuck, and she applauded. She was lovely, like a necessarily coarsened sister to my first wife, a little younger, though in pain far older. She held his hand in her very long thin fingers, on the seat, not her near thigh, between them. They had been to high school. (Two words) They had not graduated, but, oh, had they not been there, in Oklahoma? He laughed and applauded with her, an accompaniment, not a leading. Given her encouragement, he laughed a little louder. I tried to too. Meanwhile he watched her bag for her. How many times, in how many cafes and bars and bowling alleys, not her beauty parlors, had he done so! She *pressed* his hand with her lovely fingers. I had to leave the bus before them. They had just twelve more blocks to go before Municipal.

—1986

The Timing Chain

To her parents, without whom this book would not have been possible, with lasting thanks

IT WAS THE TIMING CHAIN. First he'd heard, was when they were stopped for construction on OH 101. The stout little replaced heart had skipped a beat. Just one. Perhaps she had earlier mentioned it. Certainly there had been other construction then, how else with the face of the Rockies undergoing the annual lift, the occasional, more radical prosthesis too of course; Chumly had got involved in one. He remembered peering back around the You-All for him—for them. She had had to be pushed by the grinning orange boys, had she not said? He himself, having been waved on ahead, had sat teetering, waitering on a glory edge, head tilted back, licking the sweet Teton snows of July.

Not here, this month. Here in August the sky glowed deep brown, the exhausted macadam sweat rocks. Along the once roadside the black and tan Holsteins coughed. On the once road itself, thirty or forty vehicles coughed back, their quivering tail-holes dripping disbelief. Was this their reward for observing the guidelines of emission control? Many drivers and passengers had already flung themselves out. Mostly they glared grimly ahead, wagging their chins on their craning necks. A few looked at the lineup behind, there was more satisfaction in that. They had seen the signs back yonder a mile or so—CAUTION FLAGMAN AHEAD—most of them had, but who among them could have foreseen all this? Maybe the pessimist, the mentally ill? No, it would need a real loser, the kind you see now and then parked alongside the road with a steaming radiator and two flat tires, a twelve-pack of Schlitz and no jack. Well, for better or worse, here came an orange one now.

This was no grinning boy, not this close to the Coast, on a job like this. This daddy had been around awhile. Rather small, spare, he knew to approach a vehicle slowly, right hand close to hip, left wagging his octagonal decoy turned to STOP, eyes squinting in a welcoming, anticipatory way. To those on their feet he spoke from a few paces out, a little to the driver's left, where he could squint at any passengers on the other side, shield himself from any in back. Seated drivers he approached very close, propped an elbow on the window sill, stuck his big red nose in. Those with air conditioning he encouraged to lower all the way. Let them get a little sniff of how it was out here eight to ten hours a shift. These he liked to talk to at length, from time to time sucking a little ruptured grin with his lips. One could imagine those drivers grimacing narrowly back. When at last he eased off, they waved narrowly as they reactivated the window up. Without air conditioning, all Chumly's windows were down flat; Lou sat quite still as the man narrowly approached.

"Well howdy there! A Nopel eh? '68?"

"Howdy!" Lou nodded yes. "How's it look up ahead?"

"Shouldn't be long now." He propped his left elbow on the sill, held his peeling red-and-pink beak in the shade a few inches from Lou's face. He had a bristly, sunburnt moustache that served as a little broom to sweep the flakes of dead skin away from his mouth as he talked. "The earthmover's moving again."

"Doing a little repair, are they?"

"No no. Twouldn't be worth it." He waggled his beak, from SLOW side to STOP. "That one's all wore out. We're cuttin up north this time." He swung his head to squint north. "See that big ol barn up yonder—we'll slice through that. We'll have to scatter the cows a little bit." He, they, chuckled at that. "Don't worry bout that powerline—we'll clip her off nice and short and run her underground."

"And that Indian mound?"

"Now that's our biggest hump." He tucked up the beak of his baseball cap to wipe his brow with the back of his fist, mop sweat with dust. Now he stuck his beaks inside again, squinted at Lou. "A few years back we use to clean those up nice and flat. That was before the Historics took over—they've got them on a 99-year lease. They're not saying what they want to do with them." He made a little grimace, mopping his mouth. "That's Preservation you know. Don't you worry—we'll cut her close. We'll still save you lots of miles. Save you lots of time too. You'll scarce have to drive atall to crosstate this time next year."

"You'll have it done that soon?"

"*Sooner.*" He was spraying now, and he mopped again. "I just figured you wouldn't be back through until about this time. You outlanders don't like to travel this way in wintertime—most of you don't." He squinted at Lou from three inches out. "Right?"

"I guess you're right at that."

When Lou nodded, he withdrew his beak in time to save some loose skin. "I thought. Well don't you worry—we'll haver already for you. Won't even have to change the signs. We'll just change the m's to km's and let em roll. That's Conservation right?"

"The route will be that much shorter?"

"She'll be close alright." He swung to squint at that barn again. "Conservation like that you can afford to cheat a little bit," he assured, swinging back again. "None of it's exact anyway. Take that marker there." He turned to point, squint hard at it. "Well it *use* to be there," he said, turning to squint hard at Lou. "Vandals took it I guess. It would fit easy in any trunk—even a Nopel like this." He sucked a ruptured grin, and then relaxed. "Who knows maybe those Historics took a lease on that too. Anyway it weren't anywhere near exact. None of them is. *None* of them are. It was supposed to mark the 41st parallel—well we're at 41-03 if you read your survey map. It's all shifting everyyears anyway you understand. You can blame the North Pole for that—it's out of Highway hands. Do you happen to have a Nextra cigarette?" He bent forward to sniff Lou's shirt, then back so Lou could safely bring out the pack. "Generics eh? Them's not a bad smoke. I usually smoke Marbrows myself. I usually have a pack—left it home I guess. I see your dashlight don't work—never saw a Nopel did. Happen to have a match?" Lou was preparing to light him up, but he would have none of that. He took the matchbook in his dusty talons, showed Lou how to light a cigarette without singeing broom or beak. He lit Lou up too. Now he tucked the book in his shirt while blowing out a great cloud of smoke. He waited for the air to clear. "Not a bad smoke at that," he said. "How much you pay for that?"

"$5.99 a carton, I think, plus tax."

"Here in *State*?"

"No, Colorado."

"I was going to *say*," he said, and almost did, but a horn beeped in back of him and he turned to that. "You're late man," he called, and waved his cigarette. "Be right over. Scuse me," he said to Lou, bowing to him, or to extricate. "Got to get my mail. We always let him through no matter what—unless sometimes when it snows that much. That's Dependability right?" He planted his decoy in the macadam dust at his feet, STOP side to the rear, and without it stumbled on a rock. "Hey Red," he called to the front. "Get a couple of rockhounds over here!"

The mailman had a nose like his, one side of it; he was cheerful though. He was drinking coffee from a paper cup. He offered some to his rural route patron, who stuck his head inside the truck and took a swig. Apparently it was passing hot, for he swung out just in time to lay some dust, bespittle the THIS TRUCK MAKES FREQUENT STOPS stenciled in cuneiform on the side. They laughed at that, and now they settled down to smoke and chat and sip. Some fifteen minutes later the good-natured mailman put his thermos in his thermos clip, and the full-beaked one waved his mail goodbye to him. They laughed again, mailman tucked his roach in his visor clip, patron flipped Lou's butt at the FREQUENT sign and they laughed again. OH US POST SERVICE—INDEPENDENT DELIVERY.

Now he was heading on back. He seemed to be heading for a Pinto up ahead, it being sway-backed, rock-pocked, and red, until his eye happened to catch the glint of his SLOW design; he veered toward that. He was moving more determinedly now, in a kind of knock-kneed, sway-backed ballet, a norange improvisation, backhanding his mail at the flies, booting rocks at the cows, brooming little pellets of burnt skin to the winds, missing almost everything—there being no wind—but his knees. He only stopped when he knocked into his STOP/SLOW decoy. Squinting kindly at it, he set it aright. He did not lean inside this time, for he needed both his hands to shuffle his mail.

"Mostly coupons," he said, and shuffled again. "Well that's better than draft cards, right? They've learned better than that. They only register us now. That's fair enough. They register cars. They got to do that to tell them apart. Now if they want to register guns—that'll open up a new can of noodles right? It's them Historics that's behind it you understand. They want to get control of *everything*. Once they do that there's no end to it," he said, turning to squint at the Indian mound. He turned back to Lou. "Right?"

"Right!" Lou said.

He nodded his mollified beak. "Here. Here's one for you," he said, plucking a coupon from his pack and proffering it to Lou. "I've got a hundred of those."

"Well, thanks!" Hopewell's Old Time Lip Balm and Nose Guard. Recells the Membranes While It Repels the Sunbeams.

"Hold onto that. Any trouble up ahead show it to the flagger at the other end. He'll know. He'll let you through. Cash it when you get to town. It's real good stuff when you're out in the sun." He squinted at the brown cloud above. "You'll want to wipe it off when you go indoors. It glows. When you go down on the little lady at night she'll tell you to turn off the light right?"

"Right!"

Nodding, pocketing his mail, he squinted toward the rear. There were at least fifty vehicles that one could make out back there, God and the Historics knew how many more. "Shouldn't be long now," he said, taking up his decoy.

"Take it easy!"

"You know it," he said, easing toward a two-story mobile ranch house. Lou watched in Chumly's mirror until he got his boot and his beak in the door.

There was a sign still standing up ahead to one side, and restless pedals and feet had begun to entangle. At least Lou's were still useful. Taking the keys, just in case, he walked on the left side of the once road with a hopeful eye out for traffic. To his chagrin, the cows watched him with unwarranted optimism. When he sought to wave them away, to the perhaps greener, cleaner grass around the Indian mound, they surged toward him. Shrugging, he stopped to read the sign from a distance, and they mooed at him. What, did they want him to read to them? They could see he had nothing to feed them—or could they? Lou read clearly: FOR LOCAL WEATHER AND TRAVEL INFORMATION DIAL YOUR RADIO TO 86.8 AM 103 PM. That seemed momentarily to satisfy them, their mooing had become polite coughing, but when he returned to tell Chumly they followed. Back in the car they could hear them lowing and Louing him. Guiltily he munched the peanuts and raisins she had sent along with him. The beer was up to him, and he had none.

Working lighter or no, Chumly had a sweet radio, though not PM. They tried 86.8, to be safe. Sure enough: ". . . pressure 30.20 humidity 67 percent . . . winds from the south at 1 miles per hour . . . temperature 94 beautiful degrees at 3.21 PM August 27 Year of Our Lord (*static*) . . . Now a word from our sponsor Rob's Heat and Air located just one mile south of Lower Sadusky at Four Corners . . . Rob . . ." Rob's sudden bark came on loud enough to drown out all Louing: "*Folks!* Now that summer's coming, it's time to think about *air* conditioning! Come in *today* and let us show you what we have to offer! We can install an all-new all-weather Sea Breeze Conditioner—equipped with *windblades* guaranteed for life or a whole bunch of months whichever come first—for only a fraction of the current resale value of your car truck or RV as determined by the FVC (some sub-compacts and motorcycles excluded) all in less than twenty-four hours! Courtesy vehicles provided, many with air-conditioning! Don't be sorry *tomorrow*—steam on into Rob's today and Sea Breeze *away* . . . !"

Lou had to turn it off, for up ahead the line was moving now and Chumly would want to concentrate. As would he, for he had heard the stout little heart skip a beat when they had stopped, and there were no grinning boys nearby, today, far less a beautiful girl to inspire them. No immediate need, as it turned out—Chumly started purring at once, to the cows' lament. Lou blew a kiss to them, though little likelihood of its reaching that far with so little wind. In the mirror he could see the full-beaked one a few vehicles back, flailing encouragement; from here his design sign seemed to sway GLOW / GLOW / *GLOW*. Easing into gear, they followed slowly east on a senile, degraded road that soon would see a young one slicing north. Lou flashed his coupon at the peel-nosed flagger, who waved him on.

They were moving more freely now, but over the past hour Chumly was averaging .5 mpg, scarce 2% of potential. If the choice was theirs, they would stop at a gas station soon. Lower Sadusky *had* come through loud, and in fact very soon they passed a sign for it partially defaced by vandals but not yet claimed by the Historics: Low Sad sky Pop. 2,000,000. At Four Corners they turned north, passing up Rob's Heat and Air and monster towtruck, despite ominous warnings of further construction. At least, this close to town, they did have a grinning boy in blinding red instead of orange. He stood at the base of a great earthen mound, freshly heaped, non-Indian, and used his big right hand for decoy.

"Howdy. Going into town?"

"I hope to!"

"You can make it. Just stomp er hard and keep on stomping!"

"Which way is best from here?"

"Straight on up and over."

"Oho."

"It'll be easier tomorrow, they'll have that overpass graded. But even so, most people make it."

"Ah, that's an overpass."

"Had to fill the underpass, it was always flooding. There's no need for it nowadays. That was built when there were still lots of locos."

"Ah, those are tracks up there."

"Lots of them. You don't have to worry though, the train doesn't come through till four or so."

Chumly had no more working clock than lighter, his working fuel gauge read E or so: instinct said it was time to stomp, not smalltalk. "Well, here goes," he said.

The grinning boy gave Chumly a big-handed shove to get them started. "There you go. They'll be putting up a look-and-listen sign tomorrow, to be safe," he called. "I'll take care of that from here. Just keep on st . . ."

Lou stomped out the jolly voice. Probably he wouldn't have heard it anyway, for Chumly was not purring now but growling. He attacked that mound voraciously, chewing deeply into it, spitting out the chunks that man had muddied. He seemed to welcome Lou's encouragement, but did he really need it? Almost Lou had become a backseat driver, for halfway to the top the mound became all but vertical. Chumly met the challenge bravely, taking it in leaps now, cat-like, cougar—by the time they hit the brow he was dancing, a gazelle-like prancing, high in the air and shaking big globs of earth from his face, eyes, and underside, his spinning legs treading air quite joyfully. It was only landing on those rails that slowed him, or changed his direction to a sidewise slithering, for his lately sharpened claws were mudclogged. No animus toward Firestone—he took this too in stride, one might say in slide, instinctively, duck-like, to that other brow and over, almost face-forward. It was hard to say exactly, for they were flying, again more duck- than bird-like. What he did, half-way to the bottom, was touch down tail-first, to slow them, and to some extent to steer them. He did this two or three times in quick succession, so that by the time they landed on all fours nearby the other flagger, things were well under control, and on their way by Lou glimpsed a grin well muddied.

Chumly now again was purring, heading straight for an O-Hi-O station. All tracks seemed to lead there, except those few leading to vehicles piled here and there before that. Most had made it. What mattered now was what became of those that hadn't: the place had the look of fortress. The SELF SERVE signs were tightly chained to gas pumps, the hoses themselves were armored. These were outsentries. The door to the gloomy citadel itself bore crude signs in black: NO CHECKS NO CREDIT CARDS NO CREDIT NO CHANGE AFTER 4 PM NO ADMITTANCE. Inside there was no sign of life or movement, though the one dim ceiling light did cast on the far wall a giant, immobile shadow, perhaps of a man lurking someplace invisible. Lou had a sense of being watched as he uncradled the battered nozzle, dipped it carefully into Chumly's battered gas tank. When he squeezed the lever nothing happened. This pump was still owed $11 for 7 gallons. That didn't seem quite right, at an announced price of $1.40, but he had no time to check those figures before they vanished. Now the pump was pumping eagerly, flowing over shoes and tire and parapet. Lou released the lever, depressed the cradle, to no result that he could notice, even when he joggled. When the thing cut off at $11, Chumly's tank had received perhaps 2 gallons or a quarter of the total. Amid all the fumes and flashing numbers, it was hard to figure.

Ah, here came the attendant now, perhaps with explanation. His stride did not bespeak apology. It turned out that outline on the wall had been no shadow. This knight would have seemed too tall at seven feet, had his span not been eleven. Firmly encased in steel-blue uniform from gleaming sollerets to visor, he had an arrant air about him. He had his sleeves rolled up—or the biceps prevented other.

"Well, that was cooling!" Lou said by way of greeting, smiling.

The equine face showed no reaction, but the gloved hand grasped the nozzle and crunched the cradle. The other hand indicated the nextmost pump, the $1.80 Super.

"No, that's fine!" Lou said, tightening Chumly's cap with one hand while reaching for his ill-favored wallet with the other. "That's plenty!" he assured, counting eleven dollars onto the outstretched palm from a roll of twelve.

If the man had no language, he had numbers. He shoved the bills inside his breastplate and strode back across the rampart to the stronghold, his flashlight and his tasses clinking.

They left without delay, rid of all obligation to keep track of the kilometrage. At the exit-entrance they did stop to look and listen. That mound was quaking now with wailing loco. Little wonder, when one took into account the hundred cowards it towed behind it, all rasping and overfreighted. Tomorrow was another day, and this one was replete with earthmoving anguish. They weren't at all where they intended, but they were more than halfway to Boston. After twenty forsaken hours, it was time to rest those hard-gained, sloshing gallons. There was real pavement here, the kind you could clean your claws on. The crossed eyes cleared too a little. It was the Motel Calumet that won them, its ten or twelve small shacks each separate, duly whitewashed grey, probably twenty springtimes, its lean-to carports long since turned to shade-laden bowers which only partly hid the old tires, tobacco tins, and broken shovels waiting to be rediscovered by the migrant kids of summer.

This was not a classic pre-war camp, somehow still existent, but the updated post-war image of, which he and his families had learned so well to live within together, most often. It had the little windows of yesteryear, just large enough to peer out but not let too much heat or cold through, and had the dented stovepipes out back for yearsround ventilation. These too they renewed in springtime, by banging them with broomsticks. The fresh-air nut could always leave the door ajar, doors too, if he could free the one to the smothered carport. There would not be much to see through either. A bold sign out front still boasted MODERN. A smaller, fresher one pointed out the OFFICE. Chumly purred as they parked beside that, for he was being sprayed by a manic lawn sprinkler that had lost its bearings.

The girl inside was definitely postwar, by at least a decade, with a blonde and bursting welcome. "Well, howdy, traveler," she said. "Warm enough out there for you?"

"Just about!"

"Well, I should say," she said, smiling at him, blowing stray, translucent hair away from her lips and cheeks in mock discomfort. Her voice was throatier than one could have expected, given the girl-like slenderness of her neck and shoulders; perhaps the cause was the air conditioning which fluttered her hair even more gently than her own breath did, fluttered the delicate cloth of her sleeveless blouse where it touched her cleanly shaven, or hairless, armpits, fluttered the perky unbuttoned collar above the loosely buttoned shirtfront that veiled the small but self-assured breasts delicately protruding. She was the kind whose arms alone were enough to tell one that every inch of her was perfect, down to the slender pink toes that were extensions of the exquisite ankles. He could not actually see that far, for the low counter between them—only to the slender hips just where they began their gentle rounding. "What can I do for you?" she asked, gently.

"Have you a vacant room for the night?"

"Oh, I think so," she smiling said, reaching for her file box. "How many are in the party?"

He did not immediately answer, but when she glanced up felt his forefinger rise to a fortyfive degree angle, then perhaps to fifty. His smile joined hers in some surprise, for he was not sure what he'd intended. "I'm alone," he said, watching the finger lower.

Nodding, she smiled down at the file cards. "I'll give you

Number 8," she said, and glanced up as though for his approval. "How does $10 plus tax sound?"

"It sounds like a bargain."

"The sink leaks," she said, "but it has TV and air conditioning."

"Wonderful!"

"We just took the motel over in July," she said, sliding a registration card his way, offering the pen beside it. "So far we only have air conditioning in half our units—we have to take things slowly."

"That sounds like real progress," he said, filling out the card. "How do you like the motel business?"

"I love it. It's exciting." A glance at her eyes affirmed that. "I used to spend my evenings alone watching television—my husband works the 'swing' shift." Her dainty eyebrows arched. "That's what he calls it. Now something's always happening."

"I imagine," he said, taking a twenty from a recess in his wallet.

"My husband comes home at six for supper," she said, counting change into his hand, and then the key. "We'll try to get the leak fixed for you."

"Oh, that's all right . . ."

"If that doesn't work, I'll bring around some extra toweling."

"Many thanks," he said, pocketing his wallet, and at the door he noticed the key to Number 8 was waving.

He did not have the heart to disturb Chumly for so short a purely selfish journey, left him bathing with a playful honeysuckle while he went over to look at his own accommodations. His key unlocked the warped door quite easily, once he had determined which of the four locks belonged to it: the topmost, brightest one. The eras of the others could be estimated with reasonable accuracy, late 40's, 50's, early 60's, beginning with the original, now paint-choked one at bottom, which had been opened with a big ten-cent skeleton key, when necessary a coat hanger. Inside, at the click of a shiny switch, the air conditioner began to hum quite promisingly. There was no question but what this place was MODERN: from the livingroom, hanging his nextra shirt on the hanger in the closet, he could hear a toilet chortle with constant flushing. There was a separate bedroom, with two skinny beds to choose from. Right now it was the TV that concerned him. It did come on, soon even showed a lacey picture. When traveling he never went shopping until he had checked out the cooking facilities. At thought of dinner, a brave saliva began to mingle with the dust.

It was time to trouble Chumly, who would understand, however ruefully. After five far-flung years together, it was clear to both of them that each required a separate shopping: he had had his. At least they did not have to climb that mound again, not tonight. They headed for central Lower Sadusky, turned in at the first shopping center they came to, where a Super Saver lay beside a Penneys. Given the climatic conditions, Lou bought the beer and sherry first, then the Crispos, then tomorrow morning's milk and donuts, not to thaw the Banquet dinner before its time. At the checkout stand leaned giant ladies, on either side of it, resting their lower abdomens on the counter so that their navels were all but kissing. They had gone to school together, had not seen each other since yesterday. Whew, isn't it hot today. I'll say. At least you have it a little cooler in the store here. Yes, if only that door didn't open so much. I know what you mean! Sure a lot of tourists this year, aren't there. Whew.

They did not look at Lou but eyed his perspiring Banquet next to them. Somehow this encouraged them to heave themselves partially erect until their bulk divided into separate quantities. If anything the one with the shopping bag was the smaller. Saw Goldie at the laundromat yesterday—she looked awful. Doesn't she. She goes into surgery Thursday? Yes. I go in next Monday. That soon? Well, see you at Friday sewing. Yes, if not before then. Don't forget your koala bear. Not likely! The door swished and the one with the bag rolled sidewise out. The remaining one waited for the door to inch closed again, then wiped her brow with massive forearm. Whew. Eyeing Lou's purchases, she punched keys with a swollen tenpin. She did not touch the goods, but left all that to the bagboy, who was small and quick. She did hand Lou his change—and his sales receipt after reading the time on it.

"Forty minutes to go! Have a nice evening."

"You *too,*" Lou said. The door whooshed eagerly in front

of him; now behind him he could hear it carefully collecting air from the parking lot. Whew.

He gave Chumly a proper bath on their return, despite all advice from the saliva, using the new hose at Number 7. He had earned that, and afterward looked much better; his dust had been weirdly pock-marked by that sprinkler, now he shone with the familiar rock-pocks. Lou wiped here and there with a piece of towel, the drooping right eye especially carefully. He still had all three hub caps, and his gas one. His keyholes were badly scorched, lasting memorials to the Blizzard of Chum Creek, Nebraska, but they still locked. We'll check that oil and water in the morning, promised Lou, when it will have cooled a little. Now it was time to heed saliva, cool it with a beer or two while waiting. It was newstime, coincidentally. Lou chose Channel 8, as most gracefully lacy. He put the Banquet on at once. Having no cookbook, he consulted memory: it usually takes about 2 ½ hours on a Philco grilltop (was saliva weeping?) adding approx. 30 min. in high altitude or winter. No problem there tonight—in fact he subtracted 15 min., not only cheering saliva but readying for the lady should she turn up early with nextra toweling. Some are offended at sight of TV cooking.

With grilltop models, though they are faster, your basic problem is the very slots and crevices. Even a minor drip can prove harmful to the appliance. This is especially true if you have color; at the very least you may be reduced to primaries, usually green, blue, and norange, always garish. Thus the solidtop model is recommended whenever possible, particularly if you are expecting company. Nonetheless, if you have no choice but the grilltop, even be it slanted, *don't* despair. Simply spread a clean sheet of aluminum foil upon it, crimped upward around the edges. (Save all coverings from your Banquet dinners.) If none is available, a good sturdy shopping bag can be substituted. In this case, of course, you will want to watch your dinner extra carefully. Keep your eyes, ears, and nostrils open, alert for overflow, internal sizzling, smouldering. The minute any of the above are detected, remove from the stove at once and reconsider. Your stove may simply incline at too steep an angle, allowing your gravy to slop over the edges of its container. In that case you will want to prop up the low side of the container with something sturdy (in emergency don't hesitate to use your Gideon). When cooking canned goods, sliding may be inhibited by looping a rubber band around the can, then around your aerial. On the other hand, your shopping bag may have slipped, or been joggled. Replace it squarely before continuing. Don't forget to add these lost minutes to your cooking time, saliva notwithstanding.

Luckily his Super Saver bag was double strength, relatively unwrinkled. Even so, at a knock on the door he removed it quickly, along with dinner. This did not sound to be the lady, nor promise understanding. Given the age and brittleness of the door, hard to say whether it shook in anger or timidity, or worse, in uneasy combination. Lou opened gently, yet the man was startled. He stood with towels beneath his arm, the one not raised for knocking. He seemed to hope that he was smiling. Otherwise he looked rather pleasant, still trim at thirty, just a little pale for this time of summer in Ohio. "Wanted to let you know I won't be able to get to that leak this evening," he said. "I've brought some towels."

"Oh, thanks." Lou said, accepting them. "These should do it nicely."

"I . . ." The man swung to look behind him. His lady stood in the office doorway, and there was no question about her smiling. When the man turned back to him, Lou tried to smile at both of them, politely.

"*No.*" It was a cry escaping underbreath, impotent and heart-rending. Lou had to look away. It's an appalling thing to be looked at in horror. He glanced quickly at the man, to make sure, then aside again. They had always been faithful to one another in this way, so far at least—until yesterday at least—but he knew now how it would feel when the vow was rended. He forced himself to look at the man again, share his anguish with him. They stared into one another's eyes for a moment and then they turned away, almost shrugging. "Sorry for the inconvenience," the man mumbled, heading for the office.

"Don't mention it." Quietly closing the door, Lou took the towels to the chortling bathroom before returning his dinner to the stove. They would have to add five minutes, he warned saliva, and turned the aluminum dish the other way this time.

Never neglect your *turning,* backside forward, frontside forward, every 15 or 20 minutes.

This looked to be a three-beer Happy Hour. It was time to give some attention to the news, local now. Two Saduskyites were dead in Western Pennsylvania after their VW van was sideswiped by a hijacked semi on County Road 28 ten miles northeast of Lima. They were Orville Nentram, 81, and his wife Grace, 82. The driver of the semi was in satisfactory condition. A 15-year-old youth was being held in County Hospital in connection with an alleged robbery attempt at 20th Century Liquors at Frontage Road and US 80 in the course of which Rosie Rossillini, co-owner, surprised him with a beer bottle. She said, "It was either that or Jack Daniels." Bill Balch had resigned as head football coach at Athens, to be succeeded by his offensive coordinator Buck Brock, pending approval by the Regents. Reconstruction work on Ohio 101 was continuing according to schedule, said Supervisor Elbie Sumner, completion of the first assault anticipated by late October or mid-November, December at the latest. Meanwhile the weather would continue warm and humid with the possibility of scattered thunderstorms and local dustdevils. Latenight update at 10 P.M.

That would be after dinner, barring further interruptions. The man would be returning to his 'swing' shift now; in fact Lou thought he heard him leaving. He thought not to phone tonight, though a prettily written little card offered switchboard service until 11, given the day's slowness and uncertainty. He turned from a muppet movie, turned his warming Banquet to peas and carrots. You will soon get to know your hot spots. (In winter drafts/summer airconditioning, cover meal and stove with a towel, as dry as possible.) Dinners will cook equally well on any channel, with or without a picture. This set had X-rays; he chose lower abdomen, turned down to simmer. There is still some question to what extent cooking temperature is influenced by volume, if at all, but for him any sacrifice came easily, his eardrums being even more sensitive than his taste buds, regardless of all moist cajoleries. Would she be watching their little RCA tonight? She might, while half expecting a call from him. On the other hand she had all their books but one, for on a trip like this he travelled light, with no more than he could carry on the run, or hurdle.

As for the one, he had read it years ago, and he had otherwise employed the Gideon. Perhaps she was at the movies. He didn't go so often anymore, unless lacily inhouse.

He might have bought a paper, had not the box stood in front of the motel office; not a good move for one trying to sustain ambivalence. She was very beautiful. Almost he hoped she would not visit. He turned his Banquet, a little early. The air conditioning was finally taking over, from the doorway the darkening air looked cooler. It was time for sherry. Along with the nuts and raisins, she had sent wheat thins and bean dip. In a former time, quite another marriage, it had been hard-boiled eggs and Vienna sausage. He had used to make a meal of those. That of course was before the heyday of TV cookery. Tonight he nibbled wheat thins without bean dip, only to find that he had happened upon a masticatory. Actually the Crispos had been intended for the lady. Perhaps, if not tonight, they would come in handy somewhere further along the road. He did not really think so. How he missed her! He turned his loathsome Banquet to potatoes. Avoid all dinners offering tarts, crusts, or cornbread; no goddam set has yet been invented that can brown them.

Leaning back, sipping sherry laced with an early Bond movie, he let himself relax a little. Wine almost always did that for him. If never quite his best friend, it was bent on proving itself more lasting, once again. He did not believe he could have got this far without it. Even in one like him the love of life could sometimes falter. The pain at such times seemed always sharper because the love had lasted that much longer. What he dreaded most was the possibility that the time might come when wine could no longer see him through it. He was drinking faster now, and soon the sherry encouraged him to eat his silly dinner. Never remove the container until time to serve—the cardboard not only inhibits drips, it retains the heat. It tries to. Tonight the Salisbury still showed signs of *rigor mortis,* the mashed potatoes had been air conditioned. The peas were even cooler than the carrots. Garnish with salt and pepper, oleo if you have any. Take a belt of sherry and be hearty. Keep in mind your postprandial duties. Carefully wash the aluminum foil in the leaky sink, prop to dry against the window, wring out the nextra towels in the shower, missing the latenight update. ". . . man a self-styled timebomb.

We'll tell you more about that at six tomorrow." Hey man, don't give away all the secrets. Never mind, now he could sit down alone with sherry. Saliva had long since subsided. Lou himself was almost lulled into contentment. Yet he did find himself going to the door from time to time, to check on Chumly, the thunderstorms and dustdevils, the vacancy sign in the office window. We are incorrigible toward midnight in Ohio.

It wasn't until the "swing" shift was finally over that he felt drowsy. The sherry was almost finished. Looked at from a long-range viewpoint, they weren't doing so badly. He had hoped to be in Boston by Tuesday morning, meet with Bowden in the afternoon. Well, Tuesday was simply replaced by Wednesday, both he and Chumly better rested. He wished she were here to see how easily he admitted that; she always raged at his impatience, as though he were stealing something from her. Perhaps she was right in staying behind this time, settling into the apartment. Here or there, she would probably be asleep by now. Here they would have pushed the beds together, ended up in one of them: it was quite cool enough now for cuddling. Finishing off the sherry, he turned his thoughts toward Boston. His aim was to wrap things up on Wednesday. If everything went as hoped, he would have good news to announce by evening—but would that help?

T W O

It turned out he had chosen the less voluptuous bed, which had him up and aching early. His milk at least had spent a refreshing night beside the air conditioner. She would have had to settle for tepid coffee, as he did shaving. Yet it was good he did not use an electric razor, nextra toweling notwithstanding. He waded to the toilet, squatted somewhat shyly over its enthusiastic whirlpool. If anything it felt too modern being flushed before he'd fairly started. He let his thoughts wander to Chumly's cooling system, the gentle hose of Number 7, and put this newfangled business behind him as soon as possible, not to keep the old boy waiting. By the look of it he had not had the best of nights himself, his glance at Lou seemed more than usually skew-eyed. He was very very thirsty, waterwise. Lou knew where his oil level would be before he checked it, basically the fellow was a genius. Setting his things in the passenger's seat, turning off the air conditioning and locking up Number 8, he took Chumly with him to the office.

She stood behind the counter as before, probably not in last night's blouse but one equally becoming. Her soft hair fluttered as prettily in the breezes. She smiled at him in welcome, but tentatively now, not bursting with it. Either her eyes were red or the early sun would have him think so. "Goodmorning."

"Goodmorning. Here's the key to Number 8."

"I'm sorry about last night." She said it quietly, to the counter. "My husband . . ."

"That's all right," he said as quietly. "My life is a little mixed up too. Maybe you can tell me if there's any way to get into Pennsylvania from here without climbing that damn mountain south of town."

It was the startled look of hurt in her bloodshot eyes that confirmed the involuntary challenge in his voice, piqued not so much by what she had done to him last night as by what she wanted to do to someone who loved her, had no doubt done before, would surely do again. My turn to be sorry, he tried to look as she said: "Mountain?"

"That mound of dirt at the railroad crossing."

"Oh! Let's see, there must be." She turned to a map on the wall behind her, slender neck arching studiously above hunched schoolgirl shoulders. "Well, you could go north to Old Sadusky and turn at the light there. Then you would go east to Sooner or Later and turn south on 79 until you come to The Freeway. We used to go that way sometimes with the football team."

"You were a cheerleader?"

"Me? Oh no, I was too skinny and shy for that. Just a cheerer."

"Ah." She blushed as he gazed at her admiringly. "Well, many thanks for the directions. That way sounds much better."

"It's kind of pretty."

He nodded, and from the door he waved to her, Chumly's

key this time. They were getting a good early start, and did find the light at Old Sadusky, which put them right on the road to Sooner or Later. This road was narrow, winding gently among big barns and little gas stations; it was lovely. One of the stations was still in business, with a tiny old proprietor who took the time and care to fill to the brim with no spillings at all till they pulled away, as in the old days. 19 was somewhat straighter, stiffer, though not yet a victim of rampant realignment. It was a shaded lane compared to The Freeway, an automaton designed by some local partisan for filching U.S. quarters. Usually in Pennsylvania Lou chose to spend instead on gas and eggs and scrapple, travelling by way of Route Meander, to the north and east and south a little, but these days time seemed sadly more important. At the first toll plaza he bought a roll of quarters, and from there on tossed them at the baskets. It was at the third of these he found himself behind an old lady who could not hit it; she scattered three or four of them around, soon was down to what looked like dimes and pennies. With one last jerky fling she sprayed the basket, netting several. Still no light went on; the barrier remained in front of her. Seeing that she could not open her door to retrieve her losses, Lou got out to gather them, toss one for her. "There you go!" he said, dropping the rest into her clawing fingers.

"Thank you, son!" she called, scooting away in her little lavender Whippet.

Returning to Chumly he thought to look in back to see how his shirt was going—the back seat was empty. Had the shirt blown out the window—no, he saw it now, hanging on that crippled hanger in the closet. Tossing a quarter, veering to the shoulder, he waited for the track to clear enough for him to cut across to the westbound plaza. The blonde in the booth had her hand on what looked like a siren button. "Left my shirt at the motel in Lower Sandusky!" he called to her.

"Your what?"

"*Shirt!*"

"Ah! I'll punch reuse for you!" she yelled, tearing a ticket from her waist and punching it. "That will get you to the border and back again to Toll Plaza 4."

"Many thanks!" he yelled, waving the ticket out the window.

On soon later thoughts, he was not really so happy about how things were going. It was good of her, he supposed, an efficient system, but now he had to stop at each plaza to explain his circumstances, always yelling. They in their booths seemed almost to take an interest in his story, yelled little encouragements while they punched his ticket. He felt obliged to thank them. Even 79 was tedious, from this direction; wasn't it about time they tagged it for reconstruction? Despite all drawbacks, he did relax a little on the winding road to Old Sadusky, until the radio advised him it was 8:24, 81 degrees Fahrenheit, or 28 Celsius, and that 15-year-old alleged attempting robber had been charged with possession of a controlled substance and given 11 stitches. Home Again.

"Goodmorning!"

The manager, restartled, almost spilled his coffee on the file cards. The morning light showed his eyes red too. They were looking at something behind Lou's back, perhaps the transported sprinkler caressing Chumly tearfully with honeysuckle. He seemed to force them to look away, to the clock above Lou. "Goodmorning, sir. Can I help you?"

"Sorry to bother you with something silly—I'm afraid I've left a shirt in Number 8, in the closet."

"Aha. A shirt." His eyes almost smiled as they flicked over Lou to the other window. "I see the maid's at Number 6. She'll be able to help you."

"Ah, thanks!" Lou said, going for the door.

"Have a safe trip!"

"Thanks again!" he said, waving Chumly's key at him.

The maid was singing in Number 6, something about hold me tight hold me right don't neva let me go no moe no moe. Lou knocked. The song became a quieter, almost pleasant hum, though she could not resist the no moe no moe as she opened the doe. Probably only thirtytwo or three, she had not given up all hope of being late in blooming. She still had pink pimples on her chin which matched her lipstick. Her eyes were moist, not limpid, and not just with sentimental balladry. Her tight tan hairdo had been taken from the window of The Old Sadusky Beauty Parlour. Yet her bold smile was winning. "Well, hi!" she said.

"Hi!" Lou smiled too. "Sorry to bother you. I've done

something stupid. I've locked my shirt in Number 8."

Her speaking voice was soft with smiling. "Oh, that's no bother." She joined him in the sunshine, locked Number 6 behind her. "Phew. It's going to be another hot one."

"I'm afraid so."

She had the key all ready for Number 8, knew which lock it fitted. She led the way inside, held the door for Lou. "I wish they'd fix that leaking."

"Right." He went to the closet. "I left without even looking in here. Usually I don't leave things. I guess I need a wife to look after me." He should not have said that. Unbuttoning the shirt, he could hear her murmured laughter, and turned to find her looking quite comfy on the sofa—why hadn't he slept on that—and smiling rather confidently. She had surprisingly nice legs, and enjoyed surprising. She rocked one slowly, softly on the other. Whatever infected this place was highly contagious, however benign in this case. Did the management know about this, or was this an isolated outbreak? He knew it was cruelty not to approach her, thus he stood contritely. Her smile almost faltered. How she would love to have been a cheerleader. Caught so stiffly standing there, he reached for quarters. "Here, let me give you something for your . . ."

"No no, *please,* it's no trouble." She was on her way to the door now, readying the key to Number 8, and smiling more valiantly than ever. Together they went as far as Number 6, where they waved at one another as she unlocked it. "You come back again!"

"Oh, yes!"

He walked with his shirt to Chumly, stuffed it securely in the frontseat bag where he could see it. Catching sight of Crispos, he almost went back to Number 6. That would mean knocking on the door again, interrupting singing. She would say "Well, hi again!" Then she would see what it was he offered. Instead he waved at the office, coaxing Chumly from the shower. This time they would not be back so soon—they had not been invited, of course, by everybody.

For variety, they hit the mound this time. It did seem to have settled down a little now that the red boys were gone, leaving STOP-LOOK-LISTEN signs behind them—Chumly landed on the far side with two stylish bounces. Old 101 itself was all but unencumbered with peeling flagmen and dusty earthpeelers, and met The Freeway well before Pennsylvania's plazas. Lou prepared himself for the first one, reuse ticket in left hand, ready for repunching. It was the lady he had bought his roll from. She had seemed more pleasant earlier—her main line was rolls, of course. Did she not recognize him, or did she think he had come back from the Lower World to haunt her? She glared right through him, her finger on the siren button. "Left my shirt in the motel!" he yelled up to her in the attempted explanation."

"In the *what*?"

"The *motel* in Lower Sadusky!"

"Oh hell," she seemed to say, shaking her head and punching. "You can only use these reusers once in twentyfour hours!"

"Oh right!" he called, rolling away. "Until tomorrow."

That was more than enough already, he decided, for one who had been enthralled by the Liberty Bell at the age of four in Philadelphia. Crumpling his ticket, he flung quarters across Pennsylvania. It went much faster. New York was even easier, met at lower hip level; it would have taken him most of the day and night to span those stooping shoulders, the swollen big Toe even longer. He only stopped to pee in Fishkill. To a hurrying man, Connecticut became a sliding door to Boston. Again he spent little time sightseeing archaic memories, stopped only for gas in Waterbury, half a bucket of acid rain for Chumly. Seldom had he been more pleased to see Massachusetts, this despite the dogged remembrance of their most recent visit.

In celebration they stopped at a Milton inn for a hamburger and chocolate shake, at least two gallons of water between them. The temperature had breached the 90's, in a shimmering duet with the humidity. Yet they lunched in the parking lot, where there was something like real air and room enough for both of them. Here too they had radio of their own choosing, could cheer the Red Sox all tied up with the White ones in the bottom of the fifth. The Mayor was there. A boy was singing the maid's song on another station. She would have liked that. They waited until the end before turning off the radio rather sadly.

Well, you can't sell any books this way, as they had used to say. Lou went to throw his refuse out, returning saw a puff of steam arise from Chumly into the miasma. He topped off the radiator once more before departing, or so he thought before he tried it. The ignition spoke firmly to the starter, which responded eagerly; beyond that, Chumly only whispered. They tried again. Now the starter sounded anxious. Lou got out. In the early days, in fact the second or third the three had spent together, on their first trip cross-country, the trouble had turned out to be the points. Lou had known where to find them, in the distributor, could point them out to her. It was a friendly passerby in Idaho who showed him how to gap them with a matchbook. He did that now with a proper gapper given him by a mechanic in Wyoming. He gapped exactly. Now Chumly whispered a little less forlornly, but the starter more so. Lou rocked Chumly from the doorway, thinking this might be vapor lock or dirty gas from Waterbury. If so, the rocking didn't do it. A watching couple sat nextby them, eating ice cream cones in a Pinto. Lou rocked more vigorously.

The man, on the near side, the passenger's, was licking pistachio or cashew. He had a paper napkin spread over his white shorts, but Lou approached him. The man licked warily. "Having a little trouble?"

"I think it's heat exhaustion—if I could get going about five miles an hour I'm pretty sure it would start right up."

The man waved apologetically at his shorts, his pistachio. His head shook no before he said it: "Sorry."

Lou glanced at his wife before he turned away. They all three looked disappointed in him. In the next row there was a close relative of Chumly's, several years his junior, in character especially. This couple too was eating ice cream. They had observed Lou's luckless visit, but did not look away as he approached them. The man's cone was chocolate, his shorts were blue, he had his napkin wadded. He called: "Little overheated?"

Nodding ruefully Lou bent closer. "You look like a willing man. If we could just get going about five miles an hour . . ."

The man smiled, shrugged, handed his cone to his pretty wife. "Please finish that first!" Lou said, with the wife's approval.

"That's O.K. I don't want to use the car on it, but I'll give you a hand," the man said, heaving himself out from behind the steering wheel. They had found a willing one.

Those others had not finished their cones, though the man

was surely trying. He was *sucking.* Chumly only huffed now, scarcely puffing. Lou gave him one more try: a whimper for a sucking licker. The willing one was already pushing, wholeheartedly and one-handedly. "You stay in there to catch it when we get rolling."

"Right!"

There was a little downward slope in the macadam, happy result of breaktime engineering, and they were soon rolling in a one-handed hurry. Lou waited until they were almost to the bottom to suddenly release the clutch in second. Jolted so rudely to his senses, Chumly shuddered violently. Lou stomped hard on the accelerator. For just a moment it seemed that they were running, but it was only in imagination. Chumly thought he was purring up that rise, and Lou kept feeding gas to him. In reality all the running was behind them, the power now two-handed; Lou depressed the clutch to make it easier.

Even on the upgrade they seemed to be gaining speed, but coming to a level stretch they suddenly shot forward. In the rear-view mirror Lou could see their motor charging. He must have had them rolling at ten miles an hour when Lou released the clutch again. Chumly leapt in the air this time, yelping, and Lou fed him gas with frantic gratitude, for never had he known a car with such imagination. While they shot up the next incline, their man stood a few feet behind them gasping. His eyebrows were raised as he approached them. "Well, what's the verdict?"

"I really thought we had it that time," Lou said, but those eyebrows were not convinced—at most they were sympathetic. "Maybe if we turn around and take one more run down that slope—it looks steeper than the first one."

The big man shrugged as he had on first agreeing, forced a smile through heavy breathing. "We'll try her."

Lou got out to help the turning, jumped back in as they got rolling. The slope was surely steeper than the other; by the time they reached the bottom they might almost have been ticketed for speeding on a parking lot. This time Chumly leapt that much higher, yelping even louder, but by now they had found themselves a little short on fancy. Turning off the ignition, Lou looked out at the panting man resignedly. This time they both shrugged. "Thanks for a great try," he said.

"I guess it'll take a mechanic."

"I'm afraid so. Let me pay you for your trouble."

"Oh no. Here, let's push it out of the way."

Together they pushed Chumly into a parking space, from where he eyed obliquely his distant nephew. The man's wife held his cone out the window, above a ghastly pool of chocolate dripple. "Let me buy you another cone at least."

"Oh no. I like the shell best anyway." He waved as he went to his car, hello to his wife, farewell to Lou. It took him two bites to finish his cone, and he waved again as they drove away. To Lou's answering wave his wife waved the wadded napkins.

He had a final plan, a gamble, seeing that all the ice cream eaters had departed. The exit ramp seemed to slope downhill, as though on purpose. The parking lot itself, in that direction, was almost level. If he could get them moving, they would have a quarter-mile of runway, good for several joltings. At worst they could stop just before the freeway; some Samaritan adventurer might like to push or tow them on it. Taking the mover as example, he pushed one-handed, in the doorway, saving the other for any future steering. The right hand is the loafer, and the stronger. Just here those engineers had laid the parking lot very level, an unmistakable two-hander. Chumly himself seemed to join the effort; they were inching rampward. It was like wading through a sundrift. In time they somehow made it without one ice cream helper. Lou jumped in when he felt Chumly taking over. Chumly was in a fine mood for rolling—*not* for jolting. He leapt and yelped most pitifully. His imagination had become distorted. He saw himself rolling all the way to Boston, and shook his poor deluded head in disbelief when Lou wouldn't let him try it. He wished his little friend were here.

How happy she was not to be here. Raising the hood, Lou could hear her despairing taunts at this distress signal. So he busied himself in there, puttering with everything. He adjusted the points again, the carburetor, joggled the linkage, the battery cables. From time to time he got back in the driver's seat to listen to Chumly's expiring whispers.

"Hey man, isn't it about time you got that heap to the graveyard?"

Four lounging lads loomed above them in bucket seats, tilted backward, their tanned arms and legs hanging all over their brand-new RV Gangster. It had hubcaps bigger than Chumly's wheels themselves were. Otherwise it was all motor, chassis. Its big backslung windshield was its body. Its hood was giddy gold and purple. "This is the graveyard," Lou called up to them. "Which one of you's the minister?"

Laughing, waving, they throttled forward to the freeway. They had the flaxen hair of California here in Massachusetts. Their license plates said Colorado. A roadsign read 7 miles to Cadsbury, 17 to Boston. This was a graveyard in Inferno, and Lou left Chumly to make the best of it while he sought shade beneath a giant burdock. When he went to pee behind it, he set tin cans to sizzling. Oh, wasn't she a happy one!

Here came the minister now, officially. His green door said Mass Park & Rescue. He parked alongside of Chumly to talk on radio while waiting for Lou to join him. He was from California too, Hawaii and Alaska. He was from Washington and Oregon, Arizona and Nevada. He was from New Mexico. He was from Utah and Colorado, Wyoming and Montana. He was from the Dakotas and the Minnesotas. He was from the Lone Star State and Oklahoma . . . and yes from Massachusetts. He sported government-issue polaroids. His shortcut dark hair was flecked with grey beneath his hunting cap. His face was set forever in ten thousand coffee breaks. "Trouble?" he asked of Lou.

"It seems to be the heat."

"She turn over?"

"Not recently. I think if we could get rolling about ten or—"

"I'll call for help."

"Just ten or fifteen miles an hour—"

"Have to get this vehicle back to the yard by four. I'll call for help." He was from Louisiarkabama too. He checked his visor and dialed a wizmo on his dashboard, state implanted. The radio was busy belching static, but Lou's rescuer wheezed into it with quiet confidentiality: "Got one on the Milton rampway at Kilometer 17. She don't turn over . . . 10-8 . . . 10-6 . . . 10-4." He flipped off the barking radio with his Parks Department pencil.

"What did they say?"

The dark eyes prodded him, a casualty. "Tow truck'll be here in a while." Now he double-checked his visor, eased off his clutch, merged with the freeway traffic at 10-20 kilometers below the limit, hazards blinking. After giving Chumly's starter one last opportunity, Lou rejoined the shade of burdock, waiting for the Historics to come by and plant a marker to the official flower.

If the hairy caterpillar didn't get him first. His approach was much like the flagman's, on the shady side, circumspect. He walked heavily but softly. He tested Lou's sock on his way over, but it was too brown for him. He was polite about it though, arched backward to look up at Lou's face quite cordially. He could accept the stem as a natural oddity but experience told him to continue on to a more familiar. There he began to climb off at once with confidence, weaving his upper body from side to side in graceful acknowledgement of the leaves he was passing. Those near the bottom were a little dry and dusty for his taste, even if nicely hairy. In truth he himself had not been to the parlour lately. His orange fur was crusty. He shook himself and continued upward, stopping at the topmost leaf, it seemed, only because he could go no farther. He had scarcely begun to eat a hole in it when he leaned far over backward and dove to the ground in a single gainer, landing in a hairy wad rather awkwardly. Not to hear him tell it though: he had only wanted to cool himself. He started climbing again with the same old swagger, albeit carrying more crust this time.

He soon lost his audience to another, a migrant grasshopper. This one had only one rear leg, for which the flailing antennae up front did their best to compensate. For half a rampway it seemed that Rob had crossed state lines to find them out and snare them with his clanking chains and pulleys, but at closer view one could differentiate between dried blood and the canned tomato juice of Ohio. Hall's Haul and Overhaul. Shrieking tires bit the curb in front of Chumly, flailing antennae unavailing. Even from here one could see Chumly shiver, glance the monster sidewise. Lou checked the caterpillar's carefree progress before he joined them, saying "Howdy!"

"This your Hopel?" This lad himself was built like a two-legged wrecker.

"Right."

He threw six feet of steel plate at Chumly.

"I was thinking, before we start towing—a mechanic could probably get this thing running in a minute. It would be a real help to me—I'm already late to Boston."

He looked at Chumly's dejected face, then at Lou's wallet pocket. "She turn hover?"

"Not—"

"I don't want to fool with hit." He dropped two heaps of chain in clanging punctuation. Next he dropped himself, on all fours throwing chains and snarling. "Bastard!" It took him five or six bleeding throws to chain him—Lou himself had painted this old hopper. He went up front to add a few touches to the scrapes and scratches on the driver's door. Now he wielded a lever that jolted Chumly rudely up and down, by way of testing. Auto-da-fé, trial by torture. Chumly had marvelous reflexes, glared crookedly at him from on high, eyeballs jouncing. He got an hextra jerk for that. Then it was time for radio: "Have ha Hopel—K27—headin hin."

Lou gave Chumly a last look, which he tried not to make despairing, and climbed up beside the two-legged bleeder. "Well, I hope . . ."

The radio was blaring staccato static, and the bleeder punched it off, twirled his other one up to 500 decibels of what had once been music. His look at Lou said double bastard. They jolted forward, up over the curb and back across it, merged the helter-skelter freeway traffic at 30 Ks above the limit, all hazards flashing. A quick glance out the back window saw Chumly flying sidewise cross-eyed. He was trying to get away, but the draft of the one-legged wrecker drew him on inexorably. It drew him onto the first exit ramp, toward Cadsbury.

That's what the sign had said. They seemed to be heading back to Pennsylvania, now for Canada, now Rhode Island, at 80 Ks on a narrow road Providence-sent for wreckers. Passing cars were merging with the burdocks. Each time he missed one, the bleeder turned from that road onto another narrower. He wasn't just hauling now but hunting. He had his siren on, hoping thus to flush them. He knew the country. He knew all the trails and coverts, and did not overlook any. If it was 7 Ks to Cadsbury, it was as the crow cries. She was *happy.* They only slowed when finally they came upon fellow grasshoppers.

They were milling before a high wire fence which they couldn't hop over, one-legged. It looked as though the bleeder had painted all of them as well. He knew the territory. He thrashed among them until he found a hole in that fence; swung Chumly through it. In here were all manner of other bugs and creepers, many of unidentifiable species. There were charred bodies maimed beyond recognition, half-buried carcasses. Their blood had blackened the earth around them. The bleeder thrashed among them until he found a little glass-strewn clearing. Wielding his lever, he dropped Chumly on it. Snarling he got down on all fours to grapple those chains again. The place was rife with bastards. By the time he got himself and the chains untangled, the earth, the weeds, the glasschips were all red-bespattered, and not all of it was the bleeder's. It helped that over the years Chumly had become a rock-pocked stoic. Now they watched the bleeder lever his great steel plate above him, in case he wanted to give further trouble. "What hyear his she?"

"A '68. But the motor . . ."

He wasn't interested in that. He was scrawling Chumly's license number on his clipboard with a thick stub of wrecker's pencil. Lou didn't mention that he had got it a little scrambled. "Name?"

"Mine?"

"Hyours."

"Lou Webb." Lou spelled it for him, but there was no telling if that scrawl was scrambled. Moving toward the shed with him, he was not surprised to find himself so, his gait a little hoppy. They entered through a chin-high door, the bleeder on all fours, Lou stooping. The shed was of corrugated tin, which collected heat and beamed it downward through its fissures. The only coolness came from the dim grey bulbs that dangled from the ceiling. This was a field station, not a hospital. It was where they kept the surviving patients, mostly critical. They seemed to have no attendants, unless those scattered old machines were monitoring. It seemed unlikely: their tubes were ruptured, their cables knotted. The bleeder stopped among them to wash his hand in a galvanized drip pan, soon had greasecake topped with pinkish frothing. He dried with a rag some departed attendant had discarded, led Lou through a much higher door.

The attendants were all in here, a little room with what might well have been two windows. A shoulder-high barrier, not a counter, separated outsiders from an official area, and they roamed in there in coveralls, four or five of them. They were two-legged wreckers every one, all from the same misshapen family. Each man's misshape was different, the familial tie appearing in the ability to bat that high swinging bulb with their foreheads. Only the one sitting at the desk did not bat it, though he probably could have by leaning forward. He had three piles of paper on the desk, one sheet in front of him between his smoking ashtray and his soda. The healing bleeder dropped Lou's sheet on the farthest pile, against the wall. "Hit's the Hopel."

The boss was too involved in reading, smoking, reading, sipping, reading, to look up and notice. When the radio squawked behind his back he poked a button twice with his smoking forefinger, reading. There was a little fan above his head; he poked a button with his soda forefinger. The squeak grew louder. With so much time to spare, Lou had observed that one of the five in there was not of the family. He was as large as they, better put together, yet he seemed diminished by them. His hands and clothes grew cleaner with each waiting minute. He was too clearly aware that his good-natured smile was not reflected. Watching from outside the barrier, Lou discarded smiling.

The boss one cleared his throat, his massive neck, and the boys set the bulb to balling. He cleared his chins, this time of smoke. He spoke: "The bill's four heighty."

Even now the smile persisted. "That's what you told me on the phone. As I said, I'd like to pay a hundred a week, then eighty the last week."

The boss blew smoke, rereading. Now he handed the paper to the one who had no shoulders, looked at the smiling man before him. "See hyou Tuesdays."

"Yes, Tuesdays!" he held out his check and the boss pointed to the one with sagging bumpers. "Oh!" The man carried his check and smile to that one, and Lou pushed through the barrier.

The boss was not used to seeing a stranger approach his

desk uninvited, stand beside and not before it, but he did not ask for smiling. "Hyeah?"

"I'm with that little—"

"Hwe'll look hat hit hin the morning."

"Couldn't someone—"

"Hwe're closing now, heverything hexcept the hradio."

"Ah."

"Come haround hat ten tomorrow. Leave the key." He pointed to the four-eared one.

Lou waited for him to poke the squawking radio, poke twice when it squawked again. "Can you tell me if there's a motel near here?"

"Motel? Nearest thing to a motel haround here's the jail. These roads hain't that busy."

"Aha. I'll see you at ten tomorrow."

The boss nodded hat his desk, and Lou looked around for those ears among the batters. Leaving Chumly's key with them, he went out the front door to look for the hole in the fence. Some of the "hoppers" had given up. The bleeder's was still in back. Crouched beneath that dangling plate, Chumly wasn't smiling either. He knew this was no parking lot. Furthermore, Lou took along everything of value, bag, tools, nuts, and raisins. He did check the water before he left, by way of reassurance.

Rusty tracks wormed through the burdocks beside the road, and he followed them a perspiring mile or so to what the sign on the little depot said was CADSBURY. Even in those days this could not have been an important stop. Behind the warped wooden depot lay a large, once hopeful square, or rather oblong, sustaining ten or twelve strangely tall, emaciated elm trees. Their bark was black with age and mourning. Their leaves, so high up as to seem disassociated, were probably bug infested, though even the crusty caterpillar might not have enjoyed that climb. Certainly there would have been no leaning backwards. The lawn beneath was evil looking; somebody had thought to scrape bald a section of it. All this was dominated by the Court House, three sombre granite stories. Around the edges huddled little stores, or storefronts. Ah, somebody came out of one of them. It was a policeman. He got into his patrol car and patrolled verrry slowly around the oblong. When he had done, he left three people and five parked cars behind him. All but Lou were on the storeside. Seeing that they had the public phonebooth too, he thought to join them.

It was eerie crossing over. The heat, steeped in such far-flung shade, was heavier. The lawn smelled maggoty, the bald patch of slug and snail spit. Dead and dying sow bugs crunched underfoot, emitting their own base poudours. One could scarcely feel sorry for them; a sowbug death is nasty. The occasional weed was rank with pleasure. There were no birds, not singing, near here. It was a relief to gain the blazing phonebooth. This booth had gone up with the depot, perhaps to handle the competing stagecoach traffic. They don't build them like that anymore, of real warped wood and glass, not lately. There was room to breathe in there, had there been air. The directory, what was left of it, was a few years newer. Its handful of bleached pages would not have held the A's and B's of Boston, and it took five neighboring towns to fill them, of which only Cadsbury was familiar. Twukesbury? Boss Hall was right about motels. They were mostly elsewhere, except for the Hotel Jones Motel on Fourth St. This was Fourth St. The depot was on Third. It was hard to say where the others were. Stacking the directory pages as neatly as possible on the counter, Lou headed up Fourth in the direction where lay some buildings, not just the Court House.

The jail made no mention of a vacancy; but it looked likely. The policeman was repatrolling, slowwwly. Most people had gone inside again; he parked at the café for his 4:15 coffee break. Lou strolled onward, past the sullen four-chair one-man barber shop, toward the service station. There was activity. It was a wife who was backing out of there, in a hurry. Lou had to leap aside to save her a crumpled fender. She swerved to find him. "Hey, easy, damn it!" he yelled leaping.

"Up yours!" yelled back her husband. He was not the pistachio ice cream eater; his shorts were dirty yellow.

Lou continued on more cautiously, making little mental notes for future reference. The liquor store was in the 300 block. It closed at 8. Diagonally across the street was a little diner featuring Chinese and German-American cuisine. The Caboose. It closed at 6. Down the next side street was a public phonestand, handier than the booth, better ventilated. Things should mesh pretty well if the Hotel James Motel was still on Fourth St., if this was Cadsbury. There was still the American Legion Post, the State Ployment Center, the laundromat and cleaners, the barn, the slungtailed panting dairy. He turned back toward town again.

He must have missed it the first time by, even though it was set back a few feet from the street, hmotel-like. They had ripped out the front wall and windows and put an oblong picture in there. It was straighter than its housing, but masking taped where gapping. The faded stand-in door of repressed board was laminated with dying flies and dead mosquitoes. It was far too flimsy for those ancient hinges, which still creaked atmospherically. The gloom inside was blinding, but only momentarily: too soon the penetrant eyes saw all too clearly. Lou said, "Howdy."

"Sir?" he stood sidewise to the door, at a three-and-a-half-legged table. He himself was not misshapen, in fact almost straight, and slender. In a better light his clear skin might have looked less sallow. Nice thin white teeth he had, they would have been fine for smiling. His black eyes blinked at Lou, or sunlight. Lou half-closed the door behind him. There were no pictures on the walls, no clock or calendar. There was a keyboard, on which hung every other key, three in all. The fan was bigger than Boss Hall's, which was probably what made the silence only seem uncanny. Did that explain why the fan but not the air was moving? "Sir?"

"Howdy, I'm looking for a single room with a telephone."

The man pointed to a card and a pen on the good side of the table. "All the rooms have telephones."

"Oh great. How much will that be?"

The black eyes were no longer blinking. "$20."

"Have you something a little cheaper?"

"All the rooms are $20."

"Ah. Can I give you a traveler's check?"

Lou waited with loath ardency for his yes.

"Sir?" But when Lou showed him one, he nodded and watched closely how Lou committed forgery with the chained-down ballpoint. When Lou handed out the check and registration card to him, he read with Boss Hall thoroughness. "There's a $5 key deposit," he finally said.

"$5?" Lou drew a five from his disintegrating wallet.

The man turned reluctantly to the keyboard, chose #5. "It's around back. You can leave your car back there too."

"My car's not here."

"Sir?"

Around back was a scene that might have made Chumly feel a little better about where he was to spend the night; it was remindful of the mansion in New Mexico they had stopped at briefly before taking to the street. All the half dozen cars crammed into this narrow space looked derelict with dust. Here, #5 was found at the head of an enclosed, airproof stairway, in orange light. The key was to a padlock, for management had had to chain the door closed after someone bashed it. Inside, the TV and air conditioner were bolted to the ceiling, though the air conditioner didn't work. No one would have cared to take the chair or desk or bed. At least there was no bloodstain on the carpet, no dried blood in the shower stall, no whining dog outside, patrolling before the door. It will always haunt me whether he was warning us or begging to chew the leavings. Nor had there been giggling in the office at: "You always like the plump ones—that's why you're so fat." There was no plump and pretty girl on this trip.

Perhaps they had a fan at The Caboose. He jotted his phone number on a matchbook, put his three beers to cool, to swelter, in the sink, before he padlocked up. It was good to rejoin the sun, the chartreuse glare of late afternoon in Cadsbury. The tires looked fuller. One had a current license plate. Around front, a faint blue sign in the window stuttered v-VAcancY. Wiry starlings patrolled the gutters for exploding seeds and other infiltrators. Sparrows leaped. Deep in the liquor store gleamed an heartening light. The door of The Caboose was open, for air or welcome—or neither one. As Lou stepped in, so people glanced. This was not a family restaurant. The old men hunched in separate booths. A pale mother sat in another one, opposite her weeping daughter. A young man sat at the counter. The one behind it was small and hot. Lou sat down in front of him, beneath the fan, and he moved off to stand in front of the other man.

The other smiled eagerly, spooning soup. "Pretty hot today!"

Shrugging, the small man moved back to Lou. The menu was above his head. Chop suey and sausages were the specialties. "I guess I'll have chop suey and milk," Lou said.

"Suey!" he called to wet grey hair in a hole behind his back, and drew a cloudy plastic glass of bluish milk. He brought Lou's tinware and soy sauce along with it. "Close at six o'clock."

It was 5:25 in The Caboose. Lou lit a cigarette. "About how many people are in this town?" he asked.

"What?" He was moving away again.

"What's the population of Cadsbury?"

"I don't know. I live over in Rocksbury."

"Suey!" the grey hair called.

So close to closing time, she had heaped Lou's plate, and not just with rice. There were sprouts in there, and a good glutinous sauce, the kind that sticks to the ribs, as to the throat until diluted well with soy. Lou had it all down by 5:48. The little man behind the counter took his plate, shoved it back into the grey-haired hole. He took Lou's money and his little tip. The young man had left. The old men were still gumming suey, back to back. The mother was smoking a cigarette, watching her daughter get her sausage wet. Lou headed across the street to the liquor store.

The door wasn't open, but this man said "Howdy," if warily. He had been badly beaten around the head not long ago. His face looked like the door to #5 held together with scab for chain. Luckily the sherry was right out there in front; one would have hesitated to step behind this man's back. He held both his hands beneath the cash register drawer, waited for Lou to place the bottle on the counter top. "A little sherry tonight?"

"Right."

"Anything else? Cold beer?"

"Not tonight."

"That will be $2.50 then."

Lou reached out a five to him, trying to look into his eyes without his face. "I'd much appreciate some extra quarters in the change."

"Certainly." The man scooped ten quarters with his left hand, reached them out to Lou. Then he bagged the bottle quickly with both hands. "Thank you, sir."

"Many thanks to you."

"Have a good evening!" the man called to him at the door.

"You have a good one too!"

On Charnel Street, he thought at first the phone had moved, until he saw it hidden behind the talking dude. Lou stood discreetly to one side, and lit a cigarette. People who talk on public phones acquire the eyes of owls, and prefer to use them peripherally. When looked at straight they turn their heads, which they'd rather not. This one hooted softly on until Lou had finished his cigarette. "Buzz me later," he said aloud. Nodding sidewise at Lou, he crossed the street to his big black car and waited there. Lou had no doubt he took peripheral note of the many digits tapped.

"Number please."

"I'd like to call the number I just dialed."

"What number please."

"I just dialed the—"

"What kind of call is this."

"A telephone call. I'll try again."

He did.

"What number are you calling please."

Lou gave it to her slowly, numeratim.

"What is your number please."

"I . . . Oh." He read her the other one.

"Is this pay charge or collect."

"Pay."

Now something clicked, and an electronic voice spoke slowly. "Please deposit two dollars and sev-en-ty-five cents . . . Please deposit . . ."

"Give me a few seconds!" He and the liquor man had the quarters almost right; Lou added one.

Something clicked again, and something rang her or their number at the other end. If she was there, she would wait for the second ring to spend itself before picking up the phone with whichever hand wasn't holding something else. She was there. "Hello."

"Hi," Lou said.

"Well, hi! Where are you calling from?"

"Somewhere about twenty miles or kilometers west or southwest of Boston."

She laughed. "Sounds kind of spacey."

He laughed too. "It kind of is."

"I was half-expecting you to call last night."

"I know, but I said I'd probably wait until I had some news."

"Have you seen Bowden yet?"

"Not yet."

"Well, tell me everything. How are you, first?"

"I'm fine. And how's everything with you?"

"Oh, wonderful. I love the place—the space. You'd be proud of me. I spent all day Sunday and most of last night fixing things up. I don't get to bed until I happen to fall on it . . . But tell me your adventures first."

"It'll take a while. I'm calling from a booth, a stand. Maybe it would be best for you to call me at my place. I didn't want to try from there—it was $5 for the key deposit."

"Whewy. What's the number?"

"You have a pen or pencil?"

"In my hand."

He had already guessed she was talking to her left; he read the number to her. "Give me about fifteen minutes to get into the place."

She laughed. "You make it sound difficult."

He laughed too. "It kind of is."

"Soon."

"Soon." Hanging up the phone, he turned to nod at the dude coming from his car. Around the corner, he knew the liquor man watched him from across the street. A little grey-haired lady was mopping The Caboose. The starlings and sparrows had moved to another street. The v-VAcancY sign blinked a little more boldly now. Around back, the reclaimed car had left. The heat in #5 was here to spend the night. He pulled the tin chair closer to the telephone. While he waited, he drank a beer to cool his suey if not himself. At least the taste was good, and the can looked rather decorative in here when he placed it on the desk. He had no watch, but he well knew when more than fifteen minutes passed. He decided against lifting the telephone, forfeiting his deposit for a "Sir?" He gave her a full beer's worth of time before he repadlocked.

That car had gotten back. Around front, the sign was off. Everything otherwise was much the same. The dude was seated in his car again; he caught Lou's quick approach. Was he relieved or disheartened when Lou punched O this time? Things go better when you call collect. The operator seemed rather pleased with him. She had a nice conversation with the Denver operator, several others along the way, bypassing the electronic ones. "Will you accept a collect call from Hugh Webb?"

"Yes! Hi, Hugh!"

He laughed. "Hi again."

"I tried calling you at that number. The first time, somebody answered in a language I've never heard before and then hung up. The second time somebody said 'No number 5, no number 5' and hung up again. What kind of a place is that?"

"I think you have a pretty good sense of it. I guess I should have had you call me here at the phonestand."

"We could do that now."

"Let's not try."

"Good thinking. Well, tell me all you dare to."

"Here goes. I'm in a little town called Cadsbury outside of Boston. Chumly gave out a few miles from here. It was terribly hot. I'd stopped for a hamburger along the way, then I couldn't get Chumly started again. A nice guy helped push us around the lot, but nothing happened."

"What seems to be the problem?"

"I don't know. It doesn't seem to be the points this time."

"Poor old Chumly. I wish we'd towed him from Oregon."

"I guess we should have."

"Where is he now?"

"The people who towed us have a kind of garage in Cadsbury. It looks more like a wrecking yard. They look like a family of gangsters—I watched them dealing with another customer."

"Did they give you any idea what the trouble is?"

"They won't be looking until tomorrow. They were closing."

"Maybe you can find another mechanic there."

"Maybe so."

"You usually seem to find good mechanics."

"Oh ya."

"Boy, am I glad I didn't take this trip!"

"I know. Tell me how things are there."

"I love the apartment. I've got the colors and the textures of all the curtains in my mind. You should see the living room now. You'd be proud of me—I moved the couch to the back wall all by myself. The room feels much more united, settled this way. I was sitting there when you called, making a shopping list and looking out at the sunlight on the park. You'd have loved it. Is it dark there yet?"

"No, still blazing."

"Well, you may have gathered, I'm having a ball! You know this is the first time I've ever fixed up a place from scratch, just the way I want it."

"Ah."

"Well, you know we lived for seven and a half years in little furnished places, mostly dumps."

"Mostly."

"Or slept on the floor in unfurnished ones."

"That's true."

"When we weren't living in the back of a car."

"That's true too."

She was keening now. "Or sleeping in bushes beside the road."

"Ya."

"On glass and spiders and burrs."

He laughed. "How's work?"

"Lots."

"Have you heard anything about the grant?"

"I think I blew it. He called when I was asleep and I didn't even know who was calling until halfway through. But I have other plans in mind anyway."

"Is there any interesting mail?"

"I haven't been to the post office. I'll go tomorrow."

"Are you writing?"

"I haven't had much time for that. Are you?"

"Ya, I'm writing a cookbook."

"A cookbook! What kind of a cookbook?"

"I'll wait and tell you when I see you," he said. "You know

Ma Bell is diversifying."

She laughed. "Miss you," she said.

"Miss you too."

"Well, this call is getting expensive. And rackety." The telephone was blipping.

"Yes, and there's a big dude in a big black car here who seems to use this phonestand as his office."

"When do you expect to see Bowden?"

"I hope to see him tomorrow or the next day."

"Let me hear what happens."

"Oh yes."

"Good luck with Chumly."

"And with the apartment."

"Goodnight."

"Goodnight."

He kissed, and after what was barely a pause she did. Cradling the phone softly, he turned to wave at the dude approaching. "Last call tonight."

"Right on!" The dude waved too.

On Fourth St. the liquor store gleamed at him as he went by, as did a dolorous nightlight in The Caboose. Passing the office, he decided to leave well enough alone until the morning. Around back he propped the outer door open with a broken board. He left the inner one open too, moved the chair over there. It was too hot to turn the TV on, far less think about TV cookery. He had wanted to say a few words about double boilers. Instead he took off his shirt, his shoes and socks, emptied his pockets on the bed. In the bathnook, he soaked the towel along with his jeans and himself in the shower. Draping the towel over his head, he sat down with a beer to meditate and guard the door.

She was happy.

T H R E E

He took his bag with him, and remembered to chain the door. After –5, outside seemed cool. He would not be needing his sweater though. His jeans were long since dry of course. He himself did not feel clean; he felt uneasy mean. He pushed into the office that way, left the door open wide. Nothing here had changed, even the keys hung just the same. The one slight difference was that the sidewise clerk said "Sir."

Lou said, "My wife called me twice last night. Nobody would put her through."

The man blinked at the door.

"She was calling long distance. I told you I wanted a room with a telephone. I had to go out and call her collect."

The blinks were under control. Lou tossed the key onto the table, on the crippled side, wishing the thing would tip over on him. The man reached into the table drawer and brought out last night's five. He made Lou reach for it. Lou tucked it slowly into his wallet before he turned away. From the open door he said, "Enjoy your v-VAcancY."

With the blue milk of The Caboose in mind, he found himself athirst for chocolate. With three tepid beers and a fifth of cream sherry in heavy hand, he scarcely glanced at the liquor store. He recalled seeing one that might be a little grocery store among those along the oblong, and he headed there. It was indeed a little grocery store, narrow, of frugal bent. It was the kind where routemen drop their remnant goods on Saturday afternoon before racing back to the plant. Five dusty cans of soup looked down the shelf at a rusty can of pineapple-grapefruit drink. Lou chose the last carton of chocolate milk, for thirst and vitamins, and the freshest-looking Hostess cake for calories and whatever fibre. At the cash register stood a thin lady with thinning hair. Lou offered his five to her.

"Do you have a dollar bill?"

"I'm sorry, I haven't."

She gave up all her ones to him. "Will you need a bag for that?"

"No, I've got one here." He dropped his breakfast in and took it to a far corner of the oblong, as far from the Court House and the trees as possible. He sat down to it; the sun discouraged most of the sowbugs here. The chocolate milk tasted pretty good at first, the Hostess cake had an almost satisfying chewiness: his stomach let him take his time with them. Across the way a ponderous grey powermower growled at the moribund lawn, guided by a boy of about the same age and shape, a Cadsbury boy. What held the eye, caught the breath, was a vision dancing in the air beside them. She was dancing with the mower, talking with the boy. When the boy turned the mower at the end of a row, she floated around to dance back on the other side. She was small and slender, but one could not quite make her figure out, though she seemed to be wearing a diaphanous dress. She showed no sign of self-consciousness; perhaps she thought she was walking. She moved more gracefully than any ballerina he had seen, than any deer. She was an angel deer who had strayed from the sky, footloose in enchanted Cadsbury. It took the close approach of ten o'clock to turn Lou away; he didn't look back for fear of seeing only lout and mower.

He followed the tracks back to the fence, tried to feel relief at finding Chumly and the bleeding wrecker no longer parked in there. He entered by the official door. Only Boss Hall and one bulb-batter were in here today, and Lou pushed through to the desk. In a minute or two the boss looked up from his papers. "Hyou've got hreal trouble," he said.

"Oh? What kind?"

"He'll show hyou." He meant the flat-headed one who carried his hands in his coverhauls; that way he knew where they were when he wanted to use one. Leading Lou to the shed, he grumbled, "What kind hof ha Hopel his that hanyway?"

"I guess you could call it a Chopel," Lou said. "Somebody put a Chevette engine in it."

"Hwhat hyear Chevette?" Boss Hall called.

"A '72."

Chumly looked puzzled. He stood alone in the center with a battery charger in his mouth, his air filter upside down on his head, while all around him people tinkered with others. Yet he was purring! Bending to listen, Lou's guide shook flat denial. "Hit's the carburetor," he said. He took out a hand and beckoned the shoulderless one, who slithered in behind the steering wheel. Chumly's purr grew a little louder, then stopped altogether. "See there," Flathead said. "Start her again, Snake." This time he joggled the linkage with his hand: Chumly sputtered bravely before choking out. "See there."

"It couldn't be the fuel pump, could it?"

"No, the pump his pumping. Hagain, Snake! See there. Hit's jut the carburetor won't take gas. See there!"

The bossone was coming out of his den. "Hit'll cost hyou two hundred for ha hnew hwon," he called. "Hit would take two days to get here from Boston. Hwith the Labor Day hcoming hwe couldn't hwork hon hit huntil next hweek."

"Ho. Maybe something could be done with this one," Lou suggested, "to get me moving for a while at least. I'll really need it over the weekend."

"Kneel!" Boss Hall balled. "Kneel Baruzzi. Cmere ha minute. Think hyou could get this thing going?"

Kneel Baruzzi had sharp little eyes that looked at cars not people; he was dwarfed by everyone in here, Lou as well as family. "I could give it a try this afternoon," he said quietly, a sharp finger fluttering Chumly's carburetor.

"Hyou don't think hit'll run, do hyou?"

Kneel Baruzzi thought before he spoke. "I guess not," he said. He did give Lou a sharp apologetic glance before he wandered off.

"Hit can't be fixed," Boss Hall said. "Hit'll cost hyou more than that car his worth to put hin ha hnew hwon. Hi don't think hyou hwant that."

Lou patted Chumly's fender. "Maybe we could find a rebuilt carburetor somewhere around here."

"Hi've tried that—Hi called a couple hof places. Hnowbody's got hwon."

"Maybe if we tried a few more."

"There's the phone hon the hwall there. Try hall hyou hwant. Hnobody's got hwon."

The phonebook was somewhat more complete than the one in the booth, a little less parched, greased not bleached; the light in here was just enough to read the numbers by; Lou began at the top. The word had gotten around. Nobody had one, not before the holiday. No way, not for a '72—maybe for a '78. Most heartening of all were those who took time to look. Lou patted Chumly again on his way to the office.

"Hwell, hyou hready to give hit hup?"

"How about letting it sit there a couple of hours while I look around and see what I can find."

"Hokay, hokay." Boss Hall was adjusting his fan. Hup.

She had departed. The boy and his tank were charging everywhere now, in search of grass. Black twigs and sowbugs bit the air. Machine and boy sweated their sticky gasolines in the noxious dust. Lou oblonged them this time. He bypassed the grocery store too, it being flat out of chocolate milk. He stopped at the booth, held the door open with his foot, for already it was beginning to feel like #5. The mechanics were gathered at Cadsbury Corners according to the book. He stacked it together again before he left. At the Court House he stopped before an old man seated in the sunshine on a bench. "Excuse me, can you tell me which way Cadsbury Corners is?"

The old man had been asked plenty of questions in his time, for sure, though not of late. He took off his straw hat to scratch his head, show off his full shock of white hair. He put his hat back on to point. "Must be out that way," he said. Then he turned to point the other way, where Fourth St. disappeared in grey woods. "Ain't no corners down there." He was directing Lou back to the dairy barn.

"Many thanks!"

"Just keep along that way," the old man was explaining behind his back. "You'll find them out there."

"Thanks again!" Lou called, waving. He hurried now, for the patrol car was sirening a Thunderbird merging rearlong from the service station. Lou had not planned to try there anyway. The dude was away from the office. He was in the liquor store, probably on his way to a business lunch at The Caboose. Lou slowed a little past the Hmotel Jones, trotted past the fly-warmed dairy, hiked now in open country. The old man was sending him to Boston. Oh no, not quite: high in the air ahead hung shells and flying horses. He cantered toward them. There were three of them, one on every corner, where Fourth St. went its separate ways to Burntrom and Twukesbury. The shells were left, the horses right, chevrons pointing sharply at them in the center. A man was sweeping beneath the horses as Lou approached him with "Goodmorning!"

"Hello there." It sounded like a reproach, to one who had neither horse nor carriage. "How you going?"

"I've got a little problem with an—a Chevette engine."

"What kind of problem?" The man continued sweeping.

"It runs on idle, but then it conks out when you accelerate. They say it's the carburetor—I'm not sure."

"We don't do much mechanical work here. Mostly gas and maintenance. You can try Red over there." He pointed at the chevrons. "He's a good mechanic."

"Many thanks to you."

Over there a man was pumping gas out front, another was hanging headfirst in a big car in the heart of a one-lift working space. He had the motor running beneath his face, wherever that was in the smothering steam. It was at least 110° F in here—probably his backside felt cool to him. Lou stood at the edge, under the overhanging door, waiting for him to come up for what he would think was air. His screwdriver came up first; his hand groped for a smaller one. He was adjusting the carburetor. When he turned down the idle, the smoke cleared a bit. Not satisfied, he tuned again, then grunting heaved himself out of there. He was a man built to work on compact cars. Standing on tiptoe, he fished out his trouble light hand over hand. Red no longer, Red had been. Now all the color was in his face. Lou waited while he caught his breath. "Red?"

Turning off his light, Red nodded. "Can I help you?"

"I have a little Chevette engine that doesn't want to go—it idles nicely, but then it cuts out. The people at Hall's Haul and Overhaul say it's the carburetor, but I don't know. A mechanic could tell. The Mobil man says you're a good mechanic."

"It's over at Hall's?"

"They towed me in from the freeway last night."

Red considered the steaming engine in front of him, the solemn highrise pickup just behind, the camper bonging the bell outside, then Lou, and said: "I can give it a look if you can get it over here."

"Great. Many thanks!"

He ran back to Hall's with the news, at which Boss Hall shrugged. "Hwhatever hyou hwant. Haul his forty dollars," he said, signalling the bleeder. The bleeder did it without radio, but Lou took no advantage of that. Chumly did not try to get away this time, nor complain when dropped in a narrow slot outside

Red's shop. In effect this station had three corners which met in front; everything was tightly packed inside that Y. A low cement wall in back separated it from the parking lot fanning out to a supergrocery store. That was where they kept the chocolate milk. Nonetheless Lou waited for Red, hanging by his belt in pickup smother. A well-worn wooden ladder enabled him up there. It sounded like a dual carburetor this time, the way he was gunning it. It took him ten or twenty tries to match all intakes up the way he liked. He was not a man to be easily satisfied just to save his life; when he went, things would be sounding right. He looked ready to pop when he came out, but he did not. He stared at Chumly instead. Even a brave man can pale, in any heat; bravery needs apprehension first, as does love.

"Oh no, I thought you said it was a Chevette."

"Inside it is."

Taking a deep breath he turned off his trouble light. "We'll have to push it aside to get this one out." He helped Lou do that before pushing the pickup into the street. Then he helped push Chumly onto the rack. "Start it up," he said, turning on his trouble light. He was able to stand on his feet, his toes, while he worked, and through the smoke Lou could occasionally see him adjusting things. "It isn't the carburetor," he said finally, standing up. "Somebody's been fooling with these sparkplugs though."

"Maybe they tested them at Hall's. I wasn't there when they checked it over."

"These need replacing." He showed them to Lou before placing them on his workbench, studied his parts book before selecting new ones. He seemed to enjoy this steamless respite, screwed sparkplugs judiciously. By the time he had two of them in, the office bell was mad with bonging. Red looked up to see his four pumps besieged by four cars and an RV Monster, his helper hopping among them with his sponge and rubber scraper, grabbing a hose from one tank to jab it in another, while perspiring drivers waved their credit cards and money at him. Probably a few years Red's senior, he had not yet learned his patience. Red went out to show him how to get things done in seeming leisure, enjoy the comfort of mid-afternoon fresh air and sunshine, enjoy chatting with the customers. Ten minutes later, saying something pleasant to the helper in a language Lou could not make out, he returned to the office with a handful of slips and money, a cold Pepsi in the other. Taking a swig, he placed it on his workbench, returned to Chumly's sparkplugs. When he turned on his trouble light a little later, Lou started Chumly up again. All three were heartened when a roar responded. "Hey, good work!" Lou called, but Red called back: "That's better, but still not right. Try backing up a little."

Lou eased into reverse, cautiously pressed the accelerator, felt Chumly creeping off the rack.

"Take it around the block and see what happens."

Chumly crept backward into the street, all but proudly. He couldn't wait to try going forward. Lou's foot gave him gentle encouragement. There was perhaps a slight uprise here, but they were rolling. Actually this still felt like creeping. When they reached the top of whatever rise, they levelled off at fifteen miles an hour.

Chumly simply could do no more, no matter how Lou teased him. It was as though he had developed an allergy to gasoline. They went around the block, two blocks, expecting things to suddenly clear up at any minute. Red was hanging high on the rack in a lady's car when they got back; they parked over to one side this time, and waited there with a Pepsi.

"How'd it go?" Red asked, after he had backed the lady out of there.

"We were running nice and smoothly, but couldn't do better than fifteen miles an hour, maybe twenty going downhill once."

"It's something else," Red said.

"The engine has a long history of trouble with its points."

"I'll check those later. First I want to check the timing."

He traded his trouble light for his timing light, plunged back in again. Lou caught glimpses of him from time to time through the smoke, his livid face lit up by the blinking light. To Lou it blinked with a nerve-wracking persistency, but Red kept returning to it from whatever called him, the bonging bell, the telephone, the customers, the steaming radiators, the swig of Pepsi. Lou was on his second can when Red turned off his timing light and said, "Try running it around the block again."

Things went a little better with them this time, they levelled off at eighteen miles an hour, twentytwo downhill. Red shook his head when they got back. "That's not quite it," he said, going for his timing light. Twenty minutes later he sent them out again. But they seemed to have reached their peak, were if anything a little slower on the downhill run. This time Red was waiting for them with his light. The fourth time they got back he was in the office with his helper, and he left them sitting on the rack a while before he came out. "We close at seven—I have to do the books. I'll check that distributor in the morning. I want to check the alternator too."

"Good enough," Lou said. "I guess I'll sleep in the car tonight."

"Why don't you run it back to the parking lot—I'll be locking this place up."

"Fine." Lou backed off the rack.

"We open at seven," Red called.

"Seven," Lou called, "and many thanks for your willingness."

Red waved. He had a willing smile when asked for it.

The supergrocery closed at eight. Lou got tonight's ice cream bar and Vienna sausages and tomorrow morning's chocolate milk before going to the liquor store. He ate the ice cream before they left. Chumly seemed pleased to be of help again, especially in town where everyone creeped. The V-VAcancY sign was on again; probably he thought that stutter was a wink. The old lady was mopping The Caboose. In the liquor store a friendly greeting awaited Lou. The man's face had not noticeably improved, but his hands were easier. This was an all-sherry evening. There was a lot of room out there, but he didn't want to flood the place. He bought a quart.

"Have another good night!"

"You another too!"

The patrol car was waiting for them down the street. It badly wanted to siren them, but it could not, Chumly saw to that. And Lou chose a side street in which to turn around. He did not stop at the phonestand. Perhaps there would be news tomorrow night. Tonight he would drink to her instead. Most of the parking lot was theirs by the time they got home. The few cars lined up at the cement wall were probably Red's. He parked with them and climbed in back, checked his chextra shirt over the driver's seat. He sat low back there, so that Chumly would look empty like all the rest. No one watched him eat Vienna sausages, crackers, raisins, nuts. He did not have to raise his bottle up, for he had a plastic cup. She had given him that. Thank you, honey. I'll make good use of it tonight . . .

The sun woke him early, caught sparkling in the windshield's jagged crack. When awaiting dawn in a parking lot on an important day, park facing east. He cleaned his eyes, turned on the radio, sat back to drink his quart of chocolate. The sun had moved off in quest of other cracks more southerly and higher. The radio was grumbling about the heat. He turned it off, put on his checkered shirt, for it was seven; the helper had pulled in beside them in his brown Cromagnon. His glance at Chumly was not encouraging, but he did acknowledge Lou's "Goodmorning!"

"Gamin," he said.

"O.K. if I use the men's room for shaving?

He did not say, but unlocked the door on his way to the office where bells were already bonging. When Lou came out, Red had already joined his helper, helping. He waved his sponge at Lou. "Let's get going."

"I'm due in Boston today," Lou said. "What's the surest way to get there?"

"You'd better hurry—the bus goes that way in the morning. It brings them home at night.

"Where can I catch that?"

"Somewhere in town—I'm not sure where it stops these days. Someone in there will tell you. Leave the car where it is. Leave the key in it."

"Many thanks to you!" Lou called, on the run.

The old man was seated on his sun-drenched bench, waiting for his questions. He removed his hat at Lou's approach, shook off a yellowjacket investigating his tousled mane.

"Excuse me again, sir—can you tell me where I might catch the bus to Boston?"

"Boston?" He replaced his hat, entrapping the yellowjacket. There was no need to warn him; that thatch was impenetrable. He was a little deaf too, gave no mind to the buzzing.

"Well, that'll be on the other side of the square, right there on Third there." He turned on his bench to peer over there.

"Over there by the depot?"

"No no, this side of the street, son. Just stand by that yellow trashbarrel there."

"This side? Wouldn't that be heading west?"

Peering, the old man blinked, or was that a wink? "It turns around," he said.

"Aha. Many thanks to you!"

"You'll want to get right over there, son. It's due any time now, any time between a quarter past and half."

"Thanks again!" Lou called, on his way. He took the noxious, diagonal route this time, through the fetid shade of the spindly trees, over the sticky bald spot, over the yet crunchy grass the boy's mower had chewed. And none too soon, it seemed; people were already queuing up beside the jaundiced barrel. They did not speak but nodded at one another, over the shoulder, sidewise. They nodded so at Lou as he took his place behind them. He passed it on to a stout, puffing newcomer in Hallish coverhauls. The man's head jerked sideward, but there was no one there to nod at.

Someone up front broke the silence. "There he comes."

"Right on time today."

Yet the driver seemed bent on contradicting them. His bus, scaley grey, a mutated, lopsided sowbug, appeared to be dissolving in the vapors of its own exhaust, while out the presumable window his arm waved cheerful adieu. It was not until they reappeared at the Court House that one could appreciate what forward progress they were making. Now too a reassuring squeal rent the air; the driver was already applying the brakes. Even so, he only came to a stop several feet beyond the queue, beyond the trashbarrel itself. There he awaited them, side door and grin agape. The stolid passengers boarded in turn. Most of them carried green plastic bags, whether of lunch or refuse it was impossible to say. Lou soon enough learned what the driver's contained; creased, stained, moldy as it was, one could still make out what the ticket read: GOOD ONE WAY. "Pay at the other end," the grinning driver said.

"Oh, right. What time do you head back from Boston?"

"Around five-thirty or forty. Depends on how quick I get away from Charlie's."

"Ah."

When they were mostly seated, the driver slammed the big door by hand while gunning with his foot. The bus waddled off. The old man was quite right, it did turn around, taking just a few splinters of the depot along. Soon they were passing the Court House, Cadsbury Corners after a while (Chumly was on the rack now, Red somewhere in there) and heading for Twukesbury. Even seen dimly through the sealed grey windowglass, while being pinched sharply at each jounce by the cracked leather seat, the countryside was a pleasure after so long in town. One could quite easily imagine the sky to be clear, and blue, out there. Surely these birds were singing, or railing. Why else would they perch so in a row, throw their heads back as the bus bumbled by? Why else did he himself feel his face almost relaxed, almost smiling? He was agreeably surprised, scarcely half an hour later, to find that they had gained Twukesbury. Um, for one who considered himself an intuitive man, he had been having a bad streak lately. With no Court House, this square looked rather inviting. Here trees better understood themselves, people sat in their shade. The driver stopped to pick up four or five, in exchange for a pair of departing old ladies. Only one of them dropped her plastic bag in the trashbarrel. If that had not been refuse when she boarded, she had eaten it. Not having to turn around, the Sowbug Express lurched straight ahead out of town. Of the two he had seen, Twukesbury was the prettier. Ahead lay Sudfield, Wayham, and Wenning.

He dozed off until Casterbridge, where intimations of familiarity sat him up. The iron fence he did remember, though they had taken the gate off. Inside, the grass looked less natural than formerly, even less so than on their last visit. It seemed you were no longer allowed to walk on it. He remembered himself one evening too many years ago gliding over it, coattails flying; something in the air or the grass had lent him wings for a hundred yards or so. All that was soon behind him. They were trundling Bostonward. Drivers gave wide clearance to them; they were not used to seeing such an animal here in their city . . . maybe an occasional caterpillar. This recalled to him the last rat he had seen out in the street, at night, in Cambridge, England. And it had looked a bit uneasy. They had both.

Their driver chose to drop them on a side street off Scully Square, next to a parking ramp. As his passengers filed out, he gleefully took their money and retrieved their tickets. That way he could hold the fare down to $2.98. There were a few sidewise nods as they got off the bus, but mostly they all hustled away in their predestined directions. Lou headed for a payphone at the base of that ramp, where dusty refuse stirred petulantly in a surprisingly chilly draft. There was no phonebook extant, only the everlasting blue covers—remnant pages buzzed at his ankles—but he had the number somewhere in what remained of his wallet. Kicking those insistent yellow pages aside, he did find it, and dialed—rattled it.

The voice was cheerful. "Laurence Bowden Books. Goodmorning!"

"Goodmorning. Is Larry Bowden there?"

"May I tell him who is calling?"

"Lou Webb."

"Just a minute, Mr. Webb—I'll connect you!"

Her moment lasted but seconds, the new voice was not just cheerful, hearty: "Hello there? Lou Webb?"

"Yes—Larry Bowden?"

"Speaking. Where are you?"

"I'm in Boston."

There was a pause. "What's that?"

"Boston!"

"What! Speak louder!"

"We seem to have a bad connection! I'll try rattling again!"

"What!"

Lou hung up. He was out of dimes, but, provident as always, he still had quarters left. He rerattled with a sigh.

"Laurence Bowden Books. Goodmorning!"

"Hello! It's Lou Webb again."

"Just a moment, Mr. Webb. I'll reconnect you."

Her moment took due measure this time. Finally: "Larry Bowden here."

"Hi again! Is it better now?"

"A little," Larry Bowden said. His voice was still loud,

but where was the old cheer, the gustiness? He said: "You're in from Oregon?"

"Right."

"You're coming over?"

"Yes, I'd like to."

"What time will you be here?"

"What would be a good time for you?"

"Let's see. Things are pretty busy around here, what with the holiday . . ."

"Whatever's convenient—I've got all day."

"Well, let me look . . ." He looked and looked. "Well, how about three?"

"Fine. See you at three."

"You know where we are?"

"Yes, more or less." He would have plenty of time to find out.

"O.K., then, Webb."

"See you later."

"All right," with click.

When Webb hung up, his dime came back; his quarter had been enough. It didn't cheer him much. Bowden himself had sounded quite depressed. His letter had seemed such a friendly one, as had he just now, at first. What, had a New York-Casterbridge-Canadian-English-Western accent turned him off? Had a bad connection rattled him that much? A stray yellowjacket had been buzzing him? Perhaps it was just his manner on the telephone. Lou had never cared much for the machine himself, though he generally managed to use it civilly. Intuition hinted that he should head back to Cadsbury, but as too often before it proved no match for curiosity, not to mention hope. He headed slowly toward the future through the fractured neighborhoods of the past, getting his city legs. Boston was familiar enough, what was left of it. Didn't that still look like Minski's? The Copley, the Statler, the Commons remained, the Lobster House, such places as fathers used to take them to. Where though was the Silver Dollar, the little stops on the way to it. They had wiped out the old haunts: the dim smelly bars were overlit cafeterias now, the furtive little hotels were new motels, picture windows and cinder block. Big signs out front, their crass glass most often punctured by rocks, offered a night's rest for $32, double occupancy, where once $1.50 bought three or four hours for two or more. Cars wheeled dangerously in and out. Pedestrians, mostly men and boys, kept to the alleys behind the liquor stores. The canmen clustered at the dumpsters, methodically crunching underfoot and packing their plastic sacks.

One young boy stood on the sidewalk ahead, at the curb, a pale cashmere sweater draped round his neck. He flicked one sleeve gently at a passing patrol car. The patrol car screeched through a U-turn, drew up on the other side. The big policeman hopped out. He stood squarely in front of the boy, six feet away in the street, hands on hips in his sharply-tailored summer uniform. "How old are you?" he growled.

"Fifteen."

"Why aren't you in school?"

"I'm vis-iting."

Lou strolled quietly on. Moments later he felt the patrol car rush by, toward the suburbs, glimpsed the boy's little smile in the window. They were very soon out of sight.

He located Laurence Bowden Books, on a wide, complacent street, before wandering about in search of people and shops. Just east was an even quieter avenue running north and south, dour, rather Cadsburyesque. One felt that people had once lived in those dark brick buildings, perhaps a century ago; now only the housing remained. Two massive rows faced each other across a mangy, high-elmed greenway that bisected the street, where here and there an old man slouched on a bench, peering out from under his hat. These gents were not looking for questions but quarters. Lou headed west while he still had a few. It was out there that the activity was, attracted by three or four shops and a parking lot. The people looked younger here. They perched on wire chairs in front of the snack shop, nipping their ice cream while the wire table bit little red welts in their elbows and arms, for they were all white. One sat in a little box in the middle of the parking lot, eating his cone all alone. A mother strawed her strawberry shake on the way back to the laundromat; her little boy sucked his thumb. Lou felt it was time to eat.

The shop did have chocolate milk. He carried it to a curbed patch of real grass in front of a real estate office closed for lunch.

The milk was cool and fresh, the chocolate sweet. He drank it too quickly in gulps. When he carried the empty carton to the laundromat, he spotted an ice cream machine in there. He had developed some confidence in these machines over several years on vending routes, and he was hungrier than he had thought. One of his quarters and his reclaimed dime bought him a bar with nuts on its crust. He took it back to his patch, waiting to uncover it well beyond range of the little boy's lugubrious watch. He was still eating too fast—but with his stomach's approval. At such times it is hard to take seriously good manners offended, for one cannot pat them. This time he took his trash to the snack shop, bought himself a hamburger with everything on it. He took it to his patch, for the real estate people themselves were still out to lunch. Now he could eat more decorously, though even as he did so his imagination was teased by the thought of making dessert of a hot dog. Soon after he was smiling inwardly as he went for it. Probably he would not mention this meal to Bowden; he would still have more than two hours to smoke out the onion.

And digest his burbling ingesta. Good that he did not often have too much time to kill, he'd have long ago lost his boyish figure. He began walking the blocks, rather slowly at first, clearing his throat at the occasional burp. Listless passersby, earphones plugged in, did not seem to take notice; perhaps they too were burpling. Certainly their complexions were pasty. They were going back to work, and in the preternatural light of midday in Boston their afternoon did not look promising, though he could imagine some of them quite pretty in the fluorescent glow of their offices. Meanwhile his attention mercifully wandered. What caught it was a wooden sign in the middle of the sidewalk: ACME RENTAL SERVICE $100 UP 3RD FLOOR REAR. A diversion. In fact he had told her he might try settling out here for a while, by way of easing the separation, for her at least. For himself, in his condition, it was the creaking stairs that made him feel easier. Little did it matter, for 3rd floor rear was closed. OPEN 5-6 PM LEAVE #. Having none, he creaked on down again, rejoined the thinning workward walkers.

Now he had about an hour and a half to use, and he spent some of it at a phonestand scanning those who had such things and cared to list them. In all that dense-packed million he could not right away find any he knew, not from the past. There was a scattering of new ones, but none that he cared to call just now, what with the holidays . . . etc. He knew the Arrogants of the nearby suburb. He headed now for Bowden Books by wandering ten blocks away from it, then east a few, south two, west again, and south for however many it took. He made it about on time, he felt. If he had to wait, he had time for that, and there would be a chair in there, if not a couch.

It had been an art museum once. Thus the wide and stately steps, the handrails of polished brass, the high doorway gracefully arched, the discreet sign inviting enquiries regarding office space. Certainly they had space to spare. The receptionist sat at the once curator's desk in the center of a lofty gallery to the left, where a visiting Rodin would formerly have stood. Approaching her Lou was able to take his mind off "The Kiss"; her bright greeting helped: "Goodafternoon! May I help you?"

"Goodafternoon! I'm Lou Webb. I have an appointment to meet Larry Bowden at three."

"Oh, yes! That's just down those stairs and to the right!"

"Many thanks!"

"Or would you prefer the elevator?"

"This is fine, thanks!"

Down here had been storage space, perhaps shared by a restaurant—a tea room. The ceiling was much lower here, in effect the underside of the display floor above. The interior walls were thinner too, by about a foot and a half, for Bowden had partitioned himself off. It was hard at first to find the entrance slot. Happening on it by chance, Lou entered a humming hive of electronic machines of various sizes and colors: black and ivory. Perhaps the black only seemed the more serious ones. The decor was continued throughout the low room, only interrupted here and there by a desk. Very new books were stacked in corners where old paintings had been, pastel book jackets papered the walls. In one corner a little cubicle was partitioned off, by glass in this case. Lou headed for that. The man inside might well be Bowden; he looked depressed. He was slinking out of his cage as Lou approached. A ballpoint pen hung on each of his ears, the assorted colors again. "Larry Bowden?"

"Just a minute." He moved past Lou to a man bent over a vibrating ivory machine.

They did not convene, but watched the machine, watched intently as it slowly shat into a tray. The one with the pens scooped it up, and together they studied it. Now the other man grabbed it and disgustedly squeezed it into a ball. They exchanged a few words, the taller one nodded his pens. He started back to Lou and the cage. "That's him over there," he said sliding by.

Bowden threw the wad at a wastebasket as Lou approached, booted it when it dropped on the floor.

"Larry Bowden?"

"Speaking." Now he turned around. "Oh, hello there."

"Hi." Lou put out his hand. "Lou Webb."

"Larry Bowden." The hand he offered was cool—and slippery. "You found us here."

"Oh yes."

Bowden spun to flip on the machine. "Shall we . . ." Hmmm.

"Excuse me?"

Bowden pointed to a desk: ". . . over there?" He led the way, took some books and papers from a chair, stacked them on the desk between that chair and his own. When they were seated he peered around them at Lou: "How was your . . . ?"

"My *trip*?" When Bowden nodded, Lou said: "Well, I had a little car trouble about seventeen miles west."

"*What?*"

"*Car* trouble. West of *Boston,*" Lou called, for Bowden had disappeared behind those books.

"Were you skeward?" Bowden called back.

"What's that?"

"Just a minute." A telephone was ringing, and Lou could see Bowden's sleek hand pick it up. "Bowden speaking . . . Oh. Yes. Just a minute . . ." His finger tapped a button on the side of the phone. "Now what's that? . . . Oh yes. Just a minute . . ." His hand covering the phone, he peered around the stack to wink at Lou. Of what one might call average size and shape, his personality was in his smile: thin, fixed, sharklike, yet somehow ingratiating, trying to pass for barracuda perhaps. "You might want to . . ." he said to Lou.

"Sir?"

Bowden pointed in back of Lou, above his head, at shelves. "*Books.*"

"Aha." Lou got up and went over there, while behind them Bowden boomed into the phone: "Now, where were we?" These were the Bowden Books, two of each, ten years' worth, many biographies and reminiscences, essays, the occasional novel, poetry. He drew out a novel by Ezra Brown, a fiction book, as they say in the trade. It was a handsome volume, and looked durable. He liked the heft of it, the firm way it was bound. That was what had first attracted him to the press: Bowden's aim was to make books that would last many years. He drew out another one, nonfiction this time. *Living in a Mill.* The title was not ironic, not sardonic, and had diagrams to prove it. It was by the author of *Retiring at Thirty.* On the shelves lay a variety of objets d'art; a celestial globe, of glass, stabbed by pen and pencil, of ebony and quartz; a bronzed font, as paperweight; brass books, as book ends; lead books. Fingering them Lou noted that Bowden was no longer on the phone, was now firmly plugged in. "Just a minute," he called as Lou approached, pointing at the bulky headset.

Lou sat down to read the titles of the fence Bowden had erected; these were new Bowden Books. Now Bowden put the earphones on top. "That was Bill Goslin with a new chapter for us," he shouted, tilting his head sidewise to peer at Lou. "You know his novels."

"Yes, I saw a couple over there."

"Now, we were talking . . ."

Machinery was drumming the partition at Bowden's back, and Lou shouted at that. "Yes!"

"*What?*"

"Do you do all your own printing here?"

"Oh. Only the jackets. And the one sheets. We haven't room for the rest. We have other holdings though. We're looking into air rights now. So much depends on priorities, financial short fall."

"I like your jackets."

"*What?*"

"I like them!"

"Oh good." He plucked a yellow one. "How about those graphics, hey? How do you find Boston?"

"It hasn't changed too much—a little sleeker."

"A little *what?*"

"Sleeker!"

"Sleeker? Isn't that in New York? I've lived around Boston all my life—except for four years of college." He paused to eye Lou, as though expecting comment from him.

"Oh!"

"I love Boston. I just love it, you know?"

Lou nodded encouragement.

"I wouldn't live anywhere else, not *anywhere.*"

"It's pretty nice all right."

"Pretty what?"

"Pretty nice!"

Tilted sidewise, Bowden's eyes held Lou narrowly in view. "Lean a little closer," he called. "I'm hypertropic, but I can see close hand too. What are you driving?"

Leaning forward, Lou spoke clearly: "It's a Chopel."

"How do you spell that?" Lou spelled it out while Bowden tapped a keyboard. "Married?"

"I? Well . . . yes."

"What's that?"

"Well . . ."

Bowden tapped that too. "Books?"

"I? Oh yes!"

Bowden tapped. "How many is that?"

"Ten."

Tapping Bowden kept his eyes on Lou. "Casualties?"

"Cas . . . ? Well, quite a few."

Bowden nodded and typed simultaneously. Now he fingered a gold-plated Rubik's Cube thoughtfully. "Would you care to describe them in your own words?"

"They're mostly novels," Lou said, and reached in his shirt to draw out a paper bag. "Here's the first one, the one I wrote you about reprinting."

"Oh yes." Bowden removed the book from the bag, hefted it. "I'll read it," he said.

"Fine. I hope you enjoy it."

Bowden reached behind him to tap another, larger keyboard, black. "Oops," he said, for he had set blue and white lights to flashing on an upright Retardil. "Well, might as well finish it," he said, swiveling to the machine. The game was to knock out the Unemployed—10 for Blues, 5 for Whites. Hypertropic or no, Bowden was a steeleyed sharpshooter. He flicked a little smile at Lou, before swinging to the ivory machine he had first intended. He spoke while they awaited its slow defecation: "They're trying to talk me into video vibes heads and lingerie, heavy metal, the whole byte. By the bye, there's a new video bar on Boylston. I don't know though, so much depends on the platforming. Talk about heavy metal—just for a 12-min 8mm demo clip you're talking thousands, out of pocket. Then you're into stereo clothing, sound warp, shoulder speakers—pretty heavy, actuarily speaking." Turning to Lou, he shook his heavy head.

Lou nodded in sympathy. "Then you'd get into video books?"

Bowden's face brightened. "It's an idea. That would be a good way to use the optional endings . . . Oho now." He was studying. The thing had finally come out of the machine, and it was not welcome. "We're going to have to get right onto this." He pressed a button on his desk, and out of his cage the secretary bird came stalking. Bowden shoved the thing onto his outstretched hand: "Bib, get right onto this."

Nodding to his pens, the bird stalked off with it.

Bowden stood up; he looked over the fence at Lou now. "Take some with you," he said.

"Sir?"

Bowden waved at the shelves. "Take some *books.*"

"Ah." Lou stood up too, took his paper bag with him. "Why don't you choose for me."

Bowden strode to the shelves. "Let's see." He began plucking books, not at random. "Goslin, Pound, Barley—these people *must* be published." He plucked out two more. "That should start you."

"Yes! Many thanks," Lou said, his paper bag stretched smooth now.

They were heading for the doorslot, Bowden in the lead. "I'll check yours out and get it back to you."

"No no, it's yours."

Bowden glanced back at him. "But that's valuable . . ."

"Yes," Lou said, "keep it in trade."

For once, swiftly, Bowden's smile was unsure, but "O.K. then."

Lou held out his hand for the halfshake. "Good to meet you."

"*What?*"

"Good!" Lou shouted.

"Yes!"

They waved goodbye. Lou waved at the bird sidling past. "Just a minute," he heard behind him. He dove for the slot, breathed deeply the well-preserved air. However glad to be moving, he took the stairs slowly one at a time, musing. Yes, this had happened, he had been there.

"Did you find it all right?"

"Yes, thanks!" he called, waving.

Outside on the street he lightly touched the brass railing before finding stride. Now he had no time to dawdle, he could tell by the shadows. There were people in the street now, like him leaving. He glanced at them covertly, for they would be back tomorrow. In the falling light of late afternoon, they looked realer. They were plugged in and dreaming. No, they were thinking about what had happened. They were trying to wrap it up and leave it here behind them. At home they would change their clothes and laugh with their roommates and husbands, their wives. They would pretend they had forgotten. He would have to call her. Looking down he saw his checkered shirt unbuttoned; he should never have gone back for it.

The sowbug looked greyly at the parking lot ramp, waiting for its driver. His passengers were not queued up but scattered around it citywise, and talking. Lou's little sidewise nod identified him as a stranger, but they responded. Nor was he the first to spot their driver. Now they queued, rather raggedly, and answered his jolly laughter. When he had got the heavy door open, they climbed in to retrieve their one-way tickets. Lou let them go first. When his turn came, his driver smiled affably at him, a regular. Lou asked, "What do you do at Charlie's?"

"Bounce," he said, grinning broadly.

Lou sat in back this time, behind the chatter, though he didn't feel like reading. If it was six in Boston, it was four in Denver. Presumably it was somewhere around six in Cadsbury. He would never know exactly, for by the time they got there it would be something after seven. They seemed to have lost some of this morning's sense of headway. In this direction, once they had cleared the city traffic, the hills were mostly up and seldom over. Too, it was even hotter now, the sowbug steam got all mixed up with the driver's shimmering vision. He honked a lot in precaution, precautionary greeting. Almost every truck and car responded. The joyous din spared a man from thinking.

The driver willingly let him off at Corners, charging but $2.90, smiling, waving after him. A further good omen perhaps was that Red had left Chumly in the parking lot, the key beneath the floormat. He left no note, no word of explanation. It seemed to Lou a gesture of confidence, and of pride. On the other hand, would Red trust him not to run off with the car if it were possible? Yes, Red was a trusting man, surely. But how many men are that trusting? The question remained answerless as they crept out of the parking lot and headed toward the phonestand. Red had gotten them up to twenty.

A precious few. Lou called collect. Dude was waiting.

"Hi!" she said again to him, as she had to the operator.

"Well, hi! Happy Birthday!"

"I knew it was you. Thanks for the present. I opened it last night—it was thoughtful. Where did you find it?"

"Salvation Army. I thought it might be useful in the new apartment."

"It is! It was great to have some toast with my coffee. I kind of expected you to call last night."

"Well, I'm just now back from Boston. By sowbug bus," he added.

"You saw Bowden?"

"Yes."

"But Chumly isn't . . ."

"No."

"You found a new mechanic?"

"Yes, at a service station. He worked on it all yesterday, and I guess today."

"Well, what does he have to say?"

"I got there after closing time. He has it up to twenty miles an hour."

"My my."

"Red's a really good guy, a tireless worker."

He laughed.

"Well, maybe things will go better tomorrow."

"Let's hope so."

"Tell me about Bowden. How did that go?"

"Not too well, I'm afraid."

"Oh dear. Let's hear it. What did he have to say about the book?"

"He'll check it out."

"That's something at least. What's he like?"

"Shark. He reminds me of an insurance agent I once had in Albuquerque."

"Oh, I thought he would be different."

"So did I."

"Well, you never know, maybe it will all work out."

"Oh yes."

"You're always so hypercritical. You always assume the worst of everybody."

"No, that's my main failing—I'm always over-trustful. That's why I have so many scars and missing toes."

"I know your toes, mister."

He laughed. "Tell me about yourself. How's everything going?"

"Everything's going just spiffily," she said. "Did I tell you I'm signing up for some courses at the U, media communications?"

"No. That sounds exciting."

"I know I'll enjoy it more than three heavy years of media law, and I think in the long run I'll get much more out of it."

"I think you're probably right. I'd begun to have some misgivings about the law idea. All the lawyers I've dealt with have been rather awful people."

"There you go again! But in this case I mostly agree with you. Anyway, I'm a born artist, an ecstatic—law school would only be a damper."

"Yes."

"I knew you'd agree. You're the only one who really understands me. Hon, I've been thinking . . ."

"Yes?"

"We really should stick together always—shouldn't we?"

"I always thought so."

"That's not what you usually say late at night. How many times have you told me you were going to leave me?"

"It's easy to say things late at night."

"I realize that. Has there ever been another love like ours?"

"I very much doubt it."

"We're a unique team, aren't we? There can't be another like it, certainly not in this century."

"No, there can't. We supplement one another perfectly."

"*Us.*"

"*Us.*"

They kissed.

"What else is new," she said, and laughed. "I've run into a few old friends—no real excitement though. The apartment is coming together beautifully. I've got all the curtains up, and I've put all your books and papers behind a curtain in the bedroom. You'd be proud of me."

"I am!" he said. "Thank you."

"I really love it here. By the way, it's a real delight to live in a place that doesn't stink of cigarette smoke."

"I'll bet it is."

"It's been quite a while!"

"Yes it has!"

"Well. Where are you staying tonight?"

"In the back seat again. We have a slot in the parking lot behind the station."

"Don't describe it to me, please. I'm not impressed. Are you eating?"

He described his lunch to her.

"Thanks! Gag, slurp, retch."

"As a matter of fact, I was a little burbly afterwards."

"And now you're going to climb into the backseat and sleep it off."

"Yes."

"With half a gallon of sherry to help you settle it."

"Not quite!"

"That's all you care about! Just give you sherry and cigarettes, and you can sleep anywhere."

"Not quite."

"Well . . . good luck with Chumly in the morning."

"Thanks."

"Do your best. And let me hear."

"Oh yes. Good luck to all your involvements too."

"By the way, no mail."

"Ah."

"Sleep tight."

"Sleep tight."

They kissed.

Lou waved at Dude as he turned away. He stopped only at the liquor store tonight, for a liter of dry vermouth. Those scabs were clinging.

They had been through this before.

F O U R

The windshield crack must have been a little sleepy. Everyone was pumping, sponging, wiping by the time they drove over there, all bells were bonging. Fortunately, Red had a second helper. Small and lithe, he moved among cars and hoses in a way that allowed no doubting how well he admired his father. For a moment Lou stood watching the scene in wonderment, aware he would never again see anything quite like it. Had he ever? Someone, probably the other helper, had unlocked the men's room. When Lou came out five minutes later, Red himself was waiting. "There's one more thing I want to try," he said. "If that doesn't do it, I'm through."

Lou nodded in understanding. "Fair enough," he said, and eased Chumly onto the rack.

Red climbed up there right away and lunged into the rack of Chumly's steam, with his light. He stayed in there, not coming out for bells or horns or air itself, only his arm reaching out now and then to grope for wrenches, sockets, pliers, pincers, hammer. When at last he did heave himself erect, his puffing cheeks were livid. Even his hair seemed to be turning Red again. He wiped his glittering eyes with a pale blue handkerchief from his back pocket. "You can turn it off," he said.

Lou did so.

"I'll drive it," Red said as Lou started to close the door.

Lou stepped back and watched Red carefully collect all his tools before climbing in behind the wheel. Red started the engine up, and seemed to gun it. Now he put the car in reverse and, grim-jawed, backed it off the rack, down the ramp onto the street. He shifted into first, and they began to move away. It took them a heartbreaking time to cover the first two blocks, where Red put out his arm and turned slowly out of sight. It reminded Lou of a little boy running away from home on a tricycle, pedalling valiantly. They did not soon reappear. Perhaps it was for real this time? Were they heading all-out for Canada? No, not Red. Fifteen minutes later they crept back into sight a block farther away from home. Enough was reluctantly enough, the pedalling now disconsolate.

"That's it," Red said, handing Lou the key.

Lou nodded. "It sure sounds smooth anyway."

"Oh, it's smooth."

"Do you think there's a chance in the world we could get to Denver like that, on back roads I mean?"

"Denver?"

"I keep thinking if I get it running for a while something might joggle in there and jump back to life."

Red's eyes veered toward Chumly. "Well, something might happen," he said.

"How could I head west from here without hitting the freeway?"

"Well, you could go back down Fourth and through town, then aim for Penfield and Newickton, keep west from there. That'll keep you off the freeway for a long time anyway."

"Great. I'll try it that way."

Red led the way to the office, where they took turns bribing the machine for Pepsis. Red carried his to the counter, rummaged among his papers underneath. He said, "I'm only charging you for the parts."

"But you worked hard on that car!"

"Yeah, but I didn't get it going right," Red said, leafing papers. "Only parts."

"Well, that's very good of you." Lou sat on the rusty iron chair while Red wrote out the bill. He could see the two helpers winding among the hoses and pumps, working well together, keeping up with the insistent bells and credit cards. The big grey thermometer on the wall read 92° Fahrenheit, Celsius insouciant. Outside the black-green starlings stalked the gutters coolly. "There it is," Red said, and Lou got up. Red had worked two days to get back the $21.46 he had put out in parts; he readily accepted travelers checks, would not have objected to rolls of quarters. When they had settled, Lou put out his hand. He felt the helpers were watching. "Red, you're a good man."

Red looked down as they shook hands. "I wish I could have got it going right."

"It just couldn't be done," Lou said, waving. He drove to the pumps to fill up Chumly, or watch the other helper do the filling and the washing. When that was finished, the man waved his chammy with relief. The second helper seemed to wave good luck. Red himself was high on the rack in a Chrysler. Lou would not soon forget this either.

Going back down Fourth they reviewed their recent past in glum slow-motion, in which it became the present. No one was at the doors to wave them anything. Only the patrol car watched with interest. Snuffing dogs jaywalked in front of them disrespectfully. At the Court House bench the old man did lift his hat, however briefly. Their parting scan of the oblong took long enough to insure it became indelible, as though it hadn't done that. Finally entering the grey woods marking the feudal limits was scarcely the relief one hoped for; the air was heavy with the sweat of outlaw sowbugs. The sun itself could not abide this. Only when the road began to weave a little, at least create some breeze if not escape, did the atmosphere begin to brighten. Yes, now grey trees had splashes of green on top. Lou pressed Chumly onward.

They were able to hold it at twentytwo miles an hour, mainly. At this rate, he figured Denver lay ahead about one hundred road hours, if some of the hills were favorably inclined.

Surely they weren't getting optimum mileage; some of their gas would simply evaporate in boredom. At this pace, even their oil might choose to leak. Coasting to a stop, their brake fluid would feel unwanted. He hoped the generator would be able to create some voltage, for they surely would be traveling at night. Then too there would be the expense of No-Doz. There would be savings on sherry though. This was some trip they looked forward to.

The narrow road wound ever more capriciously, dodging trees and sometimes mailboxes, discreet white signs offering antiques and seamstresses, until it came upon a sunny glade of grass and dandelions and black-eyed Susans, a stopping place for orioles. Lazing by, Lou could count the bees collecting pollen, a casual census. Ah, two ladybugs. Ants were not so easy. Presumably Chumly was attending to the right side with extra care, since she was not there to help him. Beyond, the trees grew greener, fuller, more familiar. It always surprised him on returning to find how low and dense the woods were that he'd grown up in; perhaps out west he unthinkingly accepted those new dimensions because he himself had grown much taller. Little wonder the crowded east was seeping westward. He had helped that. Now it was like coming home from years of travel to find your father and his furniture grown shorter by several inches. It made you want to pat him on the head, while seeming to wave greetings.

Lou waved as a car passed around them. There were few on the road. Whenever one did pass, it lent them a sense of progress, a suggestion that they too were moving forward. They had what seemed good proof of this when they gained Penfield at something after noontime. A sign of welcome said so; there were 697 witnesses. They all had cars which lined up peacefully at the stoplight to watch their neighbors wheel by in front of them. Chumly settled in among them; but for his plates, he belonged right here in Penfield. When the light changed, Lou almost had to apply the brakes to keep him from rear-ending a shy Toyoto. They did have to stop from time to time while the others found their parking places. Lou chose not to join them, interrupt this headway. Even so, it was quite a while before they were once again stealing through the countryside, continuing their informal census.

It could not have been two hours later that they discovered Newickton, or a most welcome apparition. The Pilgrims must have been gladdened at sight of that. It was all downhill, without a stoplight. Lou and Chumly slid on through, followed a tractor out the other end, followed it for a mile or so. Perhaps it turned off on a side road up ahead, around a bend. A sign said that they were aiming for Benton now, and gave the distance: 23. Lou liked to imagine these were kilometers. Rods would be too much to ask for: in fact at times they could see that far, passing through a straight and open space. Thus they glid on. It took until what felt like dinnertime for kilometer dreams to evaporate; half an hour later they gave up on miles. They decided these must be leagues by the time Benton yawned ahead. Its hill went in the opposite direction, and there was a stoplight at the foot of it, turning red.

This was the laziest signal Lou had faced in fortyeight states, unless it was stuck. They approached it as slowly as a car could, only to see it wait to turn green as they pulled up behind half a dozen cars patiently obeying. Even at that, the driver up front was asleep. The driver next back gave him a dainty peep, and now they all crept forward up the hill. One by one the others turned off or parked, leaving Lou and Chumly quietly gunning to a standstill. Lou let it roll back. At the foot of the hill he went through all the motions of leaping into first, and Chumly moved bravely forward. They had it up to almost ten by the time they began to slow down and stop. By now the light had turned red again, and they rolled all the way back to it. Measuring the hill, Lou gunned. Chumly attacked it in silent fury.

They hit it this time at full fifteen miles an hour, swept up the first two steep blocks of four or five, and still were moving. Three children clapped and cheered them as they reached the third. "Go! Go! Go!" They were going a mile a week now. Halfway up the third block they were going backward. Lou braked before the children in appreciation of their encouragement. "Go! Go! Go! Go! Go!" Even with that, it could not be done; maybe a foot or two. The children stopped clapping as Lou and Chumly rolled back past them. Lou backed into a little parking lot with a gentle incline, paused there. To a man headed for the Rockies this said something direful. The children were disappointed. Lou shook his head ruefully for them. He wished he had candy or ice cream bars in the trunk, as in the old days, but he had none, far less dry vermouth. He called to them. "Do you know what time it is?"

"Three. About three. Three!"

Lou waved to them, and they waved back as Chumly slid forward down the hill. He would have given a honk if Chumly had one. The light was green and they turned left toward what seemed to be Benton's congested area. Ahead were the flying balls and horses. Lou chose one less gaudy, with a MECHANIC ON DUTY sign out front. SHOCKS MUFFLERS TUNEUPS. A boy stood by the rack watching them roll in. Lou got out slowly.

"Can I help you, sir?"

"Well, I don't know." Taking a deep breath, Lou tried to explain the problem. "This car runs like a dream at twenty-two miles an hour, but I can't get it up that hill back there."

"Hm. Might be the points."

"I'm not sure," Lou said. "A mechanic in Cadsbury did quite a lot of work on it."

"Well, I can take a look at it. Want to roll it onto the rack."

"Right," Lou said.

The boy came at Chumly with a screwdriver. He raised the hood, stood listening to Chumly purring. "You can turn it off now." He got the distributor cap off, tapped in there with his screwdriver. "Those are new points," he said.

"Yes."

"The lead-in wires are new. New sparkplugs too. New fanbelt."

"Yes, he was pretty thorough."

"Try starting it up again." The boy tapped here and there, listening. "Try gunning it . . . That's good, that's good—now let it idle." He tapped again. "The carburetor's getting plenty of gas. The fuel pump's working. She's firing."

"Yes, everything seems to work fine until you need some power."

The boy stood up. "What year engine is this?"

"It's a '72 Chev."

"Is it!" He went to his book, thumbed through it thoroughly. Now he came back with his timing light. "Just let it idle." He was in there quite a while this time. When he came up, he shook his curly head. "Somebody's painted a nice new mark in there—the timing seems to be right on it."

"Ah."

The boy scratched his curls. "I wouldn't know what else to look for."

"No, neither would I. Many thanks for trying."

"I'm sorry." He lowered the hood for Lou, put away his screwdriver.

"How much do I owe you?"

"Oh, nothing. I didn't really do anything."

Lou held out five dollars. "Here—for your willingness."

"But . . ."

"Take it—you earned it."

"Well, thank you, sir!" He was smiling. "You know, there's a Chevy dealer in Newickton."

"Oh, is there! I must have missed it in all the excitement."

"Watch for it on the right—it's up on a hill."

"Oh dear! Many thanks to you!"

They were both smiling. Chumly chortled. They would like to have given the children the good news, but at the green light they turned left toward Newickton. They could wait to wave at them when they sailed back through. Already they seemed to be moving with more expression. The leagues became mere miles to them. They passed a bicycle. They could enjoy the countryside more generally, the bees being counted. They both attended to the right side. The Chevy dealer must have been on his side before, Lou admitted. He kept an eye out for it! Yet Chumly seemed to be the first to spot it, for he approached the Newickton hill with real enthusiasm. True, it was not so forbidding as the Benton, and there indeed loomed their goal atop it. BLAKEY CHEVROLET, bright blue and newly plexied. No wonder Lou had missed it—it had gone up since they last went by here. The only problem was that Blakey had chosen a side hill off the Newickton, laid a steep rampway there whose tar was still bubbling freshly. Chumly chewed it.

For the last fifteen or twenty feet it was impossible to say whether or not they were moving; but there they sat at last before the Service entrance. "Good Chumly! Good Chumly!" she used to chant, patting, drumming him on the dashboard. Now Lou patted for her.

A smiling man came out to meet them, offer his own congratulations. His new badge announced Bert Stein, Srvc Mgr. "Can I . . . Oh, I'm sorry, we don't service imports."

Lou sprang Chumly's hood. "How about this?"

"Wo. A '70?"

"A '72."

"What's the trouble?"

"It won't go over twentytwo miles an hour."

Bert Stein scratched his curls the way the boy had; his were grey and around his ears. "I'll have our Chief Mechanic check it over—he'll be back in half an hour."

"Great!"

"Can you get it over by that wall there?"

"Oh yes!"

Newickton's shopping center was at the top of the hill, its ice cream parlour at the bottom. Lou needed exercise more than Chumly did. He needed ice cream. The beer and sherry could wait till later. This was a far less gloomy town than Cadsbury, quite understandably, having gone up this noon. Perhaps the motel across the street from Blakey's had been here longer. Lou walked downhill on the left side of the road, through the startled dandelions and daisies, the red, yet bleeding, gashes left by the dozers. Only the birds were unimpressed by the recent changes; they were quite used to having machines dig up their bugs for them. Lou hoped the ice cream had had time to freeze. There was a window for drive-up customers, and he stood there to read the menu. Soon enough a pretty girl bent to peer out at him through the screen. "Can I help you?"

"A double butter pecan cone, please."

Wincing, she retreated. He could hear her clattering in there, talking to a fellow worker. "I hate to make cones," she said.

Give her a few days on the job, she'd learn to like it. On the other hand, when finally she shoved the great bulbous thing out the window he began to understand her viewpoint, it might take her years. He carried it to the shade of a tree beside Newickton's pond, or swampland. Clearly they had not had time to landscape. The water was green, and not with lilies. A stagnant scum of oil prevented one from seeing below the surface. He hated to think of tonight's mosquitoes, probably motored. Old tires and battered hubcaps seemed at home in there. Around the edges the grass grew rankly. The very tree Lou sat beneath seemed not to breathe. He traced the cause to a vast wrecking yard on beyond the ice cream parlour. Such was the foundation they had built Newickton upon. He turned toward the road to finish dinner.

Even without that the downhill hike had come much easier, but he had uphill incentive. One could almost revere the high blue BLAKEY sign. Chumly himself looked quite contented, sunning with his hosed and healthy neighbors; a little sidewise smile played around his eyes. His wheels were turned in the same direction, toward the road. When Lou lifted his hood, a boy mechanic joined them. Lou glanced sidewise at him, nodding. With Lou he looked in at Chumly's engine. "What's the trouble?"

"No power."

The boy tested the tautness of the fanbelt. "Well, Joe will know what to look for. Joe can fix anything!"

"Ah, wonderful!" Lou said, returning the boy's reassuring wave. He got in the front seat, not to seem too overanxious. He was listening to radio when another blue uniform appeared in the Service entrance, headed towards them. He was young too, but something in the way he moved said Chief Mechanic. The Jose Soto on his badge confirmed it. He went straight to Chumly's engine. "He don't go right?"

"Not above twentytwo miles an hour."

Lou set Chumly purring. Jose listened attentively for a moment, jiggled something, and held his hand up palm-forward. When Lou turned the ignition off, Jose began to operate. He had all the tools he needed in his back pockets. He took off the air filter. He took one of the new battery cables off. He stripped the new wires off the new sparkplugs, removed the plugs. Now he took the exhaust manifold off, something Lou could not recall Red's doing. Jose held a long screwdriver between one of the cylinders and the exposed battery terminal, made a switching motion with his other hand. Lou did as directed. The resulting explosion sent Jose up in the air several inches, but he came down nodding. He rubbed his left hand on his trousers; he had dropped the screwdriver. "That's the timer chain," he said.

"Ah." Lou got out to join him.

"That's too bad. I wished un otro."

"Un problema grande?"

"Cuatro horas, mas or menos."

"Any idea how much that would come to?"

"Dolares?"

"Sí."

Jose looked at Lou now, not Chumly. "Threefifty-four-hundred?" He knew Lou had wished another. He retrieved his screwdriver and they went to the Service entrance, where they could see Bert Stein talking to a prospective customer in his plexiglass compartment. It still had its stickers on it. Jose waited politely for the boss to finish, then went in there to explain to him. Lou watched him go through the motions of lifting things, many muchos of them. When he had finished, Bert Stein nodded and beckoned Lou in. "Jose's given you the news," he said.

"Yes. When could the work be done?"

"Jose can get to it on Tuesday. He has one other job for Tuesday morning."

"Hm. I'd hoped to get the car back to Colorado by Labor Day."

"We're closed tomorrow," Bert Stein said. "I'll be here in the morning, but the boys won't."

"Jose, is there any chance you could do it sometime tomorrow?"

Jose shook his head apologetically. "I have to cement my patio."

"Well, let me know what you decide," Bert Stein said.

"I will," Lou followed Jose from the office.

"Vamos," Jose said, and led him to the boy Lou had met before. "Ed, you like to work tomorrow?"

The boy put down his milk carton. "Well, I don't know," he said. He didn't even have his badge yet.

"You can put in a timer chain."

"Well, I don't know."

"First pull up the radiator." Jose made the motion. "You know?"

Ed nodded.

"Then you unscrew the big screws and pull the engine up

a poco. Then you pull out the timer. If it's all broke up you put in a new one. You make good and sure you put in the front side front. You can tell from the old one. That only takes you three or four hours."

"Well, I don't know," Ed said.

"Ed can come in the morning."

"Well, I'll be talking to my wife this evening," Lou said. He and Ed nodded at one another. "Have a good holiday, Jose."

"I have to cement that patio."

"I know you do."

Chumly looked anxious too, watching the mechanic leaving. Were they going to leave him all apart this way? Lou folded his wires and cable back inside and lowered his hood. Perhaps it would cheer him if Lou had a few beers out here with him. He went uphill for those; when he got back the salesmen were still roaming the lot in their white shirts with their perspiring customers, who were drinking pop. Lou had thought to spend the night out here. The Greene Motel began to look good to him: certainly he could use a shower (she would *agree*), a change of silly shirt (he should *never* have gone back), a cool and quiet place to think what he would say to her.

The Greene Motel indeed had been around a while, as had its proprietors. There was an antique buzzer nailed to the desk. PRESS HARD. A loud bell, a gong, brought a little white-haired lady out. Having trouble with Lou's quiet voice, she called her palsied husband out as interpreter.

"What's that?"

"Have you a single for tonight?"

"He wants a single!"

The little lady handed a card to Lou.

"How much will that be?"

"How much!"

"Twelve dollars."

"Twelve!"

"Fine!" Lou gave her cash.

"Here's your key to Number 3."

"Number 3!"

"Thanks!"

"Where's your car at?"

"Across the street."

"Over there! What's wrong with it?"

"The timing chain."

"How much will that cost you?"

"About three-fifty."

"Hundreds?"

"Yes."

"They're robbers over there! I could have warned you!"

"Well, it's a pretty big job."

"A hundred dollars an hour! Here we give you all night for twelve!"

"Twelve dollars," the lady said, and nodded.

"Yes, that's very good of you. Many thanks!" Waving he went out to find Number 3, which was justnext door. The proprietress well understood her keys, and prices. The little old fan on the dresser was droning faithfully, stirring the air around it. The windows front and back were open wide; now and then their curtains fluttered the fan encouragement. He did not question the little portable heater, but took off his shoes and socks immediately. He did not test the phone. The huge RCA console was a marvel of mahogany, with real brass fittings, a built-in clock that read *ca.* 1:05, 1936. It had preserved its voice fairly well, although it had long ago lost its knobs. It seemed the King was abdicating after all, and all the Western world was listening. Lou could hear his mother sobbing in Connecticut, as she had again at around that time when Ben Bernie came on to give his final radio show a few hours after dying. Switching the console off, Lou push-pulled a beer tab back toward the present.

The chair was comfortable enough, of a more recent era. The bed too looked newish, queensized. He wished she were here to see it; see that life with him was not all back seats, broken glass and thistles. Come now, realistically speaking, how much would this impress her? He could see from here that the linoleum floor was rather dusty around the edges. The dust on the mirror seemed long ago to have permeated. There were no drinking glasses here, only ashtrays. Smoke reclined on the stagnant air like moldy feather pillows. With the console off, mosquitoes could be heard drilling holes in the window screens. In time that might help a little. There were other noises out there too, female. They sought attention. "Number 3 is the one," he heard one advise the other with conviction. Her acute French accent lent her an air of real authority. Who could doubt her? It was time he took his shower—after one more beer to cool what the lady out the window would call his *ardour.*

He turned the C full force, not questioning the H; even so his shower water must have travelled a far distance in the sunshine on its way to spray him. He did feel a little cooler when he got out, in better contrast to the cloudy air around him. His original shirt too seemed to help some. He would wash them both tonight. Meanwhile it was probably approaching six in Denver. He put clean socks on. Outside all was quiet. Across the street he could see the white-shirted troops still parading, carefully avoiding Chumly. On this side, the fresh-scrubbed gravel of the National bankyard tried to hide its surprise beneath the errant down of dandelion and vacuum cleaner refuse. Beyond, varicenter, a partial oblong of traditional design. The supermarket, its long side, faced the road, once south, while the lesser shops and vacancies faced one another. Thus he found himself in the partial shade of a laundromat as he knelt to a telephone thoughtfully installed to the avail of the pre-school children and other handicapped. He dimed the operator, who responded to his needs with motherly compassion.

She, on the other hand, at the other end, let the phone ring five times tonight, and then said "Yes?" Then "Hi" to him.

"Hi again! How's everything?"

"You tell me."

"O.K. Red got Chumly up to twentytwo miles an hour before he gave up, so we started out. We made almost fifty miles before a hill got in the way."

"I'm not impressed."

"Well, we all did our best."

"So where are you now?"

"We came halfway back to a place called Newickton. Chumly's at a Chevrolet dealer and I'm in a little motel across the road. Actually right now I'm at a shopping center up the hill."

"Do they know what the trouble is?"

"Yes, it's the timing chain. It'll cost at least three-fifty, and they can't work on it until after the holiday."

"Oh darn."

"Yes."

"Well, what do you want to do?"

"It's a lot of money?"

"Yes it is."

"It would cost me money to hang around here four days."

"Yes it would. There's nobody around there who could fix it sooner—and for less?"

"The chief mechanic tried to talk another guy into coming in tomorrow to do the job, but I think they both doubted that the kid was up to it, and so do I. Otherwise there's not much here—this town isn't finished yet."

"You want to come home, don't you?"

"I don't know what to do. Do you want to call me here?" He read the number. The phone had a very gentle ring, not to frighten. "Hi again," he said. "It is a lot of money."

"Yes it is. Almost what we bought him for five years ago."

"I suppose they might give us a few dollars for parts."

"Ah, poor Chumly!"

"Yes!"

"Well, do what you think's best."

"Maybe I can come up with something."

"You usually do."

"Oh yes. How are things there?"

"Are you sitting down?"

"Well, I'm kneeling—this phone is about two feet off the ground."

"Here goes then: they've closed down our box in Portland."

"*What!* We paid them!"

"I just found out—David Johns neglected to give them the money."

"That bastard! You were going to call him and remind him."

"Well, I haven't had time. I have lots of things on my mind these days myself, you know."

"Damn! I suppose they've just been returning the mail?"

"I suppose so."

"*Uuhph!* We should have closed it ourselves and sent them our new address in Denver."

"Well, we didn't—we wanted to keep it for the magazine. They would have stopped forwarding the mail in six months."

"So now it's a month instead. Have you called them about it?"

"I don't think it would do any good."

"Will you call the postmaster tomorrow and try to straighten it out?"

"I'll try if you want, but I don't think—"

"Call in the morning—they'll be open until two o'clock your time."

"I'll try," she said.

"Thank you. Have you anything like good news?"

"Zilch. I didn't get the Datamaster job. That's all right with me. I want to *write.* The communications course I most looked forward to is filled. I don't know whether it would be worth spending the time and money on the other two. Now I find myself with a bigger pile of stupid typing than I can handle."

"I'm sorry to hear that. I wish I were there to help."

"Don't trouble yourself, buster. I'll take care of it. I've come to a decision lately."

"Yes?"

"As I see it, it's either your life or mine."

"That sounds pretty bloodthirsty!"

"Well, it's the way things stand. I don't want to spend my life in your shadow, the great writer's little girl with big tits. I want to be known on my own, as *myself.* You've already made it, you've published ten great books—most of them—you can die in peace with that. Now it's *my* turn!"

"*Honey!* I *want* you to be known on your own. I always do everything I can to help. You're not even thirty, and you have two wonderful books yourself."

"Ha. Look who published them. And who reads them?"

"Who reads *mine*? Most of them are out of print!"

"People who know what's going on in American literature know you. You're the best—you have fans around the world."

"Hardly anybody knows me—I get about two or three fan letters a year. Or did."

"Now it's *my* turn. *I* want to be the best."

"Don't ever worry about that! We can talk about it better when we're together, don't you think?"

"We've talked about it. I wanted you to know how I feel, and now you do. Right?"

"Right."

"How's the cookbook coming?"

"Not too well."

"Well, let me hear what happens with Chumly."

"Yes. I'll be seeing you before too long, and I'll be calling before that."

"All right. Good luck."

"And to you. You'll call the postmaster in the morning?"

"Don't worry. Goodnight."

"Goodnight."

He kissed, they clicked.

Climbing to his feet, he felt that it was sherry time, with perhaps a few beef jerkies to point the way. He carried them downhill without glancing sidewise more than once. Tomorrow morning would be soon enough to face all that. Each of us needs some time to himself. Turning in at the motel, he could see the old man nodding in a rocking chair in front of Number 1. A passing wave was not enough.

"Hello there, son!"

"Hello there!"

"You want to get that car fixed up right and cheap?"

"Yes I do."

"You just talk to the boy across the way in Number 6. He's real handy. He'll fix it up."

Lou stopped to look across at Number 6.

"He's not home just now, but he'll be back. He works at the Esso station over at Walford. Name's George, I think, drives a big wide-back Ford with Pennsylvania license plates."

"You think he'd be able to replace a timing chain?"

The old man was nodding and shaking emphatic yes. "He'll fix it up!"

"Well, I'll keep an eye out for him. Many thanks."

Number 3 had cleared a little, its lower realm at least. Lou spread his feast upon the console. Now, your console model makes a fine banquet table or smörgåsbord. He turned the chair temporarily awry from that, so he could put his feet up on the bed after taking off his shoes and socks. It was good to have a handmade cigarette again. She usually rolled them for him when he was driving, usually she had. He poured himself a full wassail cup, held it up to whomever it was in the mirror across the way. Whomever It Was returned his toast, and together they drank to love. He could not see whether he wept too.

F I V E

It was not the windshield crack's fault this time. He found that out when he surprised himself full-length on a queensize back seat, a kingsize console glooming nearby. He did not remember turning down the counterpane, nor turning out the light. He did remember being awakened in that chair by a caterwauling from the dark of the parking lot, not the old lady, not the French. "Hey where is everybody! Can't you hear me in there! Let's have a pahty! It's time for some fun! Sheet! Why doesn't somebody open up . . . What are you all a bunch of queers around here!" One would have to be queer to want to bed that voice; only her escort seemed to be enjoying it. But he was not looking for trouble himself. "Better not talk like that around here," he said chuckling quietly, and soon they drove off. Yes, he remembered turning out the light. He remembered placing cigarettes, tobacco, matches, on the floor beside the bed. After smoking a generic one he went to the shower room to make sure he had hung the shirts to dry. He was quite sure that he had, for he remembered finding only one hanger and thinking for a minute he was back in Ohio again. He had hung the nice one on top. He remembered swatting that mosquito on the wall.

He was shaved and dressed when the old man appeared at the front window, calling in: "Hello in there!"

"Hello!"

"George hasn't come back?"

"Haven't seen him."

"Well, I'll keep an eye out!"

"Thanks!"

"I'll . . ." He was looking at Lou's homemade cigarette, sniffing the screen with his incessant nod. His nose left a dent. "I'll be going now!" Waving he went. It seemed his olfactory sense had dimmed. He should have called out his wife as interpreter for that.

Chumly's tolerance too was strained. It must have seemed a long night to him. He glowered a little less sternly when Lou patted his hood and headed for Service. Bert Stein himself had had a smiling sleep, soft puffs of it were left. He welcomed Lou and waved at the coffee pot. "What have you decided?"

"Nothing quite." Lou took a moment to blow steam off the plastic mug. "Has Ed turned up?"

Bert Stein waved at the empty shop. "Nobody here but me."

"Then I guess I'd better be heading back to Colorado."

"I wish we could have been more help."

"You've been very decent, thanks," Lou said. "Could you use a good little car for your lot? It's got a perfect motor except for the timing chain—more than one mechanic has commented on that."

Bert Stein waved at the crowded lot where Chumly crouched. "We've got more cars than we need already."

Lou nodded. "Maybe one of the mechanics would like to fix it up—either for himself or resale."

Bert Stein tilted his head, gave a little shrug. "They probably have more cars than they need to. You'd have to ask them."

"I'd give it to anyone who wanted to do that."

Bert Stein stood up. "You'd have to ask them Tuesday. What we usually do with old cars is take them down the hill to Barney."

"Barney? Oh yes, I've seen that."

"He'll pay a few dollars for any car, for parts."

Lou was standing too. "What do I owe you?"

"Oh, nothing at all!"

"Well, many thanks again for your help. I guess I'll go see Barney."

Bert Stein could smile and still look sorry. "Can you get it down there?"

"We'll roll," Lou said, smiling too.

He did not look Chumly in the eye, see whether he was pleased or apprehensive. Both, he guessed, but by nature and long association not suspicious. Lou got in quickly and switched the key—out of guilt or habit? He kicked the spongy tar a hard one, slammed the door when they got rolling. Seeing no cars on either side, he let Chumly do it his way. He hit the road with a little skid and squeal of tires, off and running. He had it up to almost thirtyone by the time they reached the bottom, Lou had to brake him. Chumly tried one last yelping leap toward freedom, even with his head off. He was for going on forever, but he passed quietly enough between the high wire fences. Lou switched his key off.

It was a passive swarm of them they stared at, a glutted infestation. The only signs of life in here were the prancing dust devils, the lazy flies, the roving grasshopper. Instinct had him put Chumly quickly in reverse, but on calmer judgment he eased into neutral, not to hurt him in the towing. He climbed out slowly, quietly closed the door, went back to the trunk. He closed that quietly too when he was done. Barney's front door was open. Inside, men and boys in short-sleeved shirts ranged the counter. Lou approached the one who was not talking on telephone. "Barney?"

He pointed at a short-sleeved one with cowboy hat and bolo tie, peering from his office with squinting eyes that knew an unsaddled wrangler when they saw one.

"Suh?"

"Bert Stein sent me down. I've got a '68 Opel out there with a '72 Chevette engine."

"Has it got all its parts?"

"Everything works except the timing chain, the horn, and the lighter."

"What's with the timing chain?"

"I guess it's out of line or broken. Otherwise it's a really great little engine. You don't happen to have a mechanic free who could work on it?"

Barney chuckled, fingering his bolo. "I've got mechanics," he said, "but they don't work in that direction."

"How about after hours?"

Again he chuckled. "After hours they figure it's their turn to get smashed, especially on a three-day holiday, don't you guess?"

"I reckon so."

"I can give you $50. You have the title?"

"I have the registration. The title is back in Colorado."

Barney took the registration. "Here's my card. Send me the title when you get home."

"I will. I left the key in the ignition."

A rosy young rodeo queen appeared in the doorway, smiling widely.

"Clara dear, make out a check to Mr. Webb for $50, please. Have Buddy sign it."

Nodding, she took the registration and spun neatly out the door.

"I thank you," Lou said, following.

"She'll bring it out to you."

"Thank you." There was a rack of tires in the middle of the room, and Lou examined those while he waited. They were almost new ones.

Today the rodeo queen was not setting records; that was not her function. When at last she did come out, she presented him his check and winning smile. Accepting both, he thanked her. "Can you tell me where to catch a bus going west?"

"You mean a real one?"

"Yes."

"Going to the West west?"

"Yes."

"You'll have to go to Walford for that. That's on the freeway."

"Ah, thank you." He folded the check into his wallet before walking out the door, walking straight out the gate and down the road, as though purposefully. He had his bag with him, heavy now with tools but carried in one arm until he was out of sight. After their rolling years, a lowly hike this felt—exposed. In Chumly no one had given much attention to him. Now he could feel each car brush him by. Even at twentytwo miles an hour they had never been passed so abruptly; he had given up that magical speed for a plodding three or four? In the scraped roadside light he could see for himself that his bag had grown disgraceful. He knew that the seat of his jeans was wearing thin; a few years ago it would have been the knees that needed patching first. He stopped to test, kneel on the right one, then the left; sharp upturned rocks gouged tender flesh. Now it was his ass was calloused. He supposed there were still fields to be worked out West, perhaps a few not yet mechanized and organized, where he would be allowed to toughen his softer spots, match his patches up. Perhaps he should go back to the door-to-door instead, after buying pants to go with the shirt; good for the legs entire. She would have the typewriter. He stood up and put out his thumb, just in time to receive a honk.

It was a cousin sowbug, blue this one, surging by in yellow smoke. Lou waved at it. A little beyond, it turned out of sight, soon reappeared, surging back for him? No, now he had a passenger bound for the East. The driver and Lou toodled and waved again, while an oncoming truck plunged off the road with an OVERSIZE LOAD banner waving in front. Lou leapt aside as the truck chewed rock, a chained dozer teetering left and right on its flatbed in back. "That was a close one!" this driver called.

"Wasn't it!" Lou called, reloading his sack.

"Where are you gang?"

"Walford!"

"Clam in!" He swung the door and Lou climbed up. "New in town, are you?"

"Yes."

"So'm I—just finished scraping it."

"How long did that take?"

"Better part of a day. Hep yourself!" he said, waving his beer at a five-pack on the dash.

"I'd better wait till I've had breakfast first."

The driver waved at the bag of potato chips in the open cubby hole. His wrinkled face had the red-brown tone and texture of a fresh-shelled pecan. He propped his left foot on the dash, they wheeled out to the road. Lou leaned back too, propped his feet on the heater, chewing chips. They veered right. This way they missed the little kids on the hill; perhaps this truck needed no little help? "How far is it to Walford?"

"Don't know that yet. Can't be more than a few miles I'd guess wouldn't you?"

"I guess I would. Where you from?"

"All over too. I'm Lou."

They rolled peacefully on, Al nodding his head and tapping his foot to the radio, until he was ready to toss his beer in favor of a cooler one. He waved that at the four-pack now. "You've had your breakfast, Lou."

"Well, thanks, don't mind if I do."

They sat back with their feet up on the bar, nodding to the music, half-smiling as a basking landscape swam serenely by in the animated mirror before their bemused eyes. This had once been gorgeous country, Lou well knew, and for a few miles they were privileged to see it so. It was only when Al put his two feet on the floor and put down his beer that the bartender flicked the switch, and they could see themselves in the mirror now rolling into what was left of town. Walford, in contrast to Newickton, was an old, old town that had undergone major surgery. Bypass surgery it had been, during which it had suffered a heart attack. Thus they had cut out the heart, implanted an artificial one. The patient survived with diminished faculties, in parts.

They finished their beers before Lou climbed out; suddenly downcast he watched truck and dozer trundle off. An Esso station lay nearby, with what looked to be a wide-bed Ford out front, but he did not question that. He entered an antiques and curios shop, now dealing mainly in postal cards. A tall wan lady was aligning them in their racks. "Excuse me, can you tell me where the bus station is?"

"The bus station?" she stopped to blink her eyes and think. "Why that's across the bridge and on out that way." She waved vaguely west.

"Thank you!"

Lou was partway across the bridge when he realized a high wire fencing contained the freeway on either side. There was an exit ramp on his side, but no entrance on the other; a third wire fence cut along the median. Lou returned to the curios shop.

"Excuse me again, can you tell me the best way to get over to that?"

She blinked more practicedly this time. "Just follow the roads," she snapped.

He went out to look again. For as far as he could see on either side, wire fences ran along the roads as well, enclosing woods. Wandering the New England countryside he had used to wonder at all the low stone walls, so devoutly piled, still running all through the wooded hills. Really heavy rocks, and boulders, those. Some farmer must have spent most of his time and strength rolling and heaving them. Had they ever prevented a cow's escape? Strangely dense country for a cow to wander in. Surely the skunks and foxes weren't inconvenienced. No, those walls were intended for enclosing farmers. Now the government had made it all real. With fences like these, all mankind was enclosed, wildlife entrapped, birds garroted. Lou went to the Esso phone.

"Continental Trailways-Greyhound."

"Can you tell me about buses going toward Denver?"

"We have two a day. Next one leaves in half an hour."

He called a taxi, leaned against the curios shop while he waited. It pleased him that the driver tooted as he pulled up, and that he knew how to follow the roads and fences, however slowly. "War you headed?" "West west," Lou answered. They made it in time to buy the ticket and a quick ice cream bar, a slow bag of Planters for the journey. Seated far back in a Trailhound, he still didn't feel like reading, or much like looking. He had been on this route too recently. At least this time he didn't have to heed the traffic, hellbent to tail on Saturday. He could dream his own fitful dreams after finishing his dinner. It wasn't until he woke up in the Columbus depot, awaiting a change of Trailhounds, that he faced the question: had he anything left in either direction?

Of course there were others. He still had his lucky Canadian quarter, in his left pocket with handkerchief, pencils, matches, but he always saved that for later. He had more often tried Mexico. And Florida. It was still dark outside, darker in Denver. Time to have what they like to call a regular meal, brood thereupon. He entered the Grille, found a booth in the corner providing both a real wall and a plexi. Not to overdo things, he began with a double milk and Danish, took them slowly. Even so they began to go to his head a little; in fact parts of him felt almost cheerful. When he saw the ticket window open, he went out to cash in the remainder of his ticket for the next round. On his return his waitress had disappeared, perhaps to catch the westbound Tailhound they were announcing, taking his tip with her. He smoked a cigarette while waiting to see if she had arranged for a replacement. He wasn't really hungry now anyway, now that he thought about it. Time could be more profitably spent in exploring Columbus. Surely there must be gold out there somewhere; he took his tools with him. It did not really surprise him to find no natives lurking; he had been in enough college towns to know this was still part of Saturday. In fact they had spent a night here together. If she was still asleep it was time he awakened her, under whatever circumstances. He found a phonebooth with all its glass and door on.

"What do you want?" she began. "I've got a lot of work to do. I've been up since four."

"Ow. It sounds we both had a dull Saturday night."

"It's not the first time."

"Oh, we had some pretty wild ones."

She did not deny, but asked: "What's happening?"

"They gave me $50 for Chumly."

"The Chevrolet people?"

"The wreckers."

"Ah no."

"I'm going back. I got as far as Columbus."

"Do you think you can get him back all right?"

"No—but we'll have to."

"I'll be heading back then. Is there any good news?"

"Not really. It turns out I still have a chance at the Datamaster job, but I've decided I don't want to work there."

"I don't blame you. Anything else?"

"Not to mention. I had dinner with Janet and William last night."

"How are they?"

"Just fine. Same old Janet. He's getting fat and grizzly. I always enjoy talking to them."

"Ya, they're kind of funny sometimes. Say, did you call the postmaster?"

"It was just what I expected. He said nothing could be done about the box. Somebody already has it."

"Damn! That shyster Johns ought to be disbarred."

"You do it."

"Don't worry. I'll let him hear about it."

"I'm sure you will. At least the postmaster promised to have our mail forwarded from now on."

"Oh great. Has there been any mail to the Denver address?"

"Zip."

"I would have thought someone would write by now. Billie at least."

"You always expect people to drop everything as soon as they hear from you. Forget your own life! Attend to Lou!"

"Oh ya. Well, I'd better be hitting the road."

"How are you travelling?"

"I bussed most of the way out here, I'll hitchhike back."

"Do you have enough money to last the weekend??"

"To paraphrase, I'll have to do."

"Well, be careful. Good luck to you both."

"To you."

"Love you."

"Love you."

He kissed. She kissed and clicked.

He started hiking, after restocking dry and sweet vermouth; they always let you know where the freeway is. In Columbus's case it cut right through the heart, while a second one quartered that. They had ringed it with yet another one, trying to keep out some of the impurities. Sutures were everywhere. He stopped at one to take out the broadest Bowden Book, pencil BOS TON on the inside frontcover and flyleaf. They had done it together once, in one of his remaindered; YA LE that time, B.C., and it had worked. He had done the flagging that time too. No, more likely she had, with her glowing face. It was clear this morning that people had no time for books, inscribed or not. It had been an ununiformed chauffeur then, driving a custom-built, certainly bulletproof Cadillac. Doubtfully a reading man.

Housemovers even less likely—at first haphazard guess. This one was flagging *him*. Gathering his bag Lou ran toward the house. What, did they want books to shore it up? He smiled willingly at the hairy head, positively proving to be a reading one. "Heading for Boston are you!"

"Yes!"

"Come in!"

"Thanks!" Lou climbed up on the porch and joined him on the bearskin couch. He had no view of the man's eyes, but a firm little nose jutted out of the curly profile. His cap was coonskin. "Nice place you've got!"

"It's comfortable."

"Built it yourself, did you?"

"Well, I restored it. That's my line. A.J. Botts, House Restorer. This is a genuine Eighteenth Century cabin, out of Southern Illinois. Everything—logs, doors, windows, fittings, nails—everything is authentic, except for the floor of course. All the furniture is contemporary. We've just been on exhibition at Indianapolis. They really liked it."

"Oh, you take it along with you everywhere?"

"Oh yes." A.J. Botts released the polished wooden handbrake. "It's got over two hundred thousand miles on it," he said, moving onto the freeway. "I foresee a full half-million before I—pardon the pun—detire it. I've got a nice little spread in Northern Mass just waiting."

"That's where you're headed now?"

A.J. Botts offered a quick flash of eyes. "No, right now my home is Boston. That's where I keep my office, my equipment, my Victorian highrise and lady. You from Boston?"

"No, just visiting."

"Married?"

"Well . . ."

"Well?"

"Separating."

Botts wagged his well-washed curls. "I don't believe in that. I believe man and wife ought to stay together, no matter what. Till Death Do Us Part. They've made a contract."

Lou looked off his side of the porch at the undulating, wounded scenery. "Well, things vary. She's not even thirty yet, half my age. She has most of her life ahead of her, she has a right to make it what she wants to. She was only two-fifths my age when we got together—that's closing."

On his side Botts seemed to ruminate, or was he dozing? His right hand rested on his lap, gently stroking that. He steered one-handed, for this log cabin had automatic. Lou watched it slowly angle or wander from the freeway to a suture. Now Botts sat up and pulled the brake on. "You ever drive one of these things?"

"I don't imagine many people have. But I've driven just about everything else."

"Take over. I need some shuteye. We were exhibiting till two in the morning."

"Have a good sleep."

Yawning, Botts stepped through the front door into the cabin, and Lou slid over behind the refurbished cartwheel.

"You caught the handbrake?"

"Sure did."

"From a Pre-Revolutionary pump."

"Hm." This rig handled rather nicely, though he sensed that it might not corner well, or always stop at once. He tested that at the first service station they chanced upon, a Mobil Self-Serv. He had spotted the 50-gallon tank out back, and he wanted to top that off before the needle sank any deeper. The gas cap was high out of reach, but Botts had restored a wooden ladder; Lou squeezed $5 worth of super. That should see them through Botts's nap or most of Massachusetts, whichever took the longer. Botts was sawing wood like Davy.

"Hey, what year is that?"

"About a 1770."

"What kind of mileage?"

"Depends on the air mass."

That seemed to satisfy him; at least he took the money. In fact, it was a little strange to be driving behind a handhewn railing, after Chumly. A fine piece of isinglass kept many of the bugs out. Seen through this smoky medium the route did not look overly familiar. Mainly he recognized the highway signs and other landmarks, the background blurred a little. He did note that the flag and highwaymen had withdrawn for the holidays, relinquishing their places to side-armed Smokeys. How that beak would have enjoyed this shady porch! Waving at the smoky cows, Lou continued his sandy shuttle past Sadusky, into Pennsylvania, toward New York and nightfall, tossing pence into gaping baskets. Never, never had he done so much turning back. He stayed with the freeway until they hit that exit ramp at Walford, cornered *slowly.*

It couldn't be more than a few miles to Newickton he guessed; at any rate the odometer was right around CCCLVII and weakly lighted. At Barney's he wheeled up to the high wire gate, which even they could not look over. A hand-painted sign said OPEN 8AM TEU. In the moonlight Lou could make our Chumly crouching in that silent swarm, far off to the right, but Chumly had his back to him.

"What's up?" Botts asked, sticking his head out the door.

"Just stopped off to see an old friend."

"You can come on back here too if you want to."

"No, better keep things rolling."

"What's the name of this place?"

"Newickton."

"Never heard of it," Botts grumbled. "I'll take over."

Lou moved in to the passenger's side as Botts settled behind the wheel. "Eastern Kentucky."

"What's that?"

"The pump handle," Botts said, releasing it. He kept to the back roads, since they were on those. There was no wide-bed Ford at the Greene Motel, nor any sounds of pahty. The Penfield light was working, but only one car waited there this evening, and its driver stalled the engine as they glid by him. In the flickering light of Botts's headlamps the grey woods turned silver sinister; one could almost hear the sowbugs moaning. The Sunday pall befitted Cadsbury, where shades were drawn on darkened windows; even Dude had closed up shop. Twukesbury itself was scarcely lively. Lou would have given a liter of sweet vermouth to be back in the Cadsbury Corners lot with Chumly. Botts now was definitely ruminating. "One thing about ladies," he began at last, "you can't restore them. After a certain point the best you can do is buy them a gourmet kitchen, lend them a little style while they put the beef on. Oh, sometimes when you catch them at certain moments they'll look good to you, but mostly what you're looking at is a decaying structure, overblown, overdecorated, overpainted. It could break your heart if you allowed it. What you have to do is face it squarely: there's just no restoring ladies. Right?"

"Well, I'm not sure if it's necessary. My first wife is aging beautifully. She still looks good to me and others."

"Oh I'm not complaining mind you. I still enjoy having a good meal with her, especially dinner. We go to a lot of movies together. What happened between you and your first lady?"

"It's hard to say. We had over twenty great years together, but then we just drifted apart."

"Ah, you see there! You should have faced it squarely, like I've been telling you."

"Well, it was up to both of us."

Again Botts fell silent, ruminating, but not for long this time. "You have friends in Boston too?"

"No longer."

"You're quite welcome to stay at my place. There are lots of extra rooms. I'd like you to meet my lady."

"That's very good of you," Lou said, acknowledging the flash of eyeballs in the isinglass, "but I've been thinking of stopping off in Casterbridge. I used to know quite a few people there."

"You'd like her cooking."

"I'm sure I would. Again I thank you, but I have things to do in Casterbridge."

Botts let him off in front of the missing gate, which he probably knew had predated his sturdy railings. He peered through the gap rather gloomily. "Looks pretty quiet."

"Yes it does."

"I hear they've restored Wigglesworth."

"Oh have they?"

"Well, thanks for helping me with the toting."

"Thanks for the portage!"

Botts released the handle and rolled on toward Boston, his lamps showing the way with what looked to be about 40 candlepower. Lou passed through the imagined gate, as it was asking. They had added on to almost everything else in here, thus he found himself strolling a diminished yard. Thayer was there. Old John Stratford too, lately painted crimson, whether by way of protection, politics, or pride. The Library was closed, and so the Union. They would open again for a few hours tomorrow. In his time they would still be open now, even what with the holiday. He headed for the gatehole. The yard cops had used to lock everyone inside on Spring Riot nights; now that the riots had grown real they were clearly glad to be rid of them. The Square too was quiet tonight, crowded only by itself. No scholar slunk by with books, though a presumable whished by on her bike, in regard to thighs a real improvement, breastwise not so much so. The wonderful 5¢ hamburger joint, he noted, had somehow been enlarged though on a corner, to accommodate the $1.50 tripledecker. The spaghetti and Chianti restaurant next door now served teas and croissants. He chose the triple—speak of regular!

Emerging half an hour later, instinct and momentum carried him down toward the river where he had spent many innocent hours, playing chess with a blindfolded phenomenon, having his portrait painted by a talented nymphenomena, surprised by the patrol in the back seat of a rental car with a beauteous rental lady. He had lost a little more innocence when she blasted them to fucking hell for that. Yes, he had once known quite a few people here, now all dead or otherwise out of communication. That he no longer heard from any of them was as much his fault as theirs, though death was more theirs of course. To him in the moonlight the riverbank had a graveyard look, more pruned and kept than he remembered it. The river itself was low. He headed for the bridge.

"Hey Bridgeman! How you up there?"

"Fine enough. You down there?"

He could see them in the moon and firelight, hailing up. "Fly down a little!"

"Don't mind if I do," he said, flywalking.

There were just two of them, and young; quite old enough to smoke, however, he nosed before discerning. The little campfire brought occasional blushes to their soft, smiling faces the moonlight paled. Not one whisker between the pair of them; if anything her fuzz was stronger. Their gleaming teeth, untamed by braces, were comely crooked. "Well welcome! . . . Welcome Flyman!" they greeted almost in chorus.

"Goodevening!" he said, and sitting.

"Toke man?" host invited as hostess did the passing. Inhaling not too deeply, Lou passed it back with nodded thank you. He hesitated only briefly before bringing out a bottle. Nearby were empty cans, neatly piled. He uncapped and took a swig before he passed it.

"Man how'd you find this stuff on Sunday?"

Lou smiled. "Columbus."

Smiling too, they nodded sagely; they understood.

"Sweet what?" the girl asked.

"Vermouth," Lou said.

The boy smiled on her kindly, nodding. He knew, he knew. They watched her take a sip, lick her lips with it. "Oh neaty!"

Nodding, the boy took a swig and all but sputtered; he took a quick toke to hide that. "Good stuff, Gallo," he said a little later. "You new here?"

"Yes, this time I am—I used to live around here years ago. Have you been here long?"

"About two weeks," he said, waving at their knapsack beneath the bridge; they used their sleeping bag as a sofa. "We come down from Bangor. It's nice and warm down here."

"Still going to school?"

"Depends where we are. Sometimes when it rains or snows a lot. Or sometimes we check in for lunch."

"Get home sometimes?"

"No way. My old man's dead—her old man knocked him off. We know where *he* is! I don't know where my mother is. Carrie neither. Maybe they ran off together."

Carrie giggled.

Lou coughed smoke, took a swig to quench it. "Well, you seem to have found a comfortable spot here."

They nodded contentedly. "It's real nice for two," she said. "It's a whole family across the way there," shaking her head compassionately.

Dimly he could see them milling beneath the bridge on the other side, three or four little ones playing tag, two on teeter-totter, mother and daughter tending the open stove while father did the fishing. "They've been there awhile, have they?"

"Since before we come," the boy said.

"Almost two months, Mrs. Biddle said."

"Cops give much trouble?"

"Not much. They check in every now and then, but they know they ain't got no better place to send us."

They were passing things around quite steadily now, or it mostly seemed so. Theirs turned out to be a heavy weed, seaweed—no one had ever swum like this on Gallo Shallow. Lou found himself inhaling deeply—to help them finish with it, a remnant recess of his mind invented. "It's a weird spin, ain't it," he heard a young voice saying.

"Yes it is," he answered.

"You've been on it awhile," the boy said. "You think it ends up anywhere?"

Lou was nodding, sagely. "Everything does," he said. In the hazy firelight he could see the sage little heads agreeing.

"I guess you've been around lots of places," the girl's voice was singing.

Lou was still nodding. "Sometimes it seems like almost everywhere and back again."

They were nodding again.

"Don't copy that right away," he told them.

The boy said, "We'll probably try New York in a week or two."

She giggled, and the nodding boy bent to the dying fire to carefully pinch the tip clean, carefully tap the remnants into a lovely beaded leather bag he wore. Now the two of them leaned back against the sleeping bag together, gazing toward the surface through the seaweed, hands behind their heads, arms entwined at elbows. Lou capped the bottle, slowly standing. "You could spend the night," the boy said.

"Yes, it's beautyful," she said.

"Thanks, I think I'll do a little wandering."

"Watch the second bridge downstream—mean team in there."

"Thanks, I'll skirt it."

"Have a good night."

"Yes, beauty full," she said.

"And you," Lou said, and wandering. There seemed little problem skirting bridges, wherever they were. He saw only graveyard glowing softly, though rather rugged underfoot in places. In fact around the edges it grew bushy, hairy, and he sank down in mellow shadow. It felt kindly in here, protective. He cracked another bottle, poured himself a dry one. Next he rolled a regular, visited with the moon a while before he lit it, a small but loving signal. Yes, its beauty full. Yes, everything ends up anywhere, and starts up anywhere it ended. He had understood that well in the beginning, too often since forgot it. We get distracted pretending to slip behind a tree, and laughing. Grinning up Lou joined in, no less quietly. From time to time he returned its little winks between the branches . . .

"On the back of the car!"

He of course ignored that. Awake or dreaming, there were no cars here. They were part of the illusion, and he was prepared now to refuse it. He was having difficulty with the lights though, he could not turn them. Nor could he account for loud-voiced people. He wanted to float away from them, but of course away too was illusion.

"Stand up and place our hands on the back of the car!"

"*What?*"

"Stand up and place your hands on the back of the car!"

"*What is all this?*"

It was stand-up-and-place-your-hands-on-the-back-of-the-car-! He still could not believe it, but there were four or five of them who really thought so. Encircled by their unwavering guns and flashlights, he did what they requested. He felt hands quickly frisk him. *Him.* He was beginning to believe this, though he could not; he turned his head leftward to look at the two on that side, one of them a woman. "What's going on?" he asked more civilly.

"A girl was raped near here tonight," said the man behind him.

"Where near here?" he asked the woman.

She nodded downriver.

"I haven't been down that way. I didn't do it."

"We know you didn't." It was the talking one behind him.

"Then why are you bothering me?"

"We heard some yelling in here," said another.

"Yelling? I was asleep. If there was yelling, I didn't hear it."

"You can turn around now," said the one behind him.

Lou turned slowly. "I'm no bum," he told them.

"We know you aren't."

"I just wanted a place to sleep."

"What have you been drinking?"

"Vermouth."

"How much did you have tonight?"

Lou shrugged. "About three quarters of a liter."

"Three quarters of a liter," that one repeated, chuckling.

Seen all together now, they themselves looked rather raunchy. Only their blue pants were similar, and the woman's skirt was khaki. They wore caps of different shapes and sizes, those that had any. They wielded a motley bunch of flashlights. "What are you, yard cops?"

Some nodded. "Campus security," said another.

"Aren't you a little off your beat here?"

"We have privileges." They were busy holstering their guns and flashlights now, moving past him to the car. The girl was having difficulty clipping her big flashlight to her Batman belt. Lou slowly gathered his things. He thought he remembered remembering to cap the bottle. He followed them slowly toward the street, in a somewhat different direction, or allowing himself that illusion.

He found the freeway quite easily, a few miles away, the 24-hour Benny's by it. This time he might have arranged to have that breakfast, had he not spent the money on last night's triple. Or was this his migrant waitress from Columbus? No, she had quickly aged if so. Well, so it felt had he. In any case she stayed faithfully with him all through his coffee, waiting for him to order something gross or tip her. It wasn't until the westbound bus made its breakfast stop that she lost interest in him. He sat on sipping peacefully, waiting for the day to dawn in Denver. He supposed he should wait to give her most of his news in person. Meanwhile he tried to think of something encouraging to tell her. He was alive and free in Casterbridge, if that helped. Best that he give her another hour; he walked back to the Square to phone her.

Yet he was early, clatter told him. "Yes?"

"Goodmorning. Sorry I woke you."

"What time is it?"

"It's ten o'clock and you're in Casterbridge."

"Oh are you really. Well, what's up?"

"There have been a couple of funny ones, but I'd better save them until I see you."

"So what are you calling about?"

"Just felt like talking."

"Start talking then. Now that you've woken me up, I have lots of work to do."

"Sorry again. I wish I had a box of books here."

"We did pretty well there."

"Yes, in that way. Actually the Square is pretty quiet today, but even selling just a couple would help a lot." After a year and a half of campus tramping, they still had hundreds.

"Well, what do you want me to do, fly them to you? I resent this. Here I am laboring my ass off on a holiday for you and your car—"

"Our."

"While you loll around drinking beer and TV in some motel."

"Not quite. Do you want to make a cup of coffee and call me back?"

"No, I don't. I want to get up and get to work. If you have anything to say, say it now."

"Have you?"

"No. I went to the post office yesterday. You heard from Bowden."

"That was fast!"

"Yes. It looks like a form letter."

"Ah . . . He refused me a policy."

"He likes the book very much, but 'it would be suicidal for me to reprint a book by a little-known author.' "

"I guess he doesn't have coverage for that."

"I thought that was exactly what he claimed to be out to do."

"Oh ya. Was there any other mail?"

"Nothing interesting."

"Well, I'd better leave off now. I'll call again tomorrow."

"You do that. And by the way, I'm getting tired of all your boxes piled up in my bedroom!"

"I thought you said you had them behind a—"

"They're crowding me out of my apartment! If you don't get them out of here soon I'll throw them out the window!"

"Honey, what are you saying!"

"I'm saying I want your books and papers *out* of here! I'll pile them up in the middle of the park!"

"Honey, what are you on!"

"I'm on the floor," she said, and the litany: "I want your things out of here!"

"*All right!* I'll call tomorrow."

"*All right!*"

They clicked.

He had once offered the Library some of his books: they had answered by air mail that they had enough. At least the doors were open now. Not to trip any electronic traps, he first deposited his books in the return chute, compliments of the publisher. Vermouth they did not bother with. Inside was still sedately muted in spite of machineries encroaching. He did not wander among these tables but climbed discreetly to the second floor. Here was changed, where they had transferred the card catalogs to magic lanterns. Let your eyeballs do the flipping. Yet he found access to the stacks still possible, behind a librarian nibbling croissant. In here he caught his breath, not having prepared himself for a return to heaven. He moved gently, expecting at any moment to be ejected. Today he did not feel like reading, but was happy to stroll the familiar shapes and titles, recalling the joys of past discoveries. He noted with interest too the more recent acquisitions. Most of his friends were doing quite well, some of them exceedingly. He cached the vermouth behind his own books, thinking safety. In a wastebasket he found a smaller, nicer bag for the remainings. By now he was quite sure he would not be ejected.

Around noon, out of respect, he went to the Union to do his shaving, though the Library had complete facilities. Refreshed, he returned to heaven with a box of raisins. The croissant was still doing its duty, the librarian was sweeping into her palm, carefully crumbling in the wastebasket. From time to time he took a volume to a window, held it to the sunlight, let it see the birds still flying, the leaves already dying. That's what it's all about; they remembered. For some of them it had been quite a while.

He blew dust off. In fact he took a Simenon to the smoking room, went back for Eliots at tea time. They all sat together on a sofa, with a proper table to put their cups and pipes on, unheeded by the smoking readers. What with the holiday, the library closed at six; at five Lou excused himself, left them there while he went out for what he felt would be his final triple. He took an after-dinner stroll past the Oriental bookstore—now French boutique—where they had been grilled for half an hour beneath a blinding spotlight, then led down the street to read to 100 vermillion sleepers for $7, which he had done for her alone. This evening he did not go there but stopped off for a pack of Parliaments, to add a touch of elegance.

That he inched the sofa out from the wall on his return they did not appear to notice, far less the coughing readers. He placed his bag back there, sat down with them long enough to smoke a Parliament. When he made a sidewise somersault that landed him quietly behind the couch, they stirred uneasily; but not, he sensed, the homeward readers, who were responding to a buzzer. He lay rather rigidly, as did the Simenon and Eliots. They at least could watch the birds from there, put their feet up on the table. Not you, George—Tom and Georges. Lou himself took off his boots. He could hear heavy footsteps through the partitions, soon at the door. "The library is closed! Closed for the night!" The doorknob squeaked a little. "Is anybody in there?"

A guard could sense there was, of course, but this one did not venture to investigate. Footsteps could be heard clumping aggressively down the staircase. Lou's hope now was that this was not wastebasket night, carpet sweeping even worse. The f-ing cold drink machine had a loose bearing in its condenser fan. Fick fick fick fick. Would it go up in smoke tonight? He lay back to let things settle, not least of all the triple. Bootless he tiptoed into restless, warpful sleep, his ears alert for the flump of feet. When suddenly he sat up crookedly halfway, the smoking room had come aflame, ready to burst with sun. He held his breath, but as always it stopped short of that. All was quiet here and down below. Time now for a postap]ritif. Slipping through the mildly squeaking door, he saluted the croissant as he headed for the stacks. In here was semi-dark, but he knew by heart the path to the vermouth. Safe, of course. He took a Thoreau along on their way back, stopped to show himself in a magic lantern, with a sudden thought. Could these be worked into *TV Cookery?* Not tonight. Anyway, his raisins had already been cooked to perfection by the sun. He stopped again at the door to the smoking room. Shouldn't he have invited a Chaucer too? Should he go back? It would be polite, but if traipsed around too much up here it might stir indignation down below, they'd all be caught. Chaucer he was sure understood.

His guests seemed quite pleased by what he had brought. Thoreau himself did not look askance. They seemed not at all disturbed that Lou had but a single plastic cup. So they all sat together on the sofa now, sipping, sometimes shifting quietly, the guests no doubt glancing at one another's titles on the sly. Lou did not read but watched the setting sun. It was making faces behind some dead or dying trees. These were male and female faces, none quite recognizable, yet familiar because they looked like us. Aha, wasn't that Chaucer in the center there! Greetings. Glad you found the way! Their mood seemed mostly merry, certainly not bleak. They shimmered, changed expressions as they faded into sky, until only their benevolent eyes left burning. Soon those too disappeared, leaving behind a forest fire, which did not burn the trees. In fact they now had leaves. She would have loved this. We can be sure the Sun too has its highs, as needed, well thought out. It was having one tonight. Fire changed to smoke, pinkish white. No, that was the Sun's own smile, Goodnight, soon a rosey aftersmile. The Sun is our only friend. The rest are chance acquaintances. He of course did not mention this to his guests, or to the Moon when it showed up. . . .

Library opens at 6 o'clock. The swishing doors and whispering shoes reminded him, and he was standing up, bag in hand, boots on and laced, couch kicked back. Yes, he had remembered to put the empty bottle in a wastebasket before he slept; he left the half-empty one in the stacks, for future reference, in case. Bidding a quick fondieu to his startled guests, he mingled with the early drifters, soon was out. The Sun was still half-asleep. He headed for the freeway. That took not long, so light a bag. The westbound Trailhound was compunctioning, its driver out of sight. Lou waited for him to finish his pancake break. You stop at Walford? Certainly! Lou sat in back. It did not take his migrant waitress long to find him there. She sat down with him to rest his feet. "Sfunny how everybody always travels on the weekends!" she reported. Mmm he murmured uncommittingly, and looked out the window at the unfamiliar freeway stretch. Walford had no westbound exit ramp, but the driver stopped there anyway. He wished Lou luck. From here it couldn't be more than a few miles into Newickton he guessed wouldn't you? Chumly was still crouching there at 8 o'clock.

The cowboy was riding his desk English-style today. "Morning, partner. Howdy back."

"Howdy. I've come to take that '68 Opel back."

Barney read his watch. "You have my check?"

"Yes."

He reached for it and read, found Lou his registration. "Take her away," he said, and buzzed for the rodeo queen.

Lou hurried through the sterile hive, heading north-northeast, Chumly mostly lost to sight. All looked awful here, flat-tired, crack-windowed, dusk-encaked. They stared glazy-eyed at Lou. Even Chumly had lost his perk. He had yellow numbers scrawled on his windows, in crayon, front and back. Either this yard had opened early, or someone had scaled the fence. Despite the key they had crowbarred Chumly's trunk, to get at Lou's $20 jack. The hood too was up. They had wanted the battery, Red's new lead-in wires. Part of the carburetor was missing too. The fuel pump was gone. They had trashed Chumly's cubbyhole, ripped his ignition out. Somehow they had overlooked his sweet radio. A grasshopper roved nearby, a one-armed cowhand looking for strays to haul in with his chain lasso. He dragged them squealing to a monster machine which flattened them with one lethal *crunch* that would have made a canman's eyes pop out. "Not this one!" Lou yelled to the cowhand as he swung by. When the cowhand nodded in agreement, Lou turned and trotted for the barn. Barney was expecting him.

"Someone's been over that Opel pretty thoroughly. Lots of parts are gone—the ignition, the battery, fuel pump, part of the carburetor. Can I get replacements here?"

"You can check with Parts," Barney said.

The man behind the counter tucked up his short sleeves and bent to his keys. He leaned back to await the blinking green reply.; "I can give you the battery," he read, and said: "Maybe you can find the others out in the yard. Feel free to take whatever you can find."

It was good that he had kept his tools with him, or so at first it seemed. He found himself wandering aimlessly among dusty carcasses, some of them stripped so thoroughly they were impossible to identify. He recognized Opels best; that did him little good. He didn't really know Chevettes. His sorties grew shorter and shorter, more cursory; he was loath to leave Chumly out of sight. When he finally headed back to the barn he carried a lighter that might have worked.

"Any luck?"

"Not much." Lou held the lighter up. "I guess I'll take that battery."

Barney watched him lugging it. "Where you headed, partner?"

"Back to Blakey's."

"Give you a haul when one of the trucks gets back."

"Many thanks."

He sat outside with a cold Mountain Dew; with his back to him Chumly could not watch him gulp. Many others could. Soon a bug-eyed towtruck joined the crowd, hauling what looked to be a crocodile, probably from nearby Oily Marsh. The grasshopper stood puffing in front of Lou, itching to drop its chains. But its driver left it growling there, out its wide-open door. He sauntered to the barn past Lou, eyeing his Mountain Dew. He soon enough sauntered out again. "You the one needs a lift?"

"It sure would help."

The cowhand swung to the saddle, swung open the other door. With a great rattle of chains he dropped the crocodile. "Which way?" he asked.

"North-northeast," Lou said, and pointing.

"Yahooo!" They were off in a cloud of dust, cowhand swigging his Mountain Dew. Theirs was a careening, rattling course amongst cringing carcasses, who must have noted dimly that they were not hauling one. Chumly himself seemed cautiously delighted. He scarcely flinched at all when the cowhand swung his chains at him, jerked him up. They rode only a little more slowly now, out the yard and up Newickton Hill. Things looked rather busy at the Greene Motel, people were hurrying here and there. The wide-bed Ford was back at Number 6, and smoking. "Ya-hooo!" The cowhand took the Blakey Rise at a grinding gallop, dropped Chumly loudly at the top of it. "Yahooo!"

"How much do I owe you for that?"

"Aw forget it."

Lou checked his wallet. "Maybe it's just as well," he said, revealing its slenderness. "At least have a beer on me."

The cowhand accepted the four bits offhandedly, bucked forward down the hill. "Yahooodeeee!"

Bert Stein stood smiling at the Service door. "Decided not to sell?"

Lou nodded, his own smile rueful. "It's too great a car."

"It looks a little the worse for wear—I mean lately."

"Ya, somebody went over it pretty thoroughly."

"Well, Jose will check it over when he has a few minutes."

"Many thanks to you."

Lou secured the battery in its rack. They had not taken his plastic water jug, or his Denver *Post.* He set to work washing the yellow numbers off, and washed the unnumbered windows too. He dusted everything as best he could. The lighter did not fit. He tied down the trunk with a piece of string they'd left, returned the registration to the cubbyhole. It was Lou's turn now and he took his bag to the Service mens room, cleaned himself as best he could. At least his face could feel the air again. Bert Stein and Jose were consulting when he came out. Jose nodded a bit sorrowfully at Lou, Bert Stein's smile was sadly cheerful.

"It'll cost you $550 to get everything together again," Bert Stein said. "I don't know if you'd want to spend that much."

Lou let his breath sigh out. "It's an awful lot."

They all agreed on that.

"Jose, maybe you'd like to have the car and fix it up. It's a great car—has a perfect motor. My wife and I drove it cross-country at least half a dozen times."

"I don't want to drive cross-country," Jose said.

Lou nodded to them. "I'll call my wife."

He climbed the hill to the condescending telephone. The operator was right there, had known he would need her help. She at her end too. "Well?"

"Well, I'm back in Newickton."

"Did you get Chumly back?"

"Yes, what's left. Some scavenger went over him pretty thoroughly. Took the ignition, the fuel pump, part of the—"

"So what does that say?"

"They say at Chevrolet it will cost $550 to get everything working again."

"Oh!"

"We can't afford that."

"No, we can't."

"They let me hunt the wrecking yard for parts. All I got was a battery and a lighter that doesn't fit."

"So what are you going to do, sell it back to the wreckers?"

"I've been through all that. I'll leave it at Blakey's—I owe them some money up there anyway. Maybe Jose or someone will decide to fix it up."

"Now you haven't got a car, a wife, a publisher, a fan—anything!"

"Honey, *don't.*"

"You haven't . . ." She stopped, and he waited for her to go on. Optional endings?

"Are you still there?"

"Yes . . ." he could hear her breathing now. Finally: "We blew it, didn't we."

"Yes, I guess we did."

"Have you enough money to get back?"

"I'll get there."

"Take care."

"Oh yes."

"See you."

"See you."

They kissed and clicked. He climbed to his feet and headed west. The sun, on his back, was in heavy mood. He walked down the hill glancing sidewise only once. Chumly was watching him. He knew whose side of the road that was, he remembered their little friend who used to share that ride with him. He knew they were all three alone.

The Timing Chain was begun in a summer cabin in northern Minnesota in the winter of '83, finished in northern Arizona in the spring-summer '83.

—*D. W.*

After Words

Sandra Braman

The Fool Knows

The fool
  of the
  King's fool
    knows eternity.

The Fool minus
    one
  Was god.
        Douglas Woolf

A FEW DAYS BEFORE HIS DEATH, Douglas Woolf said:

"When it finally all comes apart, I'll have to start over."

"How will you do that?"

"I'll have to start telling myself stories." He laughed. "And because I'll be telling them to myself, they'll have to be at least partly true."

The work is "fiction," but in truth Doug wrote simply about the world in which he lived. Though only four of these pieces are explicitly autobiographical ("Note for an Autobituary," "Juncos and Jokers Wild," "Market Research," and " 'A Story I Wasn't Supposed to Tell' "), most others are very nearly so. *Hypocritic Days,* inspired by stories about a figure his first wife Yvonne knew in her adolescence in Hollywood, Doug felt was prescient of his own back pain (ultimately cured only by miles of walking) and of the importance that poet Larry Eigner would come to play in his life. (About *The Timing Chain* let me say only that much of it is exquisitely accurate, and some of it complete fabrication.)

I have found his blood bank ID card, and it is true that more than once Woolfs ate cat food ("Bank Day"). The ice cream man, the fire lookout, the groundskeeper and all the others from his biography are here in the tales. And it goes further -- as, for example, even during the last few months of his life it was possible to wake Doug from a deep sleep and watch him walk into my workroom, enclose a wasp unhurt within his fist, open a window, and let it go before returning to sleep ("The Flyman").

"The Spring of the Lamb" and "HAD" are more difficult. I do know he had intended to complete the series with the autobiography of a potato, but then had come to feel that that was a piece best written after death. For me, it is easiest to understand these tales, like his other work, as an expression of Doug's natural Buddhism. This was literally the man upon whom deer would rest their heads and butterflies would land, and to whom time was just one more dimension.

For Doug *everything* was alive. Among the unpublished writings from the last few years is a fragment written from the perspective of the numerals on the dial of a clock. At the end, Doug apologized to the trees for the tissue he then needed because of hemorrhaging. His work is a running four-decade description of our environmental degradation and the human response to it. A late poem sums it up:

The Land

Why
  we can't
    look
      the animals
        in the eyes.

Doug lived always as if within "a saving period of grace," described in the opening passage of *Hypocritic Days* as the sense that we live in that time after the Sun has gone out but during which we continue to see its light. In this last light all life is precious, and has moment. The transcendentalism of the title *Hypocritic Days,* taken from Emerson, is no accident.

Doug's attention to the Sun, and to the Light, was constant from the opening of *Hypocritic Days* to the close of *The Timing Chain.* Late, he wrote:

One of these Days I may
just run off into the
                Sun
you can look for me there

His totemic identification with the Wolf provided, for Doug, an explanation of his life habits, including moving constantly, as a loner, dedicated fiercely to a family that moved with him. He summarized:

The
      Wolf
              Runs
  four steps
        a
          head
          of
              his
                    past

Doug's work is cast within a history we share. Among his papers I found a small hand-made book that seems to be his response to the atomic bomb. Entitled "The Last Day of the World," by Thelma Virago, made my guess is in the late 1940s, the book is complete with full jacket copy (including quotes from reviews by the likes of H. G. Wells ["At last!"] as well as text [a series of colons, one centered in each page]).

The assassination of John F. Kennedy was a crisis for Doug, who wrote *John-Juan* ("John-John") in response. This fact is not in contradiction with the fact that *John-Juan* was begun in 1962, *before* the assassination, for Doug believed his prescience to be at the heart of his writing vision. (It also helped locate lost children, warn of muggings, etc.) Thus the poem he used as epigraph to *John-Juan* would have been his best epitaph, were there to have been one:

> The fast runner
> runs ever faster
> into the future
> in quest of
> present records.

Doug lived this sensibility with extraordinary integrity, clarity, and continuity. A couple weeks before his death, for example, when he could no longer leave his room to watch the fights and news on TV and so with some elaborateness of wires in my 1920s building the set was brought in, Doug looked at the tangle and said, "The future has got caught up in the present."

We spent our time together in memory. Life was lived on the road in order to see as much as possible—and then to remember it, as clearly as we could—every person, every event, every aspect of the world with which we had engaged. Though I had earlier studied Kabbalah, and deeply believe, as Doug says in *John-Juan,* that "the word is the world," it was from Doug that I came to understand the possibility of approaching infinity through language, and the role of memory in doing so. We would talk, but in any circumstance that triggered Doug's paranoia—and there were many—much of this conversation would take place in writing: poems, fragments, comments written back and forth in hours-long daily exchange for all of the years we were together. For Doug, this catching up of memory in language, dragging currents of time along in one's path as one moved through this world, was why he wrote. The two—memory and prescience—are of course related, as Doug pointed out:

> Memory
> isn't just of the past
> I went there
> I saw that
> Memory is of the future too

I'll go there
I'll do that
Perhaps I'll see you,
too

We also lived in the present, the Day—as each of Doug's book chapters celebrates. Doug loved attending to the domestic, and felt it his responsibility. A gentle and quiet man absorbed in the minutest details. In a certain perverse way he was even right that we always in fact survived the precarious situations that were a constant in the life of Douglas Woolf and those with whom he lived, whether on a macro scale, such as the explosion of Mount St. Helens, or the more micro, as the many times we slept in the streets.

When I first saw Doug's face I thought it was the most profoundly human and intelligent I had ever seen. This I believe is the quality Jeremy Prynne was referring to when, writing about Doug's work after publication of *Ya! & John-Juan,* he called it the "absolute prose of our time, so full of wit and grace and so clear of stupor and depravity that the elation it produces is simply without parallel."

While Doug lay dying in my home, a cultural studies doctoral student sat in my office and repeated the trendy line, "The author is dead." I thought, not quite yet. Doug's devotion to the written word was total, though he felt keenly that we were nearing the end of books (thus our identification of *VITAL STATISTICS* as a magazine in the sense of storehouse, etcetera). His last words were, "I have to write." *Homo scribens.*

Doug understood himself to be just passing through. He claimed he had "been born two years old" with the soul of a child who had just died, thus starting out just a little bit ahead of everybody else, and shared with his mother the feeling that the family had come from somewhere near Betelgeuse. Towards the end, "He had a sense that he was heading somewhere new, not on the run." And:

Hello, Death
What You're Really Thinking
I think G. Chaucer was like me, always aware

> of what time it was. I'm going to start wearing my $1.98 watch for 1st time (its 2-year probable life is about due to run out) so that I'll be thinking along the right lines when I meet him. No doubt he too will be miffed by all the talk about eternal timelessness—we'll go out once a month to make appropriate notches of time's passage; on a meteor or something. It will make a nice outing, a chance to get to know one another better.

On the road as a way of life. In our time, at least a couple hundred thousand miles, back and forth round and about, drive-away car after drive-away car and then Chappy (Chumly), night after midnight night in the high Rockies, the far desert, the Sierras of New Jersey.

Thus the West. Because of Doug I am one of the few of my generation (born 1951), and one of the last, I believe, to have had a chance to truly experience the West as a mood and an approach as well as a place.

None of this is to deny what have been called Doug's demons. There were reasons two women left him (with varying degrees of success) despite love, and enormous costs to those lives, and to the lives of the children. But it is an unfortunate artifact of Doug's choice of social isolation that most literary encounters were tense and as a consequence far too liquored. Few knew him in peace.

Doug was not isolated at all, actually, if one includes the constancy of his attention to those with whom he spoke via the written word, reading constantly when he wasn't writing (reading dictionaries at the end, voraciously, to make up, he said, for what he hadn't had time to do). The surprise in the Woolf archive is that while the novels and stories were all essentially written in one pass, Doug spent hours writing drafts of those letters that, as Jonathan Williams has noted, look so casual one imagines them being written with the other hand on a driving wheel. Nor was he isolated when one takes into account his relationships with all of the other beings (birds, insects, animals, plants, fellow workers, intensely with his families) within his ken.

It is worth asking why this white male who was born to

privilege received one of the first American Book Awards from the Before Columbus Foundation, when it is the very point of the awards to honor, multiculturally, "the other." I believe it was because of Doug's extraordinary ability to enter "the other" and, as Hubert Selby has noted, let each being speak for itself. In rejecting material values more sincerely and enduringly than most beatniks, hippies, monks and others, Woolf kept his vision unencumbered. Since he lived his adult life among those for whom the "we" of most of us reading this book are "the other," and reports for them, the Woolf oeuvre is thus documentation, giving voice to the voiceless. What he considered the ultimate compliment came from a Navajo, one of "the people," when after he read "Slayer of the Alien Gods" at San Francisco State in the late 1970s, the man let Doug know he'd gotten it just right.

Yvonne, Gale, and Lorraine took turns reading from "Juncos and Jokers Wild" when we took Doug's ashes behind Cabin 3 above Wallace, Idaho, still the Place he loved best. After we had picnicked, walked in the woods and picked huckleberries his grandson, Jesse, made into pancakes the next day, Yvonne took his straw hat and flung it into the woods.

I took the blue knit tocque he'd worn so much in recent years and buried it under a log deep among trees, hoping small animals would find it, for a home. I sent off this manuscript, registered, on December 31 ("The Love Letter").

Printed November 1993 in Santa Barbara & Ann Arbor for the Black Sparrow Press by Mackintosh Typography & Edwards Brothers Inc. Text set in Sabon by Words Worth. Design by Barbara Martin. This edition is published in paper wrappers; there are 200 hardcover trade copies; 100 numbered deluxe copies; & 26 lettered copies handbound in boards by Earle Gray.

Photo: Donald Braman

DOUGLAS WOOLF was born in New York City in 1922, grew up between Larchmont and the first commuters' Connecticut, boarding schools and yachts, son and grandson of pilots, with an exposure to literature and to fine things (his father edited a journal on textiles for McGraw-Hill, was a world expert on Persian rugs, his grandfather a roving journalist, his stepmother the granddaughter of Edison and an architect, Leonard Woolf a cousin, his first friend Bill Barton, son of the senator). Harvard with Mailer and JFK, and then World War II: ambulance driver in North Africa for the American Field Service, where he first learned passion for the desert, and then as navigator for the Air Force. After the war, the West, briefly working as a screen-writer in Hollywood, marrying Yvonne Elyce Stone, child of Hollywood, and toying with graduate work until *Hypocritic Days* was rejected for a master's degree at the University of New Mexico and taken by Robert Creeley as the capstone novel of The Divers Press.

From then on the pattern was set: Constantly mobile, largely West, earning money as migrant farm worker, ice cream man, groundskeeper, hawking beer and hot dogs at sports events, filling candy machines, selling eggs door to door, and Yvonne as clerk, bookkeeper, demonstrating products. When they had enough money (or thought they did), they would take to the woods or desert altogether with children Gale and Lorraine, living under blankets spread over tree branches, in ghost towns, in shacks, in the car, while Doug wrote. Migrating like wolves around the western half of the continent for a couple of decades, while Grove Press published *Wall to Wall* and *Fade Out,* a first story collection appeared (*Signs of a Migrant Worrier,* from Coyote's Journal) and the work was translated into several languages, including the Polish in which *Fade Out* became a best-seller.

Yvonne and Doug separated towards the end of the 1960s, Doug returning to New York City where he worked as a messenger while Jargon Society published *The Spring of the Lamb.* Escaping at the beginning of the 1970s, his first stop was Minneapolis, where he met poet and singer Sandra Braman and together the two took up travelling again. This time the circuit was all of North America. *Ya! & John-Juan,* remaindered by Harper & Row, was bought and then sold ("Author's 1/2-price sale") on street corners and college campuses (over 60, in 30 states), 20+ drive-away cars as transportation (Doug was one of the first drive-away drivers in the country, and all the agencies knew him). More migrant farm work and pick-up jobs, a typing service, and for the first time engagement with the literary world in person, occasional readings justifying several-month-long cross-country trips, again largely living in the car. (A few stories from those times are told in Braman's collection *A True Story,* published in 1985 by Tansy/Zelot.)

The two began Wolf Run Books, publishing a few chapbooks (including *HAD*) and the journal *VITAL STATISTICS,* and dealing in rare books, using as logo the wolf paw print Doug carved out of an electrical plug. (Woolf took seriously his identification with the Wolf.) In 1977 Black Sparrow Press published *On Us,* which tells, among other things, of Doug's experiences with the makers of Oscar-winning movie *Harry and Tonto,* sprung from *Fade Out.* In 1980 the collection *Future Preconditional,* published by Coach House Press of Toronto, Canada in 1978, received the first American Book Award. In the early 1980s, Doug and Sandra divorced but retained a life lived largely together, Doug working as a door-to-door market research interviewer until ill health (mouth and throat cancer, and arteriosclerosis) made that impossible in the mid-1980s, about when *The Timing Chain* was published by Tombouctou.

By the time of Doug's death in 1992, the Woolf publishing map was a tour of the post-war literary scene, tales appearing in the 1940s in the journals *Story, Prairie Schooner, The Span, Decade of Short Stories, Western Review*; in the 1950s in *Sir!, Perspective, New Mexico Quarterly, The California Quarterly, The Black Mountain Review, Interim, Arizona Quarterly, Southwest Review,* and *Evergreen Review*; in the 1960s continuing on with *Evergreen* and adding *Big Table, Inland, The Second Coming, Kulchur, Wild Dog, Outburst, The Outsider, Granta, El Corno Emplumado, Coyote's Journal, Delta,* and *Origin*; in the 1970s moving into *TriQuarterly, Iron, Unmuzzled Ox, Primer, Credences, Sun & Moon, Periodics, Bezoar,* and a myriad local publications encountered during the book tours; in the 1980s *The Difficulties, Hills, Island, Shearsman, Rolling Stock, Ninth Decade, Not Poetry, Bombay Gin, Imprint*;

Out of This World, from the St. Mark's Poetry Project, arrived the day of his death early in the 1990s. Countries of publication included Mexico, Spain, Germany, Poland, England, Canada, France, and Japan as well as the United States.

The point of it all, according to Doug:

> "I'm naturally devoted to the written word. It's the one thing man has that other animals do not. Parrots can talk, flies can fly, monkeys can drop things, technicians can copy them all. If there were only one reader left in the world, I would write to that one as lovingly as I do now."